Between Us and the Future

Choosing Tomorrow, Book 2

Written by Diane Kann

Brought to you by Volans Galaxy Press

© 2026 Diane Kann

All rights reserved.

No part of this publication may be reproduced, stored in a retrieval system, or transmitted in any form or by any means—electronic, mechanical, photocopying, recording, or otherwise—without prior written permission of the publisher, except in the case of brief quotations for review or educational use.

Published by Kannceptual Creations LLC

An imprint of Volans Galaxy Press

ISBN: 978-1-971356-44-0

Printed in the United States of America

First Edition, January 2026

Contents

Dedication

For everyone who has ever felt lost, uncertain, standing at the edge of something new.

For the quiet dreamers, the hopeful hearts,

and the ones still learning who they are becoming.

This book is for those who carry questions,

who stumble, who try again.

For anyone searching for a place to breathe,

a place to rest, and a place to begin.

May you always find the courage to take the next step,

even when the path feels unclear.

And may you never forget that every tomorrow

holds the possibility of something beautiful.

CHAPTER ONE

The Echoes of Yesterday

PART 1

The first blush of dawn painted the eastern sky in hues of rose and soft gold, a stark contrast to the turbulent, uncertain dawns that had characterized their arrival in Havenridge. Mara stood on the weathered porch of their modest dwelling, the cool morning air a familiar balm against her skin. One year. It felt like a lifetime and yet, in the grand sweep of things, a mere blink. The settlement, which had begun as a desperate huddle against the encroaching desolation, now possessed a quiet, determined hum. The frantic scramble for survival had mellowed into a steady rhythm of construction, cultivation, and community. Structures that had once been makeshift shelters were now solid, purposeful buildings, their timber frameworks weathered by the seasons but sturdy against the elements. Everywhere she looked, the landscape spoke of deliberate effort. Patches of vibrant green, meticulously tended gardens, promised sustenance, while the newly erected community hall stood as a silent testament to their shared aspirations.

The scent of pine, ever-present in this region, was now intertwined with the earthy aroma of turned soil and the faint, sweet perfume of the medicinal herbs Mara herself had painstakingly cultivated.

It was a fragrance of resilience, of life stubbornly taking root. As she breathed it in, a profound sense of peace, hard-won and deeply cherished, settled over her. This was no longer just a sanctuary; it was a home, built with their own hands and their shared dreams. The sunrise, once a harbinger of another day of struggle, was now a comforting ritual, a daily reminder of their enduring strength and the quiet beauty of a future they were actively creating.

A soft tread on the porch announced Eli's arrival. He didn't need to speak; their shared routines had woven a tapestry of silent understanding between them. He moved to stand beside her, his presence a grounding force, and together they watched the sun ascend, its warmth chasing away the last vestiges of the night. His arm found hers, a familiar weight that spoke of comfort and shared burdens. The easy silence between them was a language of its own, a testament to the depth of their bond, forged in shared hardship and nurtured by unwavering commitment. Yet, as the light grew, Mara felt it – a subtle shift in the atmosphere, an almost imperceptible tremor in the fabric of their peaceful existence. It was the feeling of a turning tide, a whisper of change on the wind, hinting that the relative calm they had found might soon be tested. The landscape, meticulously sculpted over the past year, now seemed poised, ready for whatever the unfolding future might bring.

The quiet energy that pulsed through Havenridge wasn't solely a product of their internal efforts; it was also a beacon. News of their self-sufficiency, their peaceful coexistence, and their burgeoning ability to thrive in what was considered a desolate fringe had, inevitably, traveled beyond their borders. This burgeoning reputation had sparked curiosity, and with curiosity often came interest from factions with their own agendas. Mara, attuned to the subtle currents of human interaction, had begun to notice it weeks ago: a new wariness in the eyes of traders who passed through, the occasional unfamiliar face lingering just a little too long at the perimeter, the quiet hum of their repurposed comms unit picking up snippets of distant, coded chatter that felt uncomfortably close.

Eli, with his keen observational skills honed by a past she still knew only fragments of, had also sensed the shift. He'd begun conducting more thorough perimeter checks, his gaze sweeping the horizon with a practiced intensity that belied the peaceful scene. His quiet review of their rudimentary defense systems, the reinforced gates and the strategically placed watchpoints, was a constant, unspoken reminder that their hard-won peace was a fragile thing. He spoke of it in low tones during their late-night discussions, his brow furrowed with a familiar pragmatism. "More travelers than usual, Mara," he'd said a few nights prior, his voice a low rumble as he meticulously mapped out supply routes on their worn table. "And their questions are... pointed. Not just about trade, but about our governance. Our resources."

Mara, tending to her beloved medicinal herb garden, felt a prickle of unease. This garden, a vibrant tapestry of healing plants, was a symbol of their vital self-reliance. Each leaf, each bloom, represented a choice to cultivate their own strength rather than depend on the unreliable currents of the outside world. As she carefully pruned a sprig of feverfew, its slightly bitter scent filling the air, she understood Eli's concern. The more successful Havenridge became, the more visible it was, and visibility, in their world, was a double-edged sword. It drew those seeking refuge, yes, but it also drew those who saw opportunity, those who might seek to exploit or control. The community council, a body born of necessity and now evolving into a formal governing entity, was already grappling with how to manage this external attention without compromising the very values that made Havenridge special. Their commitment to openness and mutual aid was a cornerstone, but how did one extend that hand without it being grasped and twisted? The quiet hum of their community was growing louder, and the world, it seemed, was finally beginning to listen.

As the seasons turned, Havenridge wasn't just a place of refuge; it was a living, breathing project. The concept of "home" deepened, expanding beyond the walls of their shared dwelling to encompass the entire settlement, the collective aspirations of its inhabitants. For Mara and Eli, it had transcended mere sanctuary. It was a shared endeavor, a future they were not just inhabiting, but actively constructing, brick by brick, seed by seed. This burgeoning sense of permanence led to conversations that delved into the very essence of their commitment.

"Do you ever... think about what 'staying' truly means?" Mara had asked one evening, the scent of woodsmoke curling around them as they sat by the hearth. It was more than just physically residing in Havenridge; it was about the investment, the sacrifices, the future they were weaving together. For her, it was intertwined with the community's future. She worried about the expansion, the inevitable influx of new people, and the potential dilution of the principles that had guided their creation. "What if we grow too fast?" she'd voiced, her gaze fixed on the dancing flames. "What if we lose what makes us, us?"

Eli had turned to her, his expression earnest, his hands reaching to cup hers. The calluses on his palms were a testament to his labor, his quiet strength a constant source of reassurance. "We won't lose it, Mara," he'd said, his voice low and steady. "Because we built it. And we'll keep building it, together." He'd reminded her of the tangible progress they had made, the carefully cultivated fields that now sustained them, the sturdy buildings that housed their growing population. He'd spoken of the sacrifices, hers and his and everyone's, that had brought them to this point, emphasizing that their shared strength, their commitment to each other and to Havenridge, was the bedrock. "We're not just surviving anymore, Mara," he'd continued, his thumb tracing circles on her skin. "We're living. And we're making choices about what that life looks like. That's the real permanence." His words, grounding and hopeful, always managed to soothe the restless anxieties that sometimes surfaced within her, anchoring her back to the present and the shared future they were determined to secure.

The responsibilities that had initially been thrust upon Mara and Eli by sheer necessity were now solidifying into recognized roles. Their input was sought not just for immediate crises, but for the long-term planning that would shape Havenridge's trajectory. The community meetings, once spontaneous gatherings around a crackling fire, were now more formalized affairs, held in the sturdy community hall. During one such meeting, Elias, a respected elder whose quiet wisdom had guided them through many a difficult decision, introduced proposals for a more structured governance system and a framework for resource allocation.

Mara felt the weight of expectation settle upon her shoulders, a familiar sensation that now carried a deeper resonance. This wasn't just about making decisions; it was about shaping the very soul of their community. Beside her, Eli meticulously took notes, his pen scratching rhythmically against the paper. His focus was always on the practicalities, the action items, the logical steps needed to translate abstract ideals into concrete reality. He would then engage with Elias, posing clarifying questions, his contributions always focused on feasibility and sustainability.

The discussions were earnest, sometimes passionate, centering on fairness, resource management, and the collective good. Debates arose about how to balance individual needs with the demands of the growing populace, how to ensure equitable distribution of essential supplies, and how to maintain their commitment to self-sufficiency in the face of increasing external pressures. Mara found herself increasingly involved in mediating these discussions, drawing upon her empathy to bridge divides and find common ground. Eli, meanwhile, would often present data-driven solutions, his pragmatic approach a crucial counterpoint to the more idealistic considerations. Together, they were laying the groundwork, not just for the coming year, but for generations to come, forging the ethical and practical frameworks that would define Havenridge's future.

As the day wound down, the structured debates of the meeting hall gave way to the quiet intimacy of their shared life. After a long day of community work and planning, Mara and Eli found a rare moment of quiet reflection by the hearth in their cabin. The scent of dried herbs hung softly in the air, a comforting constant. The fire cast dancing shadows on the walls, creating a warm, inviting ambiance that seemed to encourage a deeper conversation.

"Sometimes," Mara began, her voice soft, barely disturbing the quiet, "I worry that all of this... all these responsibilities... will pull us apart." She leaned her head against Eli's shoulder, the steady beat of his heart a familiar comfort. "We give so much to Havenridge, to everyone else. I just want to make sure we're still... us. That we still have time for us."

Eli's arm tightened around her, his touch a silent affirmation. He understood her fears, the quiet anxieties that often accompanied the immense pressure of leadership. "We built this place, Mara," he murmured, his voice a low, resonant rumble against her ear. "Together. And our partnership, our commitment to each other, that's the bedrock. Nothing we do, no matter how demanding, changes that. It just makes it stronger." He turned her gently to face him, his gaze steady and full of a love that had only deepened with every shared challenge. "Our aspirations for Havenridge are tied to our aspirations for each other. We're not sacrificing 'us' for the community; we're building a stronger 'us' *for* the community."

He spoke of the dreams they still held, not just for Havenridge, but for themselves within it. The simple dream of quiet evenings, of shared laughter, of building a life that was both purposeful and deeply personal. He acknowledged the sacrifices they had already made, the personal desires deferred, the comforts forgone, but he framed them not as losses, but as investments in a future they both believed in. Their conversation was more than just an exchange of words; it was a reaffirmation of their love, a tender acknowledgment of the pressures they faced, and a silent, profound promise to navigate whatever lay ahead, side-by-side, their bond the unwavering anchor in the storm of their unfolding lives.

The nascent strength of Havenridge, once a fragile seedling, had begun to unfurl its leaves, reaching towards the sun. This growth, however, was not without its shadows. The quiet hum of their thriving community, the tangible evidence of their resilience and self-sufficiency, had carried on the wind, reaching ears far beyond their meticulously cultivated fields. Mara felt it first, a subtle prickle of unease that settled in her gut like a stone. It was in the lingering gazes of the traders who now frequented their markets, their usual brisk transactions laced with a newfound, almost hesitant curiosity. They asked more questions now, their inquiries veering from the practicalities of trade to the intricate workings of their governance, the source of their remarkably stable resources.

Eli, his senses honed by a past shrouded in layers of caution, had also registered the shift. His days were now punctuated by more frequent and thorough perimeter checks. His gaze, often sweeping the horizon with a practiced intensity, seemed to hold a perpetual scan for anomalies. The reinforced gates, the strategically placed watchpoints – elements that had once symbolized their defense against a hostile environment – were now under constant, quiet review. He spoke of his concerns in hushed tones during their late-night discussions, the worn map spread between them a testament to their ongoing strategic planning. "More travelers than usual, Mara," he'd murmur, his brow furrowed with a familiar pragmatism. "And their questions are... pointed. Not just about trade, but about our governance. Our resources."

Mara, her hands deep in the rich earth of her medicinal herb garden, felt a answering tremor of apprehension. This garden, a vibrant mosaic of healing plants, was more than just a source of sustenance and medicine; it was a potent symbol of their hard-won independence. Each carefully nurtured leaf, each delicate bloom, represented a deliberate choice to cultivate their own strength, to rely on their own ingenuity rather than the capricious whims of the outside world. As she meticulously pruned a sprig of feverfew, its slightly bitter scent a familiar comfort, she understood Eli's apprehension. The greater their success, the more visible Havenridge became. And in their fractured world, visibility was a perilous commodity, a double-edged sword that attracted not only those seeking solace but also those who perceived opportunity, those who might seek to exploit or control.

The community council, a body born of necessity and now evolving into a more formal entity, found itself grappling with this burgeoning external attention. The very principles that defined Havenridge – its commitment to openness, to mutual aid, to fostering a sanctuary free from the predatory instincts of the old world – were now being tested. How did one extend a welcoming hand without it being grasped and twisted? How did they maintain their integrity while navigating the complex currents of external interest? The quiet hum of their community was undeniably growing louder, and the world, it seemed, was finally beginning to listen, and perhaps, to covet.

The deepening roots of Havenridge weren't just about structures and sustenance; they were about the evolution of identity. The concept of "home" had expanded, no longer confined to the intimate space of their shared dwelling but encompassing the entire settlement, the collective aspirations of every soul who called it their own. For Mara and Eli, it had long since transcended the notion of a mere sanctuary. It was a shared endeavor, a future they were actively constructing, not just inhabiting. This burgeoning sense of permanence, this tangible evidence of a life built to last, naturally led to conversations that delved into the very essence of their commitment.

It was in these moments, amidst the comforting glow of the fire and the shared warmth of their intertwined hands, that Mara found renewed strength, her anxieties quelled by the quiet certainty of their enduring connection. The echoes of yesterday, though ever-present, were fading, replaced by the steady, hopeful rhythm of a future they were building, together.

The hearth's embers pulsed with a gentle, rhythmic glow, mirroring the slow, steady beat of Mara's heart against Eli's chest. The scent of dried lavender and chamomile, harvested from her own flourishing garden, wove a calming tapestry through the air, a constant reminder of the life they had painstakingly cultivated. The outside world, with its encroaching shadows and the subtle shift in the gazes of traders, felt a world away, confined to the hushed conversations and the more formal deliberations within the community hall. Here, by the fire, in the sanctuary of their shared cabin, the concept of 'home' began to unfurl itself in its most intimate and profound sense. It was more than the sturdy walls that sheltered them, more than the fertile land that sustained them, and certainly more than the carefully chosen name, Havenridge, that symbolized their refuge. It was a living, breathing entity, woven from shared dreams, mutual respect, and the quiet understanding that had grown between them like the deepest roots of an ancient tree.

"Do you ever feel... anchored?" Mara's voice was a soft breath, barely disturbing the comfortable silence that had settled between them. She traced the worn seams of Eli's tunic, her fingers finding solace in the familiar texture. The question, though simple, held a universe of unspoken thoughts. Anchored, yes, in the steadfast presence of Eli beside her, but also in the very ground beneath their feet. Havenridge wasn't a temporary haven, a stopgap in a chaotic world. It was becoming their permanent address, their legacy, the physical manifestation of their collective will to build something lasting. This realization, both exhilarating and daunting, often led her to moments of quiet contemplation, to the edge of anxieties that she usually kept carefully guarded.

Eli shifted, his arm tightening around her, his thumb gently stroking her arm. He understood the unspoken layers of her question. The permanence they were actively creating was a double-edged sword. It offered stability, security, and the promise of a future, but it also demanded an unwavering commitment, a willingness to invest not just their labor and resources, but their very beings into the soil of this new society. "Anchored?" he echoed softly, his gaze meeting hers. The firelight flickered in his eyes, reflecting the warmth of their shared space. "Yes, Mara. I do. And it's a good feeling. It means we're not adrift anymore." He paused, his brow furrowing slightly, sensing the subtle tremor of apprehension beneath her words. "What are you feeling?"

Mara sighed, a sound that was more release than sadness. "It's just... we've built so much, Eli. More than I ever thought possible. It feels like a real place now, a real home, not just a sanctuary. And that means... staying. Truly staying. It means everything we do now shapes not just us, but everyone who lives here, and everyone who might come after us." She pulled away slightly, enough to meet his gaze fully. Her eyes, usually so bright with a vibrant energy, held a flicker of concern. "I worry about the expansion, you know? The trade that brings us more than just supplies now. The questions. What if we grow too much, too fast? What if we dilute the very things that make Havenridge special? What if we lose the... the heart of it all?"

The 'heart of it all' was a concept they had discussed countless times. It was the intangible essence of their community, the shared ethos that had guided them from the brink of despair. It was the willingness to share, to help, to prioritize the collective good. It was the quiet understanding that they were stronger together, that their interdependence was not a weakness but their greatest strength. But as Havenridge grew, as its reputation spread like tendrils of ivy across the surrounding lands, Mara feared that this delicate balance could be disrupted. The influx of new people, with their own histories and expectations, could inevitably lead to different perspectives, different needs, and potentially, different priorities. She pictured the pristine fields they had so carefully tended, the carefully constructed communal spaces, the very air of trust and mutual respect that permeated their settlement. Could these things withstand the pressure of rapid growth, of external influences that might not share their foundational values?

Eli reached out, his hand covering hers, his touch firm and reassuring. He understood her fears implicitly. They were the echoes of a world that had taught them to be wary, to be guarded, to protect what was theirs with a fierce tenacity. But Havenridge was built on the opposite principles. It was an act of audacious hope, a deliberate choice to foster openness and trust in a world that had often punished such virtues. "We won't lose it, Mara," he said, his voice steady, resonating with a conviction that always managed to calm the tempest in her soul. "Because we built it. Every single piece of it. And we built it with our eyes wide open. We knew that growth would bring challenges. We knew that visibility could attract unwanted attention."

He gestured around their small cabin, the rough-hewn beams overhead, the sturdy hearth that had seen them through countless seasons. "Look at this. Remember the first winter? We were rationing every scrap. The fear was palpable. Now…" He smiled, a genuine, heart-warming smile that crinkled the corners of his eyes. "Now we have abundance. Not excess, but enough. Enough to sustain us, to share, to build. That's not a dilution of our principles; that's the fulfillment of them."

He spoke of the sacrifices that had paved the way to their current stability. The long, arduous days in the fields, planting and harvesting under a relentless sun. The nights spent reinforcing defenses, the constant vigilance. The personal comforts they had forgone, the quiet moments of rest they had sacrificed, all for the sake of building a secure future. "Those sacrifices," he continued, his gaze intense, "they weren't just for survival. They were investments. Investments in this very permanence you're talking about. We endured the hardship so that future generations wouldn't have to. We laid the foundation, not just of buildings, but of a way of life."

He gently squeezed her hand. "The key isn't to stop growing, Mara. That would be a different kind of stagnation, wouldn't it? The key is to grow *intentionally*. To remain true to our values as we expand. It's about making conscious choices about who we welcome, about how we integrate them, about ensuring that the heart of Havenridge continues to beat strong, even as its body grows." He met her questioning gaze, his own filled with unwavering resolve. "We'll do it together. Just like we've done everything else."

Mara leaned back against him, absorbing the warmth of his presence, the strength of his words. He had a way of cutting through her anxieties, of grounding her in the tangible reality of their achievements. He reminded her that their resilience wasn't a passive state, but an active, ongoing process. The 'heart of it all,' as she called it, wasn't a fragile artifact to be protected from the world, but a living, breathing principle that needed to be nurtured and, yes, even expanded. It was about extending their core values outwards, about infusing the new with the spirit of the old, rather than allowing the new to erode it.

"But how do we do that?" she asked, the question less fraught with worry now, more a genuine inquiry into the practicalities of their shared vision. "When people arrive, they'll bring their own histories, their own fears. Not everyone will understand the need for shared resources, for collective decision-making, for... for this level of interdependence."

Eli's fingers brushed a stray strand of hair from her cheek. "We lead by example. We continue to embody those principles ourselves. And we create systems that reinforce them. Elias and the council are already working on the framework for new arrivals, aren't they? Establishing clear expectations, offering guidance, integrating them into the fabric of our community rather than just letting them exist on the fringes." He spoke of the ongoing work within the community council, the careful deliberations that were shaping the future of their governance. "It's not about building walls, Mara. It's about building bridges. Strong, well-constructed bridges that connect us, not isolate us."

He shifted, turning to face her more fully, his hands resting on her shoulders. "Remember when we first arrived here? We were strangers, adrift. The people who were already here, they didn't turn us away. They offered us a hand, a meal, a place by their fire. They shared their knowledge, their resources, their hope. That's the spirit of Havenridge. It's not something we can hoard; it's something we have to actively share and, in doing so, strengthen."

Mara pondered his words, the truth of them settling deep within her. Her anxieties stemmed from a deeply ingrained caution, a survival instinct honed by years of scarcity and uncertainty. But Havenridge was designed to be an antidote to that very scarcity, a testament to the power of abundance born from cooperation. The very act of "staying," of committing to this place, was an affirmation of their belief in its potential, not just as a refuge, but as a model for a better way of living.

"So, 'staying' means more than just planting roots," she murmured, a nascent understanding dawning. "It means actively tending to the garden of our community. It means ensuring the soil is fertile for newcomers, and that our own roots are deep enough to support their growth."

Eli smiled, his eyes conveying a wealth of shared understanding. "Exactly. It means we're not just inhabitants, Mara. We're architects. We're gardeners. We're guardians. And we're doing it together. That's the permanence. That's the home we're building." He gently drew her closer, their foreheads touching. "Our aspirations for Havenridge are intertwined with our aspirations for each other. We're not sacrificing 'us' for the community; we're building a stronger 'us' *for* the community. Our shared life, our partnership – that's the bedrock. Everything else rests on that."

The fire crackled, casting dancing shadows that seemed to dance in time with the quiet rhythm of their shared breath. The anxieties that had begun to surface in Mara's heart were not entirely vanquished, but they were significantly softened, transmuted into a quiet resolve.

The future of Havenridge, with its burgeoning challenges and its boundless potential, was no longer a source of overwhelming apprehension, but a landscape they were ready to navigate, hand in hand. The concept of home had indeed deepened, expanding from the cozy confines of their cabin to encompass the vast, hopeful expanse of the community they were forging, a community built not just of wood and stone, but of shared dreams, unwavering commitment, and the enduring strength of their love. It was a permanence rooted not in the absence of change, but in the steadfast ability to grow and adapt, together, always.

The hearth's embers pulsed with a gentle, rhythmic glow, mirroring the slow, steady beat of Mara's heart against Eli's chest. The scent of dried lavender and chamomile, harvested from her own flourishing garden, wove a calming tapestry through the air, a constant reminder of the life they had painstakingly cultivated. The outside world, with its encroaching shadows and the subtle shift in the gazes of traders, felt a world away, confined to the hushed conversations and the more formal deliberations within the community hall. Here, by the fire, in the sanctuary of their shared cabin, the concept of 'home' began to unfurl itself in its most intimate and profound sense. It was more than the sturdy walls that sheltered them, more than the fertile land that sustained them, and certainly more than the carefully chosen name, Havenridge, that symbolized their refuge. It was a living, breathing entity, woven from shared dreams, mutual respect, and the quiet understanding that had grown between them like the deepest roots of an ancient tree.

"Do you ever feel... anchored?" Mara's voice was a soft breath, barely disturbing the comfortable silence that had settled between them. She traced the worn seams of Eli's tunic, her fingers finding solace in the familiar texture. The question, though simple, held a universe of unspoken thoughts. Anchored, yes, in the steadfast presence of Eli beside her, but also in the very ground beneath their feet. Havenridge wasn't a temporary haven, a stopgap in a chaotic world. It was becoming their permanent address, their legacy, the physical manifestation of their collective will to build something lasting. This realization, both exhilarating and daunting, often led her to moments of quiet contemplation, to the edge of anxieties that she usually kept carefully guarded.

Eli shifted, his arm tightening around her, his thumb gently stroking her arm. He understood the unspoken layers of her question. The permanence they were actively creating was a double-edged sword. It offered stability, security, and the promise of a future, but it also demanded an unwavering commitment, a willingness to invest not just their labor and resources, but their very beings into the soil of this new society. "Anchored?" he echoed softly, his gaze meeting hers. The firelight flickered in his eyes, reflecting the warmth of their shared space. "Yes, Mara. I do. And it's a good feeling. It means we're not adrift anymore." He paused, his brow furrowing slightly, sensing the subtle tremor of apprehension beneath her words. "What are you feeling?"

Mara sighed, a sound that was more release than sadness. "It's just... we've built so much, Eli. More than I ever thought possible. It feels like a real place now, a real home, not just a sanctuary. And that means... staying. Truly staying. It means everything we do now shapes not just us, but everyone who lives here, and everyone who might come after us." She pulled away slightly, enough to meet his gaze fully. Her eyes, usually so bright with a vibrant energy, held a flicker of concern. "I worry about the expansion, you know? The trade that brings us more than just supplies now. The questions. What if we grow too much, too fast? What if we dilute the very things that make Havenridge special? What if we lose the... the heart of it all?"

The 'heart of it all' was a concept they had discussed countless times. It was the intangible essence of their community, the shared ethos that had guided them from the brink of despair. It was the willingness to share, to help, to prioritize the collective good. It was the quiet understanding that they were stronger together, that their interdependence was not a weakness but their greatest strength. But as Havenridge grew, as its reputation spread like tendrils of ivy across the surrounding lands, Mara feared that this delicate balance could be disrupted. The influx of new people, with their own histories and expectations, could inevitably lead to different perspectives, different needs, and potentially, different priorities. She pictured the pristine fields they had so carefully tended, the carefully constructed communal spaces, the very air of trust and mutual respect that permeated their settlement. Could these things withstand the pressure of rapid growth, of external influences that might not share their foundational values?

Eli reached out, his hand covering hers, his touch firm and reassuring. He understood her fears implicitly. They were the echoes of a world that had taught them to be wary, to be guarded, to protect what was theirs with a fierce tenacity. But Havenridge was built on the opposite principles. It was an act of audacious hope, a deliberate choice to foster openness and trust in a world that had often punished such virtues. "We won't lose it, Mara," he said, his voice steady, resonating with a conviction that always managed to calm the tempest in her soul. "Because we built it. Every single piece of it. And we built it with our eyes wide open. We knew that growth would bring challenges. We knew that visibility could attract unwanted attention."

He gestured around their small cabin, the rough-hewn beams overhead, the sturdy hearth that had seen them through countless seasons. "Look at this. Remember the first winter? We were rationing every scrap. The fear was palpable. Now..." He smiled, a genuine, heart-warming smile that crinkled the corners of his eyes. "Now we have abundance. Not excess, but enough. Enough to sustain us, to share, to build. That's not a dilution of our principles; that's the fulfillment of them."

He spoke of the sacrifices that had paved the way to their current stability. The long, arduous days in the fields, planting and harvesting under a relentless sun. The nights spent reinforcing defenses, the constant vigilance. The personal comforts they had forgone, the quiet moments of rest they had sacrificed, all for the sake of building a secure future. "Those sacrifices," he continued, his gaze intense, "they weren't just for survival. They were investments. Investments in this very permanence you're talking about. We endured the hardship so that future generations wouldn't have to. We laid the foundation, not just of buildings, but of a way of life."

He gently squeezed her hand. "The key isn't to stop growing, Mara. That would be a different kind of stagnation, wouldn't it? The key is to grow *intentionally*. To remain true to our values as we expand. It's about making conscious choices about who we welcome, about how we integrate them, about ensuring that the heart of Havenridge continues to beat strong, even as its body grows." He met her questioning gaze, his own filled with unwavering resolve. "We'll do it together. Just like we've done everything else."

Mara leaned back against him, absorbing the warmth of his presence, the strength of his words. He had a way of cutting through her anxieties, of grounding her in the tangible reality of their achievements. He reminded her that their resilience wasn't a passive state, but an active, ongoing process. The 'heart of it all,' as she called it, wasn't a fragile artifact to be protected from the world, but a living, breathing principle that needed to be nurtured and, yes, even expanded. It was about extending their core values outwards, about infusing the new with the spirit of the old, rather than allowing the new to erode it.

"But how do we do that?" she asked, the question less fraught with worry now, more a genuine inquiry into the practicalities of their shared vision. "When people arrive, they'll bring their own histories, their own fears. Not everyone will understand the need for shared resources, for collective decision-making, for... for this level of interdependence."

Eli's fingers brushed a stray strand of hair from her cheek. "We lead by example. We continue to embody those principles ourselves. And we create systems that reinforce them. Elias and the council are already working on the framework for new arrivals, aren't they? Establishing clear expectations, offering guidance, integrating them into the fabric of our community rather than just letting them exist on the fringes." He spoke of the ongoing work within the community council, the careful deliberations that were shaping the future of their governance. "It's not about building walls, Mara. It's about building bridges. Strong, well-constructed bridges that connect us, not isolate us."

He shifted, turning to face her more fully, his hands resting on her shoulders. "Remember when we first arrived here? We were strangers, adrift. The people who were already here, they didn't turn us away. They offered us a hand, a meal, a place by their fire. They shared their knowledge, their resources, their hope. That's the spirit of Havenridge. It's not something we can hoard; it's something we have to actively share and, in doing so, strengthen."

Mara pondered his words, the truth of them settling deep within her. Her anxieties stemmed from a deeply ingrained caution, a survival instinct honed by years of scarcity and uncertainty. But Havenridge was designed to be an antidote to that very scarcity, a testament to the power of abundance born from cooperation. The very act of "staying," of committing to this place, was an affirmation of their belief in its potential, not just as a refuge, but as a model for a better way of living.

"So, 'staying' means more than just planting roots," she murmured, a nascent understanding dawning. "It means actively tending to the garden of our community. It means ensuring the soil is fertile for newcomers, and that our own roots are deep enough to support their growth."

Eli smiled, his eyes conveying a wealth of shared understanding. "Exactly. It means we're not just inhabitants, Mara. We're architects. We're gardeners. We're guardians. And we're doing it together. That's the permanence. That's the home we're building." He gently drew her closer, their foreheads touching. "Our aspirations for Havenridge are intertwined with our aspirations for each other. We're not sacrificing 'us' for the community; we're building a stronger 'us' *for* the community. Our shared life, our partnership – that's the bedrock. Everything else rests on that."

The fire crackled, casting dancing shadows that seemed to dance in time with the quiet rhythm of their shared breath. The anxieties that had begun to surface in Mara's heart were not entirely vanquished, but they were significantly softened, transmuted into a quiet resolve. The future of Havenridge, with its burgeoning challenges and its boundless potential, was no longer a source of overwhelming apprehension, but a landscape they were ready to navigate, hand in hand. The concept of home had indeed deepened, expanding from the cozy confines of their cabin to encompass the vast, hopeful expanse of the community they were forging, a community built not just of wood and stone, but of shared dreams, unwavering commitment, and the enduring strength of their love. It was a permanence rooted not in the absence of change, but in the steadfast ability to grow and adapt, together, always.

Chapter Two

The Echoes of Yesterday

Part 2

The air in the community hall was thick with anticipation, a palpable buzz of collective energy that vibrated through the sturdy timber walls. It was a gathering unlike the casual conversations or impromptu problem-solving sessions that had become routine. This felt more formal, more deliberate. Mara, seated beside Eli at a long, polished wooden table, felt a familiar prickle of responsibility, a sense of being under scrutiny that was both invigorating and a little unsettling. The days of simply surviving, of focusing solely on the immediate needs of their small group, were giving way to a new phase. The necessity of leadership was morphing into a more structured, and therefore more visible, form.

Elias, his silver hair catching the light filtering through the high, arched windows, stood at the head of the hall. His presence exuded a quiet authority, earned through years of wisdom and unwavering dedication to Havenridge. He cleared his throat, his voice carrying with a resonant calm that immediately commanded attention. "My friends," he began, his gaze sweeping across the assembled faces, a mix of the original settlers and the newer arrivals who had found their way to this burgeoning settlement. "We have come a long way. From a scattered few, seeking refuge and a chance to rebuild, we have become a community. We have cultivated the land, strengthened our homes, and, most importantly, we have cultivated a spirit of togetherness."

He paused, allowing his words to sink in, the weight of their collective journey hanging in the air. "But as we grow, so too do our responsibilities. The decisions we make today will not just affect us, but those who will follow. Therefore, it is time to formalize our approach to governance and the equitable distribution of our resources."

Mara felt a surge of mingled emotions. Elias's words echoed her own deepest concerns, the very anxieties she had voiced to Eli by the hearth. This formalization was necessary, she knew, a sign of maturity and a commitment to long-term stability. Yet, the prospect of codified rules, of committees and allocations, also felt like a potential tightening, a bureaucracy that could stifle the organic spirit that had defined Havenridge.

Eli, ever the pragmatist, had already pulled out a small, leather-bound notebook and a sharpened charcoal stick. His brow was furrowed in concentration, his eyes fixed on Elias, absorbing every word, every nuance. He wasn't just listening; he was dissecting, categorizing, preparing to translate Elias's vision into actionable steps.

Elias continued, outlining proposals that had been deliberated by a small group over the preceding weeks. "We propose the establishment of a Resource Council," he announced, his voice steady. "This council will be responsible for overseeing the allocation of communal resources – the grain stores, the lumber harvested from the surrounding forest, the tools shared amongst us. Its mandate will be to ensure fair distribution, to prioritize sustainability, and to always consider the long-term needs of Havenridge."

He then presented a draft for a basic governance structure. "We are not seeking to create rigid hierarchies," Elias clarified, sensing a flicker of apprehension on some faces. "Rather, we aim to create clear pathways for decision-making, to ensure that every voice has a chance to be heard, and that collective decisions are made with transparency and consideration for all." He spoke of the need for a system that could manage disputes, that could plan for future growth, and that could represent Havenridge in its dealings with the outside world.

Mara watched Eli, noting the subtle nods, the quick scribbles in his notebook. He was already envisioning the logistics: who would be on this council, how often would they meet, what criteria would be used for resource allocation, how would surplus be managed, how would new members be integrated into the system. His mind was already at work, building the framework, anticipating potential pitfalls.

"The foundation of any thriving community lies in fairness," Elias declared, his gaze sweeping across the room again. "Fairness in how we share the fruits of our labor. Fairness in how we contribute to our collective well-being. Fairness in how we make decisions that affect us all." He elaborated on the proposed mechanisms for agricultural planning, ensuring that diverse crops were cultivated to mitigate risk, and that sufficient reserves were maintained for lean times. He spoke of shared workshops, of collective responsibility for maintaining infrastructure, and of the importance of mentorship for those learning new skills.

"Consider the recent influx of families from the eastern territories," Elias continued, his tone shifting to address a specific challenge.

"They bring with them skills, labor, and a desperate need for security. Our current system, while functional for us, may not adequately address their immediate needs nor fully integrate them into our shared vision. The Resource Council will be tasked with developing a clear onboarding process, ensuring they receive adequate support and that their contributions are recognized and valued, while also upholding the principles upon which Havenridge was founded."

Mara felt a knot of anxiety tighten in her stomach. Onboarding. Integration. These were abstract terms that represented very real people, with their own stories of hardship and their own hopes for a better future. How would fairness be measured when individuals began with such disparate starting points? How would they ensure that the spirit of openheartedness that had characterized Havenridge's early days wasn't eroded by a need for strict adherence to rules?

Eli caught her eye and offered a small, reassuring smile. He understood her unspoken concerns. His jotted notes were not just about efficiency; they were about ensuring that the *spirit* of Havenridge, the very essence of their shared success, was woven into the practicalities of their new governance. He scribbled something down, then tapped his notebook meaningfully, as if to say, "I'm thinking of that, too."

The discussion then moved to the practicalities of representation. "We propose a system of rotating representatives," Elias explained. "Each distinct area of Havenridge, each significant trade or craft, will have a voice on the council. This ensures a broad perspective and prevents any single group from wielding undue influence." He opened the floor for questions, and the ensuing dialogue was a testament to the community's engagement.

A burly man named Silas, a stonemason whose skill had been instrumental in building many of their sturdy structures, raised his hand. "Elias," he began, his voice a low rumble. "You speak of fairness. But what happens when someone cannot contribute equally? What of those who are ill, or elderly, or those who are simply not as strong as others? Do they receive less?"

Elias nodded slowly, his gaze kind. "A crucial question, Silas. Our principle of interdependence means we support one another. Those who cannot contribute labor will still receive their share. Their contribution may be in wisdom, in tending to the young, in sharing their knowledge, or simply in being a part of our community. Havenridge is built on the understanding that every member has value, in ways that extend beyond brute strength or specific skills."

Mara felt a wave of relief wash over her. That was the core, the unshakeable foundation that Elias was reinforcing. It wasn't about rigid equality of contribution, but about a shared commitment to mutual support.

A younger woman, Anya, who had arrived with her two children a few seasons ago and had quickly found her place in the communal weaving shed, spoke next. "And what about disputes?" she asked, her voice clear. "If there are disagreements between individuals, or even between a member and the council, how are they resolved?"

"That, Anya," Elias replied, "is where the council will also play a role, acting as mediators. But more importantly, we will foster a culture where open communication is encouraged, where grievances are addressed promptly and respectfully, rather than allowed to fester. We will establish clear steps for dispute resolution, starting with direct dialogue, then mediation by council members, and finally, if necessary, a community assembly to address particularly complex issues."

Eli made another series of rapid notes, his mind clearly working through the potential complexities of each stage. He wasn't just recording; he was internalizing, mentally stress-testing the proposed framework. He understood that a system, no matter how well-intentioned, was only as effective as its implementation.

The dialogue continued for some time, touching upon the management of surplus goods, the protocols for trade with external communities, and the long-term vision for education within Havenridge. Mara found herself drawn into the conversation, her initial apprehension slowly giving way to a sense of thoughtful engagement. She asked about the criteria for admitting new members, concerned that the rapid growth might dilute their core values.

"That is a point of ongoing discussion, Mara," Elias acknowledged, his gaze meeting hers with understanding. "We must be welcoming, but we must also be prudent. Newcomers will be carefully considered, their willingness to integrate and to uphold our principles will be paramount. It will not be an arbitrary process, but one guided by the needs of the community and the values we hold dear."

Eli, in his quiet way, was a powerful force in these discussions. While Elias provided the vision and the philosophical grounding, Eli translated these into practical, achievable steps. He would ask clarifying questions that often revealed subtle oversights or potential inefficiencies in the proposed plans. When Elias spoke of ensuring sufficient grain stores, Eli's notes would be detailing the precise quantities, the ideal storage conditions, and the projected consumption rates. When Elias discussed the need for shared tools, Eli would be considering their maintenance, their distribution, and the training required for their safe and effective use.

His focus was always on the 'how,' the tangible execution of the communal will. He wasn't just a follower of Elias's leadership; he was a vital partner, a builder of the practical scaffolding upon which Elias's broader vision could rest. This division of labor, this complementary approach to leadership, was one of Havenridge's greatest strengths. Elias's wisdom and foresight were balanced by Eli's grounded pragmatism and meticulous attention to detail.

As the meeting drew to a close, Elias outlined the next steps. "These proposals will be made available for review by all members of Havenridge," he announced. "We will hold further discussions, gather feedback, and make any necessary adjustments. This is not a decree; it is a framework, built by us, for us. Our collective effort in shaping it will ensure its strength."

Mara felt a quiet sense of accomplishment, a feeling that went beyond the relief of the meeting concluding. She had voiced her concerns, she had participated in the dialogue, and she felt heard. The weight of expectation was still present, but it was no longer a burden of anxiety; it was a shared responsibility, a collective endeavor.

On their walk back to their cabin, the evening air cool and carrying the scent of pine, Mara leaned her head against Eli's arm. "You were so focused," she said softly. "You always are when it comes to these practical matters."

Eli squeezed her hand. "Someone has to be," he replied with a gentle smile. "Vision is important, Mara, essential even. But without the blueprints, without the careful measurement and the sturdy joints, the grandest structures can crumble. Elias paints the sky; I build the house beneath it."

"And you do it so well," she murmured, her heart swelling with pride. She knew that their roles were evolving, that the quiet leadership they had exercised out of necessity was now becoming a more formal, and perhaps more demanding, commitment. They were no longer just survivors, but architects of a future, carefully laying the foundations, brick by painstaking brick, for generations to come. The seeds of leadership, once sown by the harsh soil of necessity, were now beginning to sprout, guided by wisdom and strengthened by unwavering partnership. The echoes of yesterday were shaping their present, not as a burden, but as a foundation upon which to build a more resilient, more equitable tomorrow.

The day had been a tapestry woven with threads of hard work and hopeful planning. Mara, her muscles aching with a pleasant weariness, found solace in the familiar warmth of their cabin. The embers in the hearth pulsed with a dying, yet comforting, glow, casting long, dancing shadows across the room. Eli sat beside her, his presence a silent anchor, a solid presence that had become the very foundation of her world. The air, still faintly scented with dried lavender from her efforts that afternoon, felt charged with the quiet hum of exhaustion and contentment. It was in these stolen moments, these pockets of stillness carved out of their demanding lives, that the true depth of their shared journey became most apparent.

"Do you ever dream anymore, Eli?" Mara's voice was a soft murmur, barely disturbing the comfortable silence that had settled between them. She rested her head on his shoulder, her gaze fixed on the shifting embers. The question felt intimate, a glimpse into the parts of herself that even she sometimes kept hidden, tucked away beneath layers of practicality and responsibility. Havenridge, as magnificent as it was, demanded so much, consumed so much of their waking hours, their energy, their very focus. She worried, sometimes, that the vibrant tapestry of their individual dreams might begin to fray, the colors fading under the relentless pressure of their communal aspirations.

Eli shifted, his arm tightening around her, a familiar gesture of reassurance. He understood, with a clarity that always amazed her, the unspoken currents beneath her words. "Dreams?" he echoed, his voice a low rumble against her ear. "Yes, Mara. I do. They're just... different now." He paused, his thumb tracing a slow, soothing circle on her arm. "I dream of the harvest being plentiful, of the new irrigation system working perfectly, of the children in the learning circle mastering their letters. I dream of Elias seeing his vision for the expanded library come to fruition. I dream of you, Mara, with your hands full of herbs, your face lit by the sun, creating something beautiful and nurturing." He sighed softly, a sound that was more contentment than weariness. "My dreams are rooted here now, in this soil, in this community we're building. They're not the solitary flights of fancy they used to be, but tangible hopes, built on the reality of what we've achieved."

Mara leaned into him, absorbing the steady beat of his heart against her. His dreams, she realized, were a reflection of their shared reality, a testament to the life they had so deliberately chosen. But her own dreams, the ones that used to flicker and spark with a wild, untamed energy, felt more elusive. She dreamt of the quiet moments before Havenridge, of long solitary walks under skies unburdened by the needs of a growing settlement. She dreamt of the freedom to simply *be*, to explore her own creative impulses without the constant undertow of communal responsibility.

"I dream of... quiet," she admitted, her voice barely audible. "Of days when the biggest decision isn't how to allocate the lumber, or how to integrate a new family. Days when I can spend hours in the apothecary, experimenting with new remedies, or days when I can simply walk through the whispering woods without a checklist running through my mind." A faint tremor ran through her as she spoke, a confession of a longing that felt almost selfish in its indulgence. Havenridge was their purpose, their shared destiny, but a small part of her yearned for the forgotten quietude of her own being, a space where her aspirations weren't dictated by the collective need.

Eli gently turned her face towards him, his eyes, usually so focused and steady, now softened by the firelight and a deep well of understanding. "I know," he said, his voice laced with a tenderness that always made her heart ache in the most beautiful way. "I know it's a lot. The weight of it all. The constant giving. It's easy to feel like you're being stretched too thin, like the parts of yourself that are just *yours* are being neglected." He brushed a stray strand of hair from her cheek, his touch sending a familiar warmth through her. "But Mara," he continued, his gaze unwavering, "those dreams you have, the ones that are just for you – they are not less important. They are, in fact, the fuel. They are what makes *us*, and therefore what makes Havenridge, whole."

He pulled her closer, her head now resting against his chest, listening to the steady rhythm of his heart. "Remember when we first arrived here? We had so little. Our dreams were simple survival, a safe place to sleep, a meal to eat. We sacrificed everything for that. Now..." He sighed again, a breath of profound gratitude. "Now we have this. We have built something. And the price of that building, the cost of this permanence, is indeed high. It demands our time, our energy, our focus. But it does not demand that we extinguish ourselves."

He paused, letting his words settle between them. "You fear that these demands will pull us apart," he stated, not as a question, but as an acknowledgment of her deepest apprehension. "And it's a valid fear. The world outside is a place that often wears down the bonds between people, that isolates and divides. But that's not the world we are building here, Mara. Our partnership, our love, it's not a casualty of this effort. It is the very bedrock upon which everything else is built. It is the source of our strength, the reason we can do any of this."

Mara closed her eyes, letting his words wash over her. He was right, of course. Their partnership was not a passive byproduct of their shared life; it was an active, vibrant force. It was in the way they anticipated each other's needs, the way they communicated with a mere glance, the way they instinctively leaned on each other when the burdens felt too heavy. Their love wasn't a fragile bloom that would wilt under the harsh sun of responsibility; it was a deep-rooted oak, its branches reaching for the sky, its foundation set firm in the earth.

"But sometimes," she whispered, her voice thick with emotion, "sometimes I feel like I'm giving so much, and I'm afraid there won't be enough left of *me* to give to you. Or enough of *you* left for me. We're both so... occupied." The word felt inadequate, a pale imitation of the consuming nature of their responsibilities. Every decision, every action, seemed to ripple outwards, affecting not just themselves, but the entire community. It was a constant act of balancing, of prioritizing, of ensuring that the needs of the many did not entirely overshadow the needs of the few, especially the two of them, who were so intrinsically linked.

Eli gently stroked her hair, his touch a balm to her weary spirit. "That fear is the echo of the world we left behind, my love. The world that taught us to be guarded, to hoard our resources, to compete for what little we had. Havenridge is an experiment in the opposite. It's an assertion that abundance comes not from scarcity, but from sharing. And that includes sharing our lives, our dreams, our burdens." He lifted his head slightly, his gaze meeting hers again, intense and unwavering. "I would not be standing here, building this life with you, if I didn't believe in the strength of what we have. Our love, Mara, it's not a finite resource that can be depleted. It's a wellspring. The more we draw from it, the deeper and more abundant it becomes."

He shifted, sitting up straighter, pulling her up with him so they were facing each other fully. The firelight danced in his eyes, mirroring the warmth that was spreading through Mara's chest. "Think about it," he urged, his voice earnest. "When you're tending to a sick neighbor, using your incredible knowledge to heal them, aren't you also nurturing the very spirit of Havenridge? When I'm working with the council, ensuring fair distribution of resources, am I not also strengthening the bonds that hold us together? These actions, they are not a drain on us. They are an expression of who we are, together. And in that expression, we find not depletion, but replenishment."

Mara considered his words, the truth of them resonating deeply within her. He was right. Her fears, while born of genuine concern, were also tinged with the old scarcity mindset, the ingrained belief that giving too much would leave one empty. But Havenridge, and their relationship within it, was a living refutation of that principle. Every act of service, every sacrifice, was an investment, a reinforcement of the very foundations they had so painstakingly laid.

"So, my dreams," she murmured, a small smile playing on her lips, "they are not selfish indulgences, then? They are... part of the plan?"

Eli chuckled, a warm, rich sound that filled the quiet cabin. "They are essential. They are the vibrant colors in the tapestry. Without them, the whole picture would be dull, wouldn't it? Your dreams of quiet study, of creative exploration – those are the dreams that will bring new discoveries, new remedies, new beauty into Havenridge. My dreams of a bountiful harvest, of robust infrastructure – those are the dreams that ensure our survival and our comfort. And our shared dream," he added, his voice softening, "our shared dream of a life together, built on trust and love, that is the very heart of it all."

He cupped her face in his hands, his thumbs gently caressing her cheeks. "We have made sacrifices, yes. We have given up much. But look at what we have gained. Look at what we have built. And the greatest gain, the most precious treasure, is not the land, or the homes, or the flourishing community. It's this. It's us. Our partnership. The fact that we can face these challenges, these demands, these dreams, together."

Mara leaned into his touch, her eyes closing for a moment, savoring the profound sense of peace that settled over her. The anxieties hadn't vanished entirely – they were deeply ingrained, a part of her history – but they had receded, replaced by a quiet confidence, a renewed sense of purpose. Eli's unwavering belief in their connection, his steadfast reassurance, was a potent antidote to her fears. He reminded her that their strength wasn't in holding back, but in giving freely, both to their community and to each other.

"I love you, Eli," she whispered, the words a simple, profound truth.

"And I love you, Mara," he replied, his voice filled with an emotion that transcended words. He lowered his head, their lips meeting in a kiss that was both tender and deeply passionate. It was a kiss that spoke of shared history, of hard-won victories, of a future they were determined to build, hand in hand. It was a promise whispered in the language of touch and breath, a silent reaffirmation of their enduring love and their unshakeable commitment to each other, and to the beautiful, demanding world they were creating together. The embers continued to glow, casting a warm, soft light on their shared sanctuary, a beacon of their enduring hope.

Chapter Three

The Shifting Tides

The scent of pine and woodsmoke, usually a comforting embrace within their modest dwelling, felt different now. It mingled with the faint, almost imperceptible aroma of something sharp and synthetic, the lingering trace of their recent visitors. Mara traced the rim of her mug, the warmth of the herbal tea doing little to soothe the unease that had settled in her stomach. Across the small, sturdy table, Eli's gaze was distant, his brow furrowed in thought. The silence between them, once a space for shared understanding, now held a palpable tension, a silent acknowledgment of the shift in their world.

"They were too smooth, Eli," Mara finally said, her voice low, the practiced calm in her tone a thin veil over her apprehension. "Too polished. Their smiles didn't quite reach their eyes." She remembered the crispness of their linens, the almost unnerving uniformity of their attire, a stark contrast to the practical, often mended, clothes of Havenridge's inhabitants. They had arrived in a manner that suggested neither urgency nor desperation, but a calculated benevolence, a desire to bestow their wisdom upon a community they deemed... in need.

Eli nodded, his eyes now meeting hers, a shared recognition passing between them. "That's exactly what struck me. The language they used – 'assistance,' 'integration,' 'shared prosperity.' It sounds benevolent on the surface, but it's a carefully crafted veneer." He leaned back in his chair, the worn wood creaking in protest. "I've seen it before, Mara. When communities start to flourish, especially those that operate outside the established norms, the larger, more established powers take notice. And they don't like competition, or even successful independence."

"They spoke of Havenridge as a 'promising venture,'" Mara continued, recalling the words with a shiver. "A place with 'untapped potential' that could be 'greatly enhanced' by their guidance. Guidance that would involve 'strategic alignment' with regional councils." She looked at Eli, her gaze searching. "It sounded an awful lot like annexation, dressed up in diplomatic finery."

"It is," Eli confirmed, his voice firm. "They don't see us as a community; they see us as a resource. Or a threat. Or both. They want to absorb us, to bring us under their control, to dictate our practices and leverage our successes for their own benefit. The 'assistance' they offer comes with strings attached, strings that will eventually bind us so tightly we won't be able to move." He recounted tales from his own past, before Havenridge, when similar delegations had arrived in nascent settlements, their promises of aid dissolving into demands for tribute and absolute compliance. The initial charm was always a potent lure, a deceptive whisper of security that masked the insidious creep of control.

Mara pictured the leader of the delegation, a man named Thorne, his hands manicured, his voice smooth as river stone. He had spoken of their 'collective responsibility' to ensure 'orderly development' across the region, implying that Havenridge's autonomous growth was somehow disruptive. He had even, with a disarming smile, offered her a position on a newly formed advisory board, a seemingly prestigious role that would have placed her directly under their watchful eyes, her innovative herbal remedies and sustainable agricultural practices subject to their approval, their eventual commodification.

"He offered me a place on their 'Regional Development Council,'" she said, a hint of incredulity in her voice. "He painted a picture of me, advising them, sharing my knowledge... It felt like a gilded cage being offered. And the 'integration' they propose for our produce – they want to 'standardize' our output. Can you imagine? They want to turn our carefully cultivated, sustainably harvested goods into mass-produced commodities, stripped of their unique properties and their connection to the land." The thought was anathema to her. Her work in the apothecary, her deep understanding of the earth's bounty, was not about mass production; it was about respect, about balance, about the subtle energies that flowed between grower, harvester, and healer.

Eli reached across the table, his hand covering hers. His touch was grounding, a familiar anchor in the swirling waters of her disquiet. "They see what we've built, Mara, and they want a piece of it. Or, more accurately, they want to control the entire pie. They don't understand that our strength lies in our independence, in our ability to adapt and innovate on our own terms. They can't comprehend a community that thrives on collaboration and shared knowledge, rather than hierarchical control and competition."

"And the children," Mara added, her voice softening as she thought of the bright, curious faces in the learning circle. "They spoke of 'educational partnerships' and 'curriculum alignment.' It sounds so innocent, but I know what that means. It means they want to mold our children, to instill in them the values and priorities of their established order, to dilute the very essence of what makes Havenridge unique." Her heart ached at the thought of her carefully nurtured seeds of independent thought being choked out by the weeds of conformity. Their learning circle was built on fostering critical thinking, on encouraging questions, on celebrating individual talents. To surrender that to an external agenda felt like a betrayal of the future.

"They see our self-sufficiency as an anomaly, a dangerous precedent," Eli stated, his thumb stroking the back of her hand. "If Havenridge can thrive independently, why should other settlements remain beholden to them? It undermines their entire power structure. So, they will try to co-opt us, to bring us into their fold, and if that fails, they will seek to undermine us." He recalled the subtle threats woven into Thorne's parting words, a veiled mention of 'resource allocation disputes' and the 'complexities of inter-settlement trade agreements' that could arise if Havenridge remained recalcitrant. It was a clear warning: comply, or face obstacles.

"The delegation was not just about offering 'help,'" Mara mused, the pieces falling into place with a chilling clarity. "It was a scouting mission, a probe. They wanted to gauge our defenses, both our material resources and our willingness to resist. They saw our prosperity, our stability, our peace, and they interpreted it as vulnerability. They believe that because we have built so much, we have more to lose."

"And they're not entirely wrong," Eli admitted, his gaze steady. "We *do* have much to lose. We have built a life here, Mara. A good life. A life of purpose, of community, of quiet dignity. That is precisely why we must be vigilant. This isn't just about Havenridge anymore; it's about the principle of what we represent. A different way of living, a way that prioritizes connection and sustainability over profit and control."

He rose from the table, walking over to the window and looking out at the darkening sky, the first stars beginning to prick through the indigo. "Their visit has amplified the external pressures, the ones we've always been aware of but have managed to keep at bay. Now, they are at our doorstep, not with open hostility, but with a far more insidious agenda. They will use diplomacy, economic leverage, and subtle manipulation. They will try to divide us, to pit factions against each other, to exploit any internal disagreements."

"How do we combat that?" Mara asked, her voice tinged with a weariness that went beyond physical exhaustion. The thought of such a battle, not with weapons, but with whispers and veiled threats, felt deeply unsettling. "We are a community built on trust and cooperation. How do we stand against an enemy that thrives on deception and division?"

Eli turned back to her, his expression resolved. "We remind ourselves of what makes us strong. Our unity. Our shared purpose. The very values that they seek to erode are our greatest defense. We engage, but we do so with open eyes and firm boundaries. We listen to their offers, but we analyze them with critical minds, always asking ourselves: 'Who truly benefits?' We do not cede our autonomy, not one inch. We share our knowledge with our neighbors, with other independent communities, fostering a network of mutual support, a counter-alliance against this kind of external pressure."

He walked back to the table, sitting down again, his presence a solid reassurance. "We will have to be more transparent within Havenridge than ever before. Every decision, every negotiation, must be brought before the council, before the community. We cannot allow them to exploit any cracks in our foundation. We must demonstrate that our unity is not a weakness, but an unbreachable fortress."

Mara felt a surge of resolve coursing through her. The fear was still there, a cold knot in her gut, but it was now tempered by a fierce protectiveness, a burning desire to safeguard what they had so painstakingly built. "And my apothecary," she said, her voice gaining strength. "My research, my experimentation… that is not just personal pursuit. It's about developing remedies that are unique to us, that can't be replicated or controlled by external forces. It's about ensuring our health and well-being are not dependent on their 'assistance.'"

"Exactly," Eli affirmed, a hint of a smile touching his lips. "Every aspect of Havenridge is a potential target for their 'integration.' Your work, the children's education, our agricultural practices, our trade routes… they will seek to bring it all under their dominion. And our response must be to strengthen those very areas, to make them more resilient, more self-sufficient, more inherently 'Havenridge.' We must prove that our way of life is not only viable, but superior."

He paused, his gaze sweeping over their small, comfortable home, the scent of herbs from the drying racks mingling with the familiar woodsmoke. "They believe they are offering us an inevitability. The natural progression of a successful settlement into a larger, more 'organized' entity. But we have already proven them wrong. We have created something new, something that doesn't fit their mold. Our success is an anomaly, and they will try to correct it. Our task now is to ensure that correction is impossible."

The weight of their responsibility felt heavier than ever, but it was a shared burden, and Eli's unwavering resolve was a beacon in the encroaching shadow. They had faced hardship, scarcity, and the raw fight for survival. Now, they faced a more subtle, perhaps more dangerous, adversary – one that sought to dismantle their spirit through seduction rather than siege. Mara met Eli's gaze, a silent promise passing between them. They would not be absorbed. They would not be assimilated. Havenridge would remain, a testament to their independence, a beacon of their chosen way of life, and they would defend it with every fiber of their being, not with weapons, but with unwavering unity and an unshakeable commitment to the values they held dear. The external pressures were mounting, but so too was their collective will to resist.

The pine-scented air, usually a balm to Mara's spirit, now seemed to carry the faint, discordant hum of differing opinions. The serene facade of Havenridge, a community forged from shared vision and collective effort, was beginning to show hairline fractures. The delegation's visit, while brief, had acted like a subtle catalyst, stirring dormant desires and anxieties among the inhabitants. Not everyone shared Mara and Eli's immediate distrust. For some, the promises of 'assistance' and 'integration' resonated with a genuine yearning for what they perceived as progress.

Among the most vocal proponents for engagement was Silas, a man who had always possessed a restless spirit, even within the confines of their peaceful settlement. He was a skilled craftsman, his hands capable of coaxing beauty from raw wood, but his mind often drifted beyond the familiar valley. Silas had been among the first to approach the delegation after their departure, his curiosity outweighing any apprehension. He had observed their meticulously crafted tools, the advanced materials they seemed to possess, and the effortless way they spoke of systems and logistics that were beyond Havenridge's current understanding.

"They offered us access to new seed strains, Mara," Silas argued animatedly, his voice carrying across the bustling marketplace where the topic of the delegation had become an unavoidable undercurrent. He gestured with a splintered piece of lumber, his eyes alight with a vision of expanded harvests and more robust crops. "Strains that are resistant to the blight that plagued our south fields last season. And their irrigation techniques... imagine, less water, better yield. Isn't that what we've always strived for? To improve our lot?"

Beside him, Elara, who managed the community's granary with an almost maternal care, nodded in agreement. She was pragmatic, her concerns rooted in the tangible realities of sustenance. "Silas is right," she stated, her voice calm but firm. "We've managed wonderfully, but there's always room for improvement. I heard them talking about energy solutions too. Solar collectors that are far more efficient than our current panels. Think of the reduced burden on our collective power stores, especially during the long winter months. It means more light for the children's studies, more heat for the elders."

Mara listened, her brow furrowed. She understood their reasoning. Their hard work had brought them security, but the siren song of enhanced efficiency and abundance was a powerful one. They had sacrificed much to build Havenridge, and the idea of easing those burdens, of introducing new innovations that could directly benefit everyone, was appealing. Yet, the way Silas and Elara spoke, it was as if the delegation had offered them a gift, unburdened by any ulterior motive.

"But at what cost, Elara?" Mara countered gently, choosing her words carefully. "They spoke of 'standardization' for our produce. What does that mean for the unique character of our berries, the specific nutrient profile of our herbs? And their energy solutions, are they readily adaptable to our existing infrastructure, or will we become dependent on their proprietary parts and technicians?" The word 'dependent' hung in the air, a stark reminder of the very thing they had sought to escape when they founded Havenridge.

"Dependency is a choice, Mara," Silas interjected, his tone a shade too sharp. "If they offer something that genuinely improves our lives, and we can manage the terms of that exchange, why shouldn't we avail ourselves of it? We can't remain in a bubble forever. The world outside is vast, and it has knowledge and resources we lack. To ignore that is to stunt our own growth." He looked around, a hopeful expression on his face, as if expecting a wave of agreement.

A ripple of murmurs went through the small crowd that had gathered around them. Some nodded along with Silas, their faces alight with possibility. Others, however, shifted uncomfortably, their gazes darting towards Mara, a silent acknowledgment of her concerns. A few even actively shook their heads, their faces etched with worry.

It was Anya, a sprightly woman whose hands were rarely still, always busy with weaving or mending, who spoke up next, her voice carrying a quiet authority. "Growth is not always outward expansion, Silas. Sometimes, it is inward deepening. What they offer might seem like a shortcut, but shortcuts often bypass the very lessons we need to learn. Our sustainability is not just about efficiency; it's about understanding the interconnectedness of our ecosystem, our community. These 'new strains' and 'techniques'... do they respect that balance? Or do they simply extract more, leaving the soil depleted in a new way, a way we might not immediately see?"

Her words resonated with a segment of the community, those who had always approached Havenridge's development with a deep reverence for its natural cycles. They remembered the initial struggles, the slow, deliberate process of learning to live in harmony with the land, a process that had forged their bonds and instilled in them a profound appreciation for what they had achieved.

The growing divergence of opinions was palpable. It was no longer just a private conversation between Mara and Eli; it was a nascent debate that was spreading through the heart of their community. The prospect of external engagement had unearthed a fundamental question: was Havenridge meant to be a self-contained utopia, or a thriving, integrated part of a larger world?

Eli, ever the pragmatist and mediator, found himself navigating these newly formed currents of dissent. He saw the genuine desire for betterment in Silas and Elara, the cautious wisdom in Anya, and the deep-seated apprehension in Mara, and he understood that each perspective held a piece of the truth. He called for a community assembly, a gathering that was usually reserved for major decisions or celebrations. This time, the air crackled with a different kind of energy – anticipation, yes, but also a nervous tension, a sense that the very foundations of their collective identity were about to be scrutinized.

The assembly was held in the central clearing, beneath the ancient oak that had witnessed the founding of Havenridge. Lumbar benches had been arranged in a semicircle, and as people settled, the quiet hum of conversation filled the space. Eli stood at the center, his presence a calming anchor in the swirling emotions. He began by acknowledging the delegation's visit, framing it not as an invitation to surrender, but as an opportunity for careful consideration.

"They presented us with a vision," Eli said, his voice clear and steady, carrying to the edges of the gathering. "A vision of connection, of shared resources, of broader opportunities. It is natural that such a vision sparks different reactions. Some see potential, others see peril. Both are valid responses, born from our shared love for Havenridge and our commitment to its future."

He then opened the floor for discussion, and the dam broke. Silas was among the first to speak, his arguments echoing his earlier sentiments. He spoke of the limitations of their current resources, the long hours spent on manual labor that could be automated, the missed opportunities for trade that could bring in much-needed goods. "We are not afraid of hard work," he declared, his voice rising, "but we should not be afraid of smart work either. If their technology can ease our burdens, if their knowledge can enhance our productivity, it would be foolish, even arrogant, to refuse it outright."

A chorus of agreement rose from a significant portion of the assembly. Faces that had always been etched with the quiet resilience of their chosen path now showed a spark of ambition, a desire for more than mere survival and quiet contentment. They had built a life, but perhaps, they thought, they could build a richer one.

Then, Anya rose, her usual warmth tempered with a steely resolve. "Our productivity is not just about numbers, Silas. It is about our connection to the land. Our 'blight-resistant' seeds might yield more, but what do they take from the soil? Their 'efficient' irrigation might save water, but does it disrupt the natural water table? We have learned to work *with* our environment, not to conquer it. We must ask if their advancements respect that hard-won wisdom." Her words drew nods of affirmation from those who valued Havenridge's unique ecological harmony.

The debate intensified. Voices rose, impassioned and firm. Arguments about self-sufficiency clashed with desires for external resources. Fears of manipulation and loss of identity were countered with appeals to progress and cooperation. Mara watched, a knot of anxiety tightening in her chest. She saw families divided, friends exchanging sharp words, the easy camaraderie that had always defined their gatherings dissolving into an us-versus-them mentality.

One faction, led by Silas, embraced the idea of cautious engagement, believing that Havenridge could strategically adopt certain advancements while maintaining its core values. They envisioned a future where they could leverage external knowledge to bolster their own strengths, creating a more resilient and prosperous community. They spoke of forming carefully negotiated trade agreements and perhaps even sending a small delegation to observe other settlements and their interactions with the outside world.

Another faction, echoing Mara's deep-seated reservations, advocated for a more insular approach. They pointed to the subtle condescension in the delegation's words, the underlying assumption that Havenridge was somehow deficient, in need of 'guidance.' They feared that any opening, however small, would inevitably lead to a gradual erosion of their autonomy, a slow assimilation into a system that did not share their values. They emphasized the importance of internal strength, of further developing their own unique solutions and fostering even tighter community bonds as their primary defense.

And then there were those in the middle, caught between the two extremes. They were wary of overtures but also acknowledged the potential benefits. They sought a balance, a path that would allow for some level of interaction without compromising their independence. Their voices, though often drowned out by the louder pronouncements of the more polarized factions, represented a significant portion of the community, a testament to the complex realities of their situation.

Eli, standing at the heart of the storm, worked tirelessly to bridge the divides. He patiently listened to each speaker, validating their concerns and acknowledging the validity of their perspectives. He didn't dismiss Silas's vision of progress, nor did he dismiss Mara's fears of assimilation. Instead, he sought common ground, urging them to remember the shared purpose that had brought them together.

"We are not defined by what we accept, but by how we choose," Eli stated, his voice cutting through the rising tide of emotion. "If we accept their innovations, do we do so with open eyes, understanding the terms and the potential consequences? Or do we accept them blindly, allowing them to dictate our future? If we choose to remain isolated, are we truly preserving our way of life, or are we merely clinging to a past that may not be sustainable in the long run?"

He proposed a compromise: a period of intense internal discussion and research. They would form specialized committees, each tasked with evaluating specific aspects of the delegation's propositions. One committee would delve into agricultural advancements, another into technological infrastructure, a third into educational outreach, and a fourth into potential trade regulations. These committees would be composed of individuals with diverse viewpoints, ensuring that all concerns were thoroughly examined. Their findings would then be presented back to the entire community for a collective decision.

"Let us gather information, not make hasty judgments," Eli urged. "Let us understand the true nature of the opportunities and the risks before we commit ourselves. Our strength has always been our unity. Let us not allow this challenge to fracture that unity, but rather to forge it anew, stronger and wiser."

Mara watched him, a profound sense of gratitude mixing with her lingering unease. Eli's calm leadership was a steadying force, a reminder that even in the face of internal discord, their commitment to reasoned discourse and communal decision-making remained. He was not dictating a path, but empowering them to find one together.

As the assembly dispersed, the conversations continued, now more nuanced, more informed by the structured debate. The factions hadn't vanished, but the edges had softened. The immediate threat of an all-or-nothing decision had receded, replaced by a shared commitment to a process of careful deliberation. Mara knew the challenges were far from over. The subtle divisions that had emerged were a testament to the complexity of their situation, a stark reminder that the external pressures were not the only ones they had to navigate. The strength of Havenridge would be tested not just by how they responded to the world beyond their valley, but by how they managed the differing hearts and minds within it. The tides were indeed shifting, and the currents of opinion within their own community were proving to be as powerful and as unpredictable as any from the outside.

The air in Eli's small study, usually a sanctuary of quiet contemplation, now felt thick with an unspoken tension. The scent of drying herbs and worn leather, so comforting moments before, seemed to recede, replaced by the metallic tang of apprehension. He had expected the delegation's leader, a man named Valerius, to be inquisitive, perhaps even probing, about Havenridge's operations and its place in the wider world. What he hadn't anticipated was the unnerving precision with which Valerius had steered the conversation, not toward communal infrastructure or agricultural yields, but towards Eli himself.

"Your reputation precedes you, Eli," Valerius had said, his voice smooth as polished obsidian, his gaze unwavering. He hadn't specified *which* reputation, and that ambiguity was precisely what sent a chill down Eli's spine. It had started subtly, with casual remarks about Eli's apparent knack for organization, his intuitive understanding of logistics, and the efficient way he managed their nascent trade routes. But then, the questions had become sharper, more personal.

"I understand you have a background in... resource management?" Valerius had asked, a slight inflection on the word 'management' that hinted at something far more complex, far less benign. Eli had offered a non-committal shrug, a carefully crafted response designed to deflect without outright lying. He'd spoken of managing supplies for a small, isolated community, of ensuring everyone had what they needed.

But Valerius had smiled, a slow, predatory unfolding of lips that made Eli's gut clench. "Of course. Essential work. But I recall... or perhaps my sources are mistaken... that your expertise extended to more... specialized applications. Strategic allocation, perhaps? The coordination of... movements?"

Eli had felt the meticulously constructed facade of his new life begin to crumble. He had worked for years to shed the skin of his past, to bury the man he once was beneath layers of honest labor and quiet anonymity. Havenridge, with its simple rhythms and its commitment to peace, had been his absolution, his sanctuary. Now, Valerius's words were like acid, eating away at the foundation. He'd felt the familiar prickle of adrenaline, a sensation he'd worked so hard to suppress, and a cold dread began to bloom in his chest. His carefully constructed anonymity wasn't just under threat; it was being systematically dismantled.

He remembered the faces, the names, the dangerous games played in the shadowed corners of a world he had desperately tried to forget. He'd been good at his old life, frighteningly good. The skills that had made him indispensable then – the ability to read people, to anticipate threats, to orchestrate complex operations with ruthless efficiency – were precisely the skills that now terrified him. Valerius's probing questions weren't idle curiosity; they were calculated moves, testing the waters, searching for the chinks in his armor.

The conversation had shifted when Eli had seen Mara approaching the open doorway, her expression one of concern as she noticed the unusual intensity of the exchange. Valerius had smoothly transitioned to discussing Havenridge's agricultural output, but the damage was done. The subtle familiarity in his tone, the way he'd looked at Eli as if recognizing an old, dangerous adversary, had left Eli unsettled to his core.

Later that evening, after Valerius and his delegation had departed, leaving behind a wake of uneasy questions and nascent divisions, Eli sought out Mara. They found themselves by the gently flowing river, the moon casting a silver path across its surface. The usual comforting murmur of the water did little to soothe the tremor in Eli's hands.

"Mara," he began, his voice rougher than he intended, "Valerius... he knows things. Things I thought were buried with my old life." He took a deep breath, the cool night air doing little to clear the fog of fear in his mind. "He spoke of 'resource management,' of 'strategic allocation.' Those aren't terms for running a farm or organizing a market day. They're terms from... from a different world."

Mara's brow furrowed, her gaze steady and expectant. She had sensed the shift in Eli during his conversation with Valerius, the subtle tension that had coiled around him. She trusted Eli implicitly, but she also knew that his past was a landscape he rarely discussed, a country he had long since exiled himself from.

"What did he mean, Eli?" she asked softly, her voice devoid of judgment, merely seeking understanding.

Eli ran a hand through his hair, the action agitated. "He was hinting, Mara. Probing. He didn't name names, but he was talking about the kind of work I used to do. Coordinating logistics for… sensitive operations. Ensuring supplies reached… difficult destinations. Orchestrating… movement." The words felt alien on his tongue, relics of a life he had fought tooth and nail to escape. "He looked at me as if he recognized me, Mara. Not as Eli, the community organizer. But as someone else. Someone dangerous."

He paused, gathering his thoughts, the images flashing through his mind – stark warehouses, hushed meetings, the cold weight of weapons, the faces of men and women driven by greed and power. "My past wasn't just about managing supplies, Mara. It was about planning, about anticipating threats, about… neutralizing them. I was good at it. Too good. And it attracted the wrong kind of attention."

He turned to face her fully, his eyes reflecting the moonlight, dark pools of a history he'd hoped would remain unseen. "Valerius is not just a representative of some external governing body. He's someone who operates in the shadows, just like some of the people I used to work for. Or against." A grimace touched his lips. "It's hard to tell sometimes, the lines are so blurred."

Mara listened, her initial apprehension solidifying into a protective resolve. She had always known Eli carried burdens, that his past was a complex tapestry. But hearing him speak of it with such raw fear, such stark recognition of danger, painted a picture far more vivid and terrifying than she had imagined. The delegation's interest, which had seemed like a political or economic concern, was suddenly much more personal, much more insidious.

"He was probing for weaknesses, Eli," Mara said, her voice firm. "Not just Havenridge's vulnerabilities, but yours. If he recognizes you, if he knows what you're capable of, then Havenridge itself becomes a target, not just for resources, but for leverage. Or worse."

Eli nodded, the dread in his heart deepening. "Exactly. There are people from that life, Mara. People who wouldn't hesitate to exploit Havenridge. They value efficiency and control above all else. They see a community like ours, so focused on peace and sustainability, as a weakness. An opportunity." He thought of specific individuals, figures from his past who wielded power with a casual cruelty, who saw people as pawns and communities as resources to be plundered.

"There's a man named Thorne," Eli continued, his voice low and intense. "He was... a competitor, then a partner, then an enemy. He's ruthless. He's built an empire on brokering illicit goods and information. He thrives on chaos and exploits vulnerability. If he catches wind of Havenridge, of our isolation, of our potential... he'd see it as a prize to be acquired, or a problem to be eliminated. He doesn't understand cooperation; he understands dominance."

He paused, picturing Thorne's cold, calculating eyes. "Then there's a woman named Anya Petrova. She was a master manipulator, skilled at sowing discord. She could turn allies against each other with a whisper. If Valerius is connected to Thorne or Petrova, or even just shares their modus operandi, then Havenridge isn't just facing an external delegation; it's facing a potential invasion, a takeover by people who have no respect for what we've built."

Mara's hand found his, her grip firm and reassuring. "We built this place together, Eli. We built it on trust and on a shared vision of a better way of life. That foundation is strong. If these threats are real, we will face them. But we face them together." Her apprehension, which had been a quiet hum, now had a name, a face, a history tied to Eli's own. The external threat was no longer an abstract possibility; it was a personal danger, a shadow reaching out from Eli's past to threaten their present and their future.

"The skills you learned in that other life, Eli," Mara said, her gaze unwavering, "they weren't just for... those operations. They were about understanding systems, about protecting what matters. You learned how to anticipate threats, how to build defenses. That knowledge, it's not inherently dangerous. It's how it's used."

Eli met her gaze, a flicker of something other than dread in his eyes – a spark of determination. "You're right. I can't let them exploit Havenridge. I can't let them destroy what we've created." He squeezed her hand. "My past is returning, Mara. But it doesn't have to dictate our future. We'll have to be more vigilant than ever. Valerius's questions weren't just about me; they were about assessing our defenses, our vulnerabilities. He's gathering intel."

The serenity of the riverside was a stark contrast to the turmoil brewing within them. The shifting tides that were beginning to stir Havenridge's community were now being compounded by a far more personal and dangerous undercurrent. The external threat was no longer a general concern about outside influence; it was a specific, insidious danger rooted in Eli's hidden history, a danger that threatened to unravel the very fabric of their sanctuary. They had to understand the true nature of this threat, to see it not just as an external force, but as a direct consequence of Eli's past life, a life that had now come knocking on their door, not with an offer of partnership, but with the chilling promise of exploitation.

The hushed urgency in Eli's voice, the stark confession of shadows from his past, had settled over Mara like a shroud. The moon, once a gentle observer of their quiet moments, now seemed to cast a cold, revealing light on the precariousness of their existence. Valerius's probing questions, Eli's palpable fear, Thorne's ruthless ambition, Anya Petrova's manipulative prowess – these were not mere geopolitical concerns for Havenridge; they were direct threats, coiled serpents preparing to strike at the heart of their hard-won peace. Eli's past, a land he had desperately sought to leave behind, had not only found him but was now actively reaching for the community he had helped to build.

Mara's mind, always attuned to the pulse of Havenridge, began to race. The initial shock of Eli's revelations gave way to a steely resolve. Fear was a natural response, but it could not be allowed to paralyze them. If Havenridge was to survive, if their vision of a self-governing, sustainable community was to endure, they needed more than just Eli's formidable skills honed in a dangerous world. They needed to fortify Havenridge from within, to build a bulwark so strong that no external force, no matter how insidious, could breach it.

"We can't just wait for the next threat to appear, Eli," Mara said, her voice resonating with a newfound conviction. They were still by the river, the water's gentle murmur a stark contrast to the storm gathering in her thoughts. "We can't rely solely on hiding or on your ability to anticipate danger. We need to be proactive. We need to make Havenridge too resilient, too self-sufficient, to be worth the effort of dismantling."

Eli turned to her, his face etched with a weariness that went beyond mere physical exhaustion. "I know. But how? We're a young community. We have basic infrastructure, agricultural knowledge, but we're still dependent on so many things. Trade routes, specialized tools, even certain kinds of medicine. Those are all vulnerabilities."

"Then we reduce those dependencies," Mara declared, her eyes alight with purpose. She pulled away slightly, her hands gesturing as she spoke, painting a picture with words. "Think about our food. We grow enough, yes, but what about preservation? What about diversifying our crops to withstand different climates or potential blight? We need more than just fields; we need robust food storage, advanced techniques for drying, fermenting, and canning. We need to be able to feed ourselves through any season, any hardship."

She began to walk slowly along the riverbank, Eli falling into step beside her. "And manufacturing. We have skilled artisans, but our capacity is limited. Imagine if we could produce more of what we need ourselves. Basic tools, spare parts for our water purification systems, even simple building materials. If we can learn to manufacture more of our own goods, we reduce our reliance on external suppliers, suppliers who could be pressured or manipulated by people like Thorne."

Eli listened, his initial despair beginning to recede, replaced by a burgeoning sense of hope. Mara's vision wasn't just about defense; it was about growth, about building a stronger, more independent Havenridge. It was a vision that resonated deeply with the core principles of their community. "Self-sufficiency," he murmured, the word tasting of potential. "It's a grand ambition, Mara."

"It's a necessary one," she corrected, her tone firm. "I've been thinking about this for a while, even before Valerius's visit. I've seen how easily outside influences can sway opinions, how a shortage of a particular good can create dependence. We're too open. We've built this place on trust and transparency, which is our strength, but it also makes us vulnerable to those who operate by deception and coercion."

She stopped and turned to him, her expression earnest. "My grandmother was a master gardener and preserver. She could store enough food to see her family through the harshest winters. I've been studying her journals, the old agricultural manuals in the community archives. There are techniques, Eli, that we've largely forgotten or never even learned. Methods for soil enrichment that go beyond simple crop rotation, ways to cultivate hardy, nutrient-rich plants that can thrive even in less-than-ideal conditions."

Mara's hands moved with animation as she described her ideas. "We could establish dedicated research plots, experimenting with heirloom seeds and forgotten farming methods. We could train more community members in advanced preservation, creating a decentralized network of storage so that no single loss would cripple us. Imagine community-wide fermentation workshops, community-run smokehouses for preserving meats and fish. It's about spreading knowledge and capacity, not concentrating it."

Eli nodded, a slow smile beginning to touch his lips. He could see the intricate web of possibilities Mara was weaving. "And the manufacturing side? That seems more complex."

"Complex, yes, but not impossible," Mara replied, her gaze fixed on the horizon, as if seeing the future unfurling before her. "We have skilled metalworkers, woodworkers, weavers. We could create a communal workshop, a place where specialized tools and machinery could be housed and maintained. We could start by identifying our most critical needs. What are the things we currently have to import that are essential for our survival and security? Water pumps? Filtration components? Basic medical supplies? We could then dedicate resources to developing local alternatives."

She paused, a thoughtful expression on her face. "I've been looking at some old schematics for simple, low-tech industrial equipment. Things like hand-cranked looms that can produce fabric more efficiently, small-scale forge designs for tool repair and creation, even basic hydraulic presses for processing materials. It's about understanding the fundamental principles and adapting them to our resources and needs."

Eli felt a surge of admiration for Mara. Her intelligence, her foresight, and her unwavering dedication to Havenridge were qualities that anchored him. He had spent so long navigating a world of duplicity and force, where survival meant anticipating and neutralizing threats. Mara's approach was different; it was about building strength, fostering self-reliance, and creating a community so robust that it would be its own best defense.

"You're talking about a paradigm shift, Mara," Eli said, his voice filled with respect. "Moving from a model of sustainable living to a model of complete self-governance and self-sufficiency. It's... it's the ideal. But it will require significant effort, resources, and buy-in from everyone."

"I know," Mara agreed. "And that's where we need to start. We need to present this not as a reaction to Valerius or the fear of external threats, but as the next natural step in our evolution as a community. We always intended to be independent, to live by our own principles. This is just accelerating that process, making it more concrete. We need to explain why this is vital for our long-term security and prosperity."

She turned to him, her eyes shining with a quiet passion. "I want to dedicate my time to this, Eli. I want to lead the charge on developing these initiatives. I can work with the agricultural guilds, with the artisans, with anyone willing to learn and contribute. I can research, I can organize workshops, I can help secure the resources we need. We can start small. A pilot program for advanced food preservation. A shared tool-making initiative. We build momentum from there."

Eli reached out and gently took her hands. They were calloused from her work, but her touch was soft and reassuring. "Mara, your vision... it's exactly what Havenridge needs. I've been so focused on the external threats, on the potential damage others could inflict. You're focused on building something so strong that those threats become irrelevant. I support this wholeheartedly. We will make it happen."

He paused, his gaze serious. "And I will do everything I can to support you. My skills... they might be less about building and more about... understanding systems, anticipating resistance, and removing obstacles. If there are those who resist these changes, or if external forces try to interfere, I will be here to protect this vision, just as I will protect Havenridge."

Mara squeezed his hands. The fear hadn't vanished entirely – it was a constant companion now, a shadow cast by the past. But with Eli's commitment and her own burgeoning plans, a new feeling began to take root: hope, strong and resilient, like the hardy crops she envisioned cultivating.

"We'll need to be strategic about how we present this," Mara mused, her mind already working through the practicalities. "We can't afford to spook people or make them feel overwhelmed. We can frame it as enhancing our existing strengths, not as a radical departure. For the agricultural side, we can emphasize increased food security, reduced waste, and greater variety for everyone. For manufacturing, we focus on reducing costs for essential items and fostering innovation and skill-sharing within the community."

She imagined the detailed plans she would draw up, the careful calculations of resources, the outreach to community leaders. She would need to visit the agricultural collectives, speak with the masters of the forge and the loom, and perhaps even consult with Elder Maeve, whose wisdom often offered a calming perspective.

"I'll start by compiling a list of the most critical goods and services we currently rely on from outside," Mara continued, her voice gaining momentum. "Then, I'll begin researching the most feasible local production methods for each. For food, I'll focus on techniques that require minimal specialized equipment initially, making them accessible to more people. Fermentation, drying, root cellaring – these are all ancient practices that are highly effective."

Eli listened, his mind already racing through the implications of her plans. He saw how her vision directly addressed the vulnerabilities Valerius had likely identified. A community that could feed itself, clothe itself, and maintain its own infrastructure was far harder to control or coerce.

"And we'll need to consider how to integrate this with our existing social structures," Eli added, thinking of the various guilds and collectives that made up Havenridge. "We don't want to create new divisions, but rather strengthen the existing ones by giving them new, vital purposes."

"Exactly," Mara affirmed. "The agricultural guilds would take the lead on expanding preservation techniques and soil enrichment. The artisan guilds could form the core of a new communal workshop, focusing on tool repair and the production of essential goods. We can create apprenticeship programs within these expanded frameworks, ensuring that knowledge is passed down and capacity grows organically."

She pictured herself surrounded by schematics and agricultural texts, the scent of ink and parchment filling her small workspace. She saw community members gathered, learning new skills, their faces alight with the satisfaction of creation and self-reliance. It was a vision of empowerment, of a community actively shaping its own destiny.

"This isn't just about defense against external threats, Eli," Mara said, her gaze meeting his with a profound sincerity. "It's about realizing the full potential of Havenridge. It's about building a truly sovereign community, one that isn't beholden to anyone, one that can stand as a beacon of what is possible when people choose cooperation and self-reliance over dependence and external control. Your past has shown us the dangers of vulnerability. My vision is to build a future where that vulnerability no longer exists."

Eli's heart swelled with a mixture of pride and affection for the woman beside him. She was not only his partner in life but a vital pillar of strength for Havenridge. While he had learned to dismantle threats, she was learning to build an unassailable future. The shifting tides were indeed upon them, but with Mara's vision for autonomy and Eli's unwavering support, Havenridge was not about to be swept away. They would stand firm, not by brute force, but by the quiet, potent power of self-sufficiency. The work ahead would be immense, but as Mara began to outline her initial proposals for food security and local manufacturing, the fear that had gripped Eli began to transform into a determined anticipation of what they could achieve, together.

The night air, crisp and carrying the faint, earthy scent of freshly turned soil from the outer fields, offered a deceptive calm. Mara and Eli stood at the precipice, not of a physical cliff, but of an existential one. The lights of Havenridge, a constellation of warm, steady glows against the encroaching darkness, pulsed with a life they had both fought to nurture. Each flicker was a testament to their shared endeavor, a silent promise whispered into the vast, indifferent expanse of the night.

Eli's hand found Mara's, his fingers interlacing with hers. The warmth was a stark contrast to the chill that had settled deep within him, a chill born not of the evening breeze, but of the specter of his former life. "Mara," he began, his voice a low rumble, tinged with an anxiety he rarely allowed to surface. "My past... it's not just a story I carry. It's a debt that others are still collecting. And I fear, with every fiber of my being, that they will find their way here. To Havenridge. To you."

He turned to her, his eyes, usually so clear and perceptive, clouded with a self-recrimination that Mara recognized instantly. It was the look of a man who believed he was a contagion, a walking plague destined to infect all he held dear. "I tried to escape it, to build something that was entirely separate, entirely clean. But it's like a shadow. It stretches, it grows, and it always finds the light."

Mara squeezed his hand, her grip a deliberate anchor against his spiraling fear. She felt the tension in his frame, the subtle tremor that betrayed the turmoil within. "Eli," she said, her voice steady, cutting through the rising tide of his apprehension. "You are not a shadow. You are the foundation upon which so much of Havenridge is built. The skills you possess, the knowledge you gained from... from that life... they are precisely why we have a chance. You saw the dangers before many of us even suspected them."

He gave a short, humorless laugh. "And now I've brought them to our doorstep. Valerius was just the first whisper. Thorne... Anya Petrova... they are the coming storm. And my past is the wind that will drive it." He looked out at the settlement, his gaze lingering on the community center, the greenhouses, the communal workshops that were so much a part of her vision. "I can't protect you from that, Mara. Not entirely. My methods were designed for destruction, for survival in a world that rewards ruthlessness. They are not suited for nurturing what we have here."

A gentle breeze rustled the leaves of a nearby oak, a soft sigh that seemed to echo his sentiment. Mara turned fully to face him, her heart aching at the burden he carried alone. "But you don't have to, Eli," she insisted, her gaze unwavering. "We don't have to carry this alone. That's the whole point of Havenridge, isn't it? We share the burdens, we share the responsibilities, and we share the strength."

She stepped closer, her shoulder brushing against his. The intimacy of the gesture was a silent declaration. "You worry about them coming for me, for us. I worry about what happens to this place if we are forced to compromise our ideals. If we have to become like them to survive. That is a sacrifice I am not willing to make, Eli. Not without a fight."

He met her gaze, and for a moment, the weariness in his eyes receded, replaced by a flicker of the fierce protectiveness she had come to know. "And I will fight with you, Mara. Always. But 'fighting' in my world often meant... eradicating. And I can't do that here. I won't let that part of me taint what we've built."

"Then we find a different way to fight," Mara said, her voice firming with conviction. "We have to. We've talked about self-sufficiency, about building resilience. That's not just about food and manufacturing, Eli. It's about our spirit. It's about refusing to be broken, refusing to be corrupted. My grandmother always said that the strongest roots grow in the hardest soil."

She reached up, her fingers tracing the line of his jaw, a touch that was both tender and resolute. "Your past is a part of you, Eli. It's the dark earth that nourishes the seed of who you are now. But it does not define the harvest. We will have to make sacrifices. There will be difficult choices. We may have to compromise on things we never imagined. But our core principles, our commitment to each other and to this community... that cannot be compromised. That is the vow we renew, not just tonight, but every day."

Eli's hand covered hers on his jaw, his thumb gently stroking her skin. The vastness of the sky above, studded with a million indifferent stars, suddenly felt less daunting, less isolating. He saw in Mara's eyes not just love, but a fierce, unwavering belief in their shared future, a future he had almost given up on. "Compromise," he murmured, the word tasting foreign on his tongue, so unlike the absolute demands he was accustomed to. "What kind of compromises, Mara?"

"The kind that strengthen us, not weaken us," she replied, her gaze earnest. "We can't afford to be naive. If Valerius can identify our vulnerabilities, Thorne and his ilk will exploit them ruthlessly. We may need to be more guarded, more discreet about certain aspects of Havenridge. We may need to invest resources in defenses we hoped we'd never need. We may even have to make difficult decisions about who we can truly trust, about who we can bring into our inner circle."

Her expression grew more serious. "And for you, Eli... it means accepting that you cannot shoulder this alone. It means allowing me to share the weight, allowing others to contribute to your protection, even if it's just by strengthening the community you're trying to shield. It means acknowledging that the 'fight' you know might not be the only fight, and perhaps not even the most effective one."

He drew a deep breath, the cool air filling his lungs, chasing away some of the tightness in his chest. "You're asking me to trust again, Mara. To trust that something other than vigilance and decisive action can protect us. To trust that building something new can be a more potent defense than tearing down what threatens it."

"I am," she confirmed, her voice soft but unwavering. "And I know it's a monumental ask, given everything you've been through. But

I have seen how you've already changed, how you've embraced the ideals of Havenridge. This is the next step. This is about accepting that this community, this life we're building, is worth protecting not just with force, but with unwavering integrity. It's about choosing what kind of future we want to defend, and then living it, even when it's hard."

Eli looked out at the distant lights, no longer seeing them as mere beacons of a settlement, but as tiny, flickering embers of hope that he, and now Mara, were determined to fan into an unquenchable fire. "The compromises will be painful," he admitted, his voice rough with emotion. "Sacrifices will be demanded. I've seen firsthand how easily people can be broken, how quickly ideals can be tarnished when faced with true desperation."

He turned back to Mara, his eyes locking with hers, a silent communion passing between them. "But you're right. This place... it's more than just a refuge. It's a promise. A promise to ourselves, to each other, and to the idea that a different way of living is possible. And if protecting that promise means changing how I approach the threats, if it means trusting in the strength of this community as much as I trust in my own skills... then I will. I will learn."

He lifted her hand to his lips, pressing a kiss to her knuckles, a gesture of reverence and deep, abiding commitment. "I vow, Mara, that I will do everything in my power to ensure that your vision for Havenridge, this beacon of self-sufficiency and integrity, is protected. And I vow that I will allow you to help me bear this burden. I will not let my past destroy our future."

Mara's heart swelled. It wasn't a dramatic declaration, no grand pronouncements echoing in the night. It was something far more profound: a quiet, shared understanding, a reaffirmation of their bond forged in the crucible of impending danger. It was a promise spoken not to the stars, but to each other, a sacred trust renewed under the vast, watchful sky.

"And I vow, Eli," she whispered, her voice thick with emotion, "that I will stand with you. We will face these shadows together. We will build our defenses, not by mirroring their darkness, but by amplifying our own light. We will make Havenridge too strong, too resilient, too full of hope, for any shadow to ever truly extinguish it."

They stood in silence for a long moment, the shared burden feeling lighter, no longer a solitary weight on Eli's shoulders, but a collective responsibility they embraced together. The distant glow of their settlement seemed to burn a little brighter now, a symbol not just of what they had built, but of what they were willing to become, together, to protect it. The shifting tides were indeed upon them, but as they held each other close, Mara felt a profound sense of peace settle over her. They were not merely surviving; they were actively choosing their future, one quiet, determined vow at a time.

The path ahead would be fraught with peril, a treacherous terrain that demanded every ounce of their ingenuity and resilience. Eli's past was a tangled knot of violence and deception, a legacy that Thorne and his ilk would undoubtedly seek to exploit, using his former allegiances and the deep-seated fear he carried as leverage. Mara understood that their plans for self-sufficiency, while vital, were not a shield against direct attack. They were a long-term strategy, a gradual strengthening of Havenridge's core, but they wouldn't deter a determined adversary overnight.

"We need to be pragmatic, Eli," Mara said, her gaze sweeping over the dimly lit perimeter of their community. "While my focus is on building our internal capacity, we also need to address the immediate threats. You've navigated these kinds of dangers before. What are the first steps you would take, not to dismantle them, but to disrupt their immediate advantage?"

Eli turned his attention from the stars to the subtle contours of the landscape, his senses already cataloging potential ingress points, the natural cover offered by the dense foliage at the edges of their territory. "Disruption is key, yes. We can't outmatch them in raw power or established networks, but we can outmaneuver them. Information is their primary weapon, both what they possess and what they glean. We need to make it harder for them to gather intelligence."

He gestured towards the natural defenses of the valley. "The natural terrain offers some cover, but we can enhance it. Hidden observation posts, camouflaged pathways that lead away from our main routes. We need to create a sense of uncertainty, make them question what they see, what they hear. A few well-placed misdirections can throw an entire operation off balance."

"So, patrols?" Mara asked, picturing them moving silently through the undergrowth.

"Not traditional patrols," Eli clarified. "More like... eyes and ears. Individuals who know the land intimately, who can move unseen and report any anomalies. People who understand the subtle signs of intrusion – disturbed foliage, unusual silence in the animal population, faint traces of passage. It's about layering our awareness, creating a distributed intelligence network that's difficult to penetrate."

He paused, his brow furrowed in thought. "And then there's the human element. Thorne will seek to sow discord, to exploit any existing grievances or fears within Havenridge. Anya Petrova will be adept at manipulation, at turning neighbor against neighbor through carefully planted rumors or offers of false security. We need to fortify our social fabric as much as our physical one."

"That's where communication and transparency become critical," Mara agreed, her mind already racing with strategies. "We need to reinforce the trust we've built. Regular, honest updates from leadership, even when the news is difficult. We need to empower community members to voice their concerns, to feel heard and valued. And we need to be prepared to counter misinformation with truth, calmly and consistently."

"Precisely," Eli said, a flicker of his old focus returning. "And if they try to use my past against me, to paint me as a liability or a danger to the community, we need a response ready. Not just denial, but a clear articulation of how my past experiences are now being channeled to protect Havenridge. It's about framing it as a strength, not a weakness, a testament to our ability to reform and rebuild, even from the darkest origins."

He looked at Mara, his gaze intense. "This will require difficult conversations, Mara. And perhaps, some difficult actions. We might have to distance ourselves from certain individuals or groups who are more susceptible to external influence. We might need to implement security protocols that feel... intrusive. These are the compromises you spoke of."

Mara met his gaze, her own reflecting a steely determination. "I understand, Eli. And I am prepared for them. We built Havenridge on the principle of collective well-being. If certain measures are necessary to ensure that well-being, then we must consider them. But we will do so with a clear conscience, ensuring that our actions remain aligned with our core values. We will not become what we oppose."

The air between them vibrated with a shared purpose, a silent pact to navigate the storm that was brewing. The stars above bore witness to their renewed vow, a quiet promise whispered against the vastness of the unknown, a commitment to protect not just their lives, but the very soul of the community they cherished. The burden was still heavy, the future uncertain, but now, it was a shared burden, a united front against the encroaching darkness, a testament to the strength that could be found not in isolation, but in unwavering solidarity. Their vow, spoken in the quiet of the night, was a seed of resilience planted in the fertile ground of their shared hope.

CHAPTER FOUR

The Weight of Decisions

The scent of damp earth and pine needles, usually a source of comfort, now felt heavy, tinged with the metallic tang of apprehension. The delegation's presence had cast a long shadow over Havenridge, a subtle but persistent erosion of the hard-won peace. They had arrived with offers of aid, their pronouncements of solidarity echoing through the community halls, but Mara, ever vigilant, had sensed the underlying agenda. Eli, too, his finely tuned instincts honed by a life lived on the knife's edge, had grown increasingly withdrawn, his silences more potent than any spoken fear.

Tonight, that apprehension crystallized into a palpable threat. A formal delegation, comprised of individuals Mara recognized from the periphery of regional power structures – men and women whose smiles never quite reached their eyes – had requested an audience in the main council chamber. They had come not with further assurances, but with a document. A proposal. It lay now on the rough-hewn table between Mara and Eli, its crisp, official letterhead a stark contrast to the worn wood and the flickering lamplight that cast dancing shadows across their faces. The air in their small cabin, usually filled with the comforting aroma of brewing tea and the faint, lingering scent of pine from the forest just beyond their walls, felt stifled, charged with unspoken anxieties.

Mara traced the embossed seal with a fingertip, her expression unreadable, but her knuckles were white where she gripped the edge of the table. The document was a masterclass in veiled coercion. It spoke of "mutual benefit," of "resource allocation for enhanced security," and of "strategic partnerships to ensure regional stability." On the surface, it was an offer too generous to refuse, a lifeline extended to a burgeoning community striving for independence. But Mara's keen intellect, her innate ability to see the currents beneath the placid surface of diplomacy, recognized the insidious tendrils of control woven into every clause.

"'Protection shall be provided against external threats, with oversight of Havenridge's defensive infrastructure by appointed regional liaisons,'" she read aloud, her voice carefully neutral, though a tremor ran beneath it. "'Resource allocation will be contingent upon adherence to approved security protocols and the integration of Havenridge's operational data into the Regional Security Network.'" She looked at Eli, her eyes, usually so vibrant, now clouded with a deep-seated concern. "Oversight, Eli. And integration. That sounds less like partnership and more like... occupation."

Eli leaned closer, his gaze fixed on a particular paragraph detailing the delegation's right to "inspect and approve any expansion or alteration of Havenridge's production facilities and resource management systems." His jaw was tight, a muscle twitching infinitesimally. He understood the implications far more acutely than Mara, his past experiences painting a chillingly clear picture of what such clauses truly meant. "They're not offering protection, Mara," he said, his voice a low, gravelly rumble that seemed to echo the unease in the room. "They're offering a gilded cage. These 'security protocols'… they'll require us to divulge our vulnerabilities, our supply chains, our operational strategies. And the 'liaisons'… they'll be their eyes and ears, reporting back, dictating our every move."

He picked up the document, his fingers brushing against the thick, high-quality paper. The scent of old parchment, mingled with a faint, almost imperceptible trace of something synthetic, something artificial, pricked at his senses. He recognized it—the scent of manufactured authority, of power wielded through carefully crafted bureaucracy. "Valerius wanted to conquer us. Thorne wants to exploit us. This delegation… they want to absorb us. To dilute what we are, to make us a compliant cog in their larger machine."

Mara nodded, her gaze sweeping over the dense text, each word a brick in the wall they were attempting to build around Havenridge. "The language is so carefully chosen. 'Strategic partnerships' to 'ensure regional stability.' They're framing their demands as necessities for our survival, for the good of the wider region. But the cost… the cost is our autonomy. Our very identity." She pointed to another section. "'All significant community decisions requiring external consultation will be routed through the appointed regional administrator, ensuring alignment with broader socio-economic objectives.'"

"Significant community decisions," Eli repeated, a humorless smile touching his lips. "That could mean anything from where we plant our next crop to who we allow to join our community. They want to control our growth, our direction, our very future. And this 'regional administrator'… that's not a title of guidance, Mara. It's a title of absolute authority." He looked at the list of signatories at the bottom of the page, names that carried weight in the fragmented political landscape beyond Havenridge. Names associated with old money, old power, and a ruthless pragmatism that prioritized control above all else. "They see our potential, Mara. They see the ingenuity, the self-sufficiency we're building. And they fear it. They fear what it represents. An independent entity, thriving outside their control."

The weight of the document felt crushing. Mara imagined the delegation's smug satisfaction, the subtle manipulations behind their polite smiles as they presented this ultimatum. They had likely observed the recent anxieties, the whispers about Eli's past, the subtle fractures that had appeared in the community's unity during the recent influx of newcomers. They had seen an opportunity, a crack in Havenridge's carefully constructed facade, and they were intent on widening it into a chasm.

"They want us to believe we need them," Mara said, her voice gaining a steely edge. "They're dangling the bait of resources – advanced agricultural techniques, manufacturing expertise, perhaps even defensive technology – knowing that we're still building our own capabilities. They're playing on our fears, on the very real threats that exist beyond our borders. They're offering a Faustian bargain, couched in the language of civic duty and shared progress."

Eli ran a hand over his tired eyes. The hours they had already spent dissecting the proposal were taking their toll. The lamplight was beginning to dim, casting longer, more distorted shadows that seemed to mirror the convoluted clauses of the document. The scent of pine had faded, replaced by the dry, papery smell of the proposal itself, a smell that spoke of compromise and capitulation. "The 'advanced agricultural techniques' likely come with mandatory crop quotas, dictated by their markets," he mused, his mind already dissecting the practical implications. "The 'manufacturing expertise' will involve technology that's proprietary, that ties us to their supply chains. And the 'defensive technology'... that's the most dangerous of all. It will come with strings attached, with conditions that will erode our freedom of action."

He tapped a finger on a particular sentence: "'Havenridge agrees to contribute a percentage of its manufactured goods and agricultural surplus to regional distribution networks, as determined by the appointed administrator.'" "So, they'll take what we produce, and decide what we keep, and what we give away. And what if we refuse? What are the consequences? They don't spell that out, do they? That's where the 'protection' clause comes in. If we don't comply, they can deem us a 'threat to regional stability,' and then their 'protection' becomes a siege."

Mara felt a cold dread seep into her bones. Eli was right. The document was a carefully constructed trap, designed to ensnare them with the illusion of partnership while slowly, inexorably, stripping them of their independence. She thought of the earnest faces of the Havenridge residents, their belief in a better way of life, their hopes for a future free from the exploitation and corruption of the old world. This proposal threatened to extinguish that hope, to replace it with the familiar, suffocating embrace of external control.

"Eli," she began, her voice softer now, laced with a weary resignation. "We cannot accept this. We simply cannot. It would be a betrayal of everything we've worked for. Of everyone who believes in Havenridge."

"I know," he replied, his gaze meeting hers, the shared understanding passing between them like a silent current. He understood the impossible position they were in. Refusal meant facing the threats they were trying to mitigate alone, potentially escalating those threats. Acceptance meant a slow, insidious death of their ideals. "But what is our alternative? They've presented this as a formal offer. To outright refuse without offering a counter-proposal, without demonstrating a willingness to negotiate... it gives them the perfect justification to label us as uncooperative, as a destabilizing force."

He gestured to the document again. "The key is in the details. We need to find a way to deflect the core of their demands, to redefine the terms of engagement without outright rejecting their offer. We need to create a counter-narrative, one that emphasizes our self-reliance, our unique contribution to the region, rather than our dependence."

Mara picked up a stylus, her mind already racing, sketching out possibilities on a scrap of parchment. "We can't offer them oversight. But perhaps we can offer them transparency, on our terms. Regular, audited reports of our production, our resource management, our security protocols. We can invite them to observe certain processes, but without direct interference." She drew a small circle, then a line connecting it to another. "And the 'regional administrator'... we can propose a joint liaison committee, with equal representation from Havenridge and the regional authorities. A committee tasked with communication and coordination, not dictation."

"And the contribution to distribution networks?" Eli asked, his brow furrowed in concentration. "That's a significant demand."

"We can frame our contribution not as a quota, but as a voluntary pledge of support, tied to specific, mutually agreed-upon needs," Mara countered, her voice gaining momentum. "We can offer surplus goods at fair market prices, or in exchange for specific resources we require. It becomes a trade, not a tribute. And our 'defensive technology'... if they offer anything, we accept it only with stringent guarantees of our sole ownership and operational control. Anything less, and we refuse it outright, citing our commitment to independent security."

The lamplight flickered again, casting long, dancing shadows that seemed to animate the figures on the page, the shadowy figures of the delegation, the concerned faces of their community. The cabin, once a sanctuary, now felt like a war room, the air thick with the scent of ink and strategy. They spent hours poring over the document, their whispered discussions a low murmur against the rustling of pages. They dissected each clause, each carefully worded phrase, searching for loopholes, for ambiguities, for the slivers of possibility that could allow them to retain their autonomy.

Eli recalled his former life, the intricate dance of negotiation and deception, the constant assessment of threats and leverage. He had always operated with a clear objective: survival, often at any cost. But here, with Mara beside him, the objective was different. It wasn't just about survival; it was about preservation. Preserving the hope, the integrity, the very soul of Havenridge. This proposal was a test, not just of their resilience, but of their ability to adapt, to innovate, to fight with words and ideas rather than with force.

"They'll push back," Eli stated, his gaze steady. "They won't simply accept our counter-proposals. They'll see it as defiance."

"Then we must be prepared to explain why our way is the better way," Mara replied, her resolve hardening with each passing moment. "We demonstrate that our self-sufficiency is not a threat, but a strength that benefits the entire region. We show them that a thriving, independent Havenridge is more valuable as a partner than as a subordinate. We make it clear that our cooperation is genuine, but it will never come at the expense of our fundamental principles."

She looked at Eli, a flicker of her usual fire returning to her eyes. "This isn't just about signing a document, Eli. It's about drawing a line. It's about showing them that Havenridge will not be easily subdued, that we are willing to fight for our independence, not with violence, but with unwavering integrity and a clear vision for our future."

The proposal lay between them, a stark symbol of the challenges they faced. The scent of pine had long since vanished, replaced by the musty aroma of the document and the faint, metallic tang of determination that settled in the air. They knew the path ahead would be arduous, fraught with the risk of misunderstanding, miscalculation, and escalating pressure. But as they continued to strategize, their voices a low, steady hum in the quiet cabin, a shared understanding solidified between them. They would not yield. They would not surrender. They would find a way to navigate this treacherous terrain, to protect the beacon of hope that was Havenridge, not by becoming what they fought against, but by becoming stronger, more resilient, and more resolute in their commitment to the ideals they held dear. The delegation's ultimatum was not an end, but a beginning. A test of their will, and a call to arms for the spirit of Havenridge.

The air in the main chamber, usually a space for collaborative planning and the gentle hum of community progress, had grown thick with an almost palpable tension. The ornate, yet functional, meeting room, with its polished wooden tables and the soft glow of its ambient lighting, had become a battleground. The delegation's proposal, once a silent threat on Mara and Eli's table, had been unveiled, its implications echoing through every corner of Havenridge. It was no longer a secret whispered in hushed tones between the community leaders; it was a public declaration, an offer that demanded a response, and in doing so, it had irrevocably fractured the unity they had so painstakingly cultivated.

The proposal's carefully worded clauses, designed to subtly erode their autonomy, had been met with a spectrum of reactions, each one a testament to the diverse hopes and fears that had propelled Havenridge into existence. For many, especially those who had arrived most recently, the promise of tangible benefits was a siren song. The constant struggle for resources, the gnawing anxiety of an uncertain future, the ever-present threat of external dangers – these were not abstract concepts for them, but lived realities. The delegation offered an escape, a lifeline thrown to those still finding their footing in this new world. They spoke of readily available supplies, of advanced technology that could revolutionize their farming and production, of a protective shield that would make their precarious existence secure.

"Think of the children," argued a woman named Anya, her voice trembling slightly as she addressed the gathered residents. Anya had arrived in Havenridge with two young ones in tow, her previous life a tapestry of hardship and loss. "No more going hungry. No more worrying if a storm will take everything we've worked for.

These people... they have the means to give us that security. Is our pride worth more than their safety?" Her words resonated with a significant portion of the assembly, particularly the families who had arrived in the latter stages of Havenridge's development, those who hadn't witnessed the raw, foundational struggles of its inception. They saw the proposal not as a cage, but as a chance to finally breathe, to build a stable future unburdened by the constant specter of scarcity.

Another resident, a burly man named Silas who had been instrumental in establishing Havenridge's early defenses, voiced his pragmatic concerns. "Mara and Eli are right to be wary, but we can't ignore the practicalities. We're still a young community. Our resources are stretched thin. The security offered by the delegation, the expertise they promise... it's not something we can replicate on our own in any reasonable timeframe. We need to consider the immediate threats. The raiders, the territorial disputes that have been brewing on our borders. This proposal offers a way to neutralize those threats, to give us breathing room." He paused, looking around the room, his gaze searching for a flicker of understanding. "It's not about giving up who we are; it's about surviving long enough to *continue* being who we are. Sometimes, you have to bend a little to avoid breaking."

These voices, fueled by a desperate need for stability and a desire for immediate relief, represented a growing faction within Havenridge. They saw Mara's caution as an impediment, a stubborn adherence to ideals that threatened to jeopardize their very survival. They felt her unwavering stance on autonomy was a luxury they could no longer afford, a romantic notion that clashed with the harsh realities of their existence. The founders, including Mara, who had personally invested everything into the vision of self-sufficiency and independence, found themselves increasingly at odds with these newer members, whose lived experiences had instilled a different set of priorities.

On the other side of the divide stood Mara and a handful of the original founders, their faces etched with a familiar blend of grim determination and weary resolve. For them, the proposal was an insidious poison, masked in the guise of a benevolent offering. They saw the thinly veiled control, the erosion of hard-won freedoms, the inevitable absorption into a larger, potentially corrupt system. Every clause, every carefully chosen word, felt like a nail in the coffin of Havenridge's unique identity.

Mara, her voice clear and steady despite the rising clamor, addressed the assembly. "They are not offering us security; they are offering us subjugation. They speak of 'mutual benefit,' but the benefit is entirely one-sided. They will gain access to our resources, our labor, our innovations, while we will lose the very essence of what makes Havenridge special. We came here to escape control, to build a society based on freedom and self-determination. To accept this proposal is to betray that founding principle, to become exactly what we sought to leave behind." She gestured to the document, which had been placed on a central lectern, a symbol of the contentious issue. "This is not a partnership; it is a blueprint for our assimilation. They want to absorb us, to dilute our strength, to make us compliant. Is that the future we envision for our children?"

Her words, though met with applause from her supporters, also drew murmurs of dissent from the other faction. The passion in her voice was undeniable, but for many, it felt like an abstract argument in the face of concrete needs. The memory of hunger pangs and the constant vigilance against external threats were far more visceral than the abstract concept of autonomy when it came at the cost of immediate well-being.

Eli, standing beside Mara, felt the weight of the fractured community pressing down on him. His role as mediator, a position he had often found challenging but manageable, had become an almost unbearable burden. He saw the genuine fears driving both sides of the debate. He understood the desperate yearning for security and stability that fueled Anya and Silas's arguments. He also felt the deep-seated commitment to freedom and self-reliance that Mara embodied, a commitment that was the very soul of Havenridge.

He stepped forward, his presence commanding a temporary hush. His voice, usually so carefully modulated, carried a note of strain. "I understand the appeal of the delegation's offer," he began, his gaze sweeping across the faces in the room, trying to connect with each individual, to acknowledge their perspective. "The promise of stability, of resources, of protection against the dangers that loom beyond our borders... these are not trivial concerns. Many of you have come to Havenridge seeking a refuge, a place where you can build a better life for yourselves and your families. It is my responsibility, and Mara's, to ensure that refuge is safe and sustainable."

He paused, letting his words sink in, acknowledging the validity of their concerns before shifting his focus. "However," he continued, his voice firming, "we must also consider the long-term implications. The proposal, as it stands, asks us to surrender a significant degree of our autonomy. It places decision-making power in the hands of individuals outside of Havenridge, individuals who may not share our vision or understand our unique needs. The founders here, those who laid the groundwork for this community, built it on the principle of self-governance. They envisioned a place where we could chart our own course, free from external interference."

Eli's attempts to find a middle ground, to bridge the growing chasm, were met with increasing difficulty. He found himself caught between the founders' unwavering commitment to their ideals and the newer residents' pressing need for security and tangible support. His attempts to reframe the proposal, to suggest modifications that would preserve their autonomy while still addressing the delegation's concerns, were often dismissed by one side or the other as either too lenient or too idealistic.

"We can negotiate the terms," Eli proposed during one particularly heated exchange, his hands held up in a gesture of conciliation. "We can propose a framework for cooperation that allows for resource sharing and joint security initiatives without ceding our right to self-governance. We can offer transparency, regular reporting, and even joint oversight committees, but the ultimate decision-making authority must remain with Havenridge."

Anya, her face flushed with frustration, retorted, "Negotiate? Eli, they've presented us with a formal proposal, not an invitation to haggle. They have the power, and they know it. If we demand too much, they'll simply withdraw their offer, and we'll be left with nothing. We'll be exposed, vulnerable, and no closer to achieving the stability we so desperately need."

"And if we accept their terms, we surrender everything we've worked for," countered a founder, his voice heavy with disappointment. "We become just another satellite community, dictated to by those who see us as a resource to be exploited, not as a people with our own aspirations. Mara is right. This is a fight for our soul."

The trust that had been the bedrock of Havenridge, forged in shared hardship and common purpose, was beginning to erode. Suspicion began to creep into their interactions. Neighbors who had once shared meals and labored side-by-side now eyed each other with doubt. The once-open doors of their homes felt a little more closed, the conversations a little more guarded. Eli noticed the subtle shifts: the averted gazes, the hushed whispers that ceased when he approached, the growing reluctance to openly discuss contentious issues for fear of being perceived as a traitor to one faction or the other.

He found himself spending more time in quiet contemplation, walking the familiar paths of Havenridge under the watchful eyes of the ancient trees, seeking solace in the natural world that had always offered him a sense of grounding. He recalled his past, a life where alliances were forged through necessity and often dissolved just as quickly, where trust was a rare commodity, earned with great difficulty and lost with terrifying speed. He had hoped that Havenridge, with its deliberate focus on community and shared values, would be different. But even the strongest foundations could be tested by the relentless pressure of external forces, and by the internal conflicts that arose when survival and ideals clashed.

The proposal had become a catalyst, exposing underlying anxieties and different priorities that had always existed, but had been largely dormant in the face of more immediate, shared challenges. Now, with the prospect of a seemingly easy solution laid before them, these differences had come to the fore, creating deep fissures within the community. Eli felt the immense pressure of his position. He was no longer just a protector; he was a reluctant arbiter, tasked with navigating the treacherous currents of a divided populace, desperately trying to steer Havenridge away from the rocks of internal conflict and external compromise, all while the very foundations of their trust were being tested. The weight of these decisions, and the fracturing of his community, pressed down on him, a burden heavier than any physical threat they had yet faced. The scent of pine, once a symbol of their freedom and sanctuary, now seemed to carry a hint of melancholy, a quiet lament for the unity they were in danger of losing.

Eli's tactical assessment began not in the grand council chambers, but in the periphery, in the quiet spaces between Havenridge's established perimeters and the delegation's temporary encampment. He moved with the practiced stealth of someone who had learned the hard way that observation was often the most potent weapon. His past life, a tapestry woven with threads of calculated risk and strategic maneuvering, had honed his senses to a razor's edge. He noted the subtle recalibration of the delegation's patrols. They had initially maintained a predictable, almost courteous rhythm, a clear demarcation of their presence. But in the last few days, a new pattern had emerged. The patrols were longer, their routes more complex, encompassing a wider sweep of the surrounding territories, pushing further than what would be necessary for mere ceremonial security. He saw the guards, no longer merely standing sentry, but actively scanning the treeline, their postures subtly shifting from passive vigilance to an almost predatory alertness. The glint of metal was more pronounced now, not just the polished surfaces of their visible weaponry, but the darker, utilitarian lines of equipment tucked away, the reinforced plating on their transport vehicles that suggested more than just civilian transport.

He'd spent hours blending into the dappled shadows, observing the mechanics of their operations. He'd seen their supply drops, not just the expected food and water, but crates of what looked suspiciously like advanced sensor arrays, compact energy cells that hummed with an unfamiliar resonance, and even what appeared to be modular defensive emplacements, designed for rapid deployment. These weren't the tools of a benevolent offer; they were the accoutrements of a force preparing for a sustained presence, and potentially, for conflict. He'd managed to get close enough to overhear fragmented conversations, snippets of jargon that spoke of "asset acquisition," "perimeter consolidation," and "pacification protocols." The words themselves were chilling, a stark contrast to the delegation's public pronouncements of partnership and mutual benefit.

He'd also noted the types of weaponry. While their standard sidearms were visible, he'd caught glimpses of heavier ordnance being carried covertly, secured within their vehicles, and even, on one occasion, a brief, unmistakable silhouette of a railgun assembly being discreetly loaded. The efficiency with which they moved, the tight communication signals, the synchronized movements of their teams – these weren't the actions of a group looking to integrate or assist. They were the hallmarks of a disciplined military unit, a force trained for strategic projection. He recognized certain tactical signatures, echoes of operations he'd witnessed and participated in during his former life, signs that spoke of a latent aggression, a readiness to enforce rather than negotiate. The delegation's outward veneer of diplomacy was a thin façade, and Eli was seeing the steel beneath.

Later, under the guise of checking the integrity of their own nascent defensive systems, Eli found Mara in their workshop, the air thick with the scent of woodsmoke and the metallic tang of mending tools. The space was a sanctuary, a testament to their hard-won independence, filled with the hum of their own repurposed technologies and the quiet satisfaction of self-reliance. He watched her for a moment, her brow furrowed in concentration as she adjusted a delicate mechanism on a new irrigation system component, her hands moving with a practiced, almost intuitive grace. He felt a pang of regret that their hard-won peace was being threatened, that the very ideals they had strived to build were being tested by such insidious forces.

He approached her, his voice low, careful not to disturb the fragile peace of the workshop. "Mara," he began, his gaze meeting hers, conveying the gravity of his findings before he even spoke the words. He gestured for her to step aside, leading her to a quiet corner where the tools were laid out neatly, a silent testament to order amidst the growing chaos. "I've been observing the delegation more closely. Their movements... they've changed. It's not just standard security anymore."

Mara's eyes, sharp and intelligent, immediately focused on him, her usual calm replaced by a flicker of apprehension. "What have you seen, Eli?" she asked, her voice hushed, reflecting the growing unease that had settled over Havenridge.

"Their patrols have expanded significantly," he continued, keeping his voice a low murmur. "They're pushing the boundaries, not just guarding their immediate vicinity, but actively scouting the surrounding territories. And their equipment... it's more than just humanitarian aid. I've seen what appear to be advanced sensor arrays, high-capacity energy cells, even modular defensive structures. They're not preparing to settle; they're preparing to occupy, or worse."

He paused, searching her face for understanding, for the shared weight of the implications. "And the chatter I've overheard. It's not about cooperation. It's about control. Terms like 'asset acquisition' and 'pacification protocols' don't sit well with the image they're projecting." He lowered his voice further, leaning in slightly. "I've also noticed specific tactical signatures. Their unit cohesion, their communication discipline, the type of secondary armament I've glimpsed... it's military grade. More than that, I recognize some of the operational patterns. They're not just a trading delegation, Mara. They're a forward operating unit, and their intentions are far more aggressive than they're letting on."

He detailed his observations, the subtle shifts in their security posture, the types of equipment they were bringing in, the language used in their hushed conversations. He spoke of the way their guards moved, no longer just maintaining a perimeter, but actively scanning the environment with a trained, almost predatory gaze. He described the specialized gear they carried, the reinforced plating on their transports that hinted at more than just cargo capacity, the discreetly deployed sensor equipment that suggested a need for constant surveillance, not just of external threats, but of Havenridge itself.

"Their security detail isn't just for show," Eli explained, his voice a low rumble that barely disturbed the ambient sounds of the workshop. "It's a projection of force. I saw one of their transport

vehicles being loaded with what looked like mobile sentry units –
automated turrets, Mara, capable of independent targeting. They're
not offering us protection; they're building their own fortresses
within our community, positioning themselves to enforce their
terms, not negotiate them."

He elaborated on the overheard conversations, piecing together
fragments of jargon that painted a disturbing picture. "They spoke of
'securing critical infrastructure' and 'integrating operational assets.'
When they mentioned resources, it wasn't in the context of sharing,
but in the context of acquisition. They're treating our innovations,
our land, our very community as something to be claimed and
controlled." He recounted a specific instance where he'd observed
a delegation member sketching detailed schematics of Havenridge's
hydroponic farms, not with the casual interest of a visitor, but with
the meticulous precision of an engineer assessing exploitable assets.

"And their patrols," he continued, his tone hardening with grim
certainty. "They've begun to deviate from their designated routes,
pushing further into the wilderness surrounding Havenridge,
mapping terrain, identifying potential ingress and egress points. It's
reconnaissance, Mara. They're not just looking for threats to us;
they're looking for vulnerabilities in our own defenses, assessing the
landscape for their own strategic advantage. I saw one patrol marking
trees with a coded spray, subtle, almost invisible to the untrained eye,
but clear indicators of surveyed routes and potential ambush points.
They're preparing for a scenario where diplomacy fails, and force
becomes their primary tool."

He described the equipment he'd glimpsed being transported under
the cover of night – not the crates of medical supplies or standard

provisions they advertised, but compact, high-frequency jamming devices, portable energy shields designed for rapid deployment, and what appeared to be advanced targeting systems integrated into their transport vehicles. "Their emphasis on 'advanced technology' in their proposal," Eli stated, his voice laced with a bitter irony, "isn't about helping us; it's about them demonstrating their technological superiority, a subtle threat of what they can bring to bear if we resist. They're not offering a handshake; they're preparing to put chains on us, gilded perhaps, but chains nonetheless."

He relayed a particularly unsettling observation: the delegation members who were supposedly 'technical advisors' were frequently seen observing the daily routines of Havenridge's inhabitants, not with the objective curiosity of researchers, but with the calculating assessment of strategists studying population behavior and logistical patterns. He'd noticed one individual meticulously documenting the shift changes at the water purification plant, another timing the movement of children to the communal learning center. "They're building a comprehensive profile of our community," Eli explained, a grim realization dawning in his eyes. "Our strengths, our weaknesses, our patterns of life. This isn't for our benefit; it's to understand how best to control us when the time comes."

Mara listened intently, her expression growing more serious with each word. She knew Eli's capabilities, his discerning eye for detail, his ability to see through deception. The implications of his assessment were far-reaching, painting a picture far more sinister than the veiled threats they had initially perceived. The proposal wasn't just about losing autonomy; it was about a calculated strategy of infiltration and eventual subjugation, masked by the guise of mutual benefit. The seeds of distrust, sown by the delegation's very presence, were now beginning to sprout into full-blown alarm. The weight of his words settled in the workshop, a palpable tension that seemed to emanate from the very tools of their self-sufficiency, reminding them of what they stood to lose.

Mara stepped out of the workshop, the metallic tang of Eli's grim report still clinging to her like the scent of the oil he'd been working with. The air outside felt lighter, cleaner, a stark contrast to the suffocating implications of his findings. Yet, the weight of his words pressed down on her, a physical manifestation of the looming threat to everything they had built. She knew she couldn't let fear paralyze them, nor could she allow the delegation's polished veneer to blind anyone to the insidious reality Eli had uncovered. The central gathering space, usually alive with the murmur of daily life and collaborative projects, felt hushed, expectant, as if sensing the shift in the atmosphere. It was here, amidst the heart of their community, that she needed to speak, to reignite the fires of their founding principles.

She found a sturdy, weathered platform that had served as a makeshift stage for countless celebrations and important announcements. The wood beneath her feet was familiar, worn smooth by generations of shared purpose. She took a deep breath, centering herself, recalling the biting winds of their early days, the gnawing hunger, the gnawing doubt that had threatened to consume them. She remembered the fierce, unyielding hope that had propelled them forward, the shared vision that had transformed a desolate patch of earth into a thriving sanctuary. She met the eyes of the people gathering, their faces etched with a mixture of curiosity and apprehension. Eli's observations, though spoken privately to her, had already begun to cast a shadow, and she knew many were feeling the unease, the subtle disquiet that had settled over Havenridge like an early frost.

"My friends," she began, her voice steady, carrying a resonance that belied the tremor in her hands. "We stand at a crossroads. You have heard whispers, perhaps seen the increased patrols, the unusual movements of our... guests." She chose her words carefully, avoiding accusatory language, for now, but letting the unspoken truth hang in the air. "They present themselves as partners, as offering solutions to problems we have already begun to solve for ourselves. They speak of progress, of advanced technology, of a shared future."

She paused, letting their own unspoken hopes and desires acknowledge the allure of such promises. "And it is tempting, isn't it? To believe that the hard path we've walked can finally give way to an easier one. To embrace the comfort and security that seems to be offered so freely." Her gaze swept across the faces, searching for any sign of wavering, any hint of the compromise she feared. "But I ask you to remember. Remember why we are here. Remember the silence that greeted us when we first arrived, the indifference of the world outside. Remember the long nights spent huddled against the cold, the gnawing emptiness in our bellies, the fear that whispered that perhaps we were fools to dream."

Her voice grew stronger, imbued with the raw power of shared memory. "We didn't seek comfort then. We sought freedom. We fought for the right to make our own choices, to chart our own course, to build a life based on our own values, not on the dictates of others. We learned to rely on ourselves, on each other. We discovered the quiet dignity of self-sufficiency, the strength that comes from knowing that what we have, we earned with our own sweat and ingenuity. We built Havenridge not just with our hands, but with our principles. Autonomy. Mutual respect. The unwavering belief that every voice matters, and that no one person, no single entity, holds all the answers."

She gestured to the surrounding structures, the intricate irrigation systems, the efficient energy conduits, the communal workshops buzzing with activity even now. "Look around you. This is not the work of a people waiting to be saved. This is the testament of a people who saved themselves. We learned to harness the rain, to coax life from the soil, to generate power from the very air we breathe. We built a society where cooperation was not a negotiation, but a natural extension of our shared humanity. We learned to value the wisdom of the elder, the strength of the laborer, the spark of the innovator, and the gentle touch of the caregiver. Every individual contribution was a vital thread in the tapestry of our survival, and now, of our prosperity."

A murmur rippled through the crowd, a shared acknowledgment of her words. She saw nods of agreement, the subtle clenching of fists, the quiet determination returning to weary eyes. Eli's report, she knew, had planted seeds of doubt, but her words were meant to water the deep-rooted plants of their identity.

"Now," Mara continued, her voice firm, her gaze unwavering, "we are presented with an offer that promises much, but at what cost? Eli's observations, which I have seen myself to be accurate, suggest that this delegation's intentions are not as altruistic as they appear. Their 'aid' comes with conditions, their 'partnership' with an unspoken hierarchy. They speak of integration, but their actions speak of control. They offer us their technology, but what if that technology becomes the very chains that bind us?"

She stepped forward, her silhouette stark against the soft twilight glow filtering through the open archways. "Consider the long-term cost of compromised integrity. If we accept their terms without question, if we allow them to dictate our path, what becomes of the freedom we fought so hard to attain? What becomes of the quiet dignity of knowing we are masters of our own destiny? Do we trade the hard-won autonomy of Havenridge for the gilded cage of dependency? Do we allow the principles that have guided us, that have made us strong, to be eroded by the convenience of appeasement?"

Her voice softened, laced with a profound sadness. "I do not dismiss the challenges we face. There are always challenges. There are always threats, both from without and from within. But our strength lies not in surrendering to external forces, but in our ability to confront those challenges with the resilience and wisdom that we have cultivated together. Our innovation, our resourcefulness, our commitment to each other – these are the true technologies that have carried us this far. They are the foundations upon which we will continue to build."

She looked directly at those who seemed most swayed by the delegation's promises, their faces reflecting a weariness she understood all too well. "It is easier, perhaps, to accept a hand reaching out to help, especially when one feels the strain of carrying a burden. But we must ask ourselves: is this a hand of partnership, or a hand seeking to guide us, then to lead us, and finally, to dictate our every step? Is the burden being shared, or is it simply being redistributed, with us holding the heavier end?"

"Our founding principles are not mere words etched on a monument," Mara declared, her voice ringing with conviction. "They are the very bedrock of our existence. They are the choices we make every single day, the decisions we take that honor our past and safeguard our future. To compromise them now, for the sake of perceived ease or superficial advancement, would be to betray the very spirit of Havenridge. It would be to declare that the freedom we bled for was not worth the sustained effort of maintaining it."

She took another breath, her gaze sweeping across the assembled faces, seeking out those who might still harbor doubts, those who might believe her words were born of fear rather than foresight. "I see the arguments in some of your eyes. 'We need their resources,' some may say. 'Their technology is far beyond our current capabilities.' And yes, we have always been open to learning, to growth. But learning from others is one thing; becoming beholden to them is another entirely. We can integrate new knowledge and tools without sacrificing our sovereignty. We can adapt and evolve without surrendering our right to self-determination."

"Remember the quiet strength of self-reliance," she implored. "It is a profound power. It is the knowledge that no matter the external circumstances, we have the capacity within ourselves to adapt, to innovate, to persevere. This is not a power that can be granted or taken away by any outside force. It is a power that resides within each of us, within our collective spirit. To trade that for the illusion of security offered by the delegation would be to extinguish the very flame that has kept us warm through the coldest nights."

Mara's voice softened again, a more personal plea now. "I believe in us. I believe in the choices we have made, and the sacrifices we have endured. I believe that the future of Havenridge lies in our continued commitment to our founding ideals, not in their abandonment. Let us not be swayed by promises that sound too good to be true, for they often are. Let us instead look to the strength within, to the bonds we share, and to the enduring power of our own collective will. Let us continue to build, to innovate, and to thrive, not as supplicants, but as sovereign architects of our own destiny. Let us honor the weight of our decisions, not by surrendering to external pressures, but by reaffirming the sacred trust we have placed in each other and in the principles that define us." The silence that followed her words was not one of confusion or disagreement, but one of deep contemplation. The seeds of doubt had been sown, but Mara had spoken words of courage, and now, the people of Havenridge had to decide which seeds would truly take root.

The moon, a sliver of bone against the velvet expanse of night, offered little illumination to the sleepless occupants of Mara's modest dwelling. The sounds of Havenridge, usually a comforting symphony of industry and communal life, had softened into a hushed murmur, the gentle exhalations of a settlement holding its breath. Outside, the air was cool and still, carrying the faint scent of pine and the distant, rhythmic pulse of the water reclamation system. Inside, however, a storm of anxious thoughts churned, mirroring the turmoil that had settled upon the community like a shroud. Mara lay beside Eli, her eyes fixed on the dark ceiling, her mind replaying every word of her address, every flicker of doubt and conviction on the faces of her people. The weight of their impending decision pressed down on her, a tangible force that made each breath a conscious effort.

Beside her, Eli shifted, the faint rustle of fabric the only indication of his wakefulness. The silence between them was heavy, laden with unspoken fears and the immense responsibility they both carried. It had been hours since they had returned to their quarters, the lingering energy of the gathered community still thrumming beneath their skin. Mara had tried to compartmentalize, to push the anxieties to the periphery, but the gnawing uncertainty of the unknown was a persistent intruder. She knew Eli was wrestling with his own demons, the confession he'd made to her earlier still echoing in the quiet. His fear – the fear that his past, a tangled knot of choices and circumstances he couldn't outrun, might be the very instrument of their undoing – was a burden she understood all too well.

"Are you awake?" Eli's voice was a low rumble, barely disturbing the stillness.

Mara turned to face him, the moonlight catching the troubled lines etched around his eyes. "Always," she replied softly. "What's on your mind?"

He sighed, a sound heavy with weariness. "Everything. The vote. What happens tomorrow, no matter which way it goes." He ran a hand through his hair, a gesture of profound agitation. "I keep thinking about what you said, about the cost of compromise. And then I think about what happens if we say no. What if they... what if they retaliate? What if their 'aid' was a front for something far more dangerous, and our refusal just ignites it?"

Mara reached out, her fingers tracing the curve of his jaw. His skin was warm, but there was a tension in him that radiated outwards. "We've faced threats before, Eli. We've always found a way."

"But not like this," he countered, his voice strained. "This isn't a rival settlement or a natural disaster. This is... a force. One that operates on a scale we can barely comprehend. And my part in it..." He trailed off, his gaze drifting to the window, as if searching for answers in the inky blackness. "The knowledge I have, the connections I made – they could be a weapon against us. If they see me, if they recognize me..."

"They won't," Mara said, her voice firm, though a sliver of her own fear pricked at her. "We've been careful. And even if they do, we face it together. That's what we've always done."

"But what if 'together' isn't enough this time?" he whispered, the raw vulnerability in his tone making her heart ache. "What if my past mistakes, my very existence, make us a target they can't ignore? I was a fool, Mara. I believed them. I thought I was doing the right thing, helping them. And now..." He shook his head, a gesture of utter despair. "Now I've brought that danger right to our doorstep. Every scrap of information I gave them, every detail about our systems, our defenses, our vulnerabilities... it could be the blueprint for our destruction. And if they learn I'm here, that I betrayed them..."

He turned his gaze back to her, his eyes dark with a desperate plea. "I'm terrified that I've doomed us. That my past is a shadow that will finally consume everything you've built, everything we believe in."

Mara pulled him closer, her arms encircling his shoulders. She felt the tremor that ran through him, the deep-seated fear that threatened to overwhelm him. She pressed her forehead against his, trying to convey through touch the strength she felt for him, for them. "Eli," she said, her voice a low, soothing balm, "look at me."

He met her gaze, his eyes swimming with unshed tears.

"Your past does not define you. Not entirely. You are more than the mistakes you made. You are the man who came back, the man who risked everything to warn us, the man who dedicates himself every single day to making this community stronger. That is who you are *now*. And if they come, if they pose a threat, we will face it with everything we have. Not just our defenses, not just our skills, but with our unity. With our belief in each other."

She felt him relax, ever so slightly, into her embrace. "But the risk..." he murmured.

"There is always risk, Eli. There was risk when we first set foot on this barren land. There was risk when we rationed our food, when we battled the elements, when we faced down despair. And yes, there is risk now. But fear of that risk cannot paralyze us. It must propel us. We choose our path based on our values, not on the potential for someone else's reprisal."

She held him a little tighter. "If we accept their terms, we risk losing ourselves. We risk becoming a shadow of what we are, dependent and controlled. That is a slow death, a surrender of the very spirit that makes us Havenridge. If we refuse, we risk conflict. But conflict, fought on our own terms, with our own people, is a chance to defend what we believe in. It's a chance to prove that our strength lies not in capitulation, but in our resilience, our ingenuity, our unyielding spirit."

"And your fear?" Eli asked, his voice a whisper against her ear. "What is your deepest fear tonight?"

Mara considered this, the cool air a stark contrast to the heat of the internal debate. "My fear," she admitted, her voice quiet, "is that I won't be strong enough. That the weight of leadership will crush me. That I will make the wrong choice, and history will judge me for it. That I will fail you all." She paused, then added, "But my *greater* fear is that we will choose the path of least resistance, the path of perceived safety, and in doing so, we will trade our soul for a comfortable cage. That is a betrayal I cannot bear to contemplate."

She pulled back slightly, her eyes searching his. "Your past is a part of you, Eli, but it's not the whole story. You are proof that people can change, that they can atone, that they can contribute something meaningful. If they come for you, they come for all of us. And we will stand together. You are not alone in this. You never have been."

He leaned his forehead against hers, a silent acknowledgment of her words, a fragile truce with his own internal war. The faint sounds of the settlement continued their quiet vigil outside. The water systems hummed, the night wind whispered through the pines, and in the distance, a lone sentinel's footsteps echoed softly on the perimeter path. These were the sounds of a community still alive, still breathing, still fighting for its future.

"I believe in you, Mara," Eli said, his voice raspy with emotion. "And I believe in us. Whatever happens tomorrow, we face it. Together."

"Always," she vowed, the word a promise forged in the crucible of shared experience and unwavering hope. She felt a flicker of peace, a small ember glowing in the darkness. The night was far from over, the decisions still lay heavy, but in that moment, holding Eli close, she found a sliver of solace. Their bond, tested and proven, was their anchor. And as dawn approached, it was that anchor, and the unwavering belief in the strength of their collective will, that would have to see them through the dawn and whatever trials it would bring. The weight of their decisions was immense, a burden shared, and as they lay there, two souls adrift in the sea of uncertainty, they held onto each other, a testament to the enduring power of connection in the face of overwhelming odds. The night was a vigil, a final, quiet communion before the storm, and in its hushed embrace, they found the strength to face the coming light, together. The quiet murmur of the settlement outside was no longer just the sound of a community holding its breath, but the subtle hum of life persevering, a reminder of what they were fighting for, a testament to the resilience that had brought them this far, and the courage that would carry them forward. Their shared sleeplessness was not a sign of weakness, but a testament to the profound responsibility they bore, a silent acknowledgement of the stakes involved, and a reaffirmation of their commitment to each other and to the future of Havenridge. The moon continued its slow descent, and as the first hint of predawn grey began to streak the eastern sky, Mara and Eli found a fragile peace in their shared wakefulness, their hands clasped, their spirits intertwined, ready to meet the challenges of the new day as one.

CHAPTER FIVE

The Crossroads

The great hall of Havenridge buzzed with a nervous energy that vibrated through the very timbers of the structure. It was a sound Mara knew intimately, the collective exhale of a community teetering on the edge of a monumental decision. Sunlight, filtering through the high, arched windows, cast long, shifting patterns on the packed earth floor, illuminating motes of dust dancing in the tense air. The usual chatter, the easy camaraderie that often filled this space, was absent, replaced by a heavy, expectant silence punctuated by the rustle of worn tunics and the soft thud of boot heels as people shifted their weight. Every face turned towards the raised platform where the voting urns stood, stark and imposing, a physical manifestation of the choice before them. Mara's gaze swept across the assembly, her heart a leaden weight in her chest. She saw the worry etched onto the weathered face of Old Man Hemlock, the usually boisterous farmer, his brow furrowed deep. She saw the hopeful, yet anxious, eyes of young Anya, whose family had always been a vocal proponent of caution, of clinging to the familiar. And then there was Silas, his jaw set, his shoulders hunched, a man who had championed the notion of self-reliance with every fiber of his being, now faced with a choice that felt like a betrayal of his core beliefs. The divisions, Mara

105

knew, ran deeper than the surface disagreements. They were carved into the very souls of Havenridge, the result of years of hard-won survival, of hard-learned lessons, and of the ever-present shadow of the unknown.

Eli stood beside her, his presence a grounding force in the swirling anxiety. He hadn't spoken much since their conversation earlier, but his hand rested lightly on the small of her back, a silent, steady reassurance. She could feel the tension in him, a coiled spring of apprehension that mirrored her own, though his was colored by the unique burden of his past. He, more than anyone, understood the precarious balance they were trying to strike, the delicate dance between security and sovereignty, between cooperation and compromise. His gaze met hers for a brief moment, and in his eyes, she saw not just fear, but a profound trust. It was a look that bolstered her, a silent affirmation that they were in this together, no matter the outcome.

"The time has come," Mara announced, her voice resonating through the hall, cutting through the oppressive silence. Her words, though amplified, felt small against the enormity of the moment. "We have heard the proposals, we have debated the implications. Now, we must cast our votes." She gestured to the voting urns, their surfaces polished smooth from countless hands. "For those who choose to accept the Alliance's offer of assistance, place your marked token in the blue urn. For those who believe Havenridge must continue on its present path, forging its own future independently, place your token in the red urn."

A collective breath was drawn in, a single, audible sigh that seemed to ripple through the crowd. The air grew thicker, charged with anticipation. The first few individuals approached the urns with measured steps, their movements deliberate, their faces masks of grim determination. Each token dropped was a tiny sound, yet it echoed like a hammer blow in the hushed hall, sealing fates, widening chasms. Mara watched each person, trying to read their intentions in the slight tremor of their hand, the way their eyes darted, the set of their jaw. The farmer, Hemlock, his hands gnarled and calloused from years of toil, hesitated for a long moment before dropping his token into the blue urn. A ripple of murmurs passed through the crowd, a subtle shift in the collective mood. Anya, her youthful face pale, followed suit, her token landing with a soft clink in the blue urn. Silas, however, walked with a resolute stride, his head held high, and with a decisive movement, dropped his token into the red urn. A small smattering of applause, tinged with defiance, rose from a section of the hall, countered by the somber silence of those who had voted blue. The votes continued to fall, each one a testament to the deeply held convictions, the individual fears, and the divergent hopes of Havenridge.

The process felt agonizingly slow, each moment stretched taut, pregnant with unspoken anxieties. Mara felt the weight of every single vote. The blue urn seemed to fill with a steady, insistent rhythm, a testament to the allure of promised security, the whispered assurances of easier times, of protection from the encroaching unknown. But the red urn, too, received its share, each token a defiant declaration of self-reliance, a fierce protection of Havenridge's hard-won autonomy, a rejection of anything that smacked of subservience. She saw families divided, friends exchanging worried glances, the subtle but undeniable fracturing of the community's once-unanimous spirit. Eli remained by her side, his presence a constant anchor, his quiet strength a balm to her frayed nerves. She could feel the unspoken questions hanging in the air, the collective yearning for a clear path, a definitive answer, a sense of resolution that felt impossibly distant.

As the last token was dropped, a hush fell over the assembly, more profound than before. The silence was now a tangible entity, a heavy cloak woven from anticipation and apprehension. Mara stepped forward, her voice steady, though her heart hammered against her ribs. "The votes have been cast," she announced. "Now, we await the count." Two elders, chosen for their impartiality, approached the urns, their faces impassive as they began the solemn task of tallying. The seconds stretched into an eternity. The sunlight shifted, casting longer shadows, painting the hall in hues of amber and rose, a beautiful, oblivious backdrop to the deeply human drama unfolding within. Mara could feel the tension radiating from every person present, a palpable force that seemed to press in on her, threatening to steal her breath. She clasped her hands together, her knuckles white, and focused on the steady rhythm of her own breathing, an attempt to anchor herself against the rising tide of anxiety. Eli's hand found hers, his fingers lacing through hers, a silent promise of shared endurance.

The elders returned to the platform, their faces unreadable. The murmuring in the hall ceased entirely, replaced by an almost reverent silence. Mara met their gaze, her own filled with a mixture of dread and determination. "The count is complete," one of the elders stated, his voice clear and steady. He held up two wooden tablets, one marked with a blue symbol, the other with a red. "By a margin of," he paused, and the hall collectively held its breath, "seventeen votes, Havenridge has chosen to accept the Alliance's offer of assistance."

A collective gasp swept through the hall. It was a sound of mingled relief and dismay, a sudden, sharp exhalation that seemed to release some of the pent-up tension, only to replace it with a different kind of unease. For a moment, the hall remained frozen, the pronouncement hanging in the air, heavy and absolute. Then, a few tentative claps began, mostly from the side where the blue urn's proponents stood, a hesitant ripple of agreement. On the other side of the hall, however, silence reigned. Faces that had been etched with hope now fell, replaced by expressions of profound disappointment, even anger. Mara saw Silas's shoulders slump, the fire in his eyes dimming, replaced by a grim acceptance. Others turned to one another, their faces etched with concern, their whispers urgent and low. The victory, if it could be called that, was hollow, achieved not by overwhelming consensus, but by a slim, fragile majority. The fissures within Havenridge had not been healed; they had been laid bare, widened by the very act of trying to bridge them.

The immediate aftermath was a stark tableau of these divisions. The air, which had been thick with anticipation, now felt heavy with unspoken anxieties and a pervasive sense of unease. Those who had voted for independence, their faces etched with worry, began to drift away from the main gathering, their conversations hushed, their movements subdued. They carried with them the palpable burden of apprehension, the fear of the unknown future that lay ahead, a future dictated by an external force, a future where their hard-won sovereignty was now a fragile memory. Mara watched them go, her heart aching for the sense of loss that seemed to emanate from them. She understood their fears, the deep-seated distrust of anything that threatened to erode the self-sufficiency they had so painstakingly cultivated.

On the other side of the hall, a different kind of atmosphere prevailed, though it was far from triumphant. There was a palpable sense of relief, a quiet exhalation from those who had been most burdened by the fear of isolation, of facing the unknown alone. They spoke in hushed tones of security, of shared resources, of a brighter, more stable future. Yet, even in their relief, there was an undercurrent of unease, a subtle awareness of the compromises that had been made, the subtle shifts in power that were already beginning to manifest. The scent of pine and earth that usually filled the hall seemed to be overlaid with something else, something fainter, more insidious – the scent of uncertainty, of a future not entirely their own.

Mara turned to Eli, her gaze searching his. The thin majority, the evident division, weighed heavily on her. "Seventeen votes," she murmured, the words tasting like ash. "It's closer than I feared, and yet... more divisive than I'd hoped."

Eli squeezed her hand, his thumb stroking the back of her palm. "It shows that people were heard, Mara. That the debate was real, and the concerns were genuine. A unanimous vote would have been easier, perhaps, but this... this is the reality of a community made of individuals with different perspectives." He looked out at the dispersing crowd, his expression thoughtful. "The challenge now is to bridge this divide, to remind them that the vote was a decision about how we face the future, not a repudiation of who we are."

"But can we, Eli?" Mara asked, her voice barely above a whisper. "Can we truly mend this when the very foundation of our decision has fractured us? Those who voted red... they feel that a part of Havenridge has been lost today. And in a way, they're not wrong."

Anya approached them, her face still pale, but her eyes now held a flicker of resolve. "Mara, Eli," she began hesitantly. "My family... we voted blue, as you know. But I understand the concerns of those who voted red. Silas and his family, they've always believed in building our own strength. And they're not wrong to fear losing that." She paused, her gaze meeting Mara's. "But we also saw the risks, didn't we? The world outside is... unpredictable. And the Alliance offered a lifeline."

"A lifeline that comes with strings, Anya," Silas said, his voice quiet but firm as he joined them, his earlier dejection tempered by a weary resignation. "Strings that could one day bind us too tightly to let us go." He looked at Mara, his gaze steady. "I respect the vote, Mara. I do. But I cannot pretend that this outcome sits well with me. We have prided ourselves on our independence, on our ability to stand on our own. Now, we have chosen dependence. And I fear the cost of that choice will be far greater than we anticipate."

Mara met his gaze, her own filled with a somber understanding. "I understand your fears, Silas. Truly, I do. And I promise you, we will not forget what brought us to this point. We will not let this alliance diminish the spirit of Havenridge. We will find a way to integrate their assistance without sacrificing our identity, without compromising the values that make us who we are."

"I hope you're right, Mara," Silas said, his voice laced with a deep skepticism. "For all our sakes, I truly hope you're right." He offered a curt nod to Mara and Eli, then turned and walked away, disappearing into the throng of those who had voted red, the embodiment of Havenridge's internal struggle.

Eli watched Silas go, a thoughtful expression on his face. "He's right, Mara," he said, his voice low. "The fear is real, and it's justified. We can't dismiss it. We have to acknowledge it, address it. This isn't just about integrating new resources; it's about managing the human element, the emotional fallout of this decision."

Mara sighed, the weight of responsibility settling heavier on her shoulders. The victory, such as it was, felt more like the beginning of a protracted conflict than an end to uncertainty. The vote had been cast, the path chosen, but the true struggle, the struggle for unity, for identity, for the very soul of Havenridge, had only just begun. The air in the hall, once alive with debate, now held a somber stillness, the scent of pine mingling with the subtle, yet undeniable, fragrance of apprehension. The Crossroads had been passed, but the road ahead was far from clear, shrouded in the lingering shadows of doubt and the stark reality of a community divided. The relief of the majority was a fragile thing, perched precariously on the precipice of apprehension for the minority. The decision had been made, but the process of healing, of reconciliation, of finding a unified path forward, was a journey that promised to be far more arduous than the vote itself. The air itself seemed to hold its breath, as if waiting to see which faction's fears would ultimately prevail, which vision of Havenridge would become the dominant reality. The echo of the votes, though silenced, resonated in the quiet, a constant reminder of the precarious balance they now had to maintain.

The quietude of the council chambers, usually a sanctuary of reasoned discourse, was now a battlefield of wills. The air, thick with the scent of polished wood and the lingering ozone of the recent storm, felt charged with a subtle, yet potent, animosity. Mara sat at the head of the long, scarred oak table, the worn surface beneath her fingertips a familiar comfort. Across from her sat the delegation, their faces impassive, their attire a stark contrast to the homespun practicality of Havenridge. They represented the Alliance, a formidable entity whose intentions, though cloaked in the language of mutual benefit, remained a source of profound unease.

Beside Mara, Eli was a study in quiet intensity. His gaze, usually warm and open, was now sharp, dissecting every subtle shift in posture, every carefully chosen word from the Alliance representatives. He understood the delicate dance they were engaged in – a negotiation, not a surrender. The vote had been close, a testament to the deep-seated pride and self-reliance of Havenridge, but it had also swung the door open, just a sliver, to the possibility of interaction. Mara's mandate was clear: to secure assistance without sacrificing sovereignty. It was a tightrope walk over a chasm of mistrust and unspoken agendas.

"We appreciate your willingness to engage," Ambassador Thorne began, his voice smooth as river stone, his eyes, a disconcerting shade of pale grey, swept across the faces gathered. "The Alliance recognizes the unique challenges faced by communities like Havenridge. Our offer is one of partnership, of shared prosperity."

Mara inclined her head, her expression neutral. "Ambassador, we have reviewed your proposal. While we acknowledge the potential benefits, certain aspects require clarification and, indeed, significant revision. Havenridge values its autonomy. Any agreement must reflect that fundamental principle." Her voice was measured, each word carefully placed, like stones building a dam against a rising tide.

Eli's hand rested on the table, his knuckles a pale white against the dark wood. He caught Mara's eye and offered a nearly imperceptible nod. It was his signal. He trusted her to articulate the core concerns, while he would be the one to sense the subtle shifts, the manipulative undertones that Thorne's polished rhetoric might attempt to conceal.

"Autonomy is a cornerstone of the Alliance," Thorne countered, a faint smile playing on his lips. "We seek to supplement, not supplant. Our intention is to provide resources, expertise, and security, allowing communities like yours to flourish even more robustly."

"Flourish, yes," Mara agreed, her gaze unwavering. "But on our own terms. The proposal, as presented, implies a level of oversight and information sharing that could, inadvertently or otherwise, compromise our internal governance. We are willing to share data pertaining to resource utilization and communal needs, but the specifics of our agricultural cycles, our water management practices, and our defense strategies will remain strictly within Havenridge's purview."

A ripple of discomfort passed through the Alliance delegation. Thorne's smile tightened, losing some of its earlier warmth. "Madam Mara, transparency is essential for effective resource allocation. To ensure equitable distribution and to prevent potential misuse, a comprehensive understanding of your operational frameworks is necessary."

Eli leaned forward, his voice a low rumble that commanded attention. "Ambassador, we understand the need for accountability. However, the 'comprehensive understanding' you seek sounds remarkably like an audit of our very existence. Havenridge has survived and thrived for generations through meticulous planning and a deep understanding of our environment. To expose those intimate details to an external body, however well-intentioned, introduces an unacceptable risk. We propose a tiered system of information exchange. Basic resource inventories and projected needs will be provided quarterly. Any requests for specialized assistance, particularly in areas you deem sensitive, will be assessed on a case-by-case basis, with detailed justification required from both sides. Furthermore, any personnel dispatched by the Alliance to assist in technical matters will operate under strict supervision, their access limited to the immediate scope of their designated task."

The room fell silent. Thorne's gaze flickered to Eli, a grudging respect warring with annoyance in his eyes. He had clearly underestimated the former scout, mistaking his quiet demeanor for a lack of strategic acumen.

"Supervision?" Thorne finally said, his tone clipped. "We are not accustomed to such... stringent conditions, Mr. Eli. The Alliance operates on trust."

"And Havenridge operates on vigilance," Eli replied smoothly. "Trust is earned, Ambassador, especially when there is an imbalance of power. We are a small community, but we are not naive. We have learned from the harsh lessons of the past. Our survival has depended on our ability to adapt, to protect our interests, and to remain masters of our own destiny. We are willing to accept aid, but we will not trade our independence for it."

Mara seized the moment. "Precisely. We propose a dedicated liaison from your delegation, someone with demonstrable expertise and a commitment to clear communication. This individual will act as our primary point of contact. All requests, all reports, all proposed interventions will flow through this single channel. This ensures efficiency and minimizes the potential for misinterpretation or unauthorized access to sensitive information." She opened a thick ledger, its pages filled with her neat, precise script. "I have prepared a draft protocol outlining the terms of engagement, including specific parameters for resource sharing, technological integration, and information exchange. We are prepared to discuss these points in detail."

Thorne's gaze shifted from Eli to Mara's meticulously prepared ledger. The sheer volume of detail, the clear articulation of Havenridge's demands, was evidently disarming. He had expected a community on its knees, grateful for any lifeline. Instead, he found a people who, while acknowledging their need, were determined to dictate the terms of their salvation.

"This is... extensive," Thorne admitted, his fingers tapping a restless rhythm on the polished table.

"It is comprehensive," Mara corrected gently. "It reflects the seriousness with which Havenridge approaches this potential partnership. We are not looking for a handout, Ambassador. We are seeking a mutually beneficial arrangement that respects our existing structures and safeguards our future."

The negotiations continued, a slow, arduous process. Each clause of Mara's draft protocol was dissected, debated, and, in many cases, fiercely contested. The Alliance delegation, accustomed to dictating terms, found themselves on the defensive, their attempts to broaden the scope of their influence met with firm, unwavering resistance. Eli, with his keen understanding of human psychology and negotiation tactics, was a formidable counterpoint to Thorne's more overt pressures. He would subtly steer the conversation, reframe arguments, and highlight the logical inconsistencies in the Alliance's demands, all while maintaining an air of polite deference.

"Regarding the proposed 'mutual defense pact'," Eli stated, his voice calm but firm, "Havenridge's security protocols are designed to address threats specific to our region. While we appreciate the Alliance's willingness to extend its protective umbrella, we must ensure that any collaborative defense strategies do not inadvertently expose us to conflicts or entanglements beyond our direct concern. We propose a mutual information-sharing agreement regarding external threats, allowing each party to assess their own response independently, rather than a blanket commitment to engage in every Alliance conflict."

Thorne bristled. "But surely, Mr. Eli, if the Alliance is providing security, it is because there are threats that transcend individual communities. To refuse to engage in mutual defense is to undermine the very purpose of our presence."

"The purpose of your presence, Ambassador," Mara interjected, her voice quiet but resonant, "is to assist Havenridge, not to absorb it. Our defense is our responsibility. Your assistance can be in the form of intelligence, advanced warning systems, or the provision of specialized defensive technologies, should we deem them necessary and appropriate for our circumstances. A mandatory engagement in every Alliance conflict is not assistance; it is subjugation. We will maintain the right to determine when and how we engage in any form of military action."

The small, sparsely furnished cabin that served as Mara's personal study, usually a haven of quiet contemplation, had been transformed into a clandestine command center. Documents, maps, and copies of the Alliance's proposals were spread across the worn wooden table, illuminated by the flickering glow of oil lamps. Eli, his brow furrowed in concentration, traced the lines of a map detailing the Alliance's known territorial holdings. Mara, her face illuminated by the lamp's warm light, meticulously cross-referenced clauses from her protocol with Thorne's counter-proposals, her quill scratching furiously across the parchment.

"They're pushing hard on the energy infrastructure," Eli murmured, tapping a specific region on the map. "Their offer to 'upgrade' our power grid seems less about efficiency and more about establishing a backdoor for their own network access. If we allow them to integrate their systems directly into ours, they'll have an unprecedented level of insight into our energy consumption patterns, our technological capabilities, even our communication frequencies."

Mara nodded, her lips pressed into a thin line. "And the agricultural sector. Their insistence on 'advising' on crop rotation and seed selection is thinly veiled interference. They want to understand our food production cycles, our storage capacities. That's not partnership, Eli, that's intelligence gathering. If they know when we are most vulnerable, when our stores are lowest, they hold a significant leverage point."

"We need to make our refusal on these points absolute, Mara," Eli said, his voice carrying the weight of their shared concern. "No room for negotiation. We can accept their help with the repair of existing infrastructure, ensuring it remains compatible with our existing systems, but any 'upgrade' that involves deeper integration is a non-starter. For agriculture, we can accept the provision of surplus seeds or nutrient supplements, but the management of our fields remains ours. We need to frame it not as suspicion, but as a matter of operational security and specialized knowledge."

"Exactly," Mara agreed, her quill poised. "We can offer them access to our agricultural research data, anonymized and generalized, of course, focusing on climate impact and soil health rather than specific yields or breeding secrets. And for the energy grid, we can accept their offer to provide advanced diagnostic tools and training for our existing technicians, but any installation of new hardware must be limited to external maintenance points. They can help us fix the leaks, but they won't be allowed to rewire the house."

The evening wore on, the lamplight casting long shadows that danced with the intensity of their focus. They worked in near silence, punctuated only by the rustle of paper and the soft scratch of Mara's quill. Eli would occasionally present a scenario, a hypothetical push from Thorne's delegation, and Mara would meticulously craft a response, a carefully worded clause designed to deflect, to redirect, to safeguard.

"What about the 'cultural exchange' initiative?" Eli asked, his brow furrowed. "It sounds benign, but I can see Thorne using it to embed 'observers' within our community, gaining insight into our social dynamics, our leadership structures, even our dissent. They could be identifying potential points of friction, individuals amenable to their influence."

Mara sighed, rubbing her temples. "It's a subtle tactic, but a dangerous one. We can agree to limited, supervised cultural exchanges. Perhaps an exchange of artisans or scholars, with strict itineraries and designated chaperones from our side. The focus must be on the exchange of crafts and knowledge, not on infiltration. We will also insist on reciprocal exchanges, allowing Havenridge citizens to visit Alliance settlements, under similar conditions, of course. That way, we gain as much insight as we give."

"And we need to be crystal clear on the definition of 'Alliance resources'," Eli added, looking up from the map. "The wording in their proposal is deliberately vague. 'Access to communal stores' could mean anything from a portion of our harvested goods to our emergency reserves. We need to define this explicitly. For instance, if they are providing energy conduits, they may require a certain allocation of energy output in return. That needs to be quantified, capped, and strictly monitored. We cannot allow them to deplete our reserves under the guise of 'resource sharing'."

Mara dipped her quill in the inkwell, her movements precise. "Agreed. Any resource provision by the Alliance will be accompanied by a clearly defined, mutually agreed-upon repayment schedule or allocation. This will be measured in units, with clear expiry dates for any such agreements. No open-ended obligations. No vague promises. Everything documented, verified, and signed by both parties. If they provide x amount of energy conduit, we will allocate y amount of energy output for a defined period, after which the obligation ceases unless renegotiated."

The weight of the task was immense, the potential for oversight a constant, gnawing fear. But with each carefully crafted clause, with each subtle redirection of the Alliance's more invasive proposals, Mara felt a surge of quiet pride. They were not caving. They were not surrendering. They were negotiating. They were carving out a space for Havenridge to exist, to receive assistance, without becoming a pawn in a larger game. Eli, sensing her resolve, reached across the table and placed his hand over hers. His touch was warm, a silent acknowledgment of the shared burden and the unwavering commitment to their community. In the flickering lamplight, amidst the scattered documents and the scent of ink and aged parchment, a fragile treaty was being forged, not of capitulation, but of careful, guarded cooperation. The path ahead was still fraught with uncertainty, but for now, they had managed to steer Havenridge away from the precipice of unconditional surrender, towards a future they might, with vigilance and unwavering resolve, still be able to call their own. The dawn was still hours away, but in the quiet intensity of their shared purpose, a new kind of light was beginning to break.

The air in Mara's study was a familiar blend of old parchment and the faint, persistent hum of the auxiliary generator that kept the essential systems running. It was a sound that had become the heartbeat of Havenridge, a constant reminder of their reliance on carefully maintained technology, a reliance that the Alliance representatives seemed determined to exploit. Eli, hunched over a scatter of schematics, his brow furrowed in a way Mara had come to recognize as the precursor to a bold, and often risky, idea, looked up.

"They're circling," he stated, his voice low, devoid of its usual warmth, replaced by a sharp edge of strategic calculation. "Thorne's delegation. They're not just asking questions about resource allocation anymore. They're probing our perimeter defenses, subtly, of course. Inquiries about patrol routes, response times during the recent storm, even the structural integrity of the northern watchtower. They're gathering intel, Mara, and not for our benefit."

Mara leaned back, the worn leather of her chair creaking in protest. She knew Eli's instincts were rarely wrong. His years as a scout had honed his ability to perceive threats before they materialized, to read the subtle shifts in the wind that signaled an approaching storm. "They are trying to ascertain our weaknesses," she confirmed, her gaze fixed on the digital display of the generator's output, a faint blue light reflecting in her eyes. "They want to know where to apply pressure if negotiations fail."

"Precisely," Eli agreed, pushing a lock of dark hair from his forehead. "And that's why I think we need to give them something to chew on. Something that will keep them occupied, misdirected, and perhaps even reveal their true objectives." He paused, gathering his thoughts, the weight of his proposition settling in the quiet room. "I have a plan. A calculated risk."

Mara's eyes narrowed, a flicker of apprehension crossing her features. Eli's 'calculated risks' had a history of being exceptionally bold, bordering on reckless, though often ultimately successful. "Calculated how, Eli?" she asked, her voice laced with caution. "What are you proposing?"

"Deception," he said simply, his gaze meeting hers. "I propose we feed them a curated narrative. Fabricated vulnerabilities. Seeds of discord. We can suggest that our recent resource strain has led to internal friction, that certain sectors of our community are... restive. We can hint at potential structural weaknesses in our outer defenses, perhaps exacerbated by the storm, that require 'urgent, internal assessment.' We let them believe they've found soft spots, cracks in our facade."

The idea, though born of desperation, sent a shiver down Mara's spine. Deception was a weapon they wielded sparingly, a tool that could easily turn against its wielder. "You want to lie to them?" she asked, her voice barely a whisper. "To actively mislead them?"

"Not lie, Mara, misdirect," Eli corrected, his tone firm. "We aren't inventing entire scenarios from scratch. We are amplifying existing concerns, presenting them in a way that will appeal to their apparent desire to 'stabilize' Havenridge. We can suggest that our water purification system, while functional, has a historical tendency to falter under sustained high demand, a 'known issue' that our current technicians are struggling to fully resolve. We can mention that there have been 'unofficial' reports of minor seismic activity in the northern sectors, nothing to worry about for us, of course, but perhaps something that an external geological survey might find... concerning."

He drew a deep breath, the scent of ozone from the generator momentarily intensifying. "The goal is to draw their attention away from our actual security protocols – the reinforced comms arrays, the hidden sensor grids, the synchronized drone patrols that were so effective during the storm. If they believe they've identified genuine weaknesses, they'll focus their efforts on those fabricated vulnerabilities, perhaps even offering 'assistance' in those areas, which would give us invaluable insight into their capabilities and their true intentions."

Mara ran a hand over the smooth, cool surface of the table. Eli's logic, though unsettling, was sound. The Alliance delegation was a chess game of sorts, and they were playing for the survival of Havenridge. Sometimes, to protect oneself, one had to present a deceptive front. "And how do you plan to 'suggest' these things, Eli? A casual conversation over dinner?"

A ghost of a smile touched Eli's lips. "Not quite. I've been cultivating a certain… relationship with one of their junior analysts. A young man named Kael. He's eager to prove himself, perhaps a little too eager. He seems to be the one collecting the 'ground truth' for Thorne. A few strategically 'overheard' conversations, a 'misplaced' report detailing minor technical glitches, a carefully worded complaint about 'resource allocation' to specific defensive posts. Nothing that can be directly traced back to us, but enough to plant seeds of doubt and curiosity."

He leaned forward, his eyes, usually so open, now held a glint of calculated cunning. "We can even hint at internal disagreements. Perhaps suggest that there are factions within Havenridge who are more… amenable to external influence. It's a dangerous game, I know, but if they believe we are fractured, divided, they might underestimate our collective resolve, or worse, try to exploit those supposed divisions, revealing their methods and their agenda in the process."

Mara remained silent for a long moment, absorbing the implications of Eli's audacious plan. The ethical tightrope they walked was becoming increasingly narrow. "And if they take the bait?" she finally asked. "If they decide to send their own technicians to 'assess' these fabricated weaknesses? What then?"

"Then we observe," Eli replied, his voice steady. "We let them show us their hand. If they send people to 'inspect' our water purification system, we'll have eyes on them at all times, noting their equipment, their methods, their questions. If they focus on the northern watchtower, we'll see what they're really looking for. It's a way to buy time, Mara, and to gain crucial intelligence without revealing our true capabilities. It's a gamble, but the stakes are too high to simply wait for them to uncover our defenses on their own terms."

He met her gaze, his expression earnest. "I understand your reservations. This goes against everything we stand for. But experience has taught me that sometimes, to protect the flock, the shepherd must become a wolf in sheep's clothing. We are not strong enough to openly defy them. We must be smarter. We must be... cunning."

Mara closed her eyes, picturing the faces of the people of Havenridge, their trust placed squarely upon her and Eli. They had survived by being resourceful, by being adaptable, and yes, by being fiercely protective of their home. This plan, as distasteful as it felt, was a form of protection. It was a calculated risk, a desperate gamble, but it was a gamble born of necessity. The scent of ozone, a byproduct of the generator's labor, seemed to mingle with the old paper and ink, a subtle reminder of the modern underpinnings of their ancient community, and the new technologies they had to contend with.

"Alright, Eli," she said, her voice firm, though a tremor of unease still lingered. "You have my permission. But tread carefully. One wrong step, and this entire carefully constructed charade could collapse, leaving us more vulnerable than before. I will be here, monitoring everything, ready to adjust the narrative if necessary. But the execution is yours. And may whatever higher powers watch over Havenridge guide your hand."

Eli offered a curt nod, his gaze already distant, focused on the intricate dance of deception he was about to initiate. The calculated risk was in motion, a subtle poison being introduced into the

Alliance's information stream, a gamble that could either save them or plunge them into deeper peril. The air in the study, once filled with the quiet hum of technology, now felt thick with the unspoken tension of their dangerous game. He would feed them a story of internal strife, of manufactured weaknesses, a narrative designed to blind them to the true strength of Havenridge, while subtly revealing the true nature of their adversaries. It was a heavy burden, this necessary deception, but one he would carry, for the sake of their community, for the sake of their survival.

The hum of the generator, once a sound of reassuring normalcy, now felt like a low thrum of anxiety beneath the surface of daily life in Havenridge. Eli's calculated risk, the intricate dance of deception he had initiated with the Alliance delegation, was a storm gathering on the horizon, unseen by most, but felt by those at the helm. While Eli navigated the treacherous currents of external diplomacy and subtle sabotage, Mara's focus turned inward, toward the very heart of Havenridge, the fragile ecosystem of its people. Her role was not one of grand strategy or calculated deception, but of quiet, persistent mending, a relentless effort to fortify the community from within.

She understood that the fear and uncertainty surrounding the Alliance's presence were insidious, capable of eroding trust and sowing discord faster than any external threat. Eli could build walls and devise traps, but it was Mara who tended the soil, ensuring that the roots of their community remained strong and deeply entwined. Her strategy was far less dramatic than Eli's, eschewing manufactured vulnerabilities for genuine connection, but it was no less vital for their survival.

Her days became a tapestry woven with countless small acts of communal nurturing. She began by revitalizing the communal meals, a tradition that had, in recent years, become less frequent, casualties of busy schedules and growing anxieties. The mess hall, a large, utilitarian space that had often echoed with the clatter of hurried meals, was transformed. Long tables were set with mismatched crockery and hand-painted placemats, the air gradually filling with the comforting aromas of slow-cooked stews, freshly baked bread, and simmering herbs. Mara herself was often in the kitchen, her hands dusted with flour, her sleeves rolled up, working alongside the cooks, her presence a visible testament to the importance she placed on this shared ritual.

It wasn't just about the food, though the hearty, nourishing meals were a balm to weary bodies and spirits. It was about the act of breaking bread together, of sharing stories, of looking into the eyes of neighbors and reminding each other of their shared humanity. She made a point of sitting at different tables each night, her laughter a warm counterpoint to the murmur of conversations. She listened to the farmers discuss the unpredictable weather patterns, to the artisans lament the scarcity of certain raw materials, to the elders recount tales of past hardships that Havenridge had overcome. Her questions were simple, open-ended, designed to draw people out, to validate their concerns, and to foster a sense of shared responsibility.

"The northern fields are showing signs of stress, Mara," murmured old Silas, his voice raspy with age, as he passed her a bowl of steaming soup. "The soil feels... tired."

Mara met his gaze, her expression sympathetic. "I've noticed. We'll need to discuss soil remediation, Silas. Perhaps the hydro-team can analyze the nutrient levels and recommend a course of action. We have the knowledge, and we have the will. We'll find a way to revitalize them." It was a promise, a small one, but it was enough to see a flicker of hope in Silas's weathered face.

Beyond the meals, Mara organized a series of skill-sharing workshops. These weren't formal classes, but informal gatherings where individuals could pass on their expertise. Elara, the community's most skilled weaver, taught a small group the intricate art of mending torn fabrics, her nimble fingers guiding hesitant hands. Jian, whose understanding of botany was unparalleled, led foraging expeditions, teaching younger generations which plants were edible, which were medicinal, and which to avoid. Even Eli, when his duties allowed, would contribute, sharing his knowledge of navigation and wilderness survival, skills that were becoming increasingly relevant in their uncertain world.

Mara saw these workshops as vital conduits, not just for knowledge transfer, but for strengthening the bonds between people. When a young man named Finn, who had always been a bit of a loner, found himself working alongside Elara, patiently learning to thread a loom, a silent understanding began to form. When a shy girl named Anya, who had previously been too timid to speak up, discovered her knack for identifying medicinal herbs with Jian, her confidence began to blossom. Mara's presence at these gatherings was often unobtrusive, a quiet observer ensuring that everyone felt included and valued, her gentle encouragement a constant, steadying force.

She also made time for individual conversations, for the quiet moments of empathy that could mend deeper wounds. She would seek out those who seemed most withdrawn, the ones whose eyes held a particular shadow of worry. She would find them by the riverbanks, in their workshops, or simply on a quiet bench beneath the ancient oak at the center of the settlement. She listened without judgment, her presence a safe harbor for their unspoken fears and anxieties.

She met with Anya's parents, their faces etched with concern for their daughter's withdrawn nature. "She's been so quiet lately, Mara," her mother confessed, her voice thick with worry. "Ever since the Alliance ships were spotted. She… she doesn't sleep well."

Mara nodded, her heart aching with understanding. "Fear can be a heavy burden for young minds. The foraging walks with Jian have been good for her, have you noticed? It's giving her a sense of purpose, a connection to the land. And with Elara's weaving, she's finding a way to express herself, to create something beautiful." She offered practical suggestions, encouraging them to involve Anya in other communal activities, to remind her of the strength and resilience that lay within their own community. She didn't offer platitudes or dismiss their worries; instead, she acknowledged the reality of their fear and offered tangible pathways toward healing and reconnection.

For Kael, the young technician who had recently lost his father in a mining accident, Mara's support was a lifeline. She remembered him from the community's harvest festival, a bright, eager young man whose laughter had been infectious. Now, his eyes were shadowed, his movements hesitant. She found him staring blankly at a broken piece of machinery in the workshop.

"It's a complex mechanism, Kael," she said softly, sitting beside him. "Your father was a master craftsman. He would have known exactly what to do."

Kael's shoulders slumped. "He always did. I... I don't have his touch."

"No, you have your own," Mara countered gently. "His wisdom, his skill, it lives on in you. Perhaps not in the exact same way, but in the way you approach a problem, the way you seek to understand. Let me help you. Let's look at this together. Your father taught you patience, didn't he? That's a skill in itself." She spent the next hour with him, not trying to solve the problem for him, but guiding him, asking him questions, prompting him to recall what he had learned, her steady presence a quiet encouragement. It was in these moments, amidst the shared effort, that Kael began to find a glimmer of his father's spirit within himself again.

Her efforts weren't always met with immediate, dramatic success. Building trust, especially in the face of fear, was a slow, arduous process. There were still murmurs of discontent, pockets of anxiety that lingered like stubborn shadows. Some individuals remained withdrawn, their experiences too deeply scarred to be easily soothed. But Mara persevered, her belief in the inherent strength of their community unwavering. She saw each shared meal, each completed workshop, each individual conversation as a small victory, a brick laid in the foundation of their resilience.

The simple act of sharing food, she discovered, was a profound ritual of reconciliation. When two neighbors, who had fallen out over a disputed water ration months prior, were seated at the same table, Mara didn't force a confrontation. Instead, she engaged them in a conversation about the surprisingly successful hydroponic yields from the west sector, a topic that had no connection to their disagreement. As they found themselves nodding in agreement, sharing a laugh at a farmer's witty observation, the ice between them began to melt. By the end of the meal, they were speaking to each other, tentatively at first, then with growing ease, the shared sustenance and the shared humanity of the moment bridging the gap that had separated them.

Mara understood that while Eli was fighting a battle of wits and deception in the shadows, her fight was in the light, in the open, nurturing the spirit of Havenridge. She was the quiet gardener, tending to the roots of their collective strength, ensuring that even as the storm gathered, the heart of their community beat strong and true. Her presence was a constant, warm, steadying force, a silent promise that they were not alone, that they were bound together, and that together, they could weather whatever came their way. She was the anchor, grounding them in their shared purpose, reminding them of who they were, and why they fought to protect their home.

The air in the council chamber had been thick with an almost unbearable tension, a palpable thing that seemed to press down on their very lungs. Each word spoken, each gesture exchanged between Eli and the Alliance delegation, had been a carefully calibrated move in a high-stakes game. Now, as the last of the Alliance officials departed, their hovercraft lifting silently into the twilight sky, a profound quiet settled over Havenridge. It wasn't the peaceful quiet of a community at rest, but the charged silence that follows a storm, the hushed anticipation of what the next gust might bring.

Eli leaned against the sturdy, polished oak of the council table, his shoulders slumping slightly as the weight of the past few days seemed to finally descend. His knuckles were white where he gripped the edge of the wood, a silent testament to the controlled fury he had held at bay. Across the room, Mara watched him, her own exhaustion a dull ache behind her eyes. The communal meals she had so diligently orchestrated, the skill-sharing workshops, the quiet conversations – all of it had been a deliberate effort to strengthen the fabric of Havenridge against the very pressures Eli had been confronting. Now, the immediate threat had receded, but the underlying fragility remained.

"They're gone," Eli's voice was a low rumble, laced with a weariness that went deeper than physical fatigue. He met Mara's gaze, and in that shared look, a thousand unspoken words passed between them. Relief, yes, a potent, heady wave of it. But beneath that, a stark, unyielding awareness. This was not a victory, not in the traditional sense. It was a reprieve.

"For now," Mara responded, her voice soft but firm. She walked towards him, her footsteps echoing softly in the suddenly cavernous space. The agreement they had struck was a precarious balancing act. Havenridge would continue its development, its vital resource extraction operations would proceed, but under the watchful, calculating eye of the Alliance. It was a concession, a carefully negotiated surrender of certain freedoms in exchange for the promise of continued autonomy. Eli had played the game masterfully, leveraging their carefully constructed self-sufficiency and the subtle, veiled threats of potential disruption to their own mining operations should they be unduly pressured. He had painted a picture of a community too valuable, too complex to simply absorb, one that would be more of a hindrance than a asset if pushed too far.

"They accepted our terms," Eli said, a ghost of a smile touching his lips. "The 'joint oversight' is minimal, the reports are to be submitted quarterly, and our internal governance remains untouched. For the moment, at least." He pushed himself away from the table, his movements stiff. "They'll be watching, though. Every move. Every decision."

"And we'll be ready," Mara replied, stepping closer. She reached out, her hand finding his, her touch grounding. His skin was cool, his grip still tight. "You did well, Eli. You bought us time. And you did it without compromising who we are."

He turned his hand, interlacing their fingers. "It was a tightrope walk, Mara. One misstep, one flicker of weakness, and they would have pounced. Your work... your work was just as crucial. Knowing that Havenridge was united, that the people were strong, that was our greatest leverage." He squeezed her hand. "They could see the order, the purpose. They saw a community that wouldn't fracture easily."

They walked out of the council chamber together, emerging into the cool evening air. The sky was a deep indigo, dusted with the first hesitant stars. The lights of Havenridge twinkled below them, a warm, inviting glow against the encroaching darkness. The generator hummed its steady, reassuring song, a counterpoint to the whispering pines that surrounded their settlement.

"It's beautiful," Mara murmured, gazing out at the familiar landscape. "And it feels so fragile tonight."

"It is fragile," Eli agreed, his arm sliding around her waist, drawing her close. He rested his chin on her head, breathing in the scent of pine and woodsmoke that clung to her. "This peace... it's a fragile thing, built on a foundation of shrewd negotiation and a desperate hope. It's not the end of the struggle, Mara. It's just a pause."

The wind rustled through the tall pines, a mournful sigh that seemed to echo their unspoken fears. The trees, ancient sentinels of this land, seemed to hold their breath, their branches swaying gently as if in contemplation of the uncertain future. The Alliance had withdrawn their physical presence, but their shadow lingered, a constant reminder of the external forces that threatened their hard-won autonomy.

"They saw us," Mara said, her voice barely audible above the wind. "They saw what we've built here. And they want a piece of it."

"They want control," Eli corrected, his jaw tight. "They see our resources, our technological advancements, and they want to integrate them into their own vast network. They don't understand the spirit of Havenridge, the independence we cherish." He tightened his embrace. "But they respect it, enough to strike this deal. That's a victory, Mara. A small one, but a victory nonetheless."

They stood in comfortable silence for a long moment, the shared experience, the shared responsibility, binding them closer than ever. The exhaustion was still there, a heavy cloak, but it was now overlaid with a fierce sense of purpose. They had faced down an immediate threat and emerged, not unscathed, but intact.

"Remember the hydro-team's report on the northern fields?" Mara suddenly asked, her mind already turning to the next challenges. "Silas was worried about the soil. That's something we can work on, something tangible."

Eli nodded, a flicker of his usual proactive energy returning. "And the new filtration system for the water reclamation plant. The prototypes are almost ready. We need to keep pushing forward, keep innovating. That's our best defense."

"Exactly," Mara agreed, a genuine smile finally gracing her lips. "We won't let fear paralyze us. We'll use this time, this fragile peace, to grow stronger. To make ourselves indispensable, not just in resources, but in spirit."

The stars above began to burn brighter as the last vestiges of twilight faded. The lights of Havenridge seemed to pulse with a renewed vibrancy, a beacon of resilience against the encroaching darkness. They were a community that had learned to thrive in adversity, to find strength in unity, and to build a future on the bedrock of their shared values.

As they turned to walk back towards their shared living quarters, the scent of woodsmoke growing stronger, Eli paused. He turned Mara to face him, his eyes serious. "This peace is a gamble, Mara. A calculated risk. But I believe in us. I believe in Havenridge."

Mara met his gaze, her own reflecting his conviction. "And I believe in you, Eli. We'll face whatever comes, together."

The path ahead was uncertain, veiled in the mists of the future. The Alliance's presence, even in its absence, was a constant pressure. But as they walked hand in hand, the gentle hum of the generator a familiar lullaby, they carried with them not just the weariness of their struggle, but the quiet, unshakeable hope that had always been the true heart of Havenridge. This fragile peace, a testament to their resilience, was not an end, but a new beginning, a chance to solidify their foundations and prepare for whatever lay beyond the horizon. The wind whispered through the pines, no longer a lament, but a promise of renewal, a reminder that even in uncertainty, life found a way to endure, to grow, and to bloom. They had navigated the crossroads, and while the path ahead was unclear, they would walk it, side by side, with their community as their guide and their shared resolve as their unwavering strength.

CHAPTER SIX

Foundations of Commitment

The lingering scent of pine and the faint hum of the generator were no longer just background notes; they were the very breath of Havenridge, a testament to the lifeblood that flowed through its veins. The council chamber, once a crucible of tension, now felt like a sanctuary, a space where the echoes of negotiation had receded, replaced by a quieter, more profound resolve. Eli and Mara, having navigated the treacherous currents of external pressure, now found themselves charting a new course, one that led inward, towards the very heart of their community and the intricate tapestry of their shared future. The Alliance had receded, like a tide that had momentarily threatened to engulf them, but its receding had not diminished the importance of what lay beneath the surface. It had, in fact, illuminated it, highlighting the need to strengthen the very bedrock upon which Havenridge stood.

"They're gone," Eli had said, his voice still carrying the weight of their recent ordeal, yet now tinged with a nascent hope. And Mara had agreed, her own weariness a silent partner to his, "For now." But the 'for now' had opened a door, a window of opportunity that they were determined to seize. The fragile peace was not an end to their struggles, but a fertile ground for growth, a chance to plant the seeds of a more robust and resilient future. It was time to turn their collective gaze inward, to examine the sinews of their community, to ensure that the foundations were not just strong enough to withstand future storms, but robust enough to foster flourishing growth.

Mara found herself drawn to the open expanse of the central clearing, a space that had seen countless community gatherings, from boisterous celebrations to somber discussions. Now, it was slated to become the beating heart of a new phase of development. The air, usually alive with the sounds of children's laughter and the gentle murmur of conversation, now carried the sharp, invigorating scent of freshly cut lumber. The rhythmic thud of hammers and the whine of saws were the sounds of progress, of tangible action being taken to solidify their shared existence. New communal buildings were beginning to take shape, their skeletal frameworks rising against the cerulean sky, each beam a deliberate choice, each nail a testament to their collective will. These structures were more than just shelters; they were physical manifestations of their renewed commitment, anchors of shared purpose in a world that often felt adrift.

Eli joined her, his movements more relaxed than they had been in weeks, the tightness in his shoulders beginning to ease. He watched the workers, his gaze steady, a quiet pride evident in the set of his jaw. "It's good to see this," he murmured, his voice a low rumble that blended with the sounds of construction. "To see us building, not just defending."

Mara nodded, a small smile playing on her lips. "It feels... right, doesn't it? Like we're finally tending to our own garden, rather than just fending off the weeds." She gestured towards the rising structures. "These will be places for learning, for healing, for simply being together. Places that reinforce why we chose to stay here, why we're investing our lives in this place."

Their conversations, once dominated by survival and negotiation, were now shifting. The focus had turned to the intricate, often complex, question of what it truly meant to *stay*. It wasn't merely about physical presence; it was about a deep-seated commitment, a conscious choice to weave oneself into the fabric of Havenridge, to contribute to its ongoing narrative. To that end, they had begun initiating a series of community-wide discussions, gatherings that spanned the spectrum of Havenridge's inhabitants, from the seasoned elders who had witnessed the settlement's very inception to the wide-eyed children who knew no other home. These weren't formal pronouncements from a governing body, but open forums, spaces where every voice could be heard, every perspective considered.

"We need to define our long-term goals, not just for the next harvest, but for the next generation," Mara had stated in one of these recent discussions, her voice carrying a quiet authority that resonated with the assembled community. "What kind of Havenridge do we want to be? What are the values that will guide us, not just in times of crisis, but in our everyday lives?"

Eli had picked up on her thread, his own vision seamlessly integrated. "And how do we ensure that our governance structures reflect those values? How do we maintain fairness, equity, and individual autonomy while ensuring the collective good?" He looked around at the sea of faces, his gaze lingering on each individual. "This isn't about imposing rules; it's about building a shared understanding, a consensus that will empower us all."

The initial discussions had been a whirlwind of ideas, some pragmatic, some idealistic, all born from a shared desire for a stable and fulfilling future. There were proposals for new educational curricula, focusing on both practical skills and the arts, ensuring that the next generation would be not only self-sufficient but also culturally rich. Debates arose about resource management, about how to ensure that Havenridge's prosperity was sustainable and ethically managed, respecting the delicate balance of their environment. The very definition of community citizenship was being re-examined, exploring what responsibilities and privileges came with being a part of Havenridge.

"'Staying' means more than just breathing the same air," Elara, a respected elder whose hands bore the indelible marks of a lifetime spent cultivating their land, had contributed during one of these sessions. Her voice, though weathered, was clear and steady. "It means planting roots, not just in the soil, but in each other. It means understanding that our individual well-being is inextricably linked to the well-being of the whole."

Young Kael, an apprentice in the engineering guild, had offered a different, yet equally vital, perspective. "For me, staying means having the freedom to innovate, to push the boundaries of what we can achieve. It means knowing that my ideas will be heard, that I have a stake in shaping our technological future, not just benefiting from it."

These diverse viewpoints, far from creating division, were weaving a richer tapestry of understanding. They were acknowledging that 'staying' was not a monolithic concept, but a spectrum of personal commitments, all of which contributed to the strength of the collective. The new communal buildings were becoming canvases for these burgeoning ideas. The planned learning center, already taking shape, was envisioned not just as a place for formal instruction, but as a hub for collaborative projects, for the cross-pollination of knowledge between different guilds and generations. The expanded communal dining hall, its roof beams now firmly in place, was destined to be more than just a place to break bread; it was to be a forum for informal dialogue, for the spontaneous connections that often fostered the deepest bonds.

Mara found herself spending more time observing these construction sites, not just as a spectator, but as an active participant in the process of envisioning the future. She'd watch the carpenters expertly join wood, their movements efficient and practiced, and see echoes of the careful precision required in community building. She'd listen to the engineers discussing load-bearing capacities and see parallels in the need for strong, well-defined governance structures.

One afternoon, as she stood near the site of what was to become the new community archive, a place dedicated to preserving their history and knowledge, Eli found her. The scent of sawdust hung heavy in the air, a comforting aroma that spoke of creation and permanence. He came to stand beside her, his arm brushing hers, a silent acknowledgement of their shared endeavor.

"The plans for the archive are impressive," he commented, his gaze sweeping over the nascent walls. "We're not just building for today, are we?"

"We're building for tomorrow, and the day after that," Mara replied, her voice soft but resolute. "We're creating a legacy. The discussions about our ethical guidelines have been particularly intense, haven't they?"

Eli chuckled, a low, rumbling sound. "Intense is an understatement. The debate on data privacy alone could have generated enough energy to power half of Havenridge for a week." He paused, his expression turning more thoughtful. "But it's necessary. We're dealing with incredibly sensitive information – our resource yields, our technological breakthroughs, our personal histories. We need a clear framework, a set of principles that ensure this information is protected, used responsibly, and never exploited."

The ethical guidelines were, indeed, a significant undertaking. They were grappling with questions that many established societies had spent centuries trying to answer, but doing so with a fresh perspective, unburdened by millennia of ingrained dogma. How would they handle intellectual property generated within the community? What were the boundaries of privacy when it came to shared resources and collective knowledge? How would they ensure that technological advancements benefited everyone, and not just a select few?

"The commitment to transparency in our decision-making processes," Mara continued, "that's crucial. It's not enough to have good intentions; we need to be able to show our work, to explain *why* certain decisions are made. That builds trust, and trust is the bedrock of any lasting commitment."

"And the principles of restorative justice," Eli added, his gaze now fixed on the intricate joinery of a window frame. "We're not looking to punish, but to repair. To understand the root causes of conflict and to find ways to heal the rifts, rather than simply severing ties. That's a powerful statement of commitment to each other, wouldn't you say?"

Mara's heart swelled with a quiet pride. This was the Havenridge she had envisioned, a place that prioritized empathy and understanding alongside efficiency and progress. "It is. It speaks to our maturity as a community, our willingness to grow and learn from our mistakes, not just repeat them." She turned to him, her eyes reflecting the warm glow of the setting sun filtering through the unfinished structure. "These new buildings, these discussions, they're all manifestations of that deeper commitment, aren't they? They're tangible expressions of what 'staying' truly means."

The scent of lumber, once merely a sign of construction, had transformed into the aroma of commitment, of a future being meticulously built, beam by beam, decision by decision. The challenges ahead were still significant, the shadow of the Alliance, though distant, was a constant reminder of the world beyond their borders. But within Havenridge, a new strength was coalescing, not just in the rising walls of their communal structures, but in the shared understanding that bloomed in the hearts and minds of its people. They were not just surviving; they were thriving, actively shaping their destiny, solidifying the foundations of a future built on intention, integrity, and an unwavering belief in the power of their collective spirit. The act of "staying" was no longer a passive state of being, but an active, vibrant verb, a continuous recommitment to the ideals and the community they had so painstakingly forged. And in that active commitment, in that shared endeavor, lay the true strength and enduring hope of Havenridge.

The scent of dried herbs, a fragrant symphony of chamomile, lavender, and mint, had become the olfactory signature of their shared living space. It wasn't merely an aesthetic choice; it was a conscious cultivation of sanctuary, a deliberate infusion of calm into the whirlwind of their expanding responsibilities. This dwelling, once a simple refuge after arduous days, had transformed into the crucible where their partnership was being reforged, tempered by the fires of recent trials and the ever-present demands of Havenridge. Mara found herself drawn to its familiar embrace after each council meeting, each strategy session, the quiet hum of its existence a balm to her often-frayed nerves. Eli, too, sought its solace, the weight of his decisions visibly lightening as he crossed the threshold.

Their conversations, once punctuated by the easy laughter of affection or the gentle murmurs of shared dreams, had deepened, their cadence shifting to accommodate the gravity of their evolving roles. The simple affirmations of love, while still cherished and essential, were now interwoven with the intricate threads of shared responsibility. They spoke not just of their feelings for one another, but of the burdens they carried, the sacrifices they were willing to make, and the intricate dance of strategy required to ensure Havenridge's continued survival and prosperity. The 'us' had expanded, not just in their hearts, but in the very fabric of their strategic thinking.

"The council is pushing for accelerated resource allocation for the hydroponic expansion," Eli stated one evening, his brow furrowed as he meticulously traced a line on a projection he'd sketched onto a salvaged piece of parchment. The soft glow of the ambient bioluminescent flora cast long shadows across their cluttered table, illuminating the earnestness in his eyes. "They argue it's the most efficient path to securing our food supply against future environmental fluctuations. But I'm concerned about the strain on our power grid, and the potential displacement of other vital projects."

Mara, who had been carefully sorting through a collection of medicinal tinctures, paused, her fingers hovering over a vial of vibrant blue liquid. "Efficiency is important, of course," she mused, her voice thoughtful, "but not at the expense of sustainability. We need to consider the ripple effects. Have you factored in the energy consumption for the filtration systems, or the waste disposal from the nutrient runoff? And what about the impact on our existing agricultural workforce? Are we providing them with alternative roles, or are we inadvertently creating unemployment?"

This was the new language of their partnership. It was a lexicon of strategic alliances, of risk assessment, of foreseeing consequences that extended far beyond the immediate benefit. Their shared affection remained the bedrock, the unwavering foundation upon which these complex discussions were built, but the edifice itself was now grander, more intricate, and built to withstand a wider spectrum of storms. Their love was not a passive emotion; it was an active force, a driving engine that propelled them forward, not just as individuals, but as a unified front.

"That's precisely my concern," Eli admitted, leaning back in his chair, the parchment momentarily forgotten. "The projections for energy output are optimistic, but they don't account for unforeseen demands. And you're right about the workforce. We can't simply discard decades of hard-won knowledge and skill. Perhaps a phased approach? Integrate the new systems gradually, retrain personnel for specialized maintenance and oversight roles. It would be slower, yes, but far more stable."

He looked at Mara, his gaze seeking not just affirmation, but her strategic input, her unique perspective that so often illuminated blind spots he might have missed. "What are your thoughts on the implications for our medical supplies? If we divert more resources to energy infrastructure, it might impact the cultivation of certain rare botanical components we rely on for advanced treatments. We spoke about needing to bolster our reserves of xylon root for the feverfew infusion, didn't we?"

Mara nodded, her mind already sifting through the intricate web of interdependencies. "The feverfew infusion is critical for managing the residual effects of the neurotoxins we encountered during the Alliance incursion. Its scarcity would leave us vulnerable. Perhaps we can explore alternative power generation methods for the hydroponics. Could we leverage geothermal vents if we identify suitable locations? Or are we still too reliant on the solar arrays, which are vulnerable to prolonged cloud cover?"

These were not hypothetical musings. These were the critical junctures where their decisions would shape the very survival of Havenridge. The challenges they had faced, the harrowing moments of uncertainty and fear, had not broken them; they had forged them. They had learned, in the crucible of crisis, that partnership was not just about holding hands, but about bearing the weight together, about shouldering the immense responsibility with an unwavering trust that the other would do the same.

"Geothermal is a long-term prospect, and the initial investment would be significant," Eli mused, tapping a finger against his chin.

"For the immediate need, perhaps we can implement more stringent energy conservation protocols across all sectors. And incentivize greater personal responsibility for energy usage. The council also needs to approve a dedicated allocation for botanical research to identify viable synthetic alternatives or supplementary cultivation methods for xylon root, even if it's just for emergency reserves."

He reached across the table, his hand covering hers. The calluses on his fingers, a testament to his own efforts in maintaining Havenridge's infrastructure, were a familiar comfort. "It's about finding that balance, isn't it? Between progress and preservation. Between ambition and prudence. And it's a balance we have to strike together."

"Always together," Mara echoed, her thumb tracing the lines on his palm. The scent of dried herbs filled the air, a quiet testament to the life they were nurturing within these walls, a life intertwined with the larger endeavor of Havenridge. Their shared dwelling wasn't just a house; it was a testament to their commitment, a space where the most crucial decisions were made not in the sterile echo of a council chamber, but in the intimate warmth of their shared existence.

The evolution of their partnership was intrinsically linked to the evolution of Havenridge itself. As the community grew, as its needs became more complex, so too did the demands on their leadership. The days of simply reacting to immediate threats were, for the moment, behind them. Now, the focus was on proactive planning, on building resilience, on creating a future that was not only secure but also thriving. This shift in focus necessitated a deeper, more nuanced understanding of what it meant to be partners, not just in love, but in the very stewardship of their collective destiny.

"I've been reviewing the proposals for the expansion of the atmospheric processors," Eli mentioned, shifting the parchment slightly to reveal a more detailed schematic. "The engineers are confident they can increase efficiency by twenty percent. However, the projected cost in rare earth minerals is substantial. We have enough for the initial deployment, but restocking will require a significant diversion of resources from other vital areas."

Mara's gaze sharpened. "Rare earth minerals. That's a bottleneck we've been aware of for some time. Have we fully explored the possibility of recycling and reclaiming materials from decommissioned machinery? And have we initiated discussions with neighboring settlements for potential trade agreements, even informal ones, for these vital resources? Relying solely on our internal reserves feels... precarious."

Her mind was already sketching out possibilities, her inherent pragmatism wrestling with the urgent need for progress. The Alliance's proximity, though less of an immediate threat, remained a stark reminder of the interconnectedness of their world, and the potential for both cooperation and conflict. "If we can establish a reliable, even if limited, supply chain for these minerals, it would alleviate the pressure on our other resource allocations. It would allow us to proceed with the atmospheric processors without compromising our ability to, for example, maintain the pharmaceutical cultivation or fund the continued development of the deep-earth geothermal survey."

Eli's eyes lit up with a familiar spark of admiration. "That's brilliant, Mara. I hadn't considered the trade angle with the same urgency. The settlements further south might have access, or perhaps even reserves they aren't utilizing effectively. It would require careful negotiation, of course. We'd need to offer something of value in return. Our advanced irrigation techniques, perhaps, or specialized agricultural knowledge?"

"Precisely," Mara confirmed, a small smile gracing her lips. "It's about identifying mutual needs and building bridges. It's about transforming potential competitors into strategic allies. And it aligns with our broader goal of fostering a network of interconnected, self-sufficient communities, reducing reliance on any single entity, including ourselves."

The conversation flowed, a seamless blend of their individual strengths. Eli, with his intuitive grasp of engineering and resource management, and Mara, with her sharp foresight in diplomacy, resource acquisition, and long-term community well-being. They were not just a couple; they were a formidable dual leadership, their private moments of connection serving as the fertile ground for public policy and community advancement.

"We also need to allocate resources for enhanced surveillance and early warning systems along those southern trade routes," Eli added, his tone becoming more serious. "If we're opening ourselves up to more external interaction, we need to be prepared for any eventuality. The Alliance may have retreated, but the underlying tensions remain. And new threats could emerge."

"Agreed," Mara said, her gaze steady. "A portion of the projected savings from more efficient atmospheric processing could be reallocated. We need to ensure our defenses are not just reactive, but also proactive. And we need to reinforce the ethical guidelines regarding external interactions. Transparency and clear protocols are paramount to avoid misunderstandings or unintentional provocations."

The dried herbs in their dwelling seemed to intensify their fragrance, a subtle reminder of the life they were fighting to protect, the peace they were working so diligently to build. Their partnership, once defined by the shared intimacy of burgeoning love, had matured into something far more profound: a strategic alliance, a pact of unwavering trust, and a shared commitment to the intricate, often daunting, task of safeguarding their future. It was a partnership built not just on shared affection, but on shared responsibility, a deep-seated understanding that their individual well-being was inextricably bound to the fate of Havenridge, and that together, they were stronger, more resilient, and more capable of navigating the complex currents of their world. They had carved out intentional time for each other, not as a luxury, but as a necessity, transforming their sanctuary into the command center of their shared vision.

The meaning of 'staying' had begun to morph, evolving from a simple declaration of presence into a deeply nuanced commitment. For Mara and Eli, it was no longer enough to simply inhabit Havenridge; their continued existence was intrinsically tied to its flourishing. This realization had spurred a series of introspection, a quiet wrestling with the personal cost and the profound rewards of such dedication. It was a concept they knew needed to be shared, not just articulated amongst themselves, but woven into the very fabric of their community's understanding.

"Staying," Mara mused one evening, her gaze sweeping across the familiar comfort of their dwelling, the scent of drying herbs a constant, grounding presence. "It's more than just not leaving, isn't it? It's about planting roots so deep that even the fiercest storm can't dislodge you."

Eli, who had been meticulously reviewing schematics for the new atmospheric processors, looked up, his eyes meeting hers with an understanding that transcended words. He set down his stylus, the familiar weight of it a counterpoint to the lightness he felt when they shared these moments of profound connection. "It's an active choice, every single day. It's about contributing, even when it's difficult. It's about investing yourself, your energy, your very being, into the collective good. And it often means making sacrifices that are deeply personal."

The notion of sacrifice, he knew, was a complex one. It wasn't always the grand, heroic gestures that defined their commitment, but the myriad of small, often unseen, concessions. It was the late nights spent poring over resource logs instead of enjoying quiet companionship, the difficult conversations with those who harbored dissent, the constant vigilance required to anticipate threats that others might not even perceive. It was a continuous offering, a dedication of self to a purpose larger than individual desires.

"I think," Mara continued, her voice a soft murmur that nevertheless carried the weight of her conviction, "we need to articulate this more clearly to everyone. Not just as leaders, but as fellow residents. The value of 'staying' needs to be understood beyond simply being present. It's about active participation, about emotional investment, about a willingness to stand for what we're building here, even when the cost feels high."

Eli nodded, the gears of his strategic mind already turning. "We need to foster a culture where 'staying' is synonymous with contributing.

Where it's understood that our collective strength is built on the dedication of each individual. Perhaps we could initiate a series of dialogues? Not formal pronouncements, but open conversations with long-term residents. Those who have chosen to remain through thick and thin, who understand the sacrifices involved."

The idea resonated deeply with Mara. She envisioned these gatherings not as interrogations, but as celebrations of shared resilience and commitment. They could share their own journeys, the personal costs they had both endured, and the profound satisfaction that came from knowing they were building something truly meaningful, something worth defending. It would be a way to reinforce the shared values that bound them, to strengthen the invisible threads that connected each individual to the larger tapestry of Havenridge.

"That's an excellent idea, Eli," she said, her enthusiasm evident. "We can invite people who embody that spirit of 'staying'. Those who have weathered storms, who have seen Havenridge through its nascent stages and its challenges. Their stories will be far more powerful than any directive we could issue. They can speak to the personal sacrifices, the moments of doubt, and ultimately, the profound sense of belonging and purpose that makes 'staying' not just a choice, but a necessity."

Their first such conversation was arranged for a crisp autumn evening, the air outside carrying the faint, metallic tang of impending frost. They chose a communal gathering space, its sturdy, reclaimed timber walls echoing with the quiet hum of anticipation. A small group had been invited, individuals who had been integral to Havenridge from its earliest days: Elara, the elder botanist whose knowledge of Havenridge's unique flora was unparalleled; Jax, the gruff but dependable engineer who had overseen much of the initial infrastructure development; and Lyra, a weaver whose intricate textiles not only clothed their community but also symbolized its interconnectedness.

Mara began, her voice warm and inviting, setting a tone of shared experience rather than formal address. "Thank you all for joining us. We wanted to have this conversation because, as leaders, we often speak about the future of Havenridge, about its growth and its security. But the foundation of that future is built by each of you, by your decision to 'stay,' to invest your lives here. And we wanted to understand, more deeply, what that means for you."

Elara, her hands gnarled with years of tending to delicate seedlings, spoke first. Her voice, though soft, carried an undeniable strength. "For me, 'staying' was never a question. When I first arrived, Havenridge was little more than a collection of hopeful structures clinging to this land. The soil was difficult, the climate unforgiving. Many saw it as a temporary refuge, a place to endure until they could find something easier. But I saw... potential. A wildness that needed to be understood, to be nurtured. My sacrifice was leaving behind the comfort of established gardens, the predictable harvests. Here, every bloom, every harvest, felt like a victory hard-won. My personal life, my relationships outside of Havenridge, they... they became secondary. It wasn't a conscious decision to abandon them, but the demands of this land, of ensuring our people had sustenance, they consumed my focus. And in a way, Havenridge became my family."

Jax, his broad shoulders filling his chair, grunted in agreement. "My story's not so different. I was a builder, always looking for the next big project. When I first came, it was all about survival. Reinforcing shelters, rigging power systems, making the impossible work with what little we had. There were times I wanted to pack up, to seek out communities where the work was easier, the resources more plentiful. But then I'd look at what we were building. The sense of shared purpose. The reliance people had on the systems I helped put in place. The sacrifices? Well, I missed seeing my younger siblings grow up. I missed the easy camaraderie of city life, the constant stream of new challenges. But here, the challenges were *ours*. And the solutions we found, they were born of necessity, of collaboration. Staying meant accepting that my personal ambitions would take a backseat to the community's needs. It meant choosing the slow, steady work of building something lasting over the fleeting thrill of novelty."

Lyra, her fingers still nimble as she demonstrated a knot on a piece of yarn, added her perspective. "My weaving, it's always been about connection. When Havenridge was young, I wove blankets, simple things to keep people warm. But as we grew, as we faced hardships, my weaving became more. It became about telling our story. Each thread, each pattern, represented a person, a family, a shared experience. 'Staying' for me meant pouring my heart and soul into that narrative. It meant sacrificing the freedom to explore new artistic avenues, to experiment with different materials. My time was dedicated to creating something that would bind us together, something that would remind us of who we were, even in the darkest hours. It meant choosing the labor of love over the pursuit of personal artistic recognition. And in doing so, I found a deeper fulfillment than I ever thought possible."

Mara and Eli listened intently, their hearts swelling with a profound sense of gratitude and recognition. These were not mere residents; they were the living embodiment of what 'staying' truly meant. Their stories, rich with personal cost and unwavering dedication, painted a vivid picture of commitment.

"Your stories are invaluable," Eli said, his voice laced with genuine emotion. "They illustrate that 'staying' is an active verb. It's not passive endurance, but a continuous process of investment, of contribution, and yes, of sacrifice. It's about recognizing that the well-being of the collective is inextricably linked to our own."

Mara picked up the thread, her gaze thoughtful. "And it highlights that the definition of 'defense' has evolved, hasn't it? It's not just about armed patrols or fortified walls anymore. It's about building a community so resilient, so deeply interconnected, that it becomes inherently defensible. It's about fostering a shared sense of ownership and belonging, where everyone has a stake in its survival and prosperity."

These conversations, they realized, were not a one-off. They needed to become a recurring aspect of community life, a way to continually reinforce the values that held Havenridge together. They began to organize more of these informal gatherings, inviting different long-term residents to share their experiences. Each story added another layer to their understanding of commitment, revealing the diverse paths individuals had taken to plant their roots.

There was Jian, a former scavenger who had learned to repurpose discarded technology, who spoke of the sacrifice of abandoning his nomadic lifestyle, the thrill of discovery replaced by the meticulous work of repair and innovation. He described the personal cost of turning down lucrative salvage opportunities outside Havenridge, choosing instead to invest his skills in maintaining their aging infrastructure, knowing that his contributions kept essential systems running. He spoke of the quiet satisfaction of seeing a vital piece of equipment brought back to life, a testament to his choice to 'stay' and contribute his unique talents.

Then there was Anya, who had initially arrived with a group planning to move on, but found herself drawn to Havenridge's burgeoning agricultural cooperative. She spoke of the difficult decision to sever ties with her original group, a painful severing of old bonds to forge new ones. Her sacrifice was the severance of a familiar support network, the risk of alienating those she had once considered her kin. But her commitment to the land, to the promise of self-sufficiency Havenridge offered, had been stronger. She described the joy of sharing her knowledge of crop rotation and soil enrichment, finding a deep sense of purpose in contributing to Havenridge's food security, a purpose that far outweighed the loneliness she had initially felt.

These narratives, shared in the intimate glow of communal spaces, began to permeate the community's consciousness. The concept of 'staying' started to shift, not as an obligation, but as a profound expression of belonging and purpose. It was a conscious decision to invest, to contribute, to defend the shared vision, not with weapons alone, but with the unwavering strength of a united people.

Mara and Eli found that these dialogues also informed their own leadership. They began to see the needs of the community not just through the lens of policy and resource allocation, but through the deeply personal experiences of those who had chosen to stay. They understood more profoundly the sacrifices involved, and the immense value of every individual's contribution. This understanding fostered a deeper empathy, a more nuanced approach to decision-making, ensuring that Havenridge was not just a functional settlement, but a vibrant, living community, sustained by the commitment and the shared spirit of its people. The meaning of 'staying' had indeed become the bedrock upon which their future was being built, a future that promised not just survival, but a thriving, enduring legacy.

The concept of 'staying' had solidified, transforming from a personal pledge into a communal cornerstone. Mara, deeply aware that Havenridge's continued existence depended on more than just a shared desire to remain, understood that survival was a proactive endeavor. It was about cultivating an environment where roots could anchor deeply, not just for them, but for every soul who called this place home. This realization had ignited a new phase of her leadership, one focused on the tangible, the infrastructural, the very scaffolding that would support Havenridge's future. She had begun to envision and implement systems that went beyond immediate needs, systems designed for endurance, for growth, for an independent future far beyond the immediate horizon.

Her focus had narrowed, coalescing around the critical infrastructure that would ensure Havenridge's long-term viability. The existing hydroponic farms, while functional, represented only a fraction of their potential. Mara's vision was expansive: to transform them into a truly self-sustaining food source, capable of feeding not just the current population, but accommodating future growth. This meant not merely expanding the physical footprint of the farms, but also meticulously optimizing every facet of their operation. She spent countless hours poring over agricultural data, studying soil composition simulations, and analyzing the energy consumption of the nutrient delivery systems. She envisioned a network of interconnected farms, each specializing in different crops, creating a diversified and resilient food ecosystem. This wasn't just about growing food; it was about cultivating a vital organ of the community, an organ that would beat with the steady rhythm of sustained nourishment.

"We need to think in terms of cycles, Eli," Mara explained one afternoon, gesturing towards a holographic projection of the expanded farm layout. "Not just daily or weekly cycles, but seasonal, annual, and even generational cycles. Our current systems are reactive; they address immediate shortages. We need to build proactive systems that anticipate needs, that regenerate resources, and that minimize waste to an absolute minimum. This expansion isn't just about increasing yield; it's about creating a robust, self-repairing agricultural engine for Havenridge."

Eli, ever the pragmatist, was already sketching improvements on a digital slate. His mind, attuned to the mechanics of creation, saw the potential for efficiency in Mara's ambitious plans. He understood that idealistic visions required practical application, and he was adept at bridging that gap. He visualized the automated harvesting arms, the precise nutrient dispensers, the closed-loop water recycling systems that would be essential to Mara's expanded farms.

"The energy requirements for such an expansion are significant," Eli stated, his brow furrowed in concentration. "We'll need to re-evaluate our entire energy grid. Current capacity is adequate for our present needs, but supporting multiple, large-scale hydroponic operations, coupled with enhanced atmospheric processors, will strain it. We need to look at not just increasing output, but also at managing demand and exploring more distributed energy generation methods."

This led Mara to her next critical focus: the optimization of their energy grid. Havenridge's power was generated through a combination of geothermal and solar arrays, a testament to their early resourcefulness. But as their needs grew, so did the demand. Mara saw the potential for a more integrated and intelligent grid, one that could dynamically allocate power, store excess energy more efficiently, and even tap into micro-generation sources within individual hab-units and communal facilities. She envisioned a system where energy was not a finite commodity to be rationed, but a flowing resource, managed with foresight and precision.

She initiated a comprehensive audit of their energy consumption, working with Jax and his engineering team to identify inefficiencies. They mapped out the power flow, pinpointing areas of leakage and wastage. Mara pushed for the installation of advanced smart meters and predictive energy management software, tools that would allow them to anticipate peak demand and proactively adjust power distribution. She also championed the development of more efficient battery storage solutions, exploring new chemical compositions and architectural designs that could hold more charge and discharge it more reliably.

"Imagine an energy grid that learns," Mara proposed during a planning session, her eyes alight with the possibilities. "One that anticipates the surge in demand when the atmospheric processors kick into high gear, or when the hydroponics require intense grow-light cycles. It could reroute power from less critical systems, or draw from dedicated energy reserves, all without direct human intervention. This isn't just about keeping the lights on; it's about ensuring the uninterrupted functioning of every system that sustains us."

Eli's contributions were invaluable in this domain. He possessed an innate understanding of electrical engineering and system architecture. He worked alongside Jax's team, translating Mara's strategic vision into actionable blueprints. He designed modular energy conduits that could be easily expanded or reconfigured, developed protocols for intelligent power allocation, and even experimented with integrating small, localized wind turbines into the community's periphery, further diversifying their energy sources. The steady hum of newly installed equipment, the whirring of automated systems, the quiet thrum of efficient energy distribution – these sounds became the soundtrack to their progress.

Beyond food and energy, Mara recognized the critical importance of material sustainability. In a closed ecosystem like Havenridge, waste was not an option. Every discarded item, every bit of refuse, represented a loss of valuable resources. She began conceptualizing a comprehensive recycling and repurposing program, aiming to move beyond simple sorting to a sophisticated system of material reclamation. This involved establishing dedicated facilities for processing different types of waste: plastics, metals, organic matter, and even complex electronic components.

"We need to treat every piece of scrap as a raw material for something new," Mara articulated, holding up a section of salvaged piping. "This isn't just metal; it's the potential for new tools, for structural reinforcement, for artistic expression. Our goal must be to achieve a near-zero waste environment, where everything that enters Havenridge can eventually be reintroduced into our ecosystem in some form."

Eli's practical genius shone here as well. He designed and oversaw the construction of compact, efficient recycling machinery. He developed specialized shredders for plastics, magnetic separators for ferrous metals, and even bio-digesters for organic waste, which would generate biogas for supplemental energy and nutrient-rich compost for the soil-based portions of their agricultural efforts. He was instrumental in designing a system for dismantling obsolete technology, extracting valuable rare earth elements and usable components that could be integrated back into the community's manufacturing and repair workshops.

The vision extended to an organized system of community participation. Mara understood that these sustainable systems would only thrive if the entire community was invested in them. She began organizing workshops and information sessions, educating residents about the importance of recycling, proper waste separation, and the potential for repurposing materials. She encouraged residents to bring their own ideas for repurposing, fostering a culture of creativity and resourcefulness.

"Think about the old atmospheric processor filters," she suggested to a group gathered in the communal workshop. "The metal casings are robust, and the filtration material, while spent, might have applications in soundproofing or even as a substrate for certain types of fungal cultivation. Don't just discard them; bring them here. Let's see what we can create."

The impact of these initiatives began to ripple through Havenridge. The expanded hydroponic farms yielded an abundance of fresh produce, reducing their reliance on stored rations and offering a wider variety of nutritious food. The optimized energy grid ensured a stable and reliable power supply, even during periods of high demand, and the exploration of new energy sources promised future independence. The recycling and repurposing program not only reduced their environmental footprint but also created a new stream of raw materials, fueling their fabrication labs and reducing the need for external resource acquisition. The hum of newly installed equipment, the steady glow of the enhanced energy grid, and the organized flow of recycled materials through their processing facilities became tangible proof of their commitment to a sustainable future.

Mara and Eli saw these efforts not merely as survival mechanisms, but as essential building blocks for the independent future they envisioned. Havenridge was no longer just a refuge; it was becoming a self-sufficient biosphere, a testament to human ingenuity and resilience in the face of adversity. Each optimized system, each reclaimed material, each kilowatt of efficiently generated power was a step towards a future where Havenridge could thrive, not just endure. It was a future built on foresight, on collaboration, and on the unwavering belief that they could not only survive but flourish, creating a legacy of sustainability for generations to come. The integration of these systems was a profound statement of their commitment, a tangible manifestation of their decision to not just stay, but to build, to nurture, and to ensure the enduring prosperity of their unique home. They were, in essence, cultivating a living, breathing testament to their collective will.

The soft, ethereal glow of Havenridge's bio-luminescent flora cast a gentle luminescence over the clearing. It was a place Mara and Eli had discovered during one of their early, clandestine explorations, a secluded pocket of tranquility where the planet's indigenous plant life bloomed with an almost otherworldly luminescence. The air was thick with the intoxicating perfume of night-blooming jasmine, a scent that always seemed to deepen their connection, a fragrant reminder of the unique ecosystem they were working so hard to protect and nurture. Tonight, this hidden sanctuary would bear witness to a different kind of growth, a quiet blossoming of their own shared future.

This was not a grand declaration, nor a public spectacle. The demands of leadership, the constant hum of infrastructure development, and the ever-present need for resource management had woven themselves into the fabric of their lives. Their commitment to Havenridge was a shared, foundational pillar, and this ceremony was a personal affirmation of that, a private acknowledgment of the profound bond that had grown between them, intertwined with the very survival and prosperity of their community. It was an intimate moment, a deliberate pause to anchor themselves amidst the ceaseless currents of their responsibilities.

Mara smoothed the simple, woven fabric of her tunic, her heart thrumming a soft rhythm against her ribs. Eli stood beside her, his presence a steady, comforting warmth. He held a small, intricately carved wooden box, its surface smoothed by countless hours of his own thoughtful labor. The setting sun painted the sky in hues of amber and rose, a fleeting spectacle that mirrored the delicate beauty of the moment they were about to share. There were no guests, no formal pronouncements, only the gentle rustle of leaves and the distant, melodic chirping of nocturnal creatures.

"It's perfect, Eli," Mara whispered, her gaze sweeping across the scene, taking in the delicate interplay of light and shadow, the serene embrace of nature that cradled them. "Just... us. And this place."

Eli turned to her, his eyes, usually alight with the sharp intelligence of an engineer, now softened with a profound tenderness. "It's a reflection of what we've built, Mara," he said, his voice a low murmur that seemed to blend with the ambient sounds. "Quiet, resilient, and deeply rooted. Just like us." He opened the wooden box, revealing two objects nestled within velvet lining. The first was a smooth, iridescent stone, a fragment of the rare crystalline structures found deep within Havenridge's caverns, imbued with a subtle energy that seemed to resonate with their own life force. The second was a small, intricately designed pendant, crafted from salvaged alloys, its form echoing the stylized wings of the native sky-gliders, a symbol of their aspirations and their shared flight towards a future they were forging together.

"This," Eli began, picking up the stone, "is from the heart of Havenridge. It's seen centuries pass, witnessed the cycles of this world. I want to give you this, Mara, as a symbol of my commitment to our enduring present, to the foundations we've laid, and to the stability I vow to always provide, just as this stone provides a constant within the earth." He gently placed the cool, smooth stone into her palm. It felt solid, grounded, a tangible connection to the planet that was now their home.

Mara closed her hand around it, feeling its weight, its inherent power. "It's beautiful, Eli. Thank you." Her voice was thick with emotion. She then reached for the pendant, her fingers brushing his as she lifted it. "And this," she continued, her own voice steady now, filled with a quiet strength. "This represents our aspirations. Our willingness to soar, to explore the possibilities that lie beyond the horizon, together. It's a promise to keep our spirits unbound, to always reach for the stars, even when our feet are firmly planted on the ground." She fastened the pendant around his neck, the cool metal resting against his skin.

"I give you my pledge, Mara," Eli said, his gaze unwavering. "Not just as your partner, but as the architect of our shared life within this sanctuary. I pledge to build with you, to innovate alongside you, and to always find solutions that strengthen our bonds and secure our future. I pledge to be your steadfast foundation, your unwavering support, and your devoted companion through every challenge and every triumph."

Mara's breath hitched. She reached up, tracing the outline of the pendant with her fingertip. "And I give you my heart, Eli," she replied, her voice a tender echo. "I pledge to love you, to nurture our connection, and to share in the immense responsibility and joy of leading this community with you. I pledge to be your creative partner, your confidante, and your refuge. Together, we are more than just survivors; we are builders, creators, and stewards of a new beginning."

They stood in comfortable silence for a moment, the unspoken understanding between them a palpable force. The small ceremony was not about binding themselves in a way that limited their freedom, but about celebrating and reinforcing the free will that had brought them to this point. It was a conscious choice, an active embrace of their shared destiny. The vows they exchanged were not of possession, but of mutual respect, shared purpose, and an unshakeable belief in each other. This quiet commitment was a profound act of hope, a testament to the fact that even in a world that had once felt defined by loss and uncertainty, love and dedication could flourish, creating an enduring legacy.

The world outside this tranquil clearing was often filled with the cacophony of their responsibilities. Mara, as the primary architect of Havenridge's long-term viability, spent her days navigating complex logistical challenges, meticulously planning resource allocation, and strategizing for future sustainability. Eli, alongside his engineering prowess, was an indispensable partner, his intuitive understanding of systems and his unwavering dedication to practical implementation making him the bedrock of so many of their ambitious projects. They were leaders, problem-solvers, and visionaries, constantly engaged in the meticulous work of ensuring Havenridge's continued existence. Yet, in this secluded space, under the soft glow of bio-luminescence, those roles momentarily receded, replaced by the simple, profound connection of two souls who had found solace and strength in each other.

The tokens they had exchanged were not mere trinkets, but potent symbols. The iridescent stone, unearthed from the planet's ancient depths, represented the enduring nature of their commitment, a connection to the very essence of Havenridge itself, a place that had weathered millennia and now stood as a testament to resilience. It was a reminder that their bond, like the planet, was built on deep, unwavering foundations, capable of sustaining life and growth through the inevitable shifts and changes. Mara held the stone, feeling its cool solidity, a grounding counterpoint to the exhilarating, sometimes overwhelming, scope of their work. It was a tangible piece of their shared history, a promise of their shared future.

Eli fingered the pendant at his throat, the stylized wings catching the faint light. It was a symbol of their shared ambition, of their willingness to push boundaries and explore the unknown. It spoke of their collective courage, their shared dream of not just surviving, but thriving. It was a constant reminder that their partnership was not just about maintaining what they had, but about actively reaching for what could be. Their lives within Havenridge were a delicate balance, a continuous negotiation between the urgent demands of the present and the hopeful aspirations for the future. This ceremony, this quiet exchange of vows and tokens, was a vital recalibration, a moment to reaffirm the personal underpinnings of their public endeavors.

The community of Havenridge was a testament to their collaborative spirit. They had not only survived the initial cataclysm but had actively cultivated a society that valued cooperation, ingenuity, and empathy. Mara and Eli's leadership was characterized by a deep understanding of these principles. They recognized that true strength lay not in individual power, but in the collective resilience of the community. Their shared vision for Havenridge was one of self-sufficiency, not just in terms of resources, but in terms of spirit and purpose. This private ceremony, while intimate, was a reflection of that broader commitment. It was a reaffirmation of the personal vows that underpinned their public dedication to the well-being of every resident.

As the last vestiges of twilight faded, and the bio-luminescent flora intensified their glow, Mara and Eli lingered in the clearing. The scent of jasmine seemed to wrap around them like a gentle embrace. They spoke softly, sharing their hopes and dreams, not just for Havenridge, but for themselves as a couple. The conversation flowed easily, punctuated by comfortable silences, a testament to the profound depth of their understanding. They spoke of the challenges ahead, the inevitable hurdles they would face, but their voices were filled with a quiet confidence, bolstered by the certainty of their shared resolve.

"We're not just building a settlement, are we?" Mara mused, her voice barely above a whisper, as she leaned her head against Eli's shoulder. "We're building a legacy."

Eli's arm tightened around her. "We are," he agreed. "And it starts here. With us. With this commitment." He lifted the iridescent stone from her hand, turning it over and over, its smooth surface a mirror to the quiet strength that emanated from it. "This," he said, his voice imbued with a quiet reverence, "is not just a promise of stability. It's a promise of enduring love. A love that will be the bedrock upon which everything else is built."

Mara looked up at him, her eyes shining in the soft light. "And the wings," she added, her fingers tracing the pendant at his neck, "are a promise of our shared journey. To always keep our hearts open to new possibilities, to embrace the adventure of life, together."

Their shared future was not a foregone conclusion, but a landscape they were actively shaping. Every decision, every effort, every sacrifice was a brushstroke on the canvas of their collective destiny. This ceremony, this quiet commitment, was not an endpoint, but a powerful affirmation, a moment to pause, to connect, and to draw strength from the unwavering bond that made them more than just leaders, but true partners in every sense of the word. It was a testament to the transformative power of love and commitment, a quiet promise that echoed through the hushed beauty of the night, solidifying the foundations of their shared life and the future of Havenridge itself. The air, thick with the scent of jasmine and the soft hum of their shared energy, seemed to hold its breath, witnessing a sacred pact, a silent testament to a love that was as resilient and as vital as the world they were determined to preserve and to build upon. Their private commitment was a silent symphony, a melody played out in the language of shared glances, gentle touches, and the quiet certainty that together, they could face whatever the future held, their hearts forever intertwined with the destiny of Havenridge.

CHAPTER SEVEN

Echoes from the Past

The gentle luminescence of Havenridge's flora, which had so recently bathed Mara and Eli in its ethereal glow during their private ceremony, now seemed to cast long, dancing shadows that played tricks on the eye. The quiet sanctuary they had chosen for their personal affirmation of commitment, a place that had felt so deeply imbued with their shared hopes and the resilience of their new home, now held a subtle disquiet. It was a disquiet that had begun to weave its way into the fabric of their lives, not with a sudden, explosive force, but with a slow, insidious creep, like tendrils of a tenacious, unwanted vine.

Mara found it first, tucked carelessly into the side pocket of her worn leather satchel, a space usually reserved for the datapads and geological samples that formed the bulk of her workday. It was a small thing, a folded piece of cheap, rough paper, the kind that snagged against the skin. The light in their cabin, a warm, inviting glow from strategically placed bio-luminescent fungi and the crackling hearth, did little to warm the paper's unnerving chill. As her fingers unfolded it, the scent of woodsmoke, usually a comforting anchor in their home, seemed to do little to mask the rising unease that prickled at the back of her neck. The message was brief, scribbled in a hurried, blocky script that lacked any discernible character, yet held a sinister anonymity.

"He thinks he's safe. He's wrong. Havenridge won't hide him forever."

Mara's breath hitched. Her initial reaction was confusion, a fleeting thought that it might be a misplaced prank, some poorly executed attempt at humor from within the community. But the carefully crafted anonymity, the impersonal nature of the threat, felt different. It felt... old. And as she looked up at Eli, who had been meticulously cleaning the filtration unit for the water recycler, she saw the subtle shift in his posture, the way his shoulders tensed almost imperceptibly. He hadn't read it, but he'd sensed her disquiet.

"Mara? What is it?" His voice was calm, but the slight furrow in his brow was a familiar indicator of his innate vigilance.

She held out the paper, her hand trembling slightly. "This. I found it in my satchel."

Eli put down his tools and walked over, his gaze falling on the folded paper. He took it from her, his movements deliberate. As he unfolded it, his expression remained neutral for a moment, then a flicker of something deep and unsettling crossed his eyes. It was a look Mara had only glimpsed a few times before, a shadow of a past she knew existed but had rarely been privy to. He didn't speak for a long moment, his fingers tracing the crude lettering, as if trying to decipher not just the words, but the intent behind them. The air in the cabin, so recently filled with the comforting sounds of domesticity and the scent of their shared life, now felt heavy, charged with an unspoken tension.

Finally, he looked up, his gaze meeting hers, and the tenderness that had been so present just hours before was now overlaid with a grim pragmatism. "I know this handwriting," he said, his voice low and measured. "Or rather, I know the style. It's... familiar. From a time I'd hoped was long buried."

Mara felt a knot tighten in her stomach. "Familiar how? Who would send something like this?"

Eli ran a hand over his jaw, his eyes scanning the room as if the walls themselves held secrets. "This isn't random, Mara. This is calculated. It's meant to unsettle. And it's meant to let us know that someone knows I'm here." He tapped the paper with his fingertip. "This cheap stock, the urgency in the strokes... it's a signature of sorts. A very unpleasant one."

He then produced a small, flat data-chip from a hidden pocket in his work vest. "I've been receiving similar messages for a few weeks now. Sporadic, always anonymous, always delivered in ways that are hard to trace. Tucked into supply crates, left on public terminals, slipped into the pockets of my work gear." He gestured to the crumpled note. "Yours is the first that's found its way to you, though. That's... significant."

Mara's mind raced, trying to reconcile the peaceful reality of Havenridge with the dark undertones of Eli's words. They had built this community from the ground up, a haven for those seeking a fresh start, a place where the ghosts of the past could be left behind. The very concept of such threats felt alien, an unwelcome intrusion into the fragile peace they had so painstakingly cultivated. "Who are they, Eli? What do they want?"

Eli sighed, a sound that seemed to carry the weight of years. "That's what we need to figure out. These messages suggest knowledge of my current activities, my location, and a clear intention to cause disruption. They're not just threats; they're warnings. And they're designed to instill fear." He sat down at their worn wooden table, the note spread before him. "The 'old dangers' I mentioned... they stem from a network, a group I was peripherally involved with before I came here. They dealt in information, in leverage, and in... silencing people."

Mara's blood ran cold. She had always known Eli had a past, that his skills and resourcefulness hinted at experiences beyond the ordinary, but she had never pressed for details, trusting his discretion and the clear intent he had shown in dedicating himself to Havenridge. Now, that discretion felt like a chasm opening beneath her feet. "And they've found you?"

"It seems that way," Eli admitted, his gaze distant. "Or at least, someone connected to them has. It could be an old associate, someone with a grudge, or someone who believes I still possess something they want. The anonymity suggests they don't want to be directly identified, but they want to make their presence felt." He paused, picking up the note again. "This is more than just a note. It's a ripple. And we need to understand where it came from, and how far it might spread."

The sense of peace that had settled over them after their ceremony felt irrevocably shattered. The bio-luminescent flora outside their cabin, which had so recently seemed to cradle them in a comforting embrace, now appeared to cast an eerie, watchful glow. The scent of woodsmoke, once a symbol of warmth and security, now felt like a weak shield against an encroaching chill. Mara looked at Eli, at the lines of worry etched around his eyes, at the careful way he was analyzing the crude script, and a fierce protectiveness surged within her. This was their home, their sanctuary, and no one was going to disrupt it.

"What can we do?" she asked, her voice firm, the initial shock giving way to a determined resolve.

Eli met her gaze, and for a fleeting moment, the old tenderness returned, a silent acknowledgment of their shared struggle. "We analyze," he said. "We cross-reference. We retrace my steps, not just here on Havenridge, but the steps that led me away from that life. And we strengthen our own security. We can't afford to be complacent."

He then began to meticulously explain his current situation, outlining the sporadic incidents he had experienced over the past few weeks, each seemingly minor on its own, but now forming a disturbing pattern. There were the subtle alterations to supply manifests that, upon closer inspection, seemed designed to misdirect resources. The unusual interest from certain off-world traders in Havenridge's developing infrastructure, an interest that bordered on surveillance. And then there were the coded transmissions he had intercepted, fragments of data that hinted at a larger network of information brokers and shadowy operatives, a world he had believed he had left behind.

"I've been keeping an eye on it," Eli continued, his voice low as he picked up a small, handheld scanner, its screen displaying complex data streams. "Trying to get a sense of who, or what, is behind it. But the sophistication of their encryption, their methods of dissemination… it's on a level I haven't encountered in years. They're professionals, and they're careful."

Mara watched him, her mind working furiously. Her own expertise lay in ecological systems, resource management, and the intricate planning of Havenridge's future. Eli's skills were more rooted in engineering, logistics, and a profound understanding of complex systems, often with a security bent. They were a formidable team, their strengths complementing each other perfectly. But this was a threat that transcended their usual challenges. This was a threat from Eli's past, a darkness that had found its way to their light.

"What about the content of the messages?" Mara asked. "They mention Havenridge, they mention you 'thinking you're safe.' Does that imply they know about the community, or just about you being here?"

Eli traced the letters on the note again. "It's deliberately vague. 'Havenridge won't hide him forever.' That could mean they know the name of the planet, or they know it's a settlement. The ambiguity is part of the intimidation. They want us to wonder, to speculate, to feel exposed." He looked around their cabin, at the shelves lined with Mara's meticulously organized samples, at the tools of his trade laid out on the workbench, at the comfortable, lived-in feel of their shared space. "The peace we've fought so hard for," he murmured, "it's built on a foundation of trust and transparency within our community. This kind of covert operation… it preys on that."

He then pulled out a more advanced decryption device, its surface cool and smooth against his palm. "I've been running analyses on the intercepted transmissions. There are faint echoes of a communication protocol I encountered a long time ago, used by a clandestine organization known as the 'Chrono-Syndicate.' They specialized in temporal anomaly detection and... extraction. Essentially, they dealt with individuals who had 'fallen through time,' or those who possessed knowledge that could alter timelines. They were ruthless, efficient, and utterly untraceable by conventional means."

Mara's eyes widened. "Temporal anomalies? Eli, what are you saying? Is this connected to... to what happened before?" The "before" was a vague, unspoken entity, a collective trauma that had shaped their lives, the cataclysm that had forced humanity to seek refuge on distant worlds like Havenridge.

"It's a possibility," Eli admitted, his gaze steady. "The Chrono-Syndicate was known to operate in the fringes of known space, acquiring individuals or artifacts that could influence the course of history. If they're still active, and if they believe I possess certain knowledge or capabilities from my past involvement with them, then it's logical they would seek me out. And if they're sending these messages now, it means they've either found me, or they're getting close."

He paused, the weight of his words settling in the quiet cabin. "The messages are designed to make me feel vulnerable, to make me question the safety of this place. It's a psychological tactic. They want to drive a wedge between me and the community, or between me and you."

Mara reached across the table and placed her hand over his. The rough paper of the anonymous note was still there, a stark contrast to the smooth metal of his skin. "They won't succeed," she said, her voice unwavering. "We built this together, Eli. We faced the unknown and created something real. We won't let shadows from your past destroy it."

Eli turned his hand, his fingers lacing with hers. "I know," he said, his grip tightening. "But we can't afford to be naive. These aren't petty criminals. They're players on a much larger, much more dangerous stage." He looked at the note again, his brow furrowed in concentration. "The paper itself... it's not standard Terran issue, nor is it from any of the common trading hubs we frequent. It's of an unusual composition, almost... synthetic, but organic in origin. And the ink... it contains trace elements that are highly anomalous. I'll need to run a full spectral analysis."

He then pulled out a small, discreet device, no larger than a thumb drive, and carefully scraped a minute sample of the ink from the note. As he worked, Mara observed him, a mixture of concern and admiration swirling within her. His methodical approach, his unwavering focus even in the face of such a direct threat, was a testament to his character. He was not someone who panicked. He was someone who solved.

"These messages," Mara mused, "if they are from this 'Chrono-Syndicate,' what would they want with you now? You've dedicated yourself to Havenridge, to building a future, not manipulating the past."

"That's the question, isn't it?" Eli replied, his eyes fixed on the device in his hand. "Perhaps they don't believe I've truly severed ties. Perhaps they think I have access to data, or technology, that could benefit them. Or perhaps this is a test. A way to gauge my reaction, my allegiances. The Chrono-Syndicate was never about simple acquisition. They were about control. And control often begins with unsettling the foundations of stability.”

He looked up at her, his gaze intense. “The irony,” he said, a wry, grim smile touching his lips, “is that they’re sending these messages to a place that represents everything I’ve strived for since leaving them. A place of growth, of hope, of a future unburdened by the machinations of the past. They’re threatening the very antithesis of their modus operandi.”

Mara felt a surge of pride in their achievement, in the haven they had created. “Then we won’t let them win,” she declared. “We’ll use everything we have to protect this place. Your knowledge, my understanding of Havenridge’s systems, our community’s resilience.”

“Exactly,” Eli affirmed, his voice regaining some of its usual strength. “This isn’t just my fight, Mara. It’s ours. And it’s Havenridge’s. If they want to threaten our peace, they’ll have to contend with all of us.” He gestured to the note and the sample device. “For now, I’ll run these analyses. We need to gather as much information as possible before we alert the council. I don’t want to cause undue panic, but we need to be prepared.”

He then returned to his workbench, his movements precise and deliberate, as he began to integrate the new data into his analytical systems. Mara watched him, the unsettling reminder of his past a cold knot in her stomach. The peace of their sanctuary had been breached, not by an external force of nature, but by the echoes of a life she had only glimpsed. Yet, as she looked at Eli, at the quiet determination in his posture, she felt a renewed sense of hope. They had faced challenges before, together. And whatever ghosts had chosen to resurface, they would face them together, their bond as a couple, and their commitment to Havenridge, serving as their unshakeable foundation. The scent of woodsmoke still filled the cabin, but now, it was mingled with the faint, metallic tang of unease, a stark reminder that even in paradise, the past could cast a long and chilling shadow. The fight for their future, it seemed, was far from over. It had just entered a new, and far more dangerous, phase. The subtle cracks in their carefully constructed peace were beginning to show, and Mara knew, with a certainty that chilled her to the bone, that they would need all their strength, and all their love, to keep them from shattering.

Eli's divided loyalties had always been a silent undercurrent, a truth he carried within him, a carefully compartmentalized aspect of his existence. Now, with the arrival of the unsettling messages, that compartment was threatening to burst open, spilling its contents into the pristine landscape of his new life with Mara and the burgeoning community of Havenridge. The weight of his past, once a manageable burden, now felt like an insurmountable mountain pressing down on his chest, stealing his breath and clouding his judgment. He had sought refuge here, a place where the shadows of his former life couldn't reach, a sanctuary built on honest labor and shared dreams. But the shadows, it seemed, were more tenacious than he had ever imagined.

He found himself watching Mara, her movements so full of purpose as she tended to the hydroponic gardens or meticulously logged new geological data, and a profound sense of guilt would wash over him. Everything he had achieved, everything he was building with her, was now at risk, not because of any failing on their part, but because of who he had been. He had never lied to Mara, not in the grand scheme of things. He had been selective with the details, omitting the darker chapters, the morally ambiguous alliances, the compromises he had made to survive. He had believed, with fervent hope, that those chapters were closed, the book sealed and locked away. But the crude script on the cheap paper, and the phantom whispers of old protocols, suggested otherwise.

"Mara," he began one evening, the words catching in his throat, the scent of roasted roots and the gentle hum of the habitat's life support suddenly feeling suffocating. They were in their small cabin, the bio-luminescent fungi casting their soft, ethereal glow, a light that usually brought him comfort but now only seemed to illuminate the growing chasm between his past and present. He had spent the better part of the day running spectral analyses on the ink and paper from the note, his analytical mind working overtime, trying to find concrete evidence, a tangible thread to pull. But the anomalies he found only deepened his unease. The synthetic compounds were unique, designed for discrete, untraceable applications, a hallmark of certain specialized organizations he had once... interacted with.

Mara turned from the console where she had been calibrating a new atmospheric sensor, her brow furrowed with concern. She had noticed the change in him, the increased tension in his shoulders, the way his gaze often drifted, lost in thoughts he couldn't articulate. "Eli? What is it? You've been quiet all day."

He hesitated, the truth a bitter pill he had to swallow. "It's more than just a warning, Mara. It's... a very specific threat, cloaked in anonymity. And I think I know *who* is behind it, or at least, who it's connected to." He paused, taking a deep breath, the air thick with unspoken dread. "There were... groups. Organizations I was involved with before I came here. Not all of them were overtly criminal, but they operated in the grey. They dealt in information, influence, and sometimes, in making inconvenient people disappear. This handwriting, the style of the message... it's reminiscent of a particularly unpleasant operative I crossed paths with years ago. A man named Kaelen. He was known for his efficiency and his absolute lack of sentimentality."

Mara's hand instinctively went to her chest, her eyes widening. "Kaelen? Is he... is he a threat to us? To Havenridge?"

"He could be," Eli admitted, the words heavy with resignation. "He worked for an entity called the Obsidian Accord. They were more of a shadow consortium, pulling strings from behind the scenes. They never showed their faces, but their reach was extensive. They dealt in resource acquisition, political manipulation, and... the suppression of emerging technologies they deemed destabilizing. Havenridge, with its unique geological resources and its burgeoning independence... it would be a prime target for them, or for Kaelen acting on their behalf."

He paced the small confines of their cabin, the familiar space suddenly feeling alien and vulnerable. "And it's not just Kaelen. There's also a network I briefly worked with, a clandestine group known as the 'Whispers.' They specialized in data extraction and intelligence brokering. They were... less violent than the Accord, but equally amoral. They'd sell anything to anyone, and if they believed I possessed knowledge they could exploit, or if they thought I was holding onto a piece of intelligence that could be valuable, they wouldn't hesitate to come after me." He stopped and looked at Mara, his eyes pleading for her understanding. "Mara, I... I was never a hero. I was a survivor. And sometimes, survival meant making deals with people I shouldn't have, operating in circles that were... compromised."

The confession hung in the air between them, a tangible manifestation of the secrets he had kept. Mara, ever the pragmatist, stepped closer, her hand reaching out to cover his. "Eli, what you did to survive then is not who you are now. You chose a different path. You chose *this* path, with me. That's what matters." But even as she said it, she saw the internal struggle warring within him. His loyalty was no longer a simple matter of commitment to Havenridge; it was a complex tapestry woven with threads of guilt, responsibility, and the deeply ingrained instinct for self-preservation that had kept him alive for so long.

"But they might not see it that way," Eli countered, his voice laced with a weariness that went beyond physical fatigue. "The Obsidian Accord, if they are indeed involved, they see people like me as assets. Assets that have gone rogue. And Kaelen, he doesn't tolerate loose ends. The Whispers, they might see me as a potential source of immense profit, or as someone who knows too much about their operations. Havenridge, with its growing autonomy and its potential... it represents something they would want to control, or exploit. Our unique geological composition, the bio-engineering advances we're making... to them, it's not progress; it's capital. And I... I am the key that could unlock it for them."

He ran a hand through his hair, the gesture one of deep distress. "The messages are designed to sow discord, Mara. To make me doubt my safety, to make me believe I've endangered you and everyone here. It's a psychological war. They want to break me down, to make me vulnerable. And if they can isolate me, or make me a pariah within the community... then Havenridge itself becomes easier to infiltrate, to manipulate.”

His words painted a chilling picture of a world far removed from the quiet resilience of Havenridge. He spoke of individuals and organizations who viewed life and progress not as a collective endeavor, but as a commodity to be traded and controlled. He described the cold calculations, the strategic maneuvering, the utter disregard for the lives of others that characterized these shadowy entities. He mentioned specific individuals within the Obsidian Accord, not by name but by their reputation and their known specialties: a ruthless logistics expert who could orchestrate the diversion of entire fleets, a propaganda specialist skilled in turning public opinion against emerging settlements, and a cyber-security operative whose intrusions were so subtle they often went undetected for months.

“There’s a woman,” Eli continued, his voice dropping to a near whisper, “known only as ‘Silas.’ She was the Accord’s primary operative for... containment. Not just of people, but of information, of technologies. If they want to prevent Havenridge from becoming a beacon of independent development, if they see us as a threat to their established order, Silas would be the one they’d send to neutralize it.” He paused, his gaze distant, as if seeing phantoms in the dimly lit cabin. “And Kaelen... he’s the muscle, the enforcer. If Silas identifies a threat, Kaelen is the one who makes it go away. Permanently.”

Mara listened, her heart a tight knot of fear, but also a steely resolve. She saw the torment in Eli’s eyes, the profound guilt he carried, but she also saw the man he had become. He was not the man who had made those compromises; he was a man who had escaped them, a man who had built a life based on principles and integrity. "Eli," she said, her voice firm, cutting through his despondency. "They want to divide us. They want to make us doubt ourselves, and each other. But we won't let them. We built Havenridge together. We are stronger than any threat they can throw at us. You are not the person you were, and neither am I. We are Havenridge now."

He looked at her, truly looked at her, and for a moment, the burden seemed to lighten. Her unwavering belief in him, in them, was a shield against the darkness he feared. "I know," he said, his voice rough with emotion. "But the danger is real. If they do come, if they try to exploit Havenridge's resources, or... or if they try to recapture me, I can't let them succeed. And I can't let them harm you or anyone here because of my past."

He sat down at their table, spreading out the few data fragments he had managed to collect – the spectral analysis reports, the cross-referenced communication logs, the faint echoes of the Whispers' data-mining protocols. "I've been trying to trace the origin of the paper and ink," he explained, his analytical mind reasserting itself. "The paper's composition... it's derived from a genetically engineered algae, cultivated in extremely controlled environments. The kind of facilities the Accord would have access to. The ink contains trace amounts of rare earth elements, also indicative of specialized manufacturing. It's a deliberate signature, meant to be recognized by those who understand their methods, but to remain opaque to outsiders."

He tapped a section of the report. "And these intercepted transmissions I've been monitoring... they're using a sophisticated encryption algorithm, far beyond standard commercial or even military-grade security. It's designed to evolve, to adapt. The Whispers were known for developing such algorithms. It's a way for them to communicate and conduct their operations without fear of interception." He sighed, a sound of deep weariness. "It all points to a coordinated effort, Mara. Not just a random threat, but a deliberate attempt to destabilize, to reclaim, or to neutralize."

The knowledge that Kaelen, Silas, and the shadowy organizations they represented were potentially aware of Havenridge and its capabilities was a chilling prospect. Eli felt a suffocating sense of responsibility. He had brought this danger to their doorstep. He had cultivated a life of peace and security, only to have it threatened by the ghosts he had tried so desperately to outrun. Sleep had become a luxury, his nights filled with restless tossing and vivid, unsettling dreams of past encounters, of choices made under duress, of betrayals, both given and received.

"What do we do, Eli?" Mara asked, her voice steady, her hand finding his again. "We can't just wait for them to arrive."

He squeezed her hand, his gaze meeting hers with a renewed sense of purpose. "We prepare. We strengthen our defenses. We discreetly monitor any unusual activity. And," he added, his voice hardening, "if they come, we fight back. Not just for me, but for Havenridge. For the future we're building. I may have made mistakes in my past, Mara, but I will not stand by and let those mistakes destroy everything I hold dear now."

He pulled up a holographic projection of Havenridge's defense grid schematics, his fingers dancing across the interface. "Our planetary defenses are robust, but they're designed for external threats, not for infiltration. We need to enhance our internal security protocols. And we need to be smart. They're counting on our surprise, on our fear. We will use their own tactics against them. We will be vigilant. We will be prepared. And we will not be broken." The internal conflict was still there, a raw ache in his chest, but it was no longer paralyzing. It was a catalyst. He would not let his divided loyalties tear him apart. He would choose. He would choose Havenridge. He would choose Mara. And he would fight for the life he had built, with every ounce of strength he possessed. The echoes from his past had found him, but they would not define his future.

The soft, persistent glow of the bio-luminescent fungi in their cabin usually soothed Eli, casting a gentle, almost comforting light on their shared space. But tonight, the ethereal luminescence only seemed to highlight the deepening shadows that had begun to gather in Mara's eyes. She watched him, her gaze steady and unwavering, as he moved through the small cabin with a restless energy, his movements betraying an internal turmoil that was becoming increasingly difficult to conceal. The quiet hum of the habitat's life support, a sound that had once represented sanctuary, now seemed to thrum with a subtle, discordant note whenever he was near. He was present, yet his mind was clearly miles away, lost in a labyrinth of memories and anxieties that she could only glimpse at the edges.

He had been distant for days, his usual engaged presence replaced by a palpable tension that coiled in his shoulders and tightened his jaw. His eyes, normally so clear and direct, now held a haunted quality, a fleeting flicker of something dark and unresolved that she had learned to recognize with a growing unease. She had tried to approach him subtly at first, offering comforting touches, brewing his favorite herbal infusions, suggesting shared stargazing from the observation deck. But he had deflected each attempt with a quiet, almost apologetic evasion, his smile not quite reaching his eyes, his words carefully chosen to keep the true depths of his distress concealed.

Tonight, however, the silence between them had become too heavy, the unspoken growing into a chasm that threatened to swallow them both. Mara approached him as he stood by the viewport, his back to her, his gaze fixed on the swirling nebulae beyond the thin layer of atmosphere. She didn't interrupt his silent vigil, but simply stood beside him, her presence a quiet anchor in the storm she sensed brewing within him. The air in the cabin, usually so familiar and welcoming, now felt charged with an invisible tension, a prelude to a confession or a confrontation.

When he finally stirred, turning to face her, the raw vulnerability in his eyes was almost more than she could bear. He looked like a man cornered, the weight of secrets pressing down on him, threatening to crush the very life out of him. He opened his mouth to speak, a rough, choked sound escaping his throat, and Mara immediately reached out, her hand finding his arm, her touch firm and grounding.

"Eli," she said softly, her voice cutting through the thick silence like a gentle blade. She didn't press for answers, didn't demand explanations. She simply offered her presence, her unwavering solidarity. "You've been carrying something heavy. I can see it."

He flinched slightly at her words, his gaze dropping to their joined hands. The confession she had been bracing for, the one she had suspected was simmering beneath the surface, was now palpable, hovering between them. He looked utterly lost, his carefully constructed composure beginning to fray at the edges.

"I... I haven't been entirely honest with you, Mara," he began, his voice barely a whisper, thick with a mixture of regret and fear. "Not about everything. My past... it's not as clean as I've let you believe."

Mara tightened her grip on his arm, her thumb stroking his skin in a gesture of reassurance. Her own heart ached for the burden he was clearly struggling to bear alone. She had known, of course, that he hadn't arrived in Havenridge a blank slate. Everyone carried their history with them, a collection of choices and experiences that shaped who they were. But she had sensed, for a while now, that Eli's past held a darker, more perilous aspect than he had initially revealed.

"Eli," she said, her voice firm but gentle, "look at me."

He finally met her gaze, and in his eyes, she saw a whirlwind of conflicting emotions: guilt, shame, and a deep-seated fear of her judgment. But she refused to let him see anything but steadfast acceptance.

"Whatever it is, whatever you've done, it doesn't change who you are now," she continued, her gaze unwavering. "We built Havenridge together. This place, this community, it's founded on the idea of second chances, of finding a new beginning. It's about looking forward, not back. And you, Eli, you are an integral part of that. You are the heart of Havenridge, just as much as I am."

A flicker of something akin to disbelief crossed his face, quickly followed by a surge of raw emotion that threatened to overwhelm him. He squeezed her hand, his knuckles white. "But this is different, Mara. This isn't just about mistakes I've made. This is about people... dangerous people. People who might still be looking for me. People who could bring their darkness here, to us."

He took a shaky breath, the confession tumbling out of him in a rush, as if a dam had finally broken. "There are... organizations. Shadow groups I was involved with before I came here. They operated outside the law, dealing in information, influence, and... more sinister things. I thought I had left them behind, truly left them behind. But the messages I've been receiving... they're a clear sign. They know where I am. They might even know about Havenridge."

He spoke of the Obsidian Accord, a clandestine consortium that pulled strings from the shadows, their tentacles reaching into every aspect of galactic resource acquisition and political manipulation. He described their ruthless efficiency, their unwavering focus on control, and their disdain for any burgeoning independent settlements that dared to defy their established order. Havenridge, with its unique geological wealth and its growing spirit of self-determination, would be precisely the kind of entity they would seek to exploit or neutralize.

And then there was Kaelen. The name itself seemed to carry a chilling resonance, a man known for his cold, calculated brutality, an operative who dealt in consequence and finality. Eli described Kaelen's reputation, the whispers of his absolute lack of sentimentality, his penchant for leaving no trace, no loose ends. Eli spoke of how Kaelen was known to be the instrument of the Accord's will, the one who carried out their most unsavory directives.

"And there are others," Eli continued, his voice growing hoarse with the effort of recounting these terrifying memories. "A group known as the 'Whispers.' They specialized in intelligence brokering, in data extraction. They were... amoral. They traded in secrets, and if they believed I possessed valuable information, or if I represented a threat to their operations, they wouldn't hesitate to silence me." He looked at Mara, his eyes wide with a desperate plea for understanding. "I wasn't always a man of principle, Mara. I was a survivor. And survival sometimes meant making compromises, associating with people who operated in the grey, people who would make anyone disappear without a second thought."

He recounted details of past encounters, of shadowy deals struck in dimly lit corners of space stations, of fleeting alliances forged out of necessity and then broken just as quickly. He spoke of the constant vigilance required to navigate those treacherous circles, the gnawing paranoia that never truly abated, even after he had thought himself free. He described the specialized equipment, the encrypted communication protocols, the sophisticated surveillance technologies that these organizations employed, all designed to maintain their secrecy and their operational dominance.

"They see people like me as assets," Eli explained, his voice laced with a weariness that seemed to seep into his very bones. "Assets that have gone rogue. And Kaelen, he's the one who cleans up messes, who eliminates any perceived threat to their agenda. The Whispers might see me as a walking data mine, or as someone who knows too much about their network." He paused, his gaze distant, as if replaying the events in his mind. "Havenridge... with its potential, its independence... it represents a deviation from their control. And I... I am the key that could unlock its secrets for them, or the obstacle they need to remove."

He walked away from the viewport, his pacing becoming more agitated, the confined space of their cabin suddenly feeling like a cage. "The messages are designed to create paranoia, Mara. To make me doubt myself, to make me believe I've endangered you and everyone here. It's psychological warfare. They want to break me down, to isolate me. If I become a pariah, if they can turn the community against me, then Havenridge itself becomes vulnerable. Easier to infiltrate, easier to manipulate."

He described the chilling efficiency with which these organizations operated, their strategic planning that was both meticulous and ruthless. He spoke of their ability to weaponize information, to sow discord, to exploit any weakness they could find. He mentioned specific operatives he had encountered, not necessarily by name, but by their function: a logistics expert capable of diverting entire fleets of cargo ships, a propaganda specialist skilled in turning public opinion against emerging settlements, and a cyber-security operative whose intrusions were so subtle they often went undetected for months.

"There's a woman," Eli continued, his voice dropping to a near whisper, his eyes darting around the cabin as if expecting unseen watchers. "Known only as 'Silas.' She was the Accord's primary operative for... containment. Not just of people, but of information, of technologies. If they see Havenridge as a threat to their established order, Silas would be the one they'd send to neutralize it. And Kaelen... he's the muscle. If Silas identifies a target, Kaelen makes it disappear. Permanently."

Mara listened, her heart a tight knot of fear and dawning understanding. She saw the torment in Eli's eyes, the profound guilt he carried, but beneath it, she also saw the unwavering integrity that had drawn her to him in the first place. He was not the man who had made those compromises; he was a man who had escaped them, a man who had chosen a different path, a path that led to her, to Havenridge.

She stepped closer, her hand reaching out to cover his once more. This time, she didn't just offer comfort; she offered a promise. "Eli," she said, her voice steady and resonant, cutting through his despair like a beacon. "They want to divide us. They want to make us doubt ourselves, and each other. But we won't let them. We built Havenridge together. We are stronger than any threat they can throw at us. You are not the person you were, and neither am I. We are Havenridge now."

He looked at her, truly looked at her, and for a fleeting moment, the crushing weight of his past seemed to lighten. Her unwavering belief in him, in their shared strength, was a shield against the darkness he feared. "I know," he said, his voice rough with emotion, a single tear tracing a path down his cheek. "But the danger is real. If they do come, if they try to exploit Havenridge's resources, or... or if they try to recapture me, I can't let them succeed. And I can't let them harm you or anyone here because of my past."

He sat down at their small table, his fingers tracing the patterns of the wood grain as if seeking solace in the tangible. He pulled up a holographic display, a complex web of spectral analysis reports, cross-referenced communication logs, and the faint echoes of data-mining protocols he had managed to intercept. "I've been trying to trace the origin of the paper and ink," he explained, his analytical mind slowly reasserting itself, finding a semblance of control in the familiar process of investigation. "The paper's composition... it's derived from a genetically engineered algae, cultivated in extremely controlled environments. The kind of facilities the Accord would have access to. The ink contains trace amounts of rare earth elements, also indicative of specialized manufacturing. It's a deliberate signature, meant to be recognized by those who understand their methods, but to remain opaque to outsiders."

He tapped a section of the report, his brow furrowed in concentration. "And these intercepted transmissions I've been monitoring... they're using a sophisticated encryption algorithm, far beyond standard commercial or even military-grade security. It's designed to evolve, to adapt. The Whispers were known for developing such algorithms. It's a way for them to communicate and conduct their operations without fear of interception." He sighed, a sound of deep weariness. "It all points to a coordinated effort, Mara. Not just a random threat, but a deliberate attempt to destabilize, to reclaim, or to neutralize."

The knowledge that Kaelen, Silas, and the shadowy organizations they represented were not just theoretical threats, but active players who might be aware of Havenridge and its capabilities, was a chilling prospect. Eli felt a suffocating sense of responsibility settle over him. He had sought refuge here, a sanctuary built on honest labor and shared dreams, only to have it threatened by the ghosts he had tried so desperately to outrun. Sleep had become a luxury he could no longer afford, his nights filled with restless tossing and vivid, unsettling dreams of past encounters, of choices made under duress, of betrayals, both given and received. The spectral figures of his past seemed to loom larger in the quiet darkness, their whispered threats a constant echo in his mind.

"What do we do, Eli?" Mara asked, her voice steady, her hand finding his again. Her calm presence was a stark contrast to the tempest raging within him. "We can't just wait for them to arrive."

He squeezed her hand, his gaze meeting hers with a renewed sense of purpose, a flicker of defiance igniting in his eyes. "We prepare. We strengthen our defenses. We discreetly monitor any unusual activity. And," he added, his voice hardening, a steely resolve replacing the despondency, "if they come, we fight back. Not just for me, but for Havenridge. For the future we're building. I may have made mistakes in my past, Mara, but I will not stand by and let those mistakes destroy everything I hold dear now."

He pulled up a holographic projection of Havenridge's defense grid schematics, his fingers dancing across the interface with renewed vigor. "Our planetary defenses are robust, but they're designed for external threats, not for infiltration. We need to enhance our internal security protocols. And we need to be smart. They're counting on our surprise, on our fear. We will use their own tactics against them. We will be vigilant. We will be prepared. And we will not be broken." The internal conflict was still there, a raw ache in his chest, a painful reminder of the man he had been, but it was no longer paralyzing. It was a catalyst. He would not let his divided loyalties tear him apart. He would choose. He would choose Havenridge. He would choose Mara. And he would fight for the life he had built, with every ounce of strength he possessed. The echoes from his past had found him, but they would not define his future. He met Mara's gaze, a silent vow passing between them, a promise of unwavering unity against the encroaching darkness. They would face this together, not as individuals burdened by past sins, but as a united front, the architects of a new beginning, determined to protect the sanctuary they had created.

The hum of the life support systems, once a comforting lullaby, now seemed to underscore the frantic energy that pulsed through their makeshift office. Dust motes, usually dormant in the controlled atmosphere, danced in the beam of Eli's diagnostic scanner as he meticulously analyzed the spectral composition of the paper fragment. The bio-luminescent fungi, a constant, gentle glow in their living quarters, were shut down in this utilitarian space, replaced by the harsh, unwavering glare of industrial-grade lamps. Mara sat opposite him, her brow furrowed in concentration, a stylus poised above a translucent data slate displaying a sprawling network of intercepted, encrypted communications. The air crackled not with an impending threat, but with a focused, determined inquiry.

"The isotopic signature is consistent with the trace elements found in the ore deposits near Sector Gamma," Eli murmured, his voice a low rumble, devoid of the tremor it had held days before. His analytical mind, a formidable weapon forged in the crucible of his past, had finally found its footing, charting a course through the labyrinth of uncertainty. "Specifically, it matches the unique blend found in the upper strata of the Kepler Vein. Not exactly common knowledge, even within Havenridge, unless one had direct access to our geological surveys."

Mara looked up from her slate, her eyes, usually so warm and empathetic, now sharp and discerning. "Which means our mole, or whoever is feeding them information, has access to our most sensitive data. This isn't just someone observing us from afar, Eli. This is someone with a level of access that suggests an insider." She traced a line on the slate with her stylus, highlighting a recurring, almost imperceptible anomaly in the communication patterns. "And these messages... they're not just designed to scare you. There's a method to their madness, a very deliberate attempt to sow discord. Look at this."

She zoomed in on a cluster of data points. "This pattern. It's almost like a coded taunt. The timing of the messages, the subtle variations in the encryption key – it's as if they're *waiting* for you to find them, to engage. It's not the work of Kaelen or Silas, not directly. Their methods are far more blunt, more efficient. This feels... personal. Like someone who knows your history, your vulnerabilities, and is trying to manipulate you into making a mistake."

Eli leaned closer, his gaze sweeping over the intricate dance of code. He recognized the underlying architecture of the encryption, a primitive yet effective variant of a cipher he had encountered years ago, favored by a small, independent data brokerage firm that had specialized in extracting sensitive information for less-than-reputable clients. They had been absorbed, or perhaps dissolved, by the Accord years ago, their operatives either integrated or eliminated. "The Whispers," he breathed, a grim certainty settling in his gut. "This particular encryption is a signature of theirs. They were masters of 'whispered' communication, their methods designed to be undetectable, to blend into the background noise of the interstellar comm net."

He pointed to a series of sub-routines he had managed to isolate. "And these little... embellishments. They're not part of the encryption itself, but they're embedded within the transmission packets. Almost like digital graffiti. They're archaic symbols, used by a specific guild of information brokers who prided themselves on their 'purity' of data acquisition. They believed in a direct, untainted line from source to recipient. These symbols... they signify 'witness.' As in, 'we are watching.'"

Mara's hand tightened around her stylus. "Witnesses to what? To your downfall? Or to Havenridge's?" The implication hung heavy in the air. Whoever was behind these messages knew Eli's past, knew his history with the Accord, the Obsidian Accord, and the Whispers. They also knew about Havenridge, its potential, and its location. The targeted nature of the threat was no longer a hypothesis; it was a chilling reality.

"They're testing the waters," Eli concluded, his voice low and steady. "They want to see how I react, how the community reacts. If they can make me an outcast, if they can paint me as a pariah, Havenridge becomes vulnerable. A community divided is a community ripe for exploitation." He recalled the psychological warfare tactics he had witnessed, the subtle erosion of trust, the systematic dismantling of social cohesion. The messages weren't just threats; they were weapons.

He spent the next few hours poring over Havenridge's internal surveillance logs, cross-referencing them with the times and inferred locations of the anonymous messages. It was a painstaking process, akin to searching for a single, misplaced star in an entire galaxy. Mara, with her uncanny ability to spot patterns where others saw only chaos, acted as his co-pilot. She had a knack for recognizing subtle shifts in behavior, for picking up on the almost imperceptible nuances of communication, both in person and through the limited digital channels they had available.

"There was a maintenance drone malfunction near the south perimeter approximately three cycles before the first message arrived," Mara stated, pointing to a log entry on her slate. "The incident was classified as a minor system glitch, quickly resolved. But the drone's flight path... it deviated significantly from its programmed route, passing close to the geological survey outpost where you store your detailed mineralogical data."

Eli's eyes narrowed. "And the timing of the subsequent messages? Did they coincide with any unusual activity around that outpost?"

"Not directly," Mara admitted, "but there was a series of encrypted data transfers from the main comms hub to an external server – untraceable, of course – that occurred shortly after each message was sent. It's as if whoever is receiving these transmissions is also using them as a trigger, or a confirmation signal, for their own data extraction."

He leaned back, rubbing his temples. The sheer audacity of it was staggering. They were not only trying to intimidate him, but to actively gather intelligence on Havenridge itself. The Obsidian Accord, with its insatiable hunger for resources and control, would undoubtedly be interested in Havenridge's unique geological wealth. And the Whispers, their information brokers, would be invaluable in facilitating such a takeover, or at least in assessing its viability.

"The algae used in the paper," Eli mused, tapping a digit on his scanner, "and the rare earth elements in the ink. It's a specific chemical signature. Our geological surveys are highly detailed, containing information on not just the presence of valuable ores, but also on the precise isotopic ratios of those deposits. If someone wanted to prove they had access to that specific information, they would need access to those surveys. And not just a casual glance, but a deep dive, to verify the composition for their own purposes.”

Mara brought up a schematic of Havenridge’s data network. “The survey outpost has a direct, albeit heavily secured, link to the main archive. Access logs are... surprisingly sparse for the period in question. There was a brief network disruption, officially attributed to a solar flare, around the time of the drone malfunction. It conveniently masked any unauthorized access during that window.”

“A solar flare,” Eli scoffed, a bitter smile touching his lips. “How convenient. The Accord and the Whispers are masters of creating plausible deniability. They don’t break down doors; they subtly manipulate the lock. They don’t steal; they orchestrate ‘disappearances.’ This ‘solar flare’ is their smokescreen.”

He began meticulously sifting through the surveillance footage from the days leading up to the first message. Hours blurred into a monotonous stream of routine activities: colonists tending crops, engineers calibrating machinery, children playing in the communal areas. It was the mundane tapestry of their lives, a stark contrast to the shadowy machinations he was uncovering. But Mara’s intuition, honed by years of reading people, was a powerful filter.

“Wait,” she said suddenly, her voice sharp. “Freeze the frame. The engineer who was recalibrating the primary comms array. Designation ‘Roric.’ He’s wearing an unfamiliar chrono-watch. It’s sleek, dark, with a polished obsidian finish. Not standard issue for Havenridge technicians.”

Eli zoomed in, his gaze fixed on the device. The design was minimalist, almost severe, but he recognized the subtle, angular styling. It was a bespoke piece, a luxury item favored by a particular echelon of operatives within the Accord, individuals who valued discretion and a certain... understated opulence. "Obsidian," he murmured, the name of the Accord's shadowy consortium echoing in his mind. "That's no coincidence."

He cross-referenced Roric's work schedule with the periods of network disruption and the purported solar flare. Roric had been assigned to the comms array maintenance precisely during those critical windows. His access logs for the main archive, however, showed no unauthorized entries.

"They're not relying on direct access for everything," Eli deduced, his mind working at lightning speed. "Roric could have been the physical conduit, the one who facilitated the network disruption or the external data transfers, perhaps unknowingly. But the detailed geological data... that would require someone with deeper knowledge. Someone who knew exactly what to look for, and how to extract it without leaving obvious traces."

Mara brought up a list of all personnel with Level 3 clearance to the geological archives. It was a short list, comprised mostly of senior scientific staff and the settlement's co-leaders. Eli's name was on that list, of course, but he had always been meticulous about his own data security, his own access logs.

"What if," Mara ventured, her voice barely a whisper, her eyes fixed on the list, "the information wasn't stolen in the traditional sense? What if it was... volunteered?"

The question hung in the air, heavy with unspoken implications. A volunteer, someone within their ranks, knowingly or unknowingly feeding information to the very entities that threatened their existence. The thought was a cold dread that coiled in Eli's stomach. He had escaped the darkness, only to find its tendrils reaching into the heart of Havenridge.

"The Whispers," Eli said, his voice hollow. "They were experts at recruitment, at coercion. They could leverage debts, fears, or even offer significant inducements to individuals who felt overlooked or undervalued. Someone with access, someone with a grievance, or someone simply blinded by greed."

He pulled up Roric's personnel file, his digital fingerprint, his medical history, his psychological evaluations. Roric was a capable engineer, a loyal member of the community, with no apparent disciplinary issues or hidden agendas. But Eli knew that even the most seemingly solid foundations could harbor hidden fissures.

"His family," Eli pointed out, scanning Roric's background. "His parents on Cygnus Prime. They've been struggling with a chronic illness, and the medical facilities there are... limited. He's been sending a significant portion of his earnings back home to support their care. The cost of advanced treatments... it's astronomical."

Mara's gaze met his, the understanding dawning between them. "They wouldn't need to force him. They could simply offer a solution. A 'generous benefactor' who would cover all his family's medical expenses, in exchange for a few simple 'favors' that wouldn't seem like much to Roric. A recalibration here, a network check there. Small acts that, when combined with the right timing and the right knowledge, could open the door for something far more sinister."

The theory solidified into a chilling narrative. Roric, the unwitting pawn, facilitating the breach. And somewhere, a more cunning architect, someone with intimate knowledge of both Havenridge and Eli's past, orchestrating the entire operation. The messages were a smokescreen, a distraction, designed to make them believe the threat was solely external, while the real danger was already within their walls, slowly, insidiously, chipping away at their security.

"We need to confirm this," Mara said, her voice firm, her resolve hardening. "Without alerting Roric, and without tipping off whoever is pulling his strings."

"We'll need to monitor his communications," Eli decided, already pulling up schematics for discreet surveillance devices. "And his movements. We can't afford to make a mistake. If we accuse him wrongly, we create the very division they're hoping for. If we're too slow, they could gain access to even more sensitive information."

He looked at the data slate, at the spectral analysis of the paper, the patterns in the encryption, the subtle anomalies in the surveillance logs. The threat was no longer an abstract fear; it was a tangible entity, with a face, a motive, and a foothold within their sanctuary. The investigation had moved from deciphering anonymous threats to unmasking a traitor, and the weight of that realization settled heavily upon them. They were not just defending Havenridge from an external enemy; they were purging a sickness from within. The night was far from over. The quiet hum of their homemade communication devices, once a symbol of their isolation and independence, now served as a constant reminder of the delicate balance they were fighting to maintain. The echoes from the past had found them, not as distant thunder, but as a storm gathering in their own backyard.

The air in Havenridge, once thick with the scent of recycled oxygen and the faint, earthy aroma of the bio-luminescent fungi, now carried a new, metallic tang. It was the smell of proactive defense, of gates reinforced with salvaged alloys and repurposed agricultural machinery, of blast shields being tested and recalibrated. This subtle shift in the environment was a tangible manifestation of the escalating danger, a danger Eli and Mara had been meticulously preparing for in the quiet hours of the night.

Mara moved with a quiet urgency through the communal hydroponics bay, her hands, usually tending to delicate sprouts, now expertly guiding a small group through a defensive drill. They were a diverse mix: a seasoned ex-miner named Jorik, his hands calloused and strong; Lyra, the settlement's sharp-witted medic, her usual calm demeanor now tinged with a focused intensity; and a handful of others, hand-picked for their loyalty, their resilience, and their quiet competence. Eli had insisted on a tight-knit core group, a "fire team" as he'd grimly termed it, chosen not for their combat experience, which was virtually non-existent in their peaceful haven, but for their ability to adapt, to follow orders, and to think under pressure.

"Remember the formations," Mara's voice was low but carried authority, cutting through the murmur of their practice maneuvers. "Maintain visual contact. Watch for flanking. Eli's analysis of their tactics suggests they'll probe for weaknesses, try to divide us." She demonstrated a hand signal, a swift flick of the wrist that indicated a need to fall back to a designated secondary position. "This isn't about fighting a pitched battle; it's about holding ground, about containment and escape. Every second counts."

The drills were grueling, held in the dead of the designated sleep cycles, minimizing the risk of discovery by the general populace. Eli believed in transparency, in shared community decisions, but this was a shadow war. Revealing their preparations prematurely could incite panic, or worse, alert their enemies to the extent of their awareness. The whispers of dissent, the subtle sabotage, had already sown seeds of unease; overt military preparedness could be the catalyst that fractured Havenridge beyond repair. So, they trained in secret, the scent of oil and metal from the newly reinforced gates a constant, grim reminder of the potential conflict looming on the horizon.

Eli, meanwhile, was on the other side of the settlement, his focus narrowed to the labyrinthine network of ventilation shafts and abandoned service tunnels that snaked beneath Havenridge. His fingers, usually deft with delicate circuitry, now grappled with ancient, corroded access panels. He wasn't just reinforcing Havenridge; he was mapping its arteries, ensuring that every potential exit, every hidden passage, remained viable. These were grim necessities he shared only with Mara, their hushed conversations in the flickering light of their private quarters carrying the weight of unspoken fears and heavy responsibilities.

"The old ventilation shafts near the eastern dome," Eli explained to Mara during one of their clandestine meetings, his voice a low rasp, the grit of the tunnels still clinging to him. He projected a schematic of the settlement onto a small, portable display. "They lead to the geological survey caves. Not ideal, but they bypass the main thoroughfares. I've rerouted power to auxiliary lighting and cleared some of the debris. They're passable, for now."

He tapped a different section of the schematic. "And the service tunnels beneath the agricultural sector. They connect to the outer perimeter access points. I've reinforced the structural integrity of key junctions, but they'll be tight, and slow. Anyone trying to move through them will be vulnerable." He paused, his gaze meeting Mara's, the unspoken question hanging between them: who would be forced to take such a desperate path?

Mara's hand rested on his arm, her touch a grounding force. "We have to believe we won't need them, Eli."

"Belief is a luxury, Mara," he replied, his voice devoid of emotion, a stark testament to the lessons learned in the crucible of his past. "Preparation is a necessity. The Obsidian Accord doesn't operate on hope; they operate on acquisition. They see Havenridge not as a sanctuary, but as a prize. And they've proven time and again that they won't hesitate to use force, or deception, to claim what they believe is theirs." He recalled the meticulous planning that had preceded the Accord's assimilation of smaller colonies, the careful cultivation of internal dissent, the systematic isolation of leadership before the final, brutal sweep.

The proactive measures they were implementing were born from a deep, visceral understanding of those past betrayals. It wasn't paranoia; it was an educated assessment of risk. Eli remembered the chilling efficiency with which the Accord had exploited a colony's reliance on a single, outdated defense system, turning their perceived strength into their ultimate weakness. He remembered the whispers of discontent amplified by Accord agents, turning neighbor against neighbor, until the community itself was too fractured to mount a unified resistance.

"We need to secure our communication channels," Eli continued, his mind already shifting to the next critical task. "The encrypted network we've been using... it's good, but it's not infallible. If they've managed to infiltrate our systems to the extent we suspect, they could be monitoring every pulse. We need a secondary, a tertiary, a system they *can't* anticipate."

This led to another secret endeavor: the creation of a localized, low-frequency comms network, using salvaged components and carefully shielded antennas. It was a painstaking process, requiring Eli's expertise in signal manipulation and Mara's ingenuity in creating discreet transmission points. They established a series of "dead drops," small, disguised relay stations hidden within the settlement's infrastructure – a faulty conduit in the hydroponics bay, a loose panel in the recycling center, a hollowed-out section of an ancient piece of machinery. Each drop was programmed with a unique, temporal activation code, ensuring that only they, and their trusted inner circle, could access the secure network.

"This," Eli explained, holding up a small, metallic disc no larger than his thumbnail, "is the access key for the tertiary network. It's keyed to our bio-signatures, but more importantly, it's keyed to a specific sequence of harmonic resonance. If you don't have the exact frequency and the precise timing, it's just inert metal. We'll distribute these to Jorik, Lyra, and the others. Only use them in absolute emergencies, or for direct communication with us."

Mara examined the disc, its surface cool and smooth against her fingertips. "It feels... significant. Like holding a piece of our future."

"It is," Eli confirmed, his gaze distant. "It's the lifeline, if things go south. The difference between surviving and being erased."

The reinforcement of the gates was a more visible, though still carefully managed, undertaking. Officially, it was presented to the community as a necessary upgrade to the settlement's aging infrastructure, a preemptive measure against the unpredictable meteor showers common in their sector. Eli, using his considerable technical acumen, oversaw the process, ensuring that the modifications were robust enough to withstand significant force without appearing overtly militaristic. He worked with the engineering teams, subtly guiding their efforts, incorporating the stronger alloys and the more resilient locking mechanisms under the guise of routine maintenance. The scent of oil and metal was stronger near the main ingress and egress points, a constant reminder of their fortified borders, a testament to their proactive measures born from a deep understanding of past betrayals.

"The outer perimeter sensors have been recalibrated to detect a wider range of energy signatures," Eli informed Mara, reviewing the final diagnostic reports. "We've also implemented a silent alarm system, linked directly to the secondary comms network. If anything breaches the outer perimeter or triggers a high-level alert, it won't be a klaxon that echoes through the settlement, but a silent alert to our secure channel. We'll have precious minutes, perhaps even an hour, before any general alarm is raised, giving us time to react, to evacuate key personnel, or to implement whatever defensive posture is necessary."

He then turned his attention to the limited arsenal Havenridge possessed. Their tools were designed for construction, for mining, for survival in a harsh environment, not for warfare. But Eli, with his knowledge of Accord weaponry and tactics, knew how to adapt. He spent hours in the fabrication workshop, painstakingly modifying mining laser cutters into more focused, if short-ranged, defensive tools. He worked with Lyra to prepare a comprehensive medical kit, far beyond their usual emergency supplies, stocked with sedatives, coagulants, and even a limited supply of nanites for rapid wound closure.

"We can't match their firepower, not directly," Eli admitted to Mara, holding up a modified plasma torch, its beam now precisely calibrated for piercing armor. "But we can make them pay for every inch they try to take. We can make this settlement a costly acquisition. And more importantly, we can ensure that we have a way out, a way to preserve what we've built, even if Havenridge itself cannot be defended."

This was the most difficult conversation, the one that weighed most heavily on his conscience. The idea of abandoning their home, their sanctuary, was a bitter pill. But the echoes from the past, the grim history of colonies that had stood their ground only to be annihilated, had taught him the harsh calculus of survival.

"I've identified a series of subterranean caves, about two days' journey west of here," Eli explained, pointing to a section of their exploratory geological surveys. "They're geologically stable, well-hidden, and contain a small, naturally occurring water source. I've seeded them with emergency rations and basic survival gear, enough for a small group to endure for several weeks. It's a fallback, Mara. A last resort. If we can't hold Havenridge, we ensure that the core of our community, the knowledge and the people who embody what we stand for, can survive to rebuild."

Mara listened, her expression a mixture of apprehension and grim understanding. She knew Eli's pragmatism, his brutal honesty about the nature of their enemies. She also knew the weight of that knowledge, the burden of carrying the possibility of failure.

"We'll make sure the designated personnel know the routes," she said, her voice steady, her gaze meeting his. "Jorik, Lyra, the families with young children. We'll ensure they are prepared, discreetly."

The reinforced gates, the silent alarms, the modified tools, the hidden escape routes – each element was a layer of defense, meticulously constructed. The scent of oil and metal was no longer just a sign of construction; it was the scent of vigilance, of a community bracing for impact, its proactive measures born from a deep, hard-won understanding of past betrayals and the unforgiving nature of the forces arrayed against them. They were preparing for the unforeseen, not with fear, but with the quiet, determined resolve of those who understood that survival was not a matter of chance, but of preparation. The echoes from the past had not just brought warnings; they had brought the blueprints for survival.

CHAPTER EIGHT

Seeds of Doubt

The carefully constructed peace of Havenridge, once as predictable as the cycle of its bio-luminescent flora, had begun to fray. The subtle hum of the settlement's life support systems, a constant, comforting presence, now seemed to carry an undertone of tension. It was a dissonance born not of any single event, but of a thousand tiny shifts, of glances that lingered too long, of conversations that ceased abruptly when footsteps approached, of a general atmosphere that had subtly, yet undeniably, altered. Eli, in his quiet intensity, had become a focal point for this burgeoning unease, his past, like a shadow cast by an unseen sun, now beginning to lengthen and distort.

Mara felt it most acutely during her visits to the central market. The vibrant stalls, usually overflowing with the bounty of their hydroponic farms and the artisan crafts of the community, now seemed muted. The air, typically thick with the mingled scents of ripening fruits, freshly baked nutrient bread, and the earthy aroma of cultivated fungi, was now laced with something less pleasant – a faint, cloying scent of anxiety. It was the smell of doubt, a subtle yet pervasive miasma that clung to the edges of every interaction. She saw it in the way people averted their eyes, in the quick, almost furtive exchange of hushed words between neighbors, in the carefully neutral expressions that masked deeper currents of apprehension.

The security enhancements, initially presented as routine upgrades, had become a significant source of speculation. Eli's meticulous planning, his almost obsessive attention to detail in reinforcing the perimeter and optimizing their defense systems, was admirable to some, but deeply unsettling to others. They had lived in Havenridge for generations, a sanctuary carved out of necessity, a haven built on mutual trust and a shared belief in a peaceful coexistence. The sudden, almost draconian measures, however well-intentioned, felt like a betrayal of that fundamental principle. Whispers began to circulate, quiet at first, like seeds carried on the wind, then growing in volume, taking root in the fertile ground of uncertainty.

"He's always been... intense," she overheard one woman confide to another near the fruit stalls, her voice barely a murmur, her eyes darting towards Mara as if she feared being overheard. "But lately, it's different. He's always looking out, always planning. It's like he's expecting the sky to fall."

The comment, innocent enough on its own, was a symptom of a larger malaise. Eli's past, a carefully guarded secret, was no longer entirely a secret. Fragments had begun to surface, like scattered debris from a long-sunken ship, hinting at a history far removed from the placid life of Havenridge. He had been instrumental in its founding, a visionary architect of their sanctuary, but the stories that now began to circulate spoke of a different Eli, a man shaped by conflict, by loss, by the harsh realities of a universe that was far less forgiving than their enclosed haven.

"They say he was... involved in something before he came here," a young man, his face earnest, confided in Jorik, the ex-miner, his voice laced with a mixture of curiosity and apprehension. "Something about... disputes. Negotiations gone wrong."

Jorik, a man of few words but keen observation, merely grunted, his weathered face impassive. He had seen the look in Eli's eyes during their training sessions, the grim calculation, the practiced efficiency. He knew that Eli's intensity was born of experience, a hard-won wisdom that transcended mere caution. But he also understood that in a community that prized harmony above all else, such an intensity could be misconstrued as aggression, as a harbinger of the very conflict they sought to avoid.

The external delegation, a recurring presence that had initially been viewed with a mixture of suspicion and cautious optimism, now became another focal point for these burgeoning rumors. Their continued interest in Havenridge, their polite but persistent inquiries into its resources and its governance, had always been a source of low-level tension. Now, with the increased security measures and Eli's heightened vigilance, their presence felt less like a diplomatic engagement and more like an assessment, a probing by potential adversaries.

"Why are they still here?" the same woman from the market, her voice now sharper, whispered to a small group gathered near the communal heating units. "What do they want with us? Havenridge is our home, our sanctuary. They have no right to keep poking around, asking questions, especially now, when we're... preparing for something."

The implication hung heavy in the air: who were they preparing for? And was Eli's past somehow intertwined with this external interest? The seed of doubt, once planted, had begun to sprout, its tendrils reaching into the hearts and minds of the community.

Mara found herself trying to counter these whispers, to reassure those who sought her out, to explain the necessity of their preparations without betraying Eli's carefully laid plans for discretion. She spoke of the unpredictable nature of their sector, of the need for robust infrastructure, of the prudent measures any responsible community would take to ensure its safety. But her words, she knew, often fell on ears already attuned to a different narrative, a narrative woven from fear and speculation.

"Mara," a woman named Elara, a respected elder and a close friend of Mara's mother, approached her after a community meeting, her face etched with concern. "I appreciate your reassurances, truly. But this... this atmosphere... it's not healthy. People are afraid. They're looking at Eli, and they're seeing not a protector, but a threat. They remember the stories, the ones whispered about what happened before he came here, before Havenridge was founded. They worry that his past will bring the conflict to our doorstep."

Mara met Elara's gaze, her heart heavy. "Elara, Eli is doing everything he can to protect us. He understands the dangers we face, dangers many of us haven't even begun to comprehend. His methods may seem... intense, but they are born of necessity. He's trying to prevent a disaster, not cause one."

"But at what cost, dear?" Elara's voice was soft, laced with a mother's concern. "At the cost of our peace? At the cost of our trust in each other? If we can't feel safe within our own walls, if we begin to eye our neighbors with suspicion, what have we truly preserved?"

The questions hung in the air, unanswered. Mara understood the validity of Elara's fears. Trust, once a cornerstone of their society, was becoming a more fragile commodity. The easy camaraderie, the open interactions, were being replaced by a guardedness, a subtle withdrawal. People were becoming more insular, more focused on their immediate circle, less willing to extend that circle to those who seemed different, or who were associated with the perceived source of the growing unease.

Eli, sensing the shift, had become even more withdrawn. He immersed himself in his work, his nights spent poring over schematics and running diagnostics, his days a blur of carefully orchestrated meetings and supervised inspections. He was a man carrying an immense burden, a burden made heavier by the knowledge that the very actions he took to protect his community were inadvertently sowing seeds of discord within it. He saw the questioning glances, the hushed conversations, the way people subtly shifted away from him when he passed. It was a familiar sensation, a chilling echo of past experiences where his perceived strengths had been interpreted as flaws, his protective instincts as aggression.

One evening, as Mara sat with Eli in their small, spartan living quarters, the hum of the settlement a distant lullaby, she voiced her concerns. "Eli, the whispers are growing louder. People are afraid, and they're looking at you. They don't understand why all this... preparation is necessary. They fear what you might have brought with you."

Eli looked up from the datapad he was examining, his eyes, usually sharp and focused, now clouded with a weariness that went beyond physical exhaustion. "I know, Mara. I see it. I feel it." He ran a hand over his tired face. "It's the price of survival, I suppose. The price of knowing what lurks in the dark. They haven't had to face it, not like I have. Their peace has been a shield, not a weapon. And now, that shield is being tested, and I'm the one holding it up. It makes me a target, not a savior."

"But they don't know your intentions, Eli," Mara pleaded, reaching out to touch his arm. "They only see the changes, the heightened security, and they connect it to… to the fragments of your past that are starting to surface. They associate your vigilance with conflict, rather than protection."

"My past is a specter that haunts every decision I make, Mara," Eli confessed, his voice a low murmur. "I came to Havenridge seeking peace, seeking a fresh start, a place where I could finally lay down the burdens I'd carried for so long. But the universe has a way of reminding you that the past is never truly buried. The Obsidian Accord… they don't forget. They don't forgive. And their reach is long."

He paused, his gaze fixed on some distant point beyond the reinforced walls of their dwelling. "The external delegation… their inquiries are not casual. They are probes. They are assessing our vulnerabilities. And if they learn of my history, if they understand the extent of what I know about the Accord's methods… they will see me not just as a leader, but as a threat to their own interests. Or worse, as a valuable asset to be acquired."

Mara's hand tightened on his arm. The weight of his words pressed down on her, a palpable force. She had always known that Eli carried deep scars, but she had never fully grasped the magnitude of the threat he believed they faced, nor how inextricably linked it was to his own history.

"So, the security upgrades…" she began, the pieces clicking into place with a terrifying clarity.

"Are a necessity," Eli finished for her, his voice firm, though tinged with regret. "I can't afford to let them exploit our naivete, Mara. I can't afford to let Havenridge become another victim of their insatiable hunger. But I also can't afford to have my community divided by fear and suspicion. It's a fine line to walk, and I'm not sure I'm succeeding."

The scent of fear in the market, the hushed conversations, the averted glances – they were all manifestations of this growing chasm. It was a subtle warfare, waged not with weapons, but with whispers, with doubt, with the insidious erosion of trust. And Mara, caught between her love for Eli and her deep-seated loyalty to her community, felt the weight of that conflict pressing down on her, a heavy, unwelcome addition to the air they all breathed. The carefully cultivated sanctuary of Havenridge was no longer just facing an external threat; it was beginning to turn inward, its own foundations being subtly undermined by the very efforts meant to secure them. The seeds of doubt, once sown, were beginning to bloom, casting long, disquieting shadows across their peaceful haven.

The polished durasteel doors of the delegation's temporary quarters slid open with a soft hiss, a sound that had become as familiar to Mara as the gentle thrum of Havenridge's life support. It had been weeks since their last official engagement, weeks marked by the escalating unease within the settlement, weeks during which Eli had poured every ounce of his energy into fortifying their defenses, and weeks during which Mara had found herself increasingly entangled in the delicate dance of reassurance and veiled truths. She had half-expected them to depart, to have concluded their 'fact-finding mission' and retreated to their own, more opulent sectors. Instead, they were back. And not just back, but seemingly more engaged, more... interested than ever before.

Ambassador Thorne, his silver uniform impeccably pressed, stood at the forefront of the small delegation. His smile, a practiced curve of his lips, was as warm and insincere as the recycled air in a poorly maintained hydroponic bay. Beside him stood a smattering of aides, their faces a study in polite neutrality, their eyes, however, constantly scanning, assessing, cataloging. Thorne's gaze, when it met Mara's, held a peculiar glint, a flicker that suggested he saw more than just the placid surface of Havenridge.

"Esteemed Mara," Thorne began, his voice a smooth baritone that seemed to resonate with an almost paternalistic concern. "We trust our absence has not caused undue disruption. We have been observing the recent... adaptations to your security protocols with considerable interest." He gestured vaguely towards the reinforced perimeter visible through the transparisteel viewport of their communal hub. "Most prudent, of course. A community as valuable as Havenridge must ensure its continued prosperity and safety."

Mara inclined her head, her own smile a carefully constructed mask. "Ambassador Thorne. Your return is... unexpected, but welcome. We have indeed been undertaking necessary enhancements to our infrastructure." She chose her words with deliberate care, aware that every syllable was being weighed. "The sector has been, shall we say, less predictable of late. Prudence is a virtue we all share, I believe."

Thorne's smile widened, a gesture that felt more like a baring of teeth than an expression of genuine pleasure. "Indeed, prudence is paramount. And it is precisely because of this shared understanding that we felt compelled to return. We have been discussing your situation amongst ourselves, and we believe we can offer... assistance." He paused, letting the word hang in the air, imbued with a subtle weight. "Assistance, of course, that would involve a greater degree of collaboration. Integration, perhaps, in certain vital areas."

The implication was clear, and it sent a chill down Mara's spine. 'Integration' was a euphemism for control. 'Collaboration' was a polite word for oversight. And the 'assistance' they offered was laced with an unspoken understanding of their own. They knew something. They *sensed* something. Perhaps it was the subtle shifts in the community's mood, the hushed conversations they'd undoubtedly overheard or intercepted. Or perhaps, and this was the more unsettling thought, their intelligence networks had finally caught wind of Eli's past, the fragments that had begun to surface like dangerous flotsam.

"Assistance?" Mara echoed, feigning mild curiosity. "We have always managed our own affairs, Ambassador. Our systems are robust, our community self-sufficient."

"Self-sufficient, yes," Thorne conceded smoothly, his eyes flicking towards a junior aide who offered a discreet nod. "But even the most robust systems can benefit from external expertise, particularly when dealing with... complex threats. Threats that might originate from unforeseen quarters. We have resources, Mara. Networks. We understand the complexities of security, the nuances of managing... challenging individuals."

The phrase 'challenging individuals' hung heavy in the air, a thinly veiled reference to Eli. Thorne's gaze, though still fixed on Mara, seemed to bore through her, as if seeking confirmation, or perhaps an admission of the very discord they were implying existed. He was offering them a solution to a problem they claimed to perceive – the perceived instability emanating from their own security chief – a solution that would entrench the delegation deeper within Havenridge's operations. It was a cunning strategy, designed to exploit the very doubts that were already beginning to fester.

"Our community is... united," Mara said, her voice firm, though a tremor of unease ran beneath the surface. "Our security measures are designed to protect us all, from any potential threat."

"Of course, of course," Thorne purred, his hand lightly touching his aide's shoulder. "And we applaud your efforts. Truly. But there are times when a fresh perspective, an objective assessment, is invaluable. Especially when one is dealing with... historical baggage. With individuals whose past experiences might, understandably, color their judgment. We have, shall we say, a keen understanding of such complexities. We have dealt with individuals who carry the weight of... prior commitments. Those who have made... difficult choices."

His words were a subtle weapon, each one honed to exploit a specific vulnerability. He was not directly accusing Eli, but he was painting a picture, a narrative that the anxious residents of Havenridge were already beginning to accept. He was offering the delegation as a stabilizing force, a neutral arbiter, to manage the perceived volatility that Eli represented. He was offering to 'help' them control the very man who was desperately trying to protect them from threats they couldn't even comprehend.

"Ambassador, if you have specific concerns regarding our security, I encourage you to present them directly, through the proper channels," Mara stated, her tone hardening. She refused to engage in this veiled chess game of insinuation.

Thorne chuckled, a dry, rustling sound. "But of course, Mara. That is precisely why we are here. We are not here to accuse, but to offer partnership. To share the burden. Consider it a gesture of goodwill. A proactive measure. We would be happy to assist in refining your security protocols, perhaps even in... advising on personnel deployment. Especially concerning individuals who may have a... complex operational history. We can offer training, support, and a more robust oversight mechanism. It would, I believe, alleviate a great deal of the underlying tension you must be experiencing."

His pronouncements were smooth, almost soothing, yet they carried the sharp edge of a predatory instinct. He was not offering help; he was offering leverage. He was making it clear that the delegation was aware, or at least suspected, the growing internal unease, and they were ready to capitalize on it. Their renewed interest was not born of altruism, but of opportunity. The seeds of doubt, which Eli had so feared, had not only sprouted, but had begun to attract the attention of those who thrived in such fertile ground.

Later that evening, the small cabin Eli and Mara shared felt both like a sanctuary and a cage. The flickering lamplight cast long, dancing shadows across the walls, mirroring the unsettling uncertainty that had begun to permeate their lives. Eli sat hunched over a datapad, his brow furrowed, his fingers tracing invisible lines on the holographic display. Mara watched him, her heart a tight knot of worry. He looked exhausted, the weight of his responsibilities etched onto his face, a burden made heavier by the insidious erosion of trust he was witnessing within his own community.

"They're back," Eli stated, his voice low, devoid of surprise. He hadn't needed to see them. He had felt their renewed focus, a subtle shift in the ambient energy of Havenridge, as palpable as a change in atmospheric pressure.

Mara sighed, sinking onto the edge of their cot. "Thorne was... more direct this time. He spoke of 'challenging individuals' and offered 'assistance' with our security. It's clear they've picked up on the whispers. Or perhaps," she hesitated, "they've heard something more concrete about you."

Eli's jaw tightened. "It's a calculated move. They see the divisions, or they suspect them, and they're ready to exploit them. Thorne's 'aid' is a poisoned chalice, Mara. He wants to integrate their oversight, to get his people into our command structures. He wants to gain direct access to our systems, to me." He looked up from the datapad, his eyes meeting hers, a flicker of the familiar intensity returning, but now tinged with a deep weariness. "He's not interested in our safety. He's interested in our resources, and he sees me as an obstacle, or worse, a potential pawn. If he believes I'm a threat to Havenridge, or that my past makes me unstable, he can use that to justify increased delegation presence, increased control."

"He implied they have experience dealing with 'difficult' people, with 'historical baggage'," Mara recounted, the words tasting like ash in her mouth. "He painted a picture, Eli, of your past being a source of instability for us. He's offering to 'manage' it, to 'advise' on personnel."

Eli ran a hand over his face, a gesture of profound exhaustion. "They've always been interested in Havenridge, in our unique bio-engineering, in our strategic location. But they've never had a foothold. Now, they see a potential opening. My past, the Obsidian Accord... it's a card they're keen to play, or at least to discover the full value of. If they can convince Havenridge that I'm a liability, that my vigilance is paranoia, that my methods are too... aggressive, they can leverage that fear to gain influence. They can present themselves as the rational, stable alternative."

He tapped a finger against the datapad. "Their 'aid' would mean their agents embedded within our security teams, monitoring our communications, observing our operations. They'd be looking for any slip-up, any sign that I'm not in control, or that Havenridge is vulnerable because of me. They want to dismantle our autonomy, piece by piece, under the guise of offering support."

"But why now?" Mara pressed, trying to understand the timing. "Have they received new intelligence?"

"Perhaps," Eli mused, his gaze distant. "Or perhaps they've simply noticed the change in our atmosphere. The increased security, the discreet patrols, your own... careful conversations. They are skilled observers, Mara. They've likely detected the subtle shifts, the ripples of unease. And Thorne, he's not a fool. He knows how to fan the flames of discontent. He'll be presenting himself as the solution to a problem that he himself is helping to create."

He leaned back, the weariness returning with full force. "It's a classic tactic. Sow discord, then offer yourself as the mediator. Undermine the existing authority, then step in to fill the vacuum. He's trying to leverage the fear of the unknown, the fear of my past, against me, and by extension, against Havenridge."

"So, what do we do?" Mara asked, her voice barely a whisper. The situation felt impossibly complex, a tangled web of external threats and internal anxieties. "We can't just ignore them. And we can't give them the leverage they're looking for."

Eli met her gaze, his own filled with a grim resolve. "We don't give them an inch, Mara. We maintain our protocols. We continue our preparations. And we reinforce the trust within Havenridge. We have to counter their narrative, not by revealing everything I've tried to shield them from, but by demonstrating our strength, our unity, and our unwavering commitment to our own security. We need to show them that their attempts to sow discord will fail."

He reached out, his hand covering hers, his touch a familiar anchor in the swirling uncertainty. "They are offering us a cage disguised as a sanctuary, Mara. We have to refuse the offer, politely but firmly. We have to make them understand that Havenridge is not for sale, and its leadership is not up for negotiation. But most importantly," his thumb stroked the back of her hand, a gesture of reassurance, "we have to make sure our own people understand that. We need to stem the tide of doubt, before Thorne's delegation can truly exploit it."

The task felt monumental. The whispers had already begun, the seeds of doubt had been sown, and now, the delegation had arrived, not to offer genuine partnership, but to cultivate the very divisions that threatened to unravel Havenridge from within. The challenge lay not just in defending against external threats, but in fortifying the hearts and minds of their own people, ensuring that the light of trust, however dimmed by fear, could not be extinguished.

The hum of the communal hub had taken on a different timbre in the past few cycles. It was no longer the steady, reassuring drone of a well-oiled machine, but a fractured melody, punctuated by anxious murmurs and hushed exchanges. Mara felt it in the way people's gazes skittered away from hers, in the forced smiles that didn't quite reach their eyes, in the palpable tension that clung to the recycled air like a persistent atmospheric anomaly. Ambassador Thorne's recent visit, with its veiled insinuations and carefully worded offers of 'assistance,' had clearly struck a nerve. The seeds of doubt he'd so expertly sown were beginning to sprout, their tendrils creeping into the very foundations of Havenridge.

She knew she couldn't let it fester. Eli was right; they couldn't afford to cede ground, not to Thorne's machinations, and certainly not to the corrosive influence of fear within their own community. While Eli focused on fortifying their physical defenses, Mara's battlefield was the hearts and minds of their people. She needed to address the growing unease directly, to counter the narrative Thorne was so artfully constructing, a narrative that painted Eli as a destabilizing force, his vigilance as paranoia, his dedication as an overreach.

The designated gathering time arrived, a standard weekly assembly where announcements were made and questions were fielded. But this time, the atmosphere was heavier, the usual buzz of communal life subdued. Residents of Havenridge, from the hydroponic farmers to the engineering technicians, filled the space, their faces etched with a mixture of apprehension and curiosity. Mara stood at the central podium, her heart thrumming a steady, determined rhythm against her ribs. She looked out at the sea of faces, a mosaic of hope, resilience, and now, vulnerability. She saw the fear in their eyes, the uncertainty that Thorne had so expertly fanned.

"My friends," she began, her voice clear and steady, projecting through the husmic silence. "I want to speak to you tonight about Havenridge. About where we are, and where we are going." She paused, letting her gaze sweep across the assembly, seeking out individuals, acknowledging their presence, their shared existence. "We have seen changes in recent cycles. Our routines have adapted, our security measures have been enhanced. I understand that change, especially when it is unexpected, can be unsettling."

A few heads nodded, tentative acknowledgments. The honesty, the directness of her opening, seemed to break the ice slightly. They weren't accustomed to such frank admissions from their leadership.

"Some of you may have heard whispers," she continued, her voice taking on a more impassioned tone. "Rumors, concerns about the direction we are taking, about the decisions being made. I want to address that directly. It is natural to question, to seek understanding, especially when the future feels uncertain. But I also want to remind you of something vital: our strength, our very survival, has always been rooted in our unity. In our trust in each other."

She could feel Thorne's insidious influence, the way he'd played on their inherent anxieties. He had arrived offering a solution to a problem that didn't truly exist, or rather, a problem he was actively exacerbating. He preyed on the fear of the unknown, and the fear of Eli's past. She wouldn't reveal the specifics of the threats they faced, not yet. That would only validate Thorne's narrative of paranoia. Instead, she would focus on the core principles that defined Havenridge.

"Havenridge is not just a settlement," Mara declared, her voice rising with conviction. "It is a shared vision. A testament to what we can achieve when we work together, when we pool our knowledge, our skills, our courage. The decisions being made, the measures being implemented, are all in service of that vision. They are designed to protect what we have built, to safeguard our future, not just for us, but for generations to come."

She met the gaze of a grizzled engineer, a man who had always been a staunch supporter, but whose brow was currently furrowed with worry. "Eli," she continued, her voice softening slightly, but losing none of its firmness, "our Chief of Security, has poured his heart and soul into ensuring our safety. His dedication is unwavering. He has seen what others have not, he has anticipated challenges that have yet to fully materialize. His commitment to Havenridge is absolute."

She chose her words carefully, weaving a narrative of loyalty and foresight, without divulging the classified nature of the threats. The Obsidian Accord, the true danger Eli represented to those who sought to exploit Havenridge, remained a carefully guarded secret. But his *dedication*, his *foresight*, his *commitment* – these were truths she could speak to, truths that should resonate with the very fabric of their community.

"His methods may sometimes seem... unconventional," Mara conceded, acknowledging the very source of the whispers that Thorne was exploiting. "He operates with a level of intensity that can be... intense. But this is not born of recklessness, but of a profound responsibility. He carries a weight, a knowledge of the dangers that exist beyond our sheltered walls, and he shoulders it so that we may continue to live in peace and prosperity."

She saw a flicker of understanding in some faces, a softening of the tension. But the doubts were deeply entrenched, fed by Thorne's insinuations and the inherent human desire for reassurance. She knew that a single speech, however heartfelt, could not erase weeks of subtle manipulation.

"We are facing challenges," she admitted, her gaze sweeping across the crowd once more. "Challenges that require us to be vigilant, to be resilient, and most importantly, to be united. The strength of Havenridge has always been its people. Your willingness to contribute, your faith in our collective future. It is this faith, this trust, that Thorne and his delegation seem to underestimate. They may offer solutions, but their solutions come with strings attached, strings that would bind us, that would dilute our autonomy, and that would ultimately compromise the very principles we hold dear."

She spoke of the delegation's 'assistance' not as a threat, but as a seductive poison, a Trojan horse of control disguised as aid. "We are a self-sufficient community. We have the intelligence, the resources, and the will to govern ourselves. We do not need external oversight that would seek to undermine our independence. We must trust our own judgment, our own capabilities, and the leadership that has guided us thus far."

The air in the hub seemed to hum with a renewed energy, a subtle shift from apprehension to a more focused contemplation. Her words weren't a magic balm, but they were a sturdy bridge, a visible attempt to reconnect the fraying threads of trust. She saw a few individuals exchange glances, not of doubt, but of thoughtful consideration.

"I know that some of you have questions about Eli's past," Mara said, choosing to directly, albeit vaguely, address the most potent source of Thorne's leverage. "And I acknowledge that his history is... complex. He has lived a life that has prepared him for the unique challenges we face here. He has made difficult choices, and he carries burdens that we can only imagine. But those experiences have forged him into the protector that Havenridge needs."

She paused, letting the weight of her statement settle. This was as close as she could get to defending him without revealing the sensitive details that could endanger them all further. "What matters most is not the shadows of his past, but the light of his dedication to our present and our future. He is committed to Havenridge, to its ideals, and to the safety of every single person within these walls. And I, along with the rest of our council, stand with him. We have faith in his judgment, and we have faith in our collective ability to navigate whatever challenges lie ahead."

She could see the effect her words were having. The rigid lines of anxiety on some faces began to soften, replaced by a thoughtful expression. They were listening. They were considering. It was not a resounding victory, not a complete dispelling of all doubt. The seeds Thorne had sown were tenacious. But Mara had planted seeds of her own – seeds of unity, of trust, of unwavering conviction.

"We must not allow fear to divide us," she urged, her voice resonating with a plea for solidarity. "We must not let external forces dictate our destiny. Havenridge is ours. Its future is ours to build, together. Let us reaffirm our commitment to each other, to our shared vision, and to the strength that lies within our unity. Let us stand as one, not out of blind obedience, but out of a deep-seated belief in what Havenridge represents, and in the courage we possess to protect it."

She stepped back from the podium, the silence that followed her speech not one of passive acceptance, but of active reflection. She saw conversations sparking, quiet debates unfolding between individuals. It was a beginning. A crucial first step in mending the social fabric Thorne sought to tear apart. She knew the fight was far from over. Thorne would continue his subtle campaigns, exploiting any lingering anxieties. But Mara had drawn a line in the sand, a public declaration of their unity and their unwavering belief in their own path. She had defended Eli, not by revealing his secrets, but by highlighting his undeniable loyalty and the vital role he played in safeguarding their home. The path ahead was uncertain, but for now, the tide of doubt had been momentarily stemmed, and the call for unity had been heard. The true test, she knew, would be in the days and weeks to come, in how well Havenridge could hold onto the strength she had so passionately invoked.

Eli moved through the shadowed corridors of Havenridge with a purpose that belied the gnawing uncertainty coiling in his gut. Mara's words, spoken to the gathered community, echoed in his mind – a desperate attempt to shore up their collective faith, to mend the cracks Thorne's insidious whispers had begun to pry open. But while Mara's battlefield was the hearts and minds of their people, Eli's lay in the unseen currents of information, in the silent war of deception he was now forced to wage. He knew Thorne wasn't just offering 'assistance'; he was probing, testing, seeking vulnerabilities. And Eli, as Chief of Security, had to act preemptively, not just to defend, but to *understand*.

His counter-intelligence operation wasn't born of aggression, but of a cold, calculated necessity. Thorne and his delegation were a carefully constructed facade, their intentions shrouded in layers of diplomatic politeness. To peel back those layers, Eli had to feed them a carefully constructed illusion of his own. He needed them to believe Havenridge was weaker than it was, to lull them into a false sense of security, or worse, to expose the true depth of their misdirection by their reactions to fabricated threats. It was a dangerous dance, a gamble where a single misstep could have devastating consequences for everything they had built.

His first recruit was Kael, the quiet, unassuming archivist whose mind was a labyrinth of data and forgotten histories. Kael possessed an uncanny ability to sift through reams of information, to find patterns where others saw only chaos. They met in the archives, a place steeped in the scent of aging paper and dry ink, the ambient hum of the data servers a low thrumming presence. Eli, cloaked in the perpetual dimness of the archive's deeper sections, spread schematics of the hydroponic bays across a long, dust-laden table.

"They're looking for weaknesses, Kael," Eli stated, his voice a low rasp. "They're looking for leverage. Thorne is too smooth, too... accommodating. It's a trap."

Kael, his fingers stained with ink, traced a line on the schematic. "The delegation's comms logs show an unusual amount of interest in our agricultural output. Specifically, the nutrient synthesis processes."

"Exactly," Eli confirmed, a grim satisfaction settling over him. "They see a potential choke point. If they can disrupt our food supply, they can destabilize us from within." He tapped a section of the schematic. "This is where we make them think the vulnerability lies. A simulated malfunction in the primary nutrient synthesizers. Nothing that would actually harm our crops, but enough to cause concern, enough to warrant 'expert intervention' from Thorne's team."

Kael nodded, his eyes sharp. "We'll need to fabricate logs, sensor readings, maintenance reports. A narrative of escalating failures. And we'll need to ensure certain... discrepancies are discoverable. A misplaced calibration report, a hastily written addendum to a safety protocol."

"Precisely," Eli agreed. "We make it look like a series of minor oversights, compounded by a lack of experienced personnel to address them. We feed them just enough rope to hang themselves. But it has to be plausible. It can't be so obvious that they dismiss it outright."

Their clandestine meetings weren't confined to the archives. They took place in the hushed glow of the lower maintenance tunnels, where the air was thick with the metallic tang of machinery and the faint scent of ozone. Here, Eli met with Lena, the head of internal security, a woman whose loyalty was as unshakeable as the bedrock beneath Havenridge. Lena was an expert in surveillance, in reading body language, in discerning truth from deception.

"They're trying to get close to the power conduits," Lena reported, her voice a low murmur as they stood beside a humming, heavily shielded generator. "Specifically, the secondary distribution hubs. They've been asking very pointed questions about emergency shutdown protocols."

Eli's jaw tightened. "The power grid. Another vital artery. If they can control our power, they control everything." He pointed to a series of diagrams on Lena's datapad. "We'll create a diversion here. A staged 'security breach' in Sector Gamma. A few tripped sensors, some automated lockdown sequences that appear to go awry. It will draw their attention, perhaps even prompt them to offer their 'assistance' in securing our infrastructure. It's a risk, but we need to see how they react. We need to gauge their willingness to involve themselves in our internal operations."

Lena's gaze was steely. "And if they accept the bait? If they try to exploit the situation?"

"Then we'll know their true intentions," Eli replied, his voice grim. "And we'll be ready. But for now, it's about misdirection. We make them chase shadows. We feed them carefully crafted whispers of vulnerability. We make them believe they're uncovering our secrets, when in reality, they're just confirming the illusions we've painstakingly constructed."

The operation required meticulous planning and an intimate understanding of Thorne's delegation. Eli, with Kael's data analysis and Lena's surveillance reports, began to build a mosaic of their interests. They noted the delegation's keen interest in Havenridge's water purification systems, their questions about waste recycling efficiency, even their seemingly innocent inquiries about the structural integrity of the domes. Each piece of information was a potential thread for Eli to exploit, a subtle lever to manipulate their perceptions.

He began anonymously leaking information through secure, untraceable channels. A heavily encrypted data packet detailing potential microbial contamination in a reservoir, complete with doctored sensor readings and a fabricated incident report. A seemingly accidental 'discovery' of schematics for a new air filtration system, subtly highlighting design flaws that would, in reality, be incredibly difficult to exploit. He even planted rumors of dissent amongst the hydroponic technicians, suggesting dissatisfaction with Eli's stringent security protocols, a narrative that played directly into Thorne's desire to portray Eli as a divisive figure.

One afternoon, Eli found himself in the quiet solitude of the hydroponics bay, the air thick with the sweet, earthy scent of ripening fruits and vegetables. The vibrant greens and reds were a stark contrast to the sterile, metallic environment of his usual work. He ran a hand over the smooth, cool surface of a nutrient feed pipe, his mind racing. Thorne's delegation had expressed a particular interest in the flow regulators.

"They're sniffing around the regulators," he murmured to himself, the words lost in the gentle whir of the climate control systems. "They think they can manipulate the nutrient flow, starve us." He paused, a dangerous spark igniting in his eyes. "Let them think that."

He made a few subtle adjustments to a secondary flow regulator, nothing that would cause actual harm, but enough to trigger a cascade of minor, easily correctable fluctuations in the nutrient delivery system. He then ensured that the logs reflecting these minor adjustments were visible to the delegation's technical liaisons, a breadcrumb trail leading them down a path of fabricated concern. He even drafted a series of internal memos, detailing the 'challenges' in maintaining precise nutrient balances, emphasizing the need for 'external expertise' – a carefully placed suggestion designed to appeal to Thorne's ego and his supposed benevolent intentions.

The pressure was immense. Each fabricated piece of intelligence, each whispered rumor, was a calculated risk. He had to maintain the illusion of Havenridge's vulnerabilities without actually compromising their security. He had to anticipate Thorne's every move, every counter-play, and weave his deceptions accordingly. It was a delicate balancing act, performed on the razor's edge between preparedness and paranoia, between protecting his people and falling prey to the very fear he was trying to combat.

One evening, while monitoring the delegation's encrypted communications, a fragment of intercepted data flickered across his console. It was a brief, almost insignificant exchange between two members of Thorne's team, discussing the 'serendipitous discovery' of certain 'internal inefficiencies.' The phrase, mundane on its own, sent a jolt of adrenaline through Eli. It was confirmation. They were taking the bait. They believed they were uncovering Havenridge's weaknesses, not realizing they were being shown carefully manufactured illusions.

He met Kael again, the latest intercepted data displayed on Kael's terminal. "They're taking the bait, Kael. The 'inefficiencies.' They think they're on the verge of something significant."

Kael's lips curved into a faint smile. "The fabricated incident reports are being analyzed. Their technical teams are expressing interest in 'assisting' with the nutrient synthesis recalibration."

"Good," Eli breathed, the tension in his shoulders easing infinitesimally. "We need to step up the pressure. Introduce a new element of uncertainty. Something about our energy reserves. A subtle implication that our primary power core is operating at suboptimal capacity."

Lena joined them, her presence a silent affirmation of their shared purpose. "Their surveillance drones have been focusing on the perimeter shield generators. They're looking for weak points in our external defenses."

"Then we give them something to worry about there," Eli decided. "A simulated anomaly in the shield harmonics. Nothing that would actually breach the system, but enough to make them believe we're more exposed than we are. We want them to expend their resources and their attention on these fabricated threats, to keep them occupied, to blind them to our true strengths and our true intentions."

The game was escalating. Eli, Kael, and Lena, working in the shadowed corners of Havenridge, were weaving a complex tapestry of deception. They were the unseen architects of a false reality, the puppeteers pulling strings that would, they hoped, distract and disarm their adversaries. The scent of damp earth and pine needles from the adjacent biodomes, carried on the recycled air, seemed to mock the synthetic nature of the battlefield they were engaged in. But in this silent war of information, in this dangerous dance of deception, Eli knew that survival depended not on brute force, but on the subtle, potent weapon of the carefully crafted lie. He was playing with fire, but it was a fire that might just keep them all from being consumed. The delegation believed they were uncovering Havenridge's vulnerabilities, but in truth, they were only seeing the shadows Eli had so expertly cast.

The sterile luminescence of Havenridge's central plaza usually offered a sterile kind of comfort, a testament to their engineered survival. But tonight, under the muted glow of the simulated twilight, it felt like a stage set for a play of uneasy compromises. Mara found Eli leaning against the cool, synthetic bark of a bioluminescent tree, his shoulders hunched, the sharp lines of his jaw softened by the dim light. He looked not like the unflinching Chief of Security she knew, but like a man weighed down by burdens too heavy for any single soul to bear.

She approached him quietly, the soft scuff of her boots on the recycled composite floor the only sound to break the manufactured tranquility. Eli's head turned, and his gaze, usually so sharp and assessing, held a raw vulnerability that stole her breath. It was a look she rarely saw, a glimpse behind the impenetrable fortress he maintained for everyone else.

"Eli," she began softly, her voice a gentle ripple in the quiet.

He offered a weak, almost imperceptible smile. "Mara. I was hoping I'd find you." He pushed away from the tree, his movements a little stiff, as if the very act of standing upright required immense effort. "Trouble sleeping?"

Mara shook her head, a faint, rueful smile touching her lips. "More like trouble *not* thinking about all the trouble we're in. Thorne's whispers are starting to sound like shouts, even when no one's speaking."

Eli's hand found hers, his fingers warm and calloused, a stark contrast to her own. He brought her hand to his lips, pressing a kiss to her knuckles. "I know. The operation... it's taking its toll."

They stood in silence for a long moment, the unspoken anxieties hanging between them like a thick fog. Mara found herself tracing the lines of his palm, the familiar terrain of his skin a strange anchor in the shifting sands of their reality. "It's not just the operation, Eli. It's... what we're becoming. To fight Thorne's deception, we're weaving our own. We're playing games with truth, and I'm starting to worry that the lines are blurring, not just for them, but for us." She looked up at him, her eyes earnest. "Are we so afraid of losing Havenridge that we're willing to change what it is?"

Eli's thumb brushed against her skin, a gesture of comfort that did little to ease the knot of dread in her own chest. He met her gaze, his eyes filled with a profound weariness. "I ask myself that every single day, Mara. Every fabricated report, every whispered lie I feed into the system... it feels like a betrayal of everything we stand for. I'm so afraid that in trying to protect them, I'm corrupting them. That I'm leading them down a path where the ends justify the means, and that's a dangerous precedent to set." He paused, his voice dropping to a near whisper. "Sometimes, I feel like I'm gambling with all of our lives, and the stakes are too high to bear."

The confession hung in the air, heavy with the weight of his guilt. Mara tightened her grip on his hand. "You're doing what you have to do, Eli. Thorne isn't playing fair. He's trying to dismantle us from the inside, and you're building walls to keep him out. It's not deception for its own sake; it's a necessary defense. You're protecting us."

"But at what cost?" he countered, his voice laced with a pain that mirrored her own. "Are we becoming the very thing we're fighting against? Are we sacrificing the integrity of Havenridge, the very principles that make us strong, just to survive this? I see it in the eyes of some of our people, Mara. They're scared. They're looking to us for answers, for reassurance, and all I can give them is a carefully constructed illusion of control. And it gnaws at me. It gnaws at me that I can't be completely honest with them, that I have to resort to these... tactics."

He ran his free hand over his face, the gesture of a man wrestling with unseen demons. "I see the fear in your eyes too, Mara. I know this isn't what you envisioned when you first stepped into leadership. It's not the open, transparent society we dreamed of. It's becoming something more guarded, more... pragmatic. And that pragmatic survival comes with a moral cost. I feel that cost acutely."

Mara stepped closer, closing the small distance between them. She could feel the tremors of his unspoken anxieties, the raw honesty of his confession. It was in these moments, stripped of their roles and their responsibilities, that she saw the true depth of the man she loved. "We dreamed of a Havenridge that could thrive, Eli. And sometimes, thriving in a hostile environment means adapting. It means finding new ways to be strong. You're not corrupting us; you're safeguarding us. You're buying us time, time to regroup, time to find a solution that doesn't involve compromising who we are at our core. The intention behind your actions is pure, and that's what matters."

She reached up, her other hand cupping his cheek. His skin was warm beneath her touch, and she could feel the slight tremor in his jaw. "And as for the cost," she continued, her voice soft but firm, "we bear it together. You're not alone in this, Eli. You can't be. Your guilt is your burden to carry, but it's not yours to carry alone. We share this. We share the fear, the uncertainty, and yes, even the compromises."

Eli's eyes, when they met hers, were still shadowed with doubt, but there was a flicker of something else there too – a nascent hope, a quiet recognition of their shared strength. He leaned into her touch, his forehead resting against hers. The hum of the plaza's environmental systems seemed to fade into the background, replaced by the steady, comforting rhythm of their shared breath.

"It's just... seeing the effect it has on you too," he murmured, his voice muffled against her skin. "You have to be the beacon of hope, the one who inspires faith, and I know these machinations are a burden on your conscience, too. I see how it weighs on you, the constant need to reassure, to rebuild trust, while I'm the one chipping away at it, however necessary it may be."

"We are a partnership, Eli," Mara said, her voice resonating with conviction. "And partnerships are built on shared burdens. You're the shield, and I'm the heart. Without both, Havenridge wouldn't stand a chance. Your strength allows me to be hopeful, and my hope fuels your determination. It's a fragile balance, I know, but it's ours." She pressed a soft kiss to his lips, a fleeting touch that conveyed more than words ever could. "Don't let the weight of your duty crush you. Let it be a reminder of why we're fighting."

He pulled her closer, his arms wrapping around her waist, holding her with a fierce possessiveness that spoke volumes. Mara melted into his embrace, the solid warmth of his body a welcome anchor against the storm of anxieties that had been raging within her. She buried her face in his chest, breathing in the familiar scent of him – a mix of clean fabric, the faintest hint of ozone from his work, and something uniquely, undeniably Eli.

"I worry that we're losing pieces of ourselves in this fight," she confessed, her voice muffled by his uniform. "That the Havenridge we're trying to save will be a different place than the one we started with. That the 'necessity' of our actions will erode the very foundations of our values."

Eli held her tighter, his chin resting on the crown of her head. "I worry about that too, Mara. Every single day. But I also believe in our capacity to endure, to adapt, and to ultimately remain true to ourselves. We're not defined by our struggles, but by how we rise above them. And we will rise above this. Together." He pulled back just enough to look at her, his eyes searching hers. "The compromises we make now are temporary. The core of Havenridge, the spirit of our community, that's what we have to protect. And that's what I'm fighting for, Mara. For you, for our people, for the future we envisioned."

He gently stroked her hair, his touch a soothing balm. "Your faith in me, even when I doubt myself, is what keeps me grounded. Your unwavering belief in our ideals is a constant reminder of what we're fighting for. I can't do this without you, Mara. You are the bedrock upon which everything else rests."

Mara leaned her forehead against his again, a profound sense of peace settling over her. The shared vulnerability hadn't erased their fears, but it had transformed them. They were no longer individual burdens, but shared challenges, a testament to the strength of their partnership. In the quiet intimacy of their embrace, surrounded by the manufactured beauty of Havenridge, they found a renewed sense of purpose, a quiet understanding that their love and their shared resolve were their greatest weapons. The seeds of doubt might be sown, but the roots of their connection ran too deep to be easily uprooted. And in the gentle reassurance of his touch, in the quiet strength of his embrace, Mara knew that no matter what Thorne threw at them, they would face it, together. The whispered fears, when spoken aloud, lost some of their power, replaced by the quiet, resolute strength of two hearts beating as one, a powerful affirmation in the face of encroaching darkness.

Chapter Nine

The Price of Stability

The hum of Havenridge's life support systems, usually a comforting constant, seemed to take on a more anxious pitch. It was a subtle shift, almost imperceptible to those not attuned to the delicate rhythms of their meticulously engineered sanctuary, but Mara felt it like a tremor in her bones. She sat across the polished expanse of the communal dining table from Eli, the flickering holo-displays showcasing meticulously curated agricultural yields casting a shifting, almost desperate light on their faces. The usual scent of processed nutrient paste, a bland but reliable staple, was now underscored by something else – a faint, metallic tang of fear, a whisper of the anxiety that had begun to permeate their carefully constructed peace.

"The atmospheric processors in Sector Gamma are running at seventy-five percent capacity, Eli," Mara stated, her voice tight with a carefully controlled weariness. She gestured to a complex graph on the display, a jagged line depicting energy consumption spiraling upwards. "And the hydroponic farms in Delta Zone are reporting a twenty percent decrease in photosynthetic efficiency. The algae blooms are... sluggish."

Eli's gaze, usually sharp and resolute, was troubled as he studied the data. The lines of strain around his eyes seemed deeper tonight. "Sluggish isn't good, Mara. Not with the population surge in the last cycle. We've absorbed close to five hundred new arrivals from the Outer Sectors. Their metabolisms are higher, their demands greater." He ran a hand through his hair, a gesture of frustration he rarely allowed himself. "And the unexpected frost in the northern agricultural domes last week... that's a significant loss of cultivated protein crops."

"Significant is an understatement," Mara replied, her tone hardening slightly. "We're looking at a projected shortfall of nearly fifteen percent for the next three rotations. That's not just about reducing portion sizes; that's about actual scarcity. People will go hungry, Eli." The words hung heavy in the air, a stark counterpoint to the manufactured abundance Havenridge was built upon.

He nodded, his jaw tight. "I've already convened the Resource Allocation Committee. Thorne's faction is, predictably, pushing for immediate, draconian cuts to non-essential energy consumption. He claims it's a 'necessary austerity measure' to ensure continued stability."

Mara scoffed, the sound sharp and disbelieving. "Thorne. Of course. His 'stability' always seems to involve making life harder for everyone else while he and his inner circle maintain their privileges. He'll demand we shut down the recreational light gardens, reduce personal climate controls to the bare minimum, maybe even restrict water purification cycles for non-critical uses."

"Precisely," Eli confirmed, his voice low. "He's using this as an opportunity to consolidate his power, to further erode the communal spirit by fostering resentment and division. He'll paint any dissenting voice as irresponsible, a threat to the very survival of Havenridge."

"And what are *we* proposing?" Mara asked, her gaze unwavering, seeking reassurance that they weren't already succumbing to Thorne's corrosive influence. "We can't just implement his draconian measures without considering the impact on morale, on the very fabric of our society. We've always prided ourselves on fairness, on shared sacrifice, not on the arbitrary imposition of hardship."

Eli leaned forward, his elbows on the table, his hands clasped tightly. "We're proposing a phased rationing system. Gradual reductions in nutrient paste density, a ten percent decrease in non-essential energy allocation across all sectors – including Thorne's residential sector, which is already generating considerable ire from his own people, I might add – and a temporary suspension of new non-essential construction projects." He met her gaze, his eyes conveying the weight of the decision. "We're also initiating a voluntary community service initiative, focusing on optimizing resource reclamation and exploring alternative nutrient synthesis methods. It's an appeal to our shared responsibility, Mara, not an authoritarian decree."

"Voluntary is a nice word for 'politely pressured' when it comes to Thorne's opposition," Mara murmured, a cynical edge to her voice. "But it's the right approach. We need to show our people that we are being transparent, that we are making decisions for the good of all, not just to appease a demagogue." She sighed, rubbing her temples. "But even with these measures, Eli, are they enough? The atmospheric processors are struggling. If we get another unexpected anomaly – a solar flare, a micrometeoroid shower impacting our shielding, anything that further strains our environmental controls – we could be looking at a systemic collapse of our life support. The growth... it's outstripping our capacity to sustain it."

"That's the question that keeps me awake at night, Mara," Eli admitted, his voice raw with fatigue. "We've designed Havenridge for resilience, for long-term sustainability, but we didn't fully anticipate the compounding effects of prolonged resource strain coupled with such rapid population growth. The simulations were always based on a stable external environment and a more controlled influx of new citizens."

"And now we're paying the price for that optimism," Mara said, her voice quiet. "The promise of Havenridge was a safe harbor, a place where ingenuity and community could thrive. But if that thriving leads to depletion, if our success becomes the very thing that unravels us, then we've failed. We haven't just built a city; we've built a promise. And that promise is starting to feel fragile."

The committee meeting that followed was a testament to the growing unease. The scent of recycled air, usually neutral, felt heavy, laden with unspoken fears. Faces around the table, a mix of elected council members and sector representatives, were drawn and anxious. Even the stoic Chief Botanist, Elara Vance, whose dedication to the hydroponic farms was legendary, looked weary.

"The nutrient solution in Dome Seven is showing signs of imbalance," Elara reported, her voice a low, steady tone that nonetheless carried an undercurrent of urgency. "We suspect it's a reaction to the increased atmospheric CO_2 levels. We're trying to compensate, but our reserves of specific trace elements are running low. We can't synthesize them fast enough on-site, and the transport delays from the central processing unit are... problematic."

A representative from the Outer Sectors, a gruff man named Kaelen who had been vocal about the perceived inequities in resource distribution, slammed his hand on the table. "Transport delays? We're talking about food, Vance! My people are already receiving smaller rations. If your algae blooms are failing, tell us now! Don't give us euphemisms and technical jargon!"

Eli's voice cut through the rising tension, firm but not aggressive. "Kaelen, I understand your frustration. We are all concerned. Elara is doing her best with the resources available. We are working on expediting the delivery of those trace elements. However, to address the systemic issue, we need to consider a broader reallocation of energy resources. The atmospheric processors in Sector Gamma are consuming an alarming amount of power, and their efficiency is declining. If we can reroute some of that energy, even temporarily, to optimize the nutrient synthesis in Delta Zone, we might alleviate the immediate crisis for the hydroponic farms."

A ripple of murmurs went through the room. Rerouting energy from atmospheric processors meant a tangible reduction in air quality and temperature regulation in Sector Gamma. This was not a minor inconvenience; it was a direct impact on daily life.

Thorne, impeccably dressed as always, his expression one of concerned paternalism, spoke up. "Eli, with all due respect, diverting power from atmospheric control seems... counterproductive. Surely, we should be focusing on increasing production, not compromising the very air we breathe. Perhaps we need to re-examine the necessity of certain... non-essential functions. The recreational lighting in the central plaza, for instance. It consumes a significant amount of energy and serves little purpose beyond aesthetic pleasure."

Mara's eyes narrowed, but she kept her voice even. "The recreational lighting is not merely aesthetic, Thorne. It contributes to psychological well-being, particularly for those who have lived through the harsh realities of the Outer Sectors. For many, it's a symbol of hope, of the peace and stability Havenridge offers. Removing it would be a blow to morale, a sign that we are already sacrificing our quality of life, not just our excess."

"Morale is a luxury we may not be able to afford if our atmospheric processors fail," Thorne countered smoothly, his gaze sweeping across the council members. "We must prioritize survival. And survival, at this juncture, demands difficult choices. Choices that may not be popular, but are undeniably necessary."

Eli turned to Elara. "Elara, the projected impact of rerouting that energy to Delta Zone? Be specific."

Elara consulted a small data slate. "If we reroute fifteen percent of Sector Gamma's energy allocation to Delta Zone's nutrient synthesis facilities, we can expect a seventy percent increase in production output within forty-eight hours. This would bring us back to a sustainable level for protein paste synthesis within the next rotation. However, Sector Gamma's atmospheric regulation will drop to sixty percent efficiency. This will result in a noticeable increase in ambient temperature and a... slightly less pure air composition. It will be noticeable, but not immediately detrimental to health, provided no other environmental anomalies occur."

A silence descended. The choice was stark: immediate discomfort for a significant portion of the population in exchange for securing their food supply, or the risk of widespread hunger if the hydroponic farms failed completely.

Kaelen spoke again, his voice rough. "My people in the Outer Sectors are used to less than sixty percent efficiency, Elara. We'll take the 'slightly less pure' air if it means we get enough to eat. Thorne wants to turn off the lights? Fine. But we need food."

The sentiment echoed among several other representatives, particularly those from sectors that had experienced the most hardship before finding refuge in Havenridge. Thorne, however, remained unyielding.

"This is a shortsighted solution," Thorne declared, his voice laced with disdain. "We are addressing a symptom, not the cause. The true cause is our unchecked growth. We are importing instability. We need to implement stricter population controls, and perhaps even consider... repurposing certain sectors to accommodate essential agricultural expansion, which would, regrettably, require the relocation of some residents."

Mara felt a cold dread creep into her gut. Repurposing sectors. Relocating residents. This was not the Havenridge she had envisioned. This was a slide into the very authoritarianism they had fled.

"Thorne, you know we cannot simply 'repurpose' residential sectors without immense social disruption and hardship," Eli stated, his voice dangerously low. "Those are not empty spaces; they are homes. We have protocols for integration and expansion, not displacement.

And population controls implemented in such a manner would be a direct violation of our founding principles."

"Principles are admirable, Eli, but they do not feed a starving populace," Thorne retorted, a hint of steel beneath his calm facade. "Stability requires pragmatism. If our current trajectory leads to collapse, then our principles must adapt. Or we perish clinging to them."

Mara finally spoke, her voice clear and resonant, cutting through the bickering. "We are not at the precipice of collapse, Thorne. We are facing a challenge, a significant one, but a challenge we can overcome through collaboration and sensible resource management. Rerouting energy to support our food production is a pragmatic, immediate solution. It prioritizes life. As for long-term sustainability, we can explore all options – optimizing existing infrastructure, developing more efficient energy sources, perhaps even initiating controlled, phased expansion into newly terraformed zones outside Havenridge, but only when we are certain we can sustain them. But we will not achieve this by sacrificing our core values, by turning our backs on our people, or by succumbing to fear-mongering."

She looked directly at Thorne, her gaze unwavering. "The energy used for the plaza lights is a fraction of what is consumed by your own private research facilities, Thorne. If we are to make sacrifices, they must be shared equally, and transparently. Let us focus on solving the immediate crisis of food scarcity, and then we can have a more productive discussion about long-term planning. But not at the expense of our humanity."

The council members shifted, some nodding in agreement, others looking uncomfortable. Thorne's carefully constructed facade of benevolent authority had been challenged, and the subtle power play was evident.

Eli seized the moment. "Mara is right. Our priority is to ensure everyone has adequate sustenance. The proposal to reroute energy from Sector Gamma to Delta Zone is approved. Implement it immediately. Kaelen, I want you to personally oversee the distribution adjustments in your sector and report back on public sentiment. Elara, keep us updated on the synthesis rates. Thorne, I expect your full cooperation in ensuring equitable energy reduction across all sectors, including your own facilities."

The meeting adjourned with a sense of uneasy resolution. The immediate crisis had been addressed, but the underlying tensions remained. The very success of Havenridge, its ability to attract and shelter more people, had brought them to this precipice. The carefully balanced systems, designed for a population that had once been much smaller, were now groaning under the strain.

Later that evening, as Mara and Eli walked through one of the less frequented corridors of Havenridge, the air was noticeably warmer. The familiar, clean scent of the recycled atmosphere was tinged with a faint, almost imperceptible humidity, a subtle indicator of the rerouted energy.

"You handled Thorne well," Eli said, his voice a low murmur in the quiet. "He's cornered, for now. But he won't forget that challenge."

"He doesn't need to," Mara replied, her hand finding his. His fingers intertwined with hers, a silent exchange of reassurance. "What matters is that we're trying to find solutions that don't involve sacrificing our principles. But Eli," she paused, her gaze meeting his, the dim corridor lights reflecting in her eyes, "this is just the beginning, isn't it? We've managed this crisis, but the fundamental issue remains. Our growth is outpacing our resources. The atmospheric processors will continue to strain, the farms will demand more, and the population will keep coming."

Eli squeezed her hand. "I know. This isn't about a single decision; it's about a fundamental reevaluation of our entire operational model. We need to invest heavily in new energy generation – advanced fusion, perhaps, or even geothermal tapping if the geological surveys prove promising. We need to explore vertical farming techniques that are even more resource-efficient. And we need to engage in honest conversations with our citizens about the limitations, about the need for responsible consumption and, perhaps, a more sustainable pace of growth."

"Honest conversations," Mara echoed, a faint smile touching her lips. "That might be the hardest part, especially with Thorne actively sowing discord. He thrives on manufactured scarcity, on creating divisions so he can exploit them."

"Then we must counter his narratives with truth and with action," Eli said, his voice firm. "We show them that collective effort, guided by integrity, is more powerful than fear and manipulation. But it will require more than just me and you, Mara. It will require the full commitment of our people, a willingness to adapt and to innovate, to redefine what 'stability' truly means in a dynamic environment."

They stopped, the corridor a quiet alcove in the vastness of Havenridge. The air here, further from the direct impact of the energy shift, was still within acceptable parameters, but the subtle change served as a constant reminder of their precarious balance.

"I worry that 'redefining stability' will involve compromises we are not prepared to make," Mara admitted, her voice barely a whisper. "We've always prided ourselves on offering refuge, on opening our doors. What happens when that generosity, when that fundamental act of welcome, becomes a threat to our own existence? Do we close the gates? Do we start turning people away? That feels like a betrayal of everything we stand for."

Eli pulled her gently towards him, wrapping an arm around her waist. She leaned into his strength, drawing solace from his presence. "We don't have to make that choice today, Mara. But we must acknowledge the possibility. We must prepare for it. Perhaps 'stability' means ensuring our own survival first, so that we can continue to be a beacon for others in the future. It's a difficult ethical tightrope, and I don't have all the answers."

He looked down at her, his expression earnest. "But I know this: whatever decisions we make, we make them together. And we face the consequences together. The weight of this responsibility... it's immense. But sharing it with you makes it bearable. It makes it, dare I say, hopeful."

"And what are

we proposing?" Mara asked, her gaze unwavering, seeking reassurance that they weren't already succumbing to Thorne's corrosive influence. "We can't just implement his draconian measures without considering the impact on morale, on the very fabric of our society. We've always prided ourselves on fairness, on shared sacrifice, not on the arbitrary imposition of hardship."

Eli leaned forward, his elbows on the table, his hands clasped tightly. "We're proposing a phased rationing system. Gradual reductions in nutrient paste density, a ten percent decrease in non-essential energy allocation across all sectors – including Thorne's residential sector, which is already generating considerable ire from his own people, I might add – and a temporary suspension of new non-essential construction projects." He met her gaze, his eyes conveying the weight of the decision. "We're also initiating a voluntary community service initiative, focusing on optimizing resource reclamation and exploring alternative nutrient synthesis methods. It's an appeal to our shared responsibility, Mara, not an authoritarian decree."

"Voluntary is a nice word for 'politely pressured' when it comes to Thorne's opposition," Mara murmured, a cynical edge to her voice. "But it's the right approach. We need to show our people that we are being transparent, that we are making decisions for the good of all, not just to appease a demagogue." She sighed, rubbing her temples. "But even with these measures, Eli, are they enough? The atmospheric processors are struggling. If we get another unexpected anomaly – a solar flare, a micrometeoroid shower impacting our shielding, anything that further strains our environmental controls – we could be looking at a systemic collapse of our life support. The growth... it's outstripping our capacity to sustain it."

"That's the question that keeps me awake at night, Mara," Eli admitted, his voice raw with fatigue. "We've designed Havenridge for resilience, for long-term sustainability, but we didn't fully anticipate the compounding effects of prolonged resource strain coupled with such rapid population growth. The simulations were always based on a stable external environment and a more controlled influx of new citizens."

"And now we're paying the price for that optimism," Mara said, her voice quiet. "The promise of Havenridge was a safe harbor, a place where ingenuity and community could thrive. But if that thriving leads to depletion, if our success becomes the very thing that unravels us, then we've failed. We haven't just built a city; we've built a promise. And that promise is starting to feel fragile."

The committee meeting that followed was a testament to the growing unease. The scent of recycled air, usually neutral, felt heavy, laden with unspoken fears. Faces around the table, a mix of elected council members and sector representatives, were drawn and anxious. Even the stoic Chief Botanist, Elara Vance, whose dedication to the hydroponic farms was legendary, looked weary.

"The nutrient solution in Dome Seven is showing signs of imbalance," Elara reported, her voice a low, steady tone that nonetheless carried an undercurrent of urgency. "We suspect it's a reaction to the increased atmospheric CO_2 levels. We're trying to compensate, but our reserves of specific trace elements are running low. We can't synthesize them fast enough on-site, and the transport delays from the central processing unit are... problematic."

A representative from the Outer Sectors, a gruff man named Kaelen who had been vocal about the perceived inequities in resource distribution, slammed his hand on the table. "Transport delays? We're talking about food, Vance! My people are already receiving smaller rations. If your algae blooms are failing, tell us now! Don't give us euphemisms and technical jargon!"

Eli's voice cut through the rising tension, firm but not aggressive. "Kaelen, I understand your frustration. We are all concerned. Elara is doing her best with the resources available. We are working on expediting the delivery of those trace elements. However, to address the systemic issue, we need to consider a broader reallocation of energy resources. The atmospheric processors in Sector Gamma are consuming an alarming amount of power, and their efficiency is declining. If we can reroute some of that energy, even temporarily, to optimize the nutrient synthesis in Delta Zone, we might alleviate the immediate crisis for the hydroponic farms."

A ripple of murmurs went through the room. Rerouting energy from atmospheric processors meant a tangible reduction in air quality and temperature regulation in Sector Gamma. This was not a minor inconvenience; it was a direct impact on daily life.

Thorne, impeccably dressed as always, his expression one of concerned paternalism, spoke up. "Eli, with all due respect, diverting power from atmospheric control seems... counterproductive. Surely, we should be focusing on increasing production, not compromising the very air we breathe. Perhaps we need to re-examine the necessity of certain... non-essential functions. The recreational lighting in the central plaza, for instance. It consumes a significant amount of energy and serves little purpose beyond aesthetic pleasure."

Mara's eyes narrowed, but she kept her voice even. "The recreational lighting is not merely aesthetic, Thorne. It contributes to psychological well-being, particularly for those who have lived through the harsh realities of the Outer Sectors. For many, it's a symbol of hope, of the peace and stability Havenridge offers. Removing it would be a blow to morale, a sign that we are already sacrificing our quality of life, not just our excess."

"Morale is a luxury we may not be able to afford if our atmospheric processors fail," Thorne countered smoothly, his gaze sweeping across the council members. "We must prioritize survival. And survival, at this juncture, demands difficult choices. Choices that may not be popular, but are undeniably necessary."

Eli turned to Elara. "Elara, the projected impact of rerouting that energy to Delta Zone? Be specific."

Elara consulted a small data slate. "If we reroute fifteen percent of Sector Gamma's energy allocation to Delta Zone's nutrient synthesis facilities, we can expect a seventy percent increase in production output within forty-eight hours. This would bring us back to a sustainable level for protein paste synthesis within the next rotation. However, Sector Gamma's atmospheric regulation will drop to sixty percent efficiency. This will result in a noticeable increase in ambient temperature and a... slightly less pure air composition. It will be noticeable, but not immediately detrimental to health, provided no other environmental anomalies occur."

A silence descended. The choice was stark: immediate discomfort for a significant portion of the population in exchange for securing their food supply, or the risk of widespread hunger if the hydroponic farms failed completely.

Kaelen spoke again, his voice rough. "My people in the Outer Sectors are used to less than sixty percent efficiency, Elara. We'll take the 'slightly less pure' air if it means we get enough to eat. Thorne wants to turn off the lights? Fine. But we need food."

The sentiment echoed among several other representatives, particularly those from sectors that had experienced the most hardship before finding refuge in Havenridge. Thorne, however, remained unyielding.

"This is a shortsighted solution," Thorne declared, his voice laced with disdain. "We are addressing a symptom, not the cause. The true cause is our unchecked growth. We are importing instability. We need to implement stricter population controls, and perhaps even consider... repurposing certain sectors to accommodate essential agricultural expansion, which would, regrettably, require the relocation of some residents."

Mara felt a cold dread creep into her gut. Repurposing sectors. Relocating residents. This was not the Havenridge she had envisioned. This was a slide into the very authoritarianism they had fled.

"Thorne, you know we cannot simply 'repurpose' residential sectors without immense social disruption and hardship," Eli stated, his voice dangerously low. "Those are not empty spaces; they are homes. We have protocols for integration and expansion, not displacement. And population controls implemented in such a manner would be a direct violation of our founding principles."

"Principles are admirable, Eli, but they do not feed a starving populace," Thorne retorted, a hint of steel beneath his calm facade. "Stability requires pragmatism. If our current trajectory leads to collapse, then our principles must adapt. Or we perish clinging to them."

Mara finally spoke, her voice clear and resonant, cutting through the bickering. "We are not at the precipice of collapse, Thorne. We are facing a challenge, a significant one, but a challenge we can overcome through collaboration and sensible resource management. Rerouting energy to support our food production is a pragmatic, immediate solution. It prioritizes life. As for long-term sustainability, we can explore all options – optimizing existing infrastructure, developing more efficient energy sources, perhaps even initiating controlled, phased expansion into newly terraformed zones outside Havenridge, but only when we are certain we can sustain them. But we will not achieve this by sacrificing our core values, by turning our backs on our people, or by succumbing to fear-mongering."

She looked directly at Thorne, her gaze unwavering. "The energy used for the plaza lights is a fraction of what is consumed by your own private research facilities, Thorne. If we are to make sacrifices, they must be shared equally, and transparently. Let us focus on solving the immediate crisis of food scarcity, and then we can have a more productive discussion about long-term planning. But not at the expense of our humanity."

The council members shifted, some nodding in agreement, others looking uncomfortable. Thorne's carefully constructed facade of benevolent authority had been challenged, and the subtle power play was evident.

Eli seized the moment. "Mara is right. Our priority is to ensure everyone has adequate sustenance. The proposal to reroute energy from Sector Gamma to Delta Zone is approved. Implement it immediately. Kaelen, I want you to personally oversee the distribution adjustments in your sector and report back on public sentiment. Elara, keep us updated on the synthesis rates. Thorne, I expect your full cooperation in ensuring equitable energy reduction across all sectors, including your own facilities."

The meeting adjourned with a sense of uneasy resolution. The immediate crisis had been addressed, but the underlying tensions remained. The very success of Havenridge, its ability to attract and shelter more people, had brought them to this precipice. The carefully balanced systems, designed for a population that had once been much smaller, were now groaning under the strain.

Later that evening, as Mara and Eli walked through one of the less frequented corridors of Havenridge, the air was noticeably warmer. The familiar, clean scent of the recycled atmosphere was tinged with a faint, almost imperceptible humidity, a subtle indicator of the rerouted energy.

"You handled Thorne well," Eli said, his voice a low murmur in the quiet. "He's cornered, for now. But he won't forget that challenge."

"He doesn't need to," Mara replied, her hand finding his. His fingers intertwined with hers, a silent exchange of reassurance. "What matters is that we're trying to find solutions that don't involve sacrificing our principles. But Eli," she paused, her gaze meeting his, the dim corridor lights reflecting in her eyes, "this is just the beginning, isn't it? We've managed this crisis, but the fundamental issue remains. Our growth is outpacing our resources. The atmospheric processors will continue to strain, the farms will demand more, and the population will keep coming."

Eli squeezed her hand. "I know. This isn't about a single decision; it's about a fundamental reevaluation of our entire operational model. We need to invest heavily in new energy generation – advanced fusion, perhaps, or even geothermal tapping if the geological surveys prove promising. We need to explore vertical farming techniques that are even more resource-efficient. And we need to engage in honest conversations with our citizens about the limitations, about the need for responsible consumption and, perhaps, a more sustainable pace of growth."

"Honest conversations," Mara echoed, a faint smile touching her lips. "That might be the hardest part, especially with Thorne actively sowing discord. He thrives on manufactured scarcity, on creating divisions so he can exploit them."

"Then we must counter his narratives with truth and with action," Eli said, his voice firm. "We show them that collective effort, guided by integrity, is more powerful than fear and manipulation. But it will require more than just me and you, Mara. It will require the full commitment of our people, a willingness to adapt and to innovate, to redefine what 'stability' truly means in a dynamic environment."

They stopped, the corridor a quiet alcove in the vastness of Havenridge. The air here, further from the direct impact of the energy shift, was still within acceptable parameters, but the subtle change served as a constant reminder of their precarious balance.

"I worry that 'redefining stability' will involve compromises we are not prepared to make," Mara admitted, her voice barely a whisper. "We've always prided ourselves on offering refuge, on opening our doors. What happens when that generosity, when that fundamental act of welcome, becomes a threat to our own existence? Do we close the gates? Do we start turning people away? That feels like a betrayal of everything we stand for."

Eli pulled her gently towards him, wrapping an arm around her waist. She leaned into his strength, drawing solace from his presence. "We don't have to make that choice today, Mara. But we must acknowledge the possibility. We must prepare for it. Perhaps 'stability' means ensuring our own survival first, so that we can continue to be a beacon for others in the future. It's a difficult ethical tightrope, and I don't have all the answers."

He looked down at her, his expression earnest. "But I know this: whatever decisions we make, we make them together. And we face the consequences together. The weight of this responsibility... it's immense. But sharing it with you makes it bearable. It makes it, dare I say, hopeful."

Mara looked up at him, the dim light catching the sincerity in his eyes. The challenges were daunting, the future uncertain, but in this shared moment of quiet reflection, amidst the humming heart of their struggling sanctuary, she found a renewed sense of purpose. The price of stability was proving to be a steep one, measured not just in energy allocations and nutrient rations, but in the constant negotiation between their ideals and the harsh realities of survival. And as they stood there, two souls bound by duty and by love, they knew that the true test of Havenridge, and of themselves, was yet to come. The resource scarcity was not just a logistical problem; it was an existential threat, a crucible that would forge their future, for better or for worse.

The gentle thrum of Havenridge's life support, a symphony of intricate machinery that had always lulled Mara into a sense of secure predictability, now seemed to carry a discordant note. It was a subtle dissonance, a whisper against the steady hum, that only those intimately familiar with its rhythms could detect. Yet, it resonated within Mara, a disquieting tremor that mirrored the growing unease in the meticulously ordered sanctuary. Across the polished expanse of the communal dining hall, Eli's presence was a grounding anchor, but even his usually unshakeable resolve seemed to waver. The holographic displays, usually a testament to Havenridge's bounty, cast an almost anxious luminescence on their faces, highlighting the deepening lines of concern etched around Eli's eyes. The bland, familiar scent of nutrient paste, the bedrock of their sustenance, was now overlaid with a faint, metallic tang—the unmistakable odor of apprehension.

"The atmospheric processors in Sector Gamma are operating at seventy-five percent capacity, Eli," Mara's voice was strained, a carefully modulated tone that barely masked the weariness within. She gestured to a complex graph on the display, a jagged line depicting energy consumption spiraling upwards with an alarming trajectory. "And the hydroponic farms in Delta Zone are reporting a twenty percent decrease in photosynthetic efficiency. The algae blooms are... sluggish."

Eli's gaze, typically sharp and decisive, was clouded with worry as he absorbed the data. He ran a hand through his close-cropped hair, a rare gesture of frustration. "Sluggish isn't a word we can afford to hear, Mara. Not with the surge in arrivals we've seen in the last cycle. We've absorbed close to five hundred new individuals from the Outer Sectors. Their metabolisms are higher, their demands greater." He sighed, the sound heavy with the weight of their shared burden. "And then there was that unexpected frost in the northern agricultural domes last week... that's a significant loss of cultivated protein crops. A loss we hadn't factored into our projections."

"Significant is an understatement," Mara replied, her tone hardening with a defensive edge. "We're looking at a projected shortfall of nearly fifteen percent for the next three rotations. This isn't just about marginally reduced portion sizes; this is about genuine scarcity. People will go hungry, Eli. The promise of Havenridge was abundance, not rationing." The words hung in the recycled air, a stark refutation of the engineered prosperity that defined their existence.

He nodded, his jaw tight, the familiar set of his shoulders betraying the immense pressure he was under. "I've already convened the Resource Allocation Committee. Thorne's faction is, predictably, pushing for immediate, draconian cuts to non-essential energy consumption. He's framing it as a 'necessary austerity measure' to ensure continued stability, a predictable play from his playbook."

Mara let out a sharp, disbelieving scoff. "Thorne. Of course. His definition of 'stability' always seems to involve making life demonstrably harder for everyone else while he and his inner circle maintain their privileged positions. He'll demand we shut down the recreational light gardens, reduce personal climate controls to the bare minimum, perhaps even restrict water purification cycles for non-critical uses. He'll weaponize our own systems against us."

"Precisely," Eli confirmed, his voice dropping to a low, serious tone. "He's using this as an opportunity to consolidate his power, to further erode the communal spirit by fostering resentment and division. He'll paint any dissenting voice as irresponsible, a threat to the very survival of Havenridge, using fear as his primary tool."

The laughter of children, echoing faintly from a distant recreational dome, served as a poignant counterpoint to their serious discussions, a reminder of what they were fighting to protect, and the profound importance of finding a way to sustain not just their lives, but their very humanity. It was a delicate balance, a tightrope walk over an abyss of scarcity, and they were only just beginning to understand the true cost of stability.

The air in the grand reception chamber, usually reserved for formal gatherings and rare diplomatic encounters, crackled with an energy that was both exciting and deeply unsettling. It was the scent of the new arrivals, a sharp, almost sterile ozone mingled with the fainter, yet distinct, aroma of exotic alloys and pressurized containment fields – the hallmark of technology far beyond Havenridge's current capabilities. This was the delegation. They had arrived not with a whisper, but with the quiet efficiency of well-oiled machinery, their transport humming softly in the external docking bay, a stark contrast to the familiar, comforting pulse of Havenridge's own systems.

Eli stood beside Mara, his posture rigid, a subtle tension in the set of his jaw that spoke volumes about his apprehension. He met her gaze, a flicker of shared understanding passing between them. This was not a visit of mutual aid; it was an overture, a carefully orchestrated move designed to leverage their current vulnerabilities. The delegation, representing a coalition of technologically advanced, though geographically disparate, settlements from the fringe sectors, had presented their offer with a veneer of magnanimity. They spoke of shared futures, of mutual prosperity, and of the inherent risks of isolation in an increasingly volatile cosmos.

"Havenridge," the lead delegate, a woman named Seraphina Thorne (no relation, Mara noted with a grim irony, to their own council member), began, her voice smooth and modulated, as if filtered through some unseen vocal enhancer, "has long been a beacon of self-sufficiency, a testament to human resilience. But the winds of change are sweeping across the sectors. Unforeseen celestial events, the resurgence of piratical elements, and the growing resource demands of burgeoning populations – these are challenges that no single entity can fully withstand alone." She gestured to a shimmering holographic display that materialized in the center of the chamber, depicting a stylized map of their known space, dotted with the various settlements, interconnected by glowing lines that pulsed with a soft, vibrant light. "We, the Consortium of Federated Systems, have observed your growth, your dedication to your people. And we wish to offer our partnership."

The 'partnership,' as Seraphina outlined it, was undeniably attractive on the surface. They offered advanced atmospheric processors, far more efficient than Havenridge's current models, capable of filtering even the most volatile atmospheric contaminants and operating at peak performance with significantly less energy expenditure. They proposed next-generation hydroponic nutrient synthesis units, promising to eliminate the very food scarcity that was currently gnawing at Havenridge's stability. Their technological package included advanced energy conduits that could harness ambient stellar radiation, reducing their reliance on internal power generation, and sophisticated terraforming schematics for potential future expansion, should Havenridge ever consider venturing beyond its current subterranean confines. It was a dazzling array of solutions, a technological panacea for their most pressing problems.

But the price, subtly woven into the fabric of their proposal, was the true catalyst for Mara's unease. "In exchange for these invaluable advancements," Seraphina continued, her gaze sweeping across the assembled council members, her smile practiced and reassuring, "we request a seat on your Resource Allocation Committee. A supervisory role, if you will, to ensure the optimal integration and utilization of these new systems. Furthermore, we would require access to your production manifests and a degree of oversight regarding your population growth projections. This is not about intrusion, but about synergistic management. To ensure that your continued prosperity does not create unforeseen imbalances within the wider regional ecosystem."

Eli's hand tightened on Mara's arm, a silent communication of alarm. 'Synergistic management' was a sanitized term for control. 'Oversight' was a polite word for dictation. He met Mara's eyes again, and this time, the shared understanding was laced with a cold dread. They were being offered a gilded cage, a comfortable dependency that would slowly, insidiously, erode their autonomy. The advanced technology was alluring, the promise of immediate relief intoxicating, but the cost was their freedom, their hard-won independence.

Mara felt it acutely, a phantom sting against her skin, the scent of ozone from the delegation's advanced technology a stark and unwelcome contrast to the familiar, earth-tinged air of Havenridge, the faint aroma of nutrient paste from the communal kitchens, the underlying scent of recycled air and the subtle, earthy notes from the hydroponic farms. This was the smell of a compromise she was loath to make. Their independence was not merely a matter of self-governance; it was woven into the very identity of Havenridge, into the spirit of its people, who had chosen this secluded existence precisely to escape the controlling tendrils of larger, more powerful entities.

"You speak of regional imbalances," Mara stated, her voice carefully measured, projecting an outward calm that belied the tempest within her. "But Havenridge has always striven for internal balance. We have grown, yes, and we face challenges, but we have faced them together, as a unified community. This offer... it suggests a distrust in our ability to manage our own affairs."

Seraphina's smile didn't waver. "Not distrust, Esteemed Mara, but shared responsibility. The sectors are becoming increasingly interconnected. A localized instability in Havenridge could, in turn, create ripples that affect us all. The Consortium's mandate is to foster stability across our sphere of influence. Your unique position, your dedication to your people, makes you an invaluable partner in this endeavor."

Eli stepped forward, his voice resonating with a quiet authority. "We appreciate the offer of technological assistance. Indeed, the advancements you propose are impressive and could alleviate many of our current pressures. However, the terms you suggest, particularly concerning governance and resource allocation, are not aligned with our foundational principles. Havenridge was established as a sanctuary, a place where its citizens could chart their own course, free from external impositions."

Another delegate, a sharp-faced man with eyes that seemed to catalog every detail of the room, chimed in. "But surely, the preservation of your people, the continued security of Havenridge, is paramount? Our assistance offers a direct path to securing that future. To reject it outright would be... short-sighted, would it not? Especially when considering the unpredictable nature of interstellar affairs. A sole entity, however well-intentioned, can be vulnerable. A united front, however, is formidable."

The implication hung heavy in the air: Havenridge, in its current state, was vulnerable. Their resource strains, their growing population, the very challenges they were grappling with, were being weaponized against them. The Consortium was presenting themselves not just as benefactors, but as saviors, offering salvation at the cost of their self-determination.

Mara felt a surge of defiance, a fierce protectiveness for the community they had built. She saw the calculating glint in Seraphina's eyes, the subtle pressure being applied. Thorne, seated in the front row of the council, offered a small, almost imperceptible nod of approval towards the delegates, his own agenda clearly aligning with their desire for centralized control. He saw an opportunity to consolidate power, not just within Havenridge, but potentially within the wider Consortium.

"We are not in need of saving, but of partnership," Mara countered, her voice firm, her gaze meeting Seraphina's directly. "And true partnership is built on mutual respect and autonomy, not on veiled demands for control. Your technology is advanced, your resources are substantial, but our independence, our right to self-governance, is not a commodity to be traded. We value our resilience, our ability to solve our own problems, even when it is difficult. Especially when it is difficult."

The scent of ozone seemed to intensify, a subtle, almost subliminal reminder of the power the Consortium wielded, the immense technological advantage they possessed. It was the scent of a superior force, offering a solution that felt suspiciously like a subjugation. The delegation's presence, their impeccably tailored uniforms, their technologically advanced accouterments, all served as a stark reminder of Havenridge's relative limitations. They were a self-made sanctuary, built on grit and ingenuity, but compared to the Consortium, they were an emerging settlement, a fledgling community still finding its footing.

Eli stepped forward again, his voice a steady anchor amidst the rising tension. "We will consider your offer of technological assistance, of course. We are always open to exploring avenues that benefit our citizens. But any agreement must respect our sovereignty and the will of our people. We will not relinquish our right to self-determination for any price, however attractive the package may seem."

Seraphina inclined her head, a subtle acknowledgment that their initial overture had been met with resistance, but not outright dismissal. "Understandable. We respect Havenridge's commitment to its principles. We will provide you with detailed schematics and performance data for our proposed technologies. Our offer of partnership remains open. We believe that in these uncertain times, unity is not merely an option, but a necessity. We await your decision."

The delegates rose, their movements precise and coordinated. The holographic display dissolved, leaving only the sterile scent of ozone lingering in the air, a silent testament to the unspoken price of their proposed stability. As they filed out of the chamber, Mara felt the weight of their offer pressing down on her, a heavy cloak of potential compromise. The immediate needs of her people, the hum of their growing population, the whisper of hunger in the communal halls, all clamored for attention. But the thought of surrendering their independence, of becoming a mere appendage to a larger, more controlling entity, felt like a betrayal of the very foundations upon which Havenridge had been built. The path ahead was fraught with peril, a delicate balance between securing their immediate future and preserving the soul of their sanctuary. The scent of ozone, once excitingly exotic, now felt like a warning, a harbinger of a future where their hard-won peace might come at the cost of their very identity. The allure of their advanced technology was a siren song, promising an end to their struggles, but Mara knew, with a certainty that chilled her to the bone, that such promises often came with strings attached, strings that could bind them tightly, suffocating the spirit of freedom that defined them.

The scent of ozone, a sharp, almost metallic tang, still clung to the air in Eli's private study, a lingering reminder of the Consortium's departure. It was a scent that had become synonymous with temptation, with a solution that promised relief but demanded surrender. He stood by the reinforced viewport, gazing out at the familiar, dimly lit tunnels of Havenridge, his reflection a distorted silhouette against the sterile glow. The silence of his study was a stark contrast to the veiled tensions of the reception chamber, a silence that now amplified the turmoil within him. He had agreed to their terms, or at least, a carefully curated selection of them. It felt like a betrayal, a chipping away at the unyielding stone of Havenridge's independence, but the alternative, outright rejection, felt like a gamble he couldn't afford to take.

He had seen the desperation in the eyes of the council, the worried lines etched on the faces of his fellow citizens when the food stores were discussed, the anxiety surrounding the failing atmospheric processors. The Consortium's offer, with its dazzling technological solutions, had been a powerful balm to those fears, a siren song promising an end to their struggles. But Mara's unwavering conviction, her fierce defense of their autonomy, had resonated deeply. He knew she was right; true freedom was a prize worth fighting for. Yet, the gnawing reality of their vulnerability, the tangible threat of widespread hardship, had gnawed at his own resolve.

The compromise had been forged in the quiet moments after the delegation had left, a hushed, tense conversation with Mara. He had seen the conflict in her eyes, the same struggle he felt in his own soul. He knew she understood his reasoning, the desperate calculus of survival, but the inherent contradiction of their situation had created a chasm between them, a silent acknowledgment of the moral cost. He had chosen to share certain technical schematics – not the core designs of their energy generation or life support, but the intricate blueprints for their advanced water reclamation systems, and limited data on their mineral extraction processes. It felt like offering up a limb, a vital part of their self-sufficiency, but he had justified it to Mara as a strategic concession, a way to buy them time, to preserve their essential autonomy while appeasing the Consortium's insatiable appetite for control.

"It's a calculated risk, Mara," he had explained, his voice raspy with fatigue and the weight of his decision. "We give them something tangible, something that demonstrates our willingness to cooperate, but we withhold the very heart of our infrastructure. It's a way to keep them engaged, to keep them invested, without fundamentally compromising our ability to govern ourselves. It's a shield, a buffer, to prevent them from pushing for more, for the control they truly crave." He had tried to imbue his words with conviction, to convince himself as much as her, that this was a pragmatic, necessary step, a shrewd negotiation born of desperation, not a capitulation.

But the words felt hollow, even to his own ears. He had always believed in the power of principle, in the unwavering pursuit of ideals. Havenridge was built on that very foundation – a sanctuary from external control, a testament to the possibility of self-determination. To now offer up even a piece of that hard-won independence felt like a dilution of their very essence. He had justified it as a means to an end, a temporary concession to secure their immediate survival, but the insidious nature of compromise worried him. Once you opened the door a crack, how easy was it to keep it from being kicked wide open?

Sleep offered no respite. His dreams were a chaotic tapestry of swirling holograms, the Consortium's schematics merging with the faces of Havenridge's citizens, their pleas for sustenance and security echoing in his subconscious. He saw himself standing at a precipice, the Consortium's advanced technology gleaming below, a golden path leading to prosperity, but at its end, a dark shadow obscured the horizon. He dreamt of Mara's disappointed gaze, of Thorne's smug satisfaction, of the quiet erosion of their self-governance, replaced by the sterile, efficient dictates of the Federated Systems. He would wake in a cold sweat, the phantom scent of ozone suffocating him, the weight of his decision a physical ache in his chest.

He understood the theory of necessity, the pragmatism of survival. He had studied the histories of countless settlements that had fallen into ruin due to their inability to adapt, to make difficult choices. But theory was a sterile thing, far removed from the lived reality of this burden. This was not a detached intellectual exercise; it was a visceral, gut-wrenching compromise of his own deeply held beliefs. He had always seen himself as a protector, a guardian of Havenridge's ideals. Now, he felt like a gatekeeper, one who had inadvertently allowed a

Trojan horse to pass through the gates, albeit with its legs bound and its mouth gagged.

The schematics he had agreed to share were complex, detailing the multi-stage filtration and purification processes of their water reclamation. They were elegant in their simplicity, a testament to Havenridge's ingenuity in repurposing and optimizing existing technologies. They represented years of tireless work by their engineers, a vital component of their closed-loop ecosystem. To hand them over, even with the understanding that the Consortium would not have direct access to the operational oversight of Havenridge's water supply, felt like surrendering a key. The Consortium could analyze them, understand their limitations, perhaps even identify vulnerabilities they hadn't considered.

The resource data was equally sensitive. It comprised detailed reports on the mineral composition of the subterranean veins they had access to, their extraction rates, and their projected yields for the next two decades. This was the lifeblood of their manufacturing, the raw materials that fueled their continued existence. By sharing this, Eli was essentially giving the Consortium a roadmap to Havenridge's resource wealth, a clear indication of what they possessed and how much they could produce. It was a calculated gamble that they would focus on the immediate technological exchange and not immediately leverage this information for their own acquisition interests.

He replayed his conversations with Mara endlessly in his mind. Her quiet resilience, her unwavering belief in their community's strength, had been a constant source of inspiration. He knew she wouldn't abandon him, wouldn't judge him harshly, but he could see the shadow of concern in her eyes. The shared understanding between them, once a source of comfort, now felt strained, laced with the unspoken acknowledgment of this moral fissure. He had tried to articulate the delicate balance he was attempting to strike, the hope that this small concession would stave off a larger, more devastating loss of autonomy.

"We are not negotiating for our survival, Mara," he had insisted, his voice low and urgent. "We are negotiating for our future. The Consortium sees potential here, resources they can exploit, technology they can integrate. By offering them these pieces, we are showing them that they can achieve their goals without needing to exert absolute control. We are demonstrating that there is a path to mutual benefit, even if that benefit is disproportionately skewed in their favor for now. It's about managing their expectations, about redirecting their avarice into a less destructive channel."

But even as he spoke, a chilling realization dawned. He was rationalizing, twisting the narrative to fit a more palatable truth. He was trading away a piece of Havenridge's soul, not for guaranteed salvation, but for a chance, a slim hope, that they could navigate these treacherous waters without drowning. The idealism that had always guided him, the unwavering belief in the inherent rightness of their chosen path, felt like a luxury he could no longer afford. The harsh realities of inter-settlement politics, of power dynamics and resource scarcity, had forced his hand.

He picked up a stylus, the cool metal a grounding sensation in his palm, and began to meticulously review the digital files he had prepared. The schematics were clear, precise, devoid of the human ingenuity that had birthed them. They were just lines and data, stripped of their context, their origin story. He felt a pang of something akin to grief, a mourning for the untainted integrity of these designs, for the spirit of self-reliance they represented.

The implications of his decision extended beyond the immediate technological exchange. He had crossed a threshold, a point of no return. He had admitted, in a way, that Havenridge was not entirely self-sufficient, that there were areas where they required external assistance, even if it was only in the form of data. This admission, however subtly framed, could embolden the Consortium, could lead them to believe that Havenridge was ripe for further influence. He had hoped to buy time, but he had also, perhaps, opened a Pandora's Box of future demands.

He thought of the long-term consequences. If these shared schematics were instrumental in the Consortium's own technological advancements, would they then credit Havenridge? Or would they simply absorb the information, integrating it into their own vast network, rendering Havenridge's contribution anonymous and insignificant? The thought gnawed at him. He had acted out of a deep-seated desire to protect his people, to ensure their continued survival and prosperity, but the methods he had employed felt tainted, a betrayal of the very principles he had sworn to uphold.

He knew Mara would accept his decision, would stand by him, but he also knew that a subtle shift had occurred between them, a new layer of complexity added to their relationship. The unwritten covenant of their shared vision had been tested, and while it had not broken, it had been irrevocably altered. He had made a choice born of necessity, a pragmatic compromise that sat heavy on his conscience. The scent of ozone, once a symbol of exotic possibilities, now represented a Faustian bargain, a chilling reminder of the moral compromises required when idealism collided with the unforgiving realities of survival in a universe that rarely offered easy answers. The price of stability, he was learning, was often paid in the currency of one's own soul. He closed his eyes, the weight of that truth pressing down on him, a silent promise of many more sleepless nights to come.

The whispers began subtly, like a tremor beneath the polished surface of Havenridge's carefully constructed calm. They slithered through the hydroponic gardens, coiled in the recycled air of the communal halls, and buzzed with an almost audible intensity in the marketplace. The news, even carefully filtered, had spread like wildfire: Eli, their trusted leader, had struck a deal. A deal with *them*. The Consortium. And the heart of that deal, the part that festered most, was the sharing of resources. Not the core energy matrix, not the life-support schematics, but the intricate blueprints of their water reclamation systems and the precise mapping of their mineral extraction.

At first, it was a murmur of disbelief, then a chorus of outrage. "Betrayal!" the shouts echoed in the cavernous primary plaza, the word amplified by the sheer shock of it. "They're selling us out!" "Our autonomy, gone!" Faces that had always held a quiet pride now contorted with suspicion and fear. The very foundation of Havenridge, its hard-won independence, felt suddenly fragile, like a delicate spun-glass sculpture dropped on solid rock. The Consortium, a distant, monolithic entity that represented everything they had strived to escape, was now being invited, in part, into their inner sanctum.

Mara found herself at the epicenter of the storm. Her role as Second Representative, a position that had always demanded diplomacy and a steady hand, now felt like being a human shield against a tidal wave of emotion. She stood on the raised platform in the plaza, the air thick with unspoken accusations, her heart a heavy, leaden weight in her chest. Eli's decision had been a difficult one, a pragmatic gamble born of a dire necessity she understood all too well, but explaining that to a populace teetering on the brink of panic was a monumental task.

"I understand your anger," she began, her voice, though amplified, carried a tremor of her own unease. "I feel it too. The idea of giving any part of our hard-won independence, of sharing what makes us unique, is deeply unsettling. But I implore you, listen." She paused, scanning the sea of anxious faces. "Eli made a choice, a difficult one, not out of weakness, but out of a profound responsibility to ensure our survival. The Consortium's offer was not a demand we could ignore. It was a complex negotiation, a balancing act between our principles and our very existence."

The words seemed to land like pebbles against a fortress wall. "Survival? At what cost, Mara?" a man in the front row, a grizzled miner named Silas, shouted, his voice raw with indignation. "Our ingenuity, our self-sufficiency – those are the cornerstones of our survival! You hand over our water tech, our mineral maps, and what are we? Just another resource node for the Consortium's empire!"

A ripple of agreement spread through the crowd. The carefully guarded knowledge, the ingenuity born of necessity that had allowed Havenridge to thrive in its isolation, was now being laid bare. The water reclamation systems, a marvel of closed-loop efficiency, were the result of countless hours of dedicated work by their engineers, a testament to their ability to make something from nothing. The mineral reports, detailing the veins of precious ore that fueled their manufacturing and sustained their economy, represented their tangible wealth, their ability to stand on their own. To share these was not merely a concession; it felt like a fundamental breach of trust, a surrender of the very essence of their identity.

Mara's shoulders sagged for a fleeting moment, the weight of the collective disillusionment pressing down on her. She saw the fear in their eyes, the deeply ingrained mistrust of any external authority, a mistrust forged in the very crucible of their founding. "We did not give them everything," she countered, her voice gaining strength, fueled by a desperate need to anchor them to the truth. "The core of our energy, the heart of our life support, our strategic defense systems – those remain sacrosanct. Eli negotiated fiercely, ensuring that the most vital elements of our autonomy are protected. What we shared are schematics, data points, not operational control. The Consortium will analyze them, perhaps learn from them, but they will not dictate how we use them, nor will they gain direct access to our systems."

She could see the doubt still lingering. The Consortium was known for its insatiable appetite, its ability to twist any agreement to its advantage. The fear was not just of what was given, but of what this concession would inevitably lead to. "They see us as a valuable asset," she continued, choosing her words carefully. "By demonstrating our willingness to engage, to share certain knowledge, Eli's intent was to satisfy their immediate curiosity and perhaps their need for technological advancement, thus diverting them from more intrusive demands. It's a way to build a bridge, however precarious, rather than an impenetrable wall that they will inevitably try to break down."

The explanation, while logical, felt insufficient against the tide of raw emotion. The word "betrayal" hung heavy in the air, a phantom limb that ached with the memory of past injustices. Some in the crowd turned away, their faces set in grim determination, their whispers now laced with a new, dangerous resolve. Others, however, remained, their eyes searching Mara's for reassurance, for a flicker of the hope she so desperately tried to project.

In the days that followed, Mara found herself in a constant state of motion, a whirlwind of meetings and conversations. She moved from the bustling workshops where fabricators discussed potential impacts on their material procurement, to the quiet residential blocks where families worried about the long-term security of their community. She held informal gatherings, not on the grand plaza, but in smaller, more intimate spaces, seeking to foster dialogue rather than pronouncements.

One evening, she found herself in the community kitchen, the air thick with the comforting aroma of freshly baked bread. It was a scent that had become an unspoken symbol of Havenridge's self-sufficiency, a tangible manifestation of their ability to create sustenance from their own carefully managed resources. A group of bakers, their aprons dusted with flour, had gathered, their faces etched with worry.

"We've always been proud of what we can do here, Mara," old Mrs. Gable, her hands gnarled but still nimble, said, her voice soft but firm. "This bread... it's more than just food. It's a promise. A promise that we can feed ourselves, that we don't need to rely on anyone else."

Mara nodded, taking a deep breath of the warm, yeasty air. "And that promise remains unbroken, Mrs. Gable. The bread is still made with our grain, our yeast, our ovens. This deal, as difficult as it is, is not about diminishing our ability to bake bread. It's about ensuring we have the flour, the water, the energy to keep the ovens burning for generations to come."

She began to weave a new narrative, one that shifted the focus from loss to resilience, from capitulation to a renewed sense of internal strength. "We must see this not as an end, but as a catalyst," she urged, her voice resonating with a newfound conviction. "A catalyst for us to become even more resourceful, to innovate further, to strengthen our internal systems even more than before. If the Consortium is watching, let them see that Havenridge does not falter. Let them see that our spirit of ingenuity burns brighter when challenged."

She proposed a series of community-led initiatives, not just to appease the Consortium, but to empower Havenridge from within. "Let's form a task force," she suggested, her gaze sweeping across the bakers. "A task force dedicated to optimizing our current water reclamation processes even further, to find efficiencies we haven't yet discovered. Let's have another focused on exploring new mineral extraction techniques, perhaps more sustainable ones, or even identifying new, untapped sources within our existing territory. Let us show ourselves, and them, that our greatest resource is not what lies beneath the ground, but the minds and hands of our people."

The idea began to take root. The immediate anger, though not entirely quelled, began to transform into a more constructive energy. The bakers, inspired, started discussing ways to reduce water usage in their dough preparation, exploring new leavening agents that might require less moisture. The miners, initially resistant, began to talk about collaborative projects, sharing their expertise on geological surveying and extraction methods, pooling their knowledge to identify safer, more efficient methods.

Mara organized a series of forums, not just to explain the agreement, but to brainstorm. These weren't passive lectures; they were interactive sessions where citizens could voice their concerns, propose solutions, and contribute to the collective effort. She invited Eli to these forums, not to defend his decision, but to listen, to be present, and to reaffirm their shared commitment to Havenridge's future.

During one such forum, held in a repurposed research lab, a young engineer, Kai, stepped forward. He was one of the brilliant minds behind the water reclamation systems, and the prospect of sharing his designs had clearly pained him. "Mara," he began, his voice hesitant but clear, "I've been re-examining the schematics we've provided. There are redundancies, points of optimization within our own system that we've overlooked because, frankly, we've been operating at peak efficiency with our existing technology. Perhaps, in analyzing what we've given them, we can learn to improve what we still have."

This was the turning point. The fear of external exploitation was slowly being replaced by a sense of internal empowerment. The shared blueprints, rather than being a symbol of their vulnerability, were becoming a challenge. A challenge to innovate, to push their own boundaries, to prove that their self-sufficiency was not a static state but a dynamic, evolving force.

The scent of fresh bread, once a simple comfort, now carried a deeper meaning. It was a reminder of their roots, of their fundamental strengths, and of the enduring promise of self-determination. It was the aroma of resilience, wafting through the halls of Havenridge, a fragrant testament to their collective will to not just survive, but to thrive, even in the face of difficult compromise. Mara knew the path ahead would not be easy. The whispers of doubt might never fully disappear, and the shadow of the Consortium would always loom. But as she watched her people engage, not with anger, but with a renewed sense of purpose, she felt a flicker of hope. They were not just enduring; they were rebuilding, reinforcing their foundations, and rediscovering the true meaning of their autonomy, one loaf of bread, one shared idea, at a time.

CHAPTER TEN

Forging the Future

The air in Havenridge's primary research hub, usually a hum of controlled activity, now vibrated with an almost palpable energy. It was a symphony of focused creation, a testament to the collective will that had been ignited by necessity. The recent concessions, though still a source of lingering unease for some, had undeniably spurred a fervent drive towards self-improvement. Mara, her brow furrowed in concentration, meticulously examined a holographic projection of a novel filtration membrane. Its intricate lattice structure, designed to mimic the natural osmotic processes found in extremophile organisms, shimmered before her. This wasn't just about improving their existing water reclamation; it was about a paradigm shift, a leap towards a system so efficient it would render them virtually impervious to external resource fluctuations.

"The nanocarbon matrix is holding up under simulated pressure, Mara," Kai, the young engineer whose insights had been so crucial in reframing their perspective, reported from his console. His voice, usually tinged with a youthful exuberance, now carried a gravitas that belied his years. "We're seeing a purity index exceeding ninety-nine-point-nine percent, even with the simulated contaminants we introduced from the deep-well samples."

Mara nodded, a small smile touching her lips. "Excellent, Kai. And the energy expenditure for the osmotic pumps? Are we seeing the projected reduction?"

"We are. By nearly thirty percent compared to our current tertiary filtration. It's... it's remarkable, Mara. It feels like we're not just cleaning water; we're conjuring it from the very essence of the elements." He paused, then added, a touch of awe in his tone, "It's as if we've learned to speak the language of the planet's own lifeblood."

This was the heart of their renewed innovation: drawing inspiration from nature's most resilient systems. The salvaged Earth-based archives, once a repository of historical curiosities, had become a goldmine of biological and geological blueprints. Engineers and scientists pored over data on mangrove root systems, desert succulents, and deep-sea vent organisms, seeking to understand how life thrived in the harshest environments. The goal wasn't simply to replicate, but to synthesize, to adapt these principles to Havenridge's unique subterranean existence.

Eli, his usual meticulous demeanor amplified by the urgency of their situation, was overseeing a different, yet equally vital, aspect of their future-proofing. He stood amidst a cluster of workers in the structural engineering bay, his hands, usually reserved for precise schematics, now dusted with fine concrete powder. He pointed to a section of a massive, arching support beam, its surface a complex weave of bio-integrated composites.

"The tensile strength is holding beautifully, Mara," Eli called out, his voice carrying over the low thrum of machinery. "We're reinforcing the primary habitation domes with this new composite. It's designed to absorb seismic shock far more effectively than the original alloys.

Plus, the integrated nutrient channels will allow for auxiliary vertical farming to be incorporated directly into the dome's infrastructure. Think of it as a living, breathing shield."

Mara walked over, the scent of ozone and a faint, metallic tang of newly formed composites filling her nostrils. She ran a gloved hand over the beam's surface. "A living shield," she echoed, appreciating the dual purpose. "So, if we experience another tremor like the one that threatened Sector Gamma, these domes will not only withstand it but potentially offer a secondary food source if surface agriculture is impacted?"

"Precisely," Eli confirmed, his eyes alight with the satisfaction of a problem solved. "We're not just building structures; we're building ecosystems. Self-sustaining, resilient, and adaptable. We're future-proofing Havenridge against geological instability, against atmospheric shifts, against any unforeseen environmental challenge that the Great Unsettling might throw at us."

The workshops were a testament to this holistic approach. In one corner, fabricators meticulously wove intricate solar-collecting threads into flexible materials, designed to be integrated into clothing and structural coverings. These weren't the rigid, land-intensive panels of old Earth; these were adaptable, efficient energy harvesters that could function even in Havenridge's diffused ambient light. The process involved delicate nano-assembly, a far cry from the brute-force manufacturing of the past.

In another bay, biologists and chemists worked in tandem, exploring bio-luminescent algae strains that could not only provide sustainable, low-energy lighting for communal areas but also contribute to air purification. The idea was to create a symbiotic environment where every element served multiple purposes, minimizing waste and maximizing utility. The air was thick with the mingled aromas of ionized air from the 3D printers, the subtle, earthy scent of nascent bio-cultures, and the sharp, invigorating scent of ozone from the advanced welding processes.

"The challenges we face have forced us to look beyond the obvious," Mara mused aloud, gesturing towards a team of young technicians calibrating a new atmospheric moisture condenser. This unit, unlike their current models, utilized a complex series of bio-mimetic surfaces and phase-change materials to extract moisture with unprecedented efficiency, even from the relatively arid subterranean air. "We're not just trying to replace what we've shared; we're trying to surpass it. We're striving for a level of ingenuity that makes our past achievements seem rudimentary."

Kai joined her, wiping a smudge of lubricant from his cheek. "It's the pressure, isn't it? Knowing that our systems are being scrutinized, it's like an invisible deadline. But it's also a motivator. We want to prove that our capacity for innovation isn't diminished by sharing; it's amplified. It's like a competitive spirit has been awakened."

Eli chimed in, his voice a deep rumble of agreement. "And it's not just about technology. It's about mindset. We're retraining our engineers, our technicians, to think in terms of closed-loop systems, of biomimicry, of radical efficiency. We're fostering a culture where every problem is an opportunity for groundbreaking solutions, not just a setback."

He picked up a small, intricately machined component. "This housing for the new atmospheric sensor array, for example. It's made from a recycled polymer infused with a self-repairing microbial agent. If a micro-fracture occurs due to stress, the microbes activate, re-bonding the polymer. It's a small component, but it embodies the philosophy: resilience, sustainability, and intelligent design."

The commitment to sustainability was woven into every facet of their innovation. The materials used in the new designs were predominantly recycled or bio-derived. Waste products from one process were meticulously routed as feedstock for another. The energy capture systems were being diversified – beyond the enhanced solar collection, they were experimenting with geothermal taps, leveraging the planet's internal heat, and even exploring kinetic energy capture from water flow in their subterranean infrastructure.

Mara often found herself spending late hours in the research hub, drawn by the quiet dedication of the people working there. She'd watch as teams collaborated, their initial frustrations melting away as they found elegant solutions to complex problems. The scent of soldering irons, a familiar aroma in any engineering bay, was now overlaid with something fresher, something more organic, as bio-integration became commonplace.

One evening, she observed a small group working on a prototype for a bio-integrated filtration system. They were using a carefully cultivated strain of specialized fungi, known for its ability to break down complex organic compounds, to pre-process greywater before it entered the main purification cycle. The air around their station carried a faint, earthy, almost mushroom-like aroma, a stark contrast to the sterile, metallic scent that usually dominated such labs.

"It's surprisingly efficient, Mara," a biologist named Lena explained, her eyes shining with enthusiasm. "These fungi are incredibly robust. They thrive on the very contaminants that would clog our mechanical filters. And the byproduct... it's a nutrient-rich biomass that can be fed back into our hydroponic systems. It's a perfect symbiotic loop."

Mara felt a surge of pride, not just in the technological advancements, but in the collaborative spirit that fueled them. This wasn't just about survival; it was about thriving, about creating a more sophisticated, more sustainable existence than they had ever imagined. The deal with the Consortium, while a difficult pill to swallow, had indeed acted as a catalyst, forcing them to look inward and to unlock the full potential of their own ingenuity.

The drive for innovation extended beyond the tangible. There was a palpable shift in their collective consciousness. The fear of external dependence was slowly giving way to a fierce pride in their internal capabilities. They were demonstrating that their self-sufficiency wasn't a static state of being, but a dynamic, evolving process. The shared knowledge, rather than being a source of vulnerability, had become a benchmark against which they constantly strove to improve.

Eli's contribution wasn't limited to the physical infrastructure. He was also a keen observer of social engineering, and he recognized that resilience also meant fostering adaptability within the populace. He began initiating pilot programs for cross-training citizens in essential technical skills – basic hydroponics maintenance, emergency power grid operation, water system diagnostics. The idea was to create a distributed network of expertise, making Havenridge less reliant on specialized roles and more capable of adapting to unforeseen disruptions.

"If our primary water reclamation specialists are incapacitated, we need to have a significant portion of our population capable of stepping in, at least to maintain basic functionality," Eli explained to Mara during one of their strategy sessions, the scent of recycled polymers a constant companion in his office. "It's about redundancy, but it's also about empowering individuals. It gives them a sense of agency, a deeper understanding of how their community functions, and a stake in its continued operation."

The workshops continued to hum with activity. The scent of solder and ozone became a comforting background noise, a reminder of the ceaseless effort to build a more secure and sustainable future. Every new prototype, every refined process, was a defiant statement against the uncertainty that lay beyond their subterranean haven. They were not merely surviving; they were actively forging a future, brick by bio-integrated brick, circuit by intricate circuit, driven by the unwavering belief that their greatest resource was not in the earth beneath them, but within the minds and hands of their people. The lessons learned, the compromises made, were now being transformed into a blueprint for an even more robust and self-reliant Havenridge, a testament to their unyielding spirit of innovation.

The hum of the communal workspace had shifted. It was no longer the invigorating thrum of innovation, but a low, persistent buzz of tension that radiated from the delegation's assigned quarters. Eli's small cabin, usually a sanctuary of organized thought, had become the focal point of this unease. Mara sat across from him, the soft glow of a data slate illuminating her thoughtful expression. The concessions they'd made had been a necessary evil, a hard-won reprieve. But the price, it seemed, was an even deeper dissection of their inner workings, and Eli, with his unique history, was the primary target.

"They're digging, Eli," Mara stated, her voice low but firm. "The data we shared, the concessions regarding resource allocation and transparency... it's all been a key to unlock the next level of interrogation." She tapped a finger on the slate. "Their questions are becoming more... pointed. Less about current capabilities, more about historical predispositions."

Eli leaned back in his chair, a familiar, practiced calm settling over him. He'd anticipated this. The delegation, a collection of individuals representing various factions within the broader, fractured societal structure that had emerged from the Great Unsettling, were inherently suspicious. They operated on a foundation of distrust, a legacy of broken promises and territorial disputes. Eli's own past, a tapestry woven with threads of service to entities whose motives were now questionable at best, made him a prime candidate for their focused scrutiny.

"What specifically are they asking?" he inquired, his tone even. He knew the game. They wanted leverage, a weakness to exploit, a chink in his armor that could destabilize Havenridge's fragile autonomy. He had spent years honing the art of strategic disclosure, of presenting a version of himself that was both truthful and strategically benign.

"They're referencing your early training protocols," Mara replied, scrolling through a series of transcribed inquiries. "Specifically, the advanced tactical simulations and your proficiency in... let's call them 'unconventional problem-solving scenarios.' They're framing it as a need to understand the full spectrum of Havenridge's defensive and operational readiness. But the subtext is clear: they want to know if you're capable of, or inclined towards, actions that might be perceived as aggressive, or if your skills could be turned against them in the future."

Eli closed his eyes for a brief moment, a faint crease appearing between his brows. The simulations. They were designed to push the boundaries of human response under extreme duress, to forge individuals capable of operating in environments where standard protocols were irrelevant. He had excelled, not out of a thirst for conflict, but out of a deep-seated need to understand how to survive, how to protect, and ultimately, how to build something stable from the chaos.

"The training was designed to foster adaptability," Eli stated, his gaze meeting Mara's. "It was about understanding threats, de-escalating where possible, and neutralizing them when necessary. It was about preserving life, not taking it. That is the core principle I carried forward."

"And how do you convey that nuance to them?" Mara pressed. "They're not interested in philosophical discussions about the ethics of combat training. They want tangible assurances. They want to know if Eli, the architect of Havenridge's structural integrity, is also Eli, the highly skilled operative who can execute a pre-emptive strike."

This was where their strategy came into play. Eli's past was a minefield, but one he had meticulously mapped. He had chosen his affiliations carefully, prioritizing those that aligned with his core values, even if those affiliations operated in morally grey areas.

He had never been a blindly loyal soldier; he had always been a pragmatist, a problem-solver.

"We focus on the outcomes," Eli said, his voice gaining a quiet authority. "My tactical training was a means to an end: ensuring the safety and security of those I was tasked with protecting. The simulations honed my ability to assess risk, to identify vulnerabilities, and to devise solutions that minimized collateral damage and maximized survival rates. Those are skills directly applicable to Havenridge's current mission: fortifying our infrastructure, optimizing our resource management, and ensuring the well-being of our citizens."

He paused, letting the words sink in. "We emphasize the constructive application of those skills. The resilience of the domes against seismic activity, the efficiency of the water filtration systems – these are direct descendants of the analytical and problem-solving methodologies I refined during my training. We frame my past not as a testament to aggression, but as proof of my capacity for rigorous, results-oriented problem-solving under pressure."

Mara nodded slowly. "So, when they ask about the 'Ghost Protocol' simulations – the ones designed for deep-cover infiltration and extraction – we frame it as an exercise in understanding covert operational weaknesses, thus enabling us to better defend against them. And your success in those scenarios is presented as a testament to your ability to identify and neutralize such threats, not as a demonstration of your intent to employ them."

"Precisely," Eli confirmed. "And when they inquire about my brief tenure with the Meridian Collective – a group known for its... assertive approach to resource acquisition – we highlight our fundamental disagreements regarding their methods. We emphasize that I left because their path was unsustainable and ethically compromised. We present my departure as a proactive choice to align with a more principled and enduring vision of community building.”

He continued, outlining their narrative. “We acknowledge my skills in advanced navigation and environmental adaptation. These were crucial for the exploratory missions I undertook, missions that ultimately provided Havenridge with vital intelligence about subterranean resource deposits and potential geological hazards. We spin it as a foundation for our current exploration and expansion efforts, not as preparation for warfare.”

The air in the cabin grew thicker with the weight of their strategic discussion. It wasn't just about deflecting questions; it was about proactively shaping the narrative, about weaving a consistent and compelling story that aligned Eli’s past with Havenridge’s present and future.

“They’re also probing about your relationship with Silas Vance,” Mara added, her tone hardening slightly. Vance. The name still carried a phantom chill. A former mentor, a man whose ambition had outstripped his ethics, Vance had been instrumental in shaping a generation of operatives, Eli among them. Their paths had diverged years ago, a painful but necessary separation.

“Vance represented a path I chose not to take,” Eli stated, his voice devoid of emotion. “His focus was on control and domination. Mine has always been on creation and preservation. My interactions with him were limited, and my departure from his sphere of influence was definitive. We can state that our association was professional, that I learned valuable lessons from his operational acumen, but ultimately rejected his ideological trajectory."

He looked at Mara, his gaze steady. "The key, Mara, is controlled honesty. We do not lie. But we select the truths that serve our purpose. We present the facets of my past that demonstrate my loyalty to Havenridge, my commitment to its survival and prosperity, and my dedication to a future built on collaboration, not coercion."

Mara leaned forward, a flicker of admiration in her eyes. "You've built an impressive facade, Eli. Or rather, a carefully constructed truth. It's remarkable how you can distill years of complex experience into a narrative that is both accurate and disarming."

"It's a skill honed by necessity," Eli replied. "The ability to assess a situation, identify the critical factors, and present a clear, actionable path forward. It's what I do for Havenridge's infrastructure, and it's what I must do for my own history." He gestured towards the data slate. "These questions are designed to uncover a weapon. We must instead present them with a shield. My past achievements are not evidence of potential aggression; they are proof of my capacity to overcome obstacles and to build a secure future."

Their cabin, filled with the quiet intensity of their shared purpose, became a crucible. The delegation's probes were the fire, and Eli and Mara's carefully crafted responses were the forge. They meticulously reviewed each query, each veiled accusation, each attempt to unearth a vulnerability. They dissected Eli's training logs, his personnel files, even his personal correspondence, looking for any detail that could be twisted or misinterpreted.

"What about the incident at Outpost Gamma?" Mara asked, her brow furrowed. "They've cross-referenced it with data from the external archives. They're implying a degree of... unauthorized initiative."

Eli sighed, the memory sharp. Outpost Gamma. A desperate situation, a critical failure of command from a higher echelon, and a difficult choice that had saved lives but defied direct orders. "That was a situation where protocol failed, and human lives were at stake," he explained. "The established chain of command was compromised, and inaction would have resulted in significant casualties. I made a judgment call based on the immediate threat assessment and the available resources. The outcome was successful. The 'unauthorized initiative' was simply a deviation from a flawed plan in order to achieve a desired outcome: survival."

He continued, his voice firm. "We frame it as decisive leadership in a crisis. We highlight the successful preservation of life and matériel. We acknowledge that it was an unconventional response, but one necessitated by extraordinary circumstances. We emphasize that my actions were always guided by the principle of protecting those under my care."

The process was draining. Every carefully worded response, every strategic omission, required immense focus and a deep understanding of the delegation's underlying motivations. They weren't just defending Eli; they were defending Havenridge's right to self-determination, to operate without constant external interference fueled by paranoia.

"They're asking about your network," Mara said, her gaze intense. "Your contacts from your previous affiliations. They want to know who you still have ties to, who might be loyal to you outside of Havenridge."

This was a particularly sensitive area. Eli had cultivated a network of individuals who valued integrity and competence, people who had, like him, grown disillusioned with the prevailing ideologies of the fractured world. He had maintained discreet contact, not for nefarious purposes, but as a source of intelligence and potential future alliances should Havenridge ever need them.

"We acknowledge the existence of professional relationships," Eli stated, choosing his words with precision. "We categorize them as sources of information and expertise, particularly concerning geological stability, atmospheric anomalies, and advanced materials science – areas that directly benefit Havenridge. We emphasize that these contacts are purely professional, transactional, and bound by mutual respect for discretion. We explicitly state that there are no personal allegiances that supersede my commitment to Havenridge."

He met Mara's gaze. "We can even offer limited, anonymized data exchange with a select few, those whose expertise is demonstrably beneficial and whose trustworthiness has been independently verified by our own internal security protocols. This demonstrates transparency and a willingness to collaborate, while carefully controlling the flow of information and safeguarding the identities of those who might be put at risk."

Mara tapped her stylus against the data slate, a thoughtful expression on her face. "So, we're not just deflecting; we're strategically engaging. We're offering glimpses behind the curtain, but always from a position of control. We're showing them that Eli is not a hidden threat, but a valuable asset whose history, when understood through the lens of Havenridge's objectives, is a source of strength, not weakness."

"Exactly," Eli confirmed. "My past is not a weapon to be feared, but a foundation upon which I've built my current contributions. The skills I acquired were not for conquest, but for resilience. The lessons I learned were not about subjugation, but about the critical importance of order and sustainability. And my network is not a cabal of conspirators, but a quiet alliance of individuals dedicated to progress and stability in a fractured world."

He leaned forward, his hands clasped on the table. "We must ensure that every piece of information they receive paints a consistent picture: Eli, the unwavering architect of Havenridge's future. A man whose past experiences, however challenging or ethically complex, have forged him into the most capable guardian of this community. We are not hiding; we are curating. We are not evading; we are strategically revealing."

The intensity of their shared work was palpable. The cabin, usually a place of quiet planning, had become a hub of strategic defense. Each question from the delegation was met with a carefully considered answer, a judicious blend of disclosed facts and strategic omissions. They were navigating a labyrinth of suspicion, guided by the unwavering conviction that Eli's past, when presented correctly, was not a liability, but a testament to his strength and his dedication to Havenridge. Their future, and Eli's place within it, depended on their ability to control the narrative, to turn scrutiny into a demonstration of their unwavering resolve.

The quiet hum of Havenridge was punctuated by a new sound, a sound that had been absent for too long in the sterile efficiency of their post-Unsettling existence: the unrestrained, joyous peals of children's laughter. It echoed through the repurposed sector that Mara had designated as the nascent learning space, a testament to a future being actively cultivated, not merely hoped for. This was the culmination of weeks, months even, of intense deliberation, of poring over fragmented educational philosophies salvaged from the old world and attempting to synthesize them into something entirely new, something intrinsically *Havenridge*. The delegation's relentless scrutiny of Eli's past had underscored a critical vulnerability, not of their defenses, but of their very being: a potential erosion of identity if the next generation wasn't consciously imprinted with the values and history that made them distinct.

Mara, who had always possessed a fierce, protective streak, found this particular endeavor resonating with a deep, instinctual drive. She moved through the learning space, her steps light, observing the early interactions. A group of younger children were gathered around a weathered holographic projector, their faces illuminated by a flickering, monochromatic image of a sky-scanner drone navigating a treacherous atmospheric current. Their instructor, a young woman named Anya with a patient smile, was patiently explaining the principles of atmospheric stratification, relating it directly to the safety protocols for dome integrity. Mara remembered the initial discussions, the hesitant proposals for formal education. Some had argued for prioritizing only practical, hands-on vocational training – the mechanics of the filtration systems, the hydroponic cultivation cycles, the structural maintenance of the habitat. But Mara had pushed for more.

"We are not merely survivors," she had argued, her voice carrying the weight of conviction in one of the initial community forums. "We are builders. And what we build will be hollow if it lacks a soul, a guiding conscience. Our children need to understand *why* we do what we do, not just *how*." The memory of the silence that followed, then the slow, thoughtful nods, still warmed her. It had been a consensus built on a shared, unspoken understanding that survival was not an end in itself, but a means to a greater purpose.

Her vision for Havenridge's education was a tapestry woven from multiple threads. There were, of course, the essential survival skills – the intricate knowledge of their habitat's life-support, the foraging and cultivation techniques adapted to their unique environment, the first-aid and emergency response protocols that were as instinctive as breathing. These were non-negotiable, the bedrock upon which all other learning would be built. But intertwined with these practical necessities were lessons in ethical governance, drawing directly from the hard-won experience of the Great Unsettling and the subsequent years of fragile coexistence. They needed to understand the nuances of resource allocation, the complexities of equitable decision-making, and the absolute imperative of communal responsibility.

Then there was the history. Not a dry recitation of dates and names, but a living narrative. Mara was meticulously piecing together oral histories, digitizing salvaged fragments of pre-Unsettling data, and, most importantly, weaving in the story of Havenridge itself. The sacrifices made, the innovations born from desperation, the philosophical shifts that had guided their establishment – all of it needed to be passed down. This history was their anchor, a reminder of how far they had come and a bulwark against repeating the mistakes of the past. She envisioned lessons that explored the societal collapse, not to instill fear, but to foster critical thinking about the systems that had failed. They would dissect the ethical dilemmas faced by the early settlers, debating the choices made and the consequences that followed.

"We need to teach them to question," Mara had confided to Eli during one of their late-night strategy sessions, the faint glow of their data slates illuminating their faces. "Not to be rebellious, but to be discerning. To understand the 'why' behind every rule, every decision. If they only know to follow, they are susceptible to manipulation, to the same forces that led to the Unsettling." Eli, ever pragmatic, had nodded, recognizing the parallel to their current dealings with the delegation. A citizenry that understood its own history and values would be a far more resilient and unified entity, less easily swayed by external pressures or internal dissent.

The learning space itself was a testament to this collaborative spirit. The tables and seating had been salvaged and repurposed from abandoned sectors, their surfaces smoothed and reinforced. Shelves, constructed by skilled artisans from reclaimed polymers, held a growing collection of learning materials. Anya's holographic projector was a salvaged piece of technology, painstakingly restored and calibrated. Other community members had contributed in their own ways. Kael, the master hydroponicist, was developing a series of interactive modules on sustainable agriculture, complete with miniature self-contained grow units for hands-on experimentation. Lyra, the former archivist, was leading the effort to catalogue and digitize salvaged historical records, her careful fingers brushing over fragile data chips as if they were ancient artifacts. Even some of the delegation members, under Mara's careful guidance, had contributed – a geologist offering insights into subterranean structures, a former medical technician sharing knowledge of basic trauma care. It was a slow, arduous process, but each contribution was a brick laid in the foundation of their educational future.

Mara watched as a group of slightly older children, perhaps ten or eleven years old, were engaged in a mock council meeting. They were debating the equitable distribution of a newly discovered mineral vein. Each child had been assigned a role – a representative of the engineering guild, the agricultural collective, the resource management division, and so on. They were using salvaged data pads to track resource allocation, referencing simulated environmental impact reports, and earnestly presenting their arguments. Their voices, though young, held a surprising gravity. There were disagreements, of course, animated debates that required a designated facilitator to keep them on track, but the underlying respect for the process was evident. They were learning to negotiate, to compromise, to understand that the needs of the collective often superseded individual desires. This, Mara thought with a surge of pride, was the essence of ethical governance in practice.

"How is the historical archiving coming along, Lyra?" Mara asked, approaching the woman who was meticulously cleaning a data shard.

Lyra looked up, her eyes bright with enthusiasm. "It's coming along, Mara. I've managed to recover fragments of pre-Unsettling news feeds. It's... sobering. The sheer disconnect between the public narratives and the underlying systemic failures is astonishing. And the seeds of the Unsettling are so evident, even then. The rampant consumerism, the political polarization, the willful ignorance of impending ecological collapse..." She trailed off, shaking her head. "But it's crucial. Understanding what led to the collapse is our best defense against repeating it. I'm working on creating comparative modules – showing the pre-Unsettling societal structures alongside our own, highlighting the divergence and the lessons learned."

Mara nodded, a thoughtful expression on her face. "That's exactly what we need. Not just the facts, but the analysis. The critical lens. The children need to understand the fragility of systems, and the constant vigilance required to maintain them. And this history... it's not just about the past. It's about shaping our present and future."

She then turned her attention to Anya, who was now guiding the younger children through a simulation of a controlled atmospheric breach. The projector displayed a rapidly de-pressurizing section of the dome, alarms blaring softly. The children, their faces a mixture of concentration and mild apprehension, were instructed to identify the breach points, to seal emergency bulkheads, and to guide simulated inhabitants to designated safe zones.

"It's fascinating," Anya remarked as Mara approached. "Their initial reactions are often instinctive – a sense of panic. But within minutes, they fall back on the protocols we've drilled. They remember the sequence, the safety checks. And they help each other. The older ones instinctively guide the younger ones. It's proof that these lessons are sinking in, not just as memorization, but as ingrained responses."

Mara's gaze swept across the room, taking in the scene: children learning, collaborating, their young minds actively engaged in understanding the world and their place within it. The laughter, the earnest debates, the focused concentration – it was a symphony of hope. This wasn't just a learning space; it was a nursery for a new kind of citizenry, one forged not in the crucible of immediate survival alone, but in the thoughtful cultivation of knowledge, ethics, and a profound understanding of their shared heritage.

The delegation's inquiries, while probing and at times unnerving, had inadvertently highlighted a critical need. By scrutinizing Eli's past, they had forced Havenridge to confront the potential for its own future to be misunderstood, to be misrepresented. Mara's vision for education was a proactive countermeasure, a way of inscribing their identity, their values, and their history so deeply into the next generation that no external force, however persuasive, could easily erase it.

She walked over to a corner where a few of the older children were examining a collection of geological samples, comparing them to holographic models of subterranean formations. They were discussing the potential risks and rewards of further tunneling, their conversation a blend of technical jargon and nascent scientific reasoning. One boy, no older than twelve, was excitedly pointing out a unique crystalline structure on a piece of rock, his explanation peppered with terms like 'pressure crystallization' and 'mineral composition.'

"See how the facets are so perfectly formed?" he explained to his peers, his voice full of wonder. "It tells us about the intense pressure and the specific chemical environment deep underground. It's like a story written in stone, isn't it?"

Mara smiled. A story written in stone. That was precisely what she hoped to impart. A deep understanding of their world, its past, its present, and its potential future, written not just in stone, but in knowledge, in ethics, and in the shared narrative of Havenridge. The challenges were immense, the resources finite, but the laughter of these children, echoing through the newly established learning space, was a powerful testament to the enduring human spirit and the unwavering hope for a brighter, more informed tomorrow. Her work was far from over, but in the eyes of these engaged young learners, Mara saw not just the future of Havenridge, but the very embodiment of its enduring resilience and its unwavering commitment to building a better world, one lesson at a time.

The air in Havenridge, once thick with the palpable tension of isolation, was beginning to carry the subtle, yet distinct, aroma of change. It wasn't the harsh, metallic tang of recycled air or the earthy scent of hydroponic crops, but something richer, more evocative – the ghost of exotic spices, a whisper of distant lands and the promise of connection. Mara stood on a newly constructed observation platform, overlooking the main docking bay, a space that had recently transformed from a purely utilitarian zone into a hub of nascent commerce. Crate after crate, once filled with the necessities of survival, were now being meticulously inventoried, their contents a testament to successful negotiations and carefully cultivated relationships with settlements beyond their immediate, insulated sphere.

This shift wasn't born of recklessness, but of a carefully considered evolution in their survival philosophy. The Unsettling had taught them the brutal efficacy of self-reliance, the absolute necessity of defending their borders. Yet, the stark reality of their existence in the post-collapse world was that complete autarky was a Sisyphean endeavor. True resilience, Mara had come to believe, lay not in building impenetrable walls, but in forging sturdy bridges. Bridges of trade, of knowledge, and of mutual respect.

Eli, his face etched with the familiar lines of strategic contemplation, stood beside her. His presence was a constant, grounding force, a reminder of the careful planning and calculated risks that underpinned every one of Mara's more outward-looking initiatives. "The caravan from Atheria arrived an hour ahead of schedule," he reported, his voice a low murmur against the steady thrum of activity below. "Their textiles are as fine as advertised, and their processed medicinal herbs are already being cataloged by Anya's team. In return, we've dispatched the latest shipment of our nutrient paste enhancers and the water purification modules. A fair exchange, considering the rarity of their flora."

Mara nodded, a small smile playing on her lips. "Atheria understands the value of specialization. They have the climate for their unique crops, and we have the expertise in nutrient synthesis. It's a natural symbiosis, one that benefits both our communities." She watched as a team of Havenridge workers, their movements efficient and practiced, guided a lev-cart laden with their own goods towards the waiting Atherian traders. There was a sense of purposeful cooperation, a shared understanding of the mutual benefit that transcended mere transactional exchange.

The decision to actively seek out partnerships hadn't been met with universal acclaim, of course. Vestiges of the old Havenridge, the one defined by extreme caution and an almost pathological fear of outsiders, still lingered in some corners. Whispers of suspicion, of the old adage that "no good can come from beyond the walls," still surfaced. Mara had addressed these concerns head-on, not by dismissing them, but by acknowledging their validity and then presenting a compelling alternative.

"The delegation's persistent scrutiny of Eli's past, their delving into the vulnerabilities of our security protocols, it served as a stark reminder," Mara had articulated during a recent community forum, her voice resonating with quiet authority. "They sought to expose our weaknesses, to find cracks in our defenses. But what if our greatest strength lies not in our walls, but in the relationships we build beyond them? What if our ultimate security is found in a network of allies, each contributing their unique strengths, each invested in the well-being of the others?"

She had then outlined the criteria for selecting potential partners. Not just any settlement would do. They had to demonstrate a commitment to similar ethical frameworks, a respect for communal well-being, and a willingness to engage in transparent and fair dealings. It was a delicate balancing act, a process of careful vetting that Eli had spearheaded, utilizing salvaged pre-Unsettling data streams and discreet reconnaissance when necessary.

"The settlement of Solara has expressed interest in our hydroponic cultivation techniques," Eli continued, referencing a portable data slate. "They're facing persistent issues with soil degradation due to atmospheric particulate contamination. Lyra has prepared a series of instructional modules, detailing our closed-loop systems and our specialized nutrient cycling. She believes they can adapt our methods with some modifications."

"And in return?" Mara prompted, her gaze still fixed on the bustling bay.

"They possess advanced solar energy capture technology. Their arrays are significantly more efficient than ours, and they've developed a novel method for energy storage that could drastically improve our grid stability, especially during prolonged atmospheric obscuration events," Eli explained. "It's a risk, of course. Their

technological reliance is deep, and their social structures are...
different. But their leadership has proven pragmatic and their people
seem genuinely invested in finding sustainable solutions."

Mara found herself nodding. This was precisely the kind of
calculated risk she was willing to take. It wasn't about blind faith,
but about informed trust. They weren't just trading goods; they were
trading knowledge, sharing the hard-won lessons of their existence,
and in doing so, reinforcing the very values that defined Havenridge.
It was an active affirmation of their identity, a declaration to the
world that they were not just survivors, but contributors, innovators,
and collaborators.

The scent of spices, carried on a gentle breeze that snaked through
the docking bay, seemed to intensify. It was the aroma of cardamom,
of star anise, of something earthy and sweet that Mara couldn't quite
place. It spoke of trade routes stretching further than anyone in
Havenridge had dared to imagine in the immediate aftermath of the
Unsettling. It was the scent of possibility.

"Kael has also been in contact with the Ironwood Collective,"
Eli added, his tone carrying a hint of professional admiration.
"They've developed some incredibly robust alloys for structural
reinforcement, using a unique blend of salvaged metals and
bio-engineered resins. Their materials are far superior to anything
we can currently produce. They're interested in our advanced
atmospheric filtration systems, believing they can adapt them to
purify the air in their subterranean mining operations."

"The Ironwood Collective," Mara mused. "They're known for
their stoicism and their almost monastic dedication to their craft.
A good match for our engineering principles. But their social

structure is highly hierarchical. We'll need to be exceptionally clear about our own governance model, our emphasis on communal decision-making."

"Precisely," Eli confirmed. "Transparency is key. We've provided them with detailed schematics of our filtration systems, but also with explanations of the community oversight that dictates their maintenance and deployment. Lyra is preparing a comparative analysis of societal structures, highlighting the differences and the potential areas of friction, alongside the proposed benefits of collaboration."

Mara appreciated Eli's meticulous approach. He was the anchor that kept her ambitious visions tethered to reality, ensuring that every bridge built was on solid ground. He understood that cooperation wasn't simply about exchanging resources; it was about aligning values. If a settlement's core principles were antithetical to Havenridge's – if they were exploitative, aggressive, or disregarded the well-being of their own people – then no amount of mutually beneficial trade would be worth the risk.

"The delegation has been observing these developments with... keen interest," Eli stated, his voice dropping slightly. "They've asked for detailed reports on our trade partners, their capabilities, and their perceived threat levels."

Mara's jaw tightened almost imperceptibly. The delegation. Their presence, while ostensibly focused on evaluating Havenridge's long-term viability, remained a constant undercurrent of unease. They represented the old world's way of thinking – the fragmented, competitive, often predatory mindset that had contributed to the Unsettling in the first place. Their interest in Havenridge's burgeoning network of alliances was understandable, but it was also a potential avenue for manipulation.

"Let them observe," Mara said, her voice firm and resolute. "Let them see that we are not simply hoarding resources or cowering behind our walls. Let them see that we are building a future, not just for ourselves, but as part of a larger, interconnected web. If they believe that our strength lies in our isolation, they will underestimate us. And that, Eli, is a far greater defense than any physical barrier."

She gestured towards the docking bay, where a group of Atherian traders, identifiable by their brightly colored, woven headscarves, were engaged in animated discussion with a Havenridge logistics officer. The air, previously filled with the utilitarian sounds of cargo handling, now carried snippets of unfamiliar languages, the rise and fall of different intonations, a testament to the growing diversity within their orbit.

"These aren't just trade agreements, Eli," Mara continued, her gaze sweeping over the scene with a profound sense of satisfaction. "These are seeds of a new kind of world. A world where cooperation is not a weakness, but a cornerstone of survival. Where shared knowledge isn't a risk, but an investment. Where our children can grow up understanding that the world beyond Havenridge isn't something to be feared, but something to be engaged with, to be understood, and to be improved, collectively."

The exotic spices seemed to weave their way into every breath, a fragrant reminder of the tangible progress being made. It was the scent of cinnamon, of cloves, a warm, comforting aroma that spoke of stability and shared prosperity. It was a stark contrast to the sterile, controlled environment of their past, a testament to the conscious decision to embrace a wider world.

"We've also initiated discussions with the Lumina Enclave regarding shared research into advanced bioluminescent cultivation for ambient lighting," Eli added, his tone shifting to a more technical focus. "Their expertise in bio-engineering is unparalleled, and they've expressed a keen interest in our atmospheric pressure regulation systems, which they believe could be adapted for their deep-sea research facilities."

Mara's mind raced, connecting the dots. Lumina Enclave, known for their reclusive nature and their pioneering work in bio-sciences, and Havenridge, with its mastery of controlled environmental systems. The potential for groundbreaking discoveries was immense. "Have we shared our data on the atmospheric scrubber efficiency during periods of high solar flare activity?" Mara inquired, her mind already formulating the next steps. "That particular challenge has always been a bottleneck for them, if I recall correctly from Lyra's initial assessment."

"Yes," Eli confirmed. "And in return, they've offered us access to their genetic sequencing database. Anya believes it could revolutionize our crop yield optimization, allowing us to develop strains even more resistant to nutrient deficiencies and subtle environmental shifts."

The implications were far-reaching. It wasn't just about immediate needs; it was about investing in long-term advancements, about pushing the boundaries of what was possible in their post-Unsettling world. This was the essence of building bridges, not walls. It was about acknowledging that no single settlement, no matter how self-sufficient, possessed all the answers. True progress, true security, lay in the collaborative pursuit of solutions.

The docking bay continued its symphony of organized chaos. The clatter of machinery, the hum of lev-carts, the distant calls of workers – all interwoven with the subtle, yet persistent, aroma of distant lands. It was a scent that spoke of a future actively being forged, a future where Havenridge was not an isolated fortress, but a vital node in a network of mutual support and shared progress. Mara inhaled deeply, drawing in the fragrance of saffron, of ginger, of a hundred other exotic notes that promised a world beyond their current horizons. They were no longer just surviving; they were building. And with every carefully constructed bridge, with every exchanged piece of knowledge, they were laying the foundations for a more resilient, more connected, and ultimately, more hopeful future. The whispers of suspicion were slowly being drowned out by the chorus of collaboration, and the scent of possibility was growing stronger with every passing day.

The setting sun cast long, benevolent shadows across Havenridge, painting the sturdy, utilitarian structures in hues of amber and rose. The day's ceaseless hum of activity had softened into a more gentle murmur, the sounds of the settlement settling into a rhythm of evening routine. Mara and Eli stood on the newly reinforced observation platform, a structure that had itself been a testament to collaboration, built with materials sourced from the Ironwood Collective and designed with insights from Solara's engineers. The air, still carrying the faint, intriguing scents of Atherian spices and Lumina's bio-engineered flora from the earlier trade discussions, now also held the crispness of approaching twilight.

Their conversation, which had begun amidst the bustling energy of the docking bay, had gradually shifted, mirroring the descent of the sun, moving from the broader strokes of community development to the finer, more intimate lines of their own shared existence. The initial pronouncements of strategy and diplomacy had softened, replaced by the quiet resonance of understanding between two souls who had weathered storms that would have shattered lesser bonds.

"Remember the first time we stood here?" Mara asked, her voice a low, melodic current against the fading sounds of the day. Her gaze was not on the horizon, but on Eli, her eyes reflecting the warm, fading light. "Before the shields were fully functional, before Anya's team had perfected the atmospheric filtration. It felt... precarious. Every breath was a calculated risk, every night a vigil."

Eli's hand found hers, his grip firm and familiar. The calluses on his palm were a testament to his own steady work, his own commitment to the physical manifestation of their survival. "Precarious is an understatement," he replied, a ghost of a smile touching his lips. "We were living on borrowed time, held together by sheer will and a healthy dose of desperation. The concept of a 'future' then was simply 'tomorrow.' Beyond that was a nebulous, terrifying unknown."

He squeezed her hand gently. "And now? Look at us. We've not only survived, Mara, we've thrived. We've built something beyond mere existence. We've cultivated hope." He gestured to the lights that were beginning to twinkle to life across the settlement, a testament to Solara's energy grid improvements. "Those aren't just lights, they're symbols. Symbols of resilience, of innovation, of a willingness to reach out and connect."

Mara leaned her head against his shoulder, the subtle scent of his worn leather jacket, mingled with the clean, sharp aroma of Havenridge's recycled air, a comforting presence. "It wasn't easy," she murmured, the weight of those past struggles settling for a moment. "The sacrifices... some were immense. The days when we rationed even the synthesized protein, the constant threat of resource depletion, the emotional toll of knowing that a single miscalculation could unravel everything."

"And the risks we took," Eli added, his gaze now sweeping across the valley, the shadows deepening, concealing and revealing the landscape in equal measure. "Trusting the Lumina Enclave with our atmospheric data, especially given their reputation for being so fiercely independent. Negotiating with the Ironwood Collective, knowing their societal structure was so rigidly defined. Every step forward was a leap of faith, a calculated gamble."

He turned to face her fully, his expression earnest. "But we made those leaps together. And the community... they've trusted us. They've embraced the change, even when it was difficult. That trust is our most valuable currency, Mara. More than any energy cell or nutrient synthesiser."

The memory of the community forums, the initial hesitant questions, the eventual surge of collective will, flashed through her mind. She remembered the fear in some eyes, the deep-seated skepticism born of decades of isolation. But she also remembered the spark of understanding, the dawning realization that a different path was not only possible, but necessary.

"It's the choices, Eli," Mara said, her voice regaining its characteristic clarity, though now tinged with a profound tenderness. "It's always been about the choices. The choice to believe in something more than just survival. The choice to extend a hand, even when our instincts screamed to pull back. The choice to define our future not by what we feared, but by what we aspired to become."

She met his gaze, her own filled with an unwavering affection that had been forged in the crucible of shared adversity. Their love story wasn't one of serendipitous meetings or grand romantic gestures, but of quiet companionship, of shared burdens, of mutual respect that had deepened with every challenge they had overcome. It was a love built on the bedrock of shared responsibility and an unshakeable belief in each other's strength and integrity.

"And our choices now," she continued, her tone shifting, a gentle optimism infusing her words. "They're still defining us. We choose to continue these alliances, to foster these connections. We choose to invest in knowledge, to share our expertise. We choose to be a beacon, not a fortress. It's a different kind of strength, isn't it? One that draws power from connection, rather than isolation."

Eli brought her hand to his lips, pressing a soft kiss to her knuckles. The gesture was a silent affirmation, a testament to the unspoken language that had developed between them over the years. "It's a strength that cannot be easily broken," he agreed. "The delegation, they may see our network as a vulnerability, a series of potential weak points. But they fail to understand that a web, when intricately woven, is far more resilient than a single, isolated thread. Each connection strengthens the whole."

He paused, his brow furrowing slightly. "Their continued scrutiny... it's a reminder. A reminder of the old ways of thinking, the competitive, zero-sum game that led to the Unsettling. They want to understand our 'advantage,' our 'power.' They don't yet grasp that our greatest advantage is our willingness to share, our commitment to collaboration."

"And our greatest power," Mara added softly, her eyes now fixed on the first stars appearing in the darkening sky, "lies in our unwavering commitment to each other, and to the principles we've chosen to uphold. We are not bound by fear, Eli. We are bound by purpose. By a shared vision of a future where Havenridge is not just a sanctuary, but a catalyst for a better world."

She felt a profound sense of peace settle over her, a quiet contentment that was more potent than any euphoria. The uncertainty of the future remained, as it always would. The Unsettling had taught them that much. But now, that uncertainty was not a source of dread, but an open canvas, a space for continued creation, for further exploration. They had the tools, the knowledge, and most importantly, the collective will to paint whatever future they chose.

"We've come so far," Eli said, his voice a low rumble of contentment. "From the brink of extinction to this. To a place where we can afford to discuss the finer points of interstellar trade agreements and the ethical implications of advanced bio-engineering, all while ensuring our people are safe, fed, and healthy."

He gently pulled her closer, their bodies aligning in a familiar, comforting embrace. The warmth that spread through Mara was not just physical, but emotional, a deep wellspring of love and gratitude. This was more than just a partnership; it was a fusion of destinies, two souls inextricably linked by the arduous journey they had undertaken.

"And we'll continue to choose," Mara whispered, her voice muffled against his chest. "We'll choose to learn, to grow, to adapt. We'll choose to trust, to connect, to build. We'll choose to face whatever comes next, not as isolated individuals, but as a united force, guided by the choices we make together."

The stars were now a dazzling tapestry overhead, a silent, vast expanse that held both the promise of the unknown and the comfort of eternity. The scents of the day's trade – the spices, the floral notes, the metallic tang of new alloys – had all merged into a complex, yet harmonious, olfactory landscape. It was the scent of possibility, the perfume of a future meticulously crafted, choice by choice, embrace by embrace.

Eli tilted her chin up, his eyes meeting hers, reflecting the starlight. "Our future, Mara," he said, his voice thick with emotion, "defined by our choices. And I wouldn't want to define it with anyone else."

He kissed her then, a kiss that spoke of shared history, of unwavering commitment, and of the boundless potential of the future they were actively, deliberately, forging together. It was a promise whispered in the twilight, a silent vow made beneath the watchful gaze of a thousand distant suns, a testament to the enduring power of love and the unyielding strength of a future defined by choice. The vastness of the sky above mirrored the vastness of the possibilities that lay before them, and in that moment, standing on the precipice of the night, they knew they were ready for it all.

Their journey was far from over, but with each other, and with the community they had so painstakingly built, they were more than prepared. They were empowered. They were hopeful. They were, in the truest sense of the word, free to choose their destiny.

The choices they had made had led them here, to this quiet moment of profound connection, and the choices they would continue to make would guide them through whatever lay ahead, a testament to the enduring power of their shared future.

CHAPTER ELEVEN
The Reckoning

The subtle maneuvering had failed. The delegation, comprised of representatives from the more established, power-hungry systems that had historically dictated terms across the sector, had clearly exhausted their patience for diplomacy. What began as a series of seemingly benign overtures, veiled in the language of cooperation and shared prosperity, had solidified into a stark, unvarnished demand. Mara and Eli found themselves in their study, the sanctuary of quiet contemplation, the air thick with the scent of aged vellum and the faint, metallic tang of an imminent crisis. The late afternoon sun, which had only hours before cast a warm, benevolent glow, now seemed to highlight the stark reality of their situation, each beam of light a spotlight on the precipice they were being pushed towards.

"'Complete integration'," Eli read aloud, his voice a low, measured rumble, though the tension in his jaw was a telltale sign of his inner turmoil. He held the communication tablet, the holographic projection of the delegation's final proposal shimmering between them. "'Or face severe sanctions, including the immediate withdrawal of all technological and logistical assistance, and the potential for the enforcement of regional security protocols to ensure compliance.'" He looked up at Mara, his gaze sharp, dissecting her expression for any hint of doubt, any flicker of wavering resolve. He found none.

Mara traced the rim of her thermal mug, the warmth seeping into her fingers a stark contrast to the chilling implications of the words on the screen. "They've revealed their hand," she stated, her voice steady, betraying none of the anxiety that coiled in her gut. The polite, almost deferential approach of Ambassador Valerius had been a masterful performance, designed to lull them into a false sense of security, to foster a dependency that could then be leveraged. But Havenridge, built on a foundation of hard-won self-reliance and a deep understanding of true independence, was not easily swayed by veiled threats. "The 'assistance' they've been so keen to offer was never about aid, Eli. It was about leverage. A leash, patiently extended."

Eli nodded, his fingers clenching around the tablet. "And now they're pulling it taut. The Ironwood Collective, their reliance on Havenridge for refined ores and skilled fabrication is no secret. The Lumina Enclave, dependent on our atmospheric processors and advanced bio-filters. Even the smaller agricultural collectives, reliant on our energy grid stability. They threaten to cut off the very lifelines we've so carefully cultivated, the very connections that have allowed us to thrive." He ran a hand through his hair, a gesture of frustration. "They're not just threatening Havenridge; they're threatening the delicate balance we've established across this entire region."

"They believe our interconnectedness is our weakness," Mara continued, her eyes fixed on the projected text, her mind already dissecting the delegation's strategy. "They see the web we've woven and assume it's a fragile thing, easily torn. They fail to comprehend that a truly interwoven fabric, made of mutual reliance and shared purpose, is far more resilient than any single, isolated thread. Their power comes from coercion; ours comes from collaboration."

"But coercion has its own brutal efficacy," Eli countered, his voice grim. "Especially when backed by the sheer military might of systems like Cygnus Prime. Their 'security protocols' are a euphemism for armed intervention. They've always preferred brute force over genuine negotiation when their dominance is challenged." He leaned back in his chair, the leather creaking softly. "Valerius, for all his practiced charm, is a mouthpiece for those who believe might makes right. He's not a negotiator; he's a pronouncer of decrees."

Mara stood and walked to the viewport, gazing out at the settlement. The lights of Havenridge, usually a beacon of progress and community, now seemed to flicker with a newfound vulnerability. She saw the bustling activity in the hydroponic domes, the hum of the fabrication plants, the gentle glow emanating from the residential sectors. Each light represented a life, a family, a shared dream. The delegation's ultimatum wasn't just a political threat; it was a threat to the very existence of everything they had built.

"They underestimated us," she said, her voice barely a whisper, but filled with a conviction that resonated through the room. "They saw a fledgling settlement, struggling for resources, ripe for exploitation. They didn't see the ingenuity, the resilience, the sheer force of will that brought us here. They didn't see the community that has forged itself in the crucible of shared adversity. They don't understand that our strength isn't just in our technology or our resources; it's in our people. It's in our refusal to be subjugated."

Eli joined her at the viewport, his arm sliding around her waist, a comforting anchor in the rising tide of uncertainty. "So, what is our play, Mara? We can't simply capitulate. Our principles would be compromised, and that would break the spirit of Havenridge. But a direct refusal... it opens the door to the very aggression they're threatening."

"We don't refuse, Eli," Mara said, turning to face him, her eyes alight with a fierce determination. "We don't accept their terms either. We counter. We shift the paradigm. They want integration? We offer a different kind of unity. They threaten sanctions? We leverage our network, not as a tool of control, but as a testament to our shared strength."

He searched her face, the wheels of strategy turning in his mind. "You're thinking... of formalizing the alliances? Presenting a united front, not as a defensive maneuver, but as a declaration of intent?"

"Precisely," Mara confirmed, her gaze unwavering. "We've spent years building trust, fostering interdependence. The Lumina Enclave values their autonomy, but they also understand the benefits of our shared infrastructure. The Ironwood Collective relies on our skilled labor and advanced processing techniques. Our trade agreements, our collaborative research initiatives, our mutual defense pacts – these are not mere transactions; they are the sinews of a new kind of regional governance. A voluntary federation, built on mutual respect and shared benefit, not on domination."

"But the delegation represents established powers," Eli mused, the complexity of the challenge becoming clearer. "They have the infrastructure for large-scale enforcement, the historical precedent for imposing their will. A voluntary federation, while noble, might be seen as a challenge to their established order. They might view it as an act of defiance."

"And it is," Mara stated, a spark igniting in her eyes. "It is an act of defiance against the old ways. Against the exploitative systems that led to the Unsettling. We don't need to match their might with brute force. We can match their arrogance with undeniable unity. We can demonstrate that a different path is not only possible, but demonstrably more prosperous and stable."

She walked back to the study table, her movements purposeful. "We convene an emergency council. Not just with the heads of our closest partners, but with representatives from across all the systems we've established ties with. We present them with the delegation's ultimatum, and then we present them with our alternative: the Charter of Sovereign Alliances. A document that outlines our commitment to mutual defense, shared resource management, and cooperative development, all while preserving the autonomy and unique identity of each member system."

Eli stood, a slow smile spreading across his face. The tension in his shoulders began to ease, replaced by a burgeoning sense of possibility. "You're proposing we don't just defend ourselves, Mara, but that we proactively redefine the political landscape. They're trying to force us into their mold, and you want to break the mold and create an entirely new one."

"Exactly," Mara said, her voice gaining momentum. "The delegation believes they hold all the cards. They're counting on fear, on division, on the inherent self-interest of isolated entities. We will counter that with unity, with shared vision, and with the undeniable strength of a community that chooses to stand together. We will show them that our 'assistance' was not a tool of subjugation, but a seed of true partnership, and that seed has now blossomed into a formidable alliance."

She picked up a stylus, her fingers hovering over a blank section of the data slate. "We draft a response to the delegation. A polite, yet firm, refusal of their terms. We clearly state that Havenridge, and indeed the burgeoning network of allied systems, will not be integrated into their existing governing body. Then, we extend an invitation. An invitation for them to engage with us on our terms, to recognize the Charter of Sovereign Alliances as the legitimate governing framework for this sector. We offer them a seat at the table, not as overlords, but as equals, if they are willing to shed their archaic notions of dominance."

Eli came up behind her, placing his hands on her shoulders, his presence a solid reassurance. "And if they refuse? If they escalate?"

"Then we face that with the unified strength of our alliances," Mara replied, her gaze meeting his in the reflection of the data slate. "We've spent years preparing for this, Eli. Not just technologically, but politically and socially. We've built relationships, fostered trust, and demonstrated the tangible benefits of cooperation. They can try to sever our connections, but they cannot sever the bonds of mutual respect and shared purpose that now tie us together. Their ultimatum is not an end; it is merely the catalyst for our final play."

The air in the study seemed to hum with a renewed energy, the scent of old paper now overlaid with the invigorating aroma of strategic planning. The delegation's threat, meant to destabilize and intimidate, had instead galvanized them. It had forced their hand, yes, but it had also revealed the true depth of their strength, a strength that lay not in military might or political maneuvering, but in the unwavering commitment of a people who had chosen to build a future together, brick by painstaking brick, alliance by unbreakable alliance. The reckoning was coming, but Havenridge, and its growing confederation, would be ready to meet it, not with fear, but with a united, unyielding resolve. The sun had dipped below the horizon, but a new dawn was breaking, not just for Havenridge, but for an entire sector, a dawn illuminated by the principles of self-determination and collective power.

The weight of the delegation's ultimatum pressed down, a suffocating blanket over Havenridge. Mara and Eli had formulated a brilliant counter-strategy, a bold declaration of unity that promised to reshape the sector. Yet, as Eli replayed the intercepted communications, the unsettling truth gnawed at him. The delegation's unnerving precision, their uncanny knowledge of Havenridge's internal workings, and the subtle but potent leverage they wielded – it all pointed to a source far more intimate than mere political maneuvering. It reeked of betrayal, of ghosts from his own shadowed past clawing their way back into his life, and by extension, into the fragile peace he had fought so hard to build.

He remembered the whispers, the carefully placed rumors, the insidious suggestions that had always seemed to follow him, even before he'd found solace on Havenridge. They were echoes of a life he had tried to bury, a life of calculated risks and morally ambiguous alliances. Now, those echoes had materialized into a tangible threat, personified by faces he had long hoped to forget. Kaelen, with his silken tongue and his talent for dissecting weaknesses with surgical precision. Lyra, whose ambition burned as brightly as the nebulae she claimed to chart, and whose loyalty was as fickle as stellar winds.

They were the architects of his downfall, the ones who had profited from his desperation and who now saw Havenridge as another lucrative acquisition. Their involvement wasn't just an escalation of the delegation's demands; it was a personal vendetta, a sinister game where Havenridge was merely the board, and he, Eli, was the pawn they were determined to sacrifice.

The realization struck him with the force of a physical blow. He couldn't allow his personal history, his past mistakes, to jeopardize the future of thousands. Mara's strength, her unwavering belief in their collective vision, deserved more than a leader compromised by secrets. The community council, the very heart and soul of Havenridge, needed to know the full scope of the danger they faced. Hiding this, attempting to manage this threat alone, would be the ultimate betrayal. It would be a replay of his past failures, a testament to his inability to truly break free. The time for subterfuge was over. The time for confession, for radical honesty, had arrived. The rain outside intensified, each drop a drumbeat against the hull of their study, mirroring the storm gathering within him.

The council chambers, usually a place of robust debate and thoughtful deliberation, felt charged with a different kind of energy. The familiar faces of Havenridge's elected representatives, farmers, engineers, educators, and artisans, were etched with a newfound gravity. They had been briefed on the delegation's ultimatum, on Mara's brilliant counter-strategy, but the undercurrent of unease that had permeated the settlement for cycles now threatened to crest into a wave of full-blown anxiety. The holographic displays flickered, showcasing projected trade routes, resource distribution charts, and the intricate network of alliances that Mara had so painstakingly woven. Yet, beneath the surface of these reassuring visuals, a darker narrative was unfolding, one that only Eli could fully articulate.

Eli stood before them, the weight of his past a physical burden pressing down on his shoulders. Mara was by his side, her presence a silent, unwavering support. He met the gaze of each council member, seeing not judgment, but a shared commitment to the well-being of their home. He began to speak, his voice steady, though the tremor in his hands was a betraying sign of the turmoil within. He spoke of his life before Havenridge, not in broad strokes, but in granular detail, eschewing the carefully crafted anonymity he had adopted. He spoke of the precarious balance of power in the outer systems, the insatiable hunger of the core worlds, and the desperate measures he had taken to survive, and sometimes, to thrive.

"You know me as Eli Vance, a citizen, a partner in building Havenridge," he began, his voice echoing in the hushed chamber. "But that is not the entirety of my story. My past is... complicated. I was once known by other names, and I was associated with individuals who operated in the shadows, individuals who believed that power was best wielded through manipulation and fear." He paused, allowing the implication to settle. The rain outside had become a torrential downpour, drumming against the transparisteel of the chamber, a raw, untamed sound that seemed to amplify the vulnerability of his confession.

He spoke of Kaelen and Lyra, not as abstract threats, but as specific individuals with a history intertwined with his own. He described their methods, their ruthlessness, their uncanny ability to exploit any weakness, any vulnerability. "Kaelen," Eli continued, his voice hardening with a mixture of resentment and regret, "is a master strategist, a weaver of narratives. He thrives on sowing discord, on turning allies against each other. He sees systems like ours, independent and idealistic, as ripe for the plucking. He was instrumental in the destabilization of the Kepler Federation, a prosperous network that fell apart from within, thanks to his machinations." He glanced at a council member, an elder named Anya, whose family had been displaced during the Kepler collapse. Her expression was unreadable, but the subtle clench of her jaw spoke volumes.

"Lyra," he went on, "possesses a keen understanding of technological vulnerabilities and resource dependencies. She has a network of informants that spans countless systems. She's not driven by ideology, but by pure, unadulterated profit. She was the one who identified the critical infrastructure points in the Cygnus Prime supply lines, enabling a swift and devastating blockade that crippled their economy for cycles. The delegation's knowledge of our energy grid, our atmospheric processors, our hydroponic systems – that is Lyra's handiwork. She's not just feeding them information; she's guiding their strategy, identifying our softest underbellies."

The council members exchanged uneasy glances. The abstract threat of the delegation had suddenly become terrifyingly concrete, infused with the personal animosity of men and women Eli had once called... associates. The scent of ozone from the rain outside seemed to prickle the air, mirroring the electric tension that now crackled within the chamber.

Eli described the specific threats these individuals posed, not just to Havenridge's autonomy, but to the very lives of its citizens. He detailed the potential for sophisticated cyber-attacks, designed to cripple their infrastructure and sow panic. He revealed their propensity for exploiting social divisions, for amplifying existing anxieties within the population, turning neighbor against neighbor. He spoke of the psychological warfare they were capable of, the insidious whispers designed to erode trust and create an atmosphere of pervasive fear.

"They will not simply bombard us with warships, though that is a possibility," Eli stated, his gaze sweeping across the faces of the council. "Their primary weapon is subversion. They will exploit our reliance on off-world resources, our internal communication networks, even our own democratic processes. They know my history with them. They know my past weaknesses, my former allegiances. They are using that knowledge to apply pressure, not just to you, but to me, hoping to exploit my guilt, my desire to protect you all. They believe they can break me, and through me, break Havenridge."

He took a deep breath, the scent of rain and damp earth seeping into the sterile air of the chamber. "This is why I can no longer hide. The risk of exposure, of revealing the darker chapters of my life, is far outweighed by the risk of facing this threat unprepared, without your full knowledge and trust. My past is not just my burden; it has become a threat to our collective future. I have spent years trying to outrun it, but it has finally caught up. And it has brought with it the most dangerous adversaries I have ever faced."

He looked directly at Mara, his eyes filled with a profound plea for understanding. "Mara believed in me when I barely believed in myself. She saw past the shadows and recognized the man I aspired to be. But these individuals... they remember the man I was.

And they are leveraging every scar, every regret, every mistake to undermine everything we have built together. They are the 'experts' the delegation hired, the 'consultants' who know exactly how to destabilize a frontier system, how to dismantle a nascent republic from the inside out."

The council members listened intently, their faces a mosaic of emotions. Shock was evident, a visceral reaction to the revelation that their quiet, unassuming partner was entwined with such dangerous figures. But beneath the shock, a steely resolve began to harden. The scent of the rain outside, which had initially seemed to reflect an internal gloom, now felt like a cleansing force, washing away the pretense and preparing them for the difficult task ahead. They had been lulled into a false sense of security, believing the delegation's threats were purely political. Now, they understood the true depth of the danger, a danger that was both external and deeply personal.

"The delegation is not merely an economic or political entity," Eli concluded, his voice resonating with a newfound authority born of brutal honesty. "They are a front. A shield for individuals who have a vested interest in seeing independent systems like ours fail. Kaelen and Lyra, and others like them, thrive in chaos. They profit from the subjugation of free peoples. And they have chosen Havenridge, and by extension, all of us, as their next target. They believe that by threatening me, by exposing my past, they can shatter the unity you and Mara have worked so hard to build. They are wrong. They have underestimated our resilience. They have underestimated our commitment to each other. And they have underestimated the power of the truth, no matter how painful."

A heavy silence descended upon the chamber, broken only by the insistent drumming of the rain. The council members processed the information, the implications rippling through them. The trust they had placed in Eli, the belief in his integrity, had been tested, but in his vulnerability, he had forged a new, deeper bond. The revelation was a risk, a gamble with their collective security, but as Eli had said, honesty was their only viable path forward. They had been shown the true face of the enemy, a face twisted by malice and ambition, but also a face that, in its very exposure, offered a glimmer of hope. They knew now what they were truly up against, and with that knowledge came the clarity to fight, not just for their survival,, but for the principles upon which Havenridge was founded. The storm outside raged, but within the council chambers, a quiet determination began to solidify, a collective will forged in the crucible of Eli's confession.

The hum of the settlement, usually a comforting symphony of daily life, had been replaced by a hushed, anxious murmur. The news of Eli's past, delivered with such raw honesty to the council, had inevitably seeped through Havenridge like a contagion. Fear, a sly and insidious visitor, had begun to take root in the fertile ground of uncertainty. Mara felt it in the averted gazes, the strained conversations, the subtle tightening of community bonds as people instinctively sought solace in familiar faces, but also the nascent fracturing as old suspicions, long dormant, began to stir. It was a delicate moment, a precipice where Havenridge could either solidify its foundations or crumble under the weight of apprehension. Eli's confession, while courageous, had exposed a vulnerability, a chink in their armor that their adversaries were undoubtedly poised to exploit.

Mara stood on the elevated platform in the central plaza, the heart of Havenridge, the place where celebrations were held and where pronouncements of hope were made. Today, the air thrummed with a different energy, a volatile mixture of apprehension and a desperate yearning for reassurance. The rain had finally abated, leaving behind a clean, crisp scent of damp earth and the faint, sweet perfume of the pine forests that encircled their valley. This natural fragrance, usually a source of comfort, now seemed to carry a subtle whisper of resilience, a reminder of the enduring strength of the wild places. She looked out at the sea of faces – farmers whose hands were calloused from coaxing life from the soil, engineers whose minds charted the intricate pathways of their technology, artisans whose craft breathed beauty into their existence, educators who nurtured the minds of their future. They were the embodiment of Havenridge, its strength and its soul.

Her own heart beat a steady, determined rhythm against her ribs. She met Eli's gaze from where he stood amongst the council members, a silent anchor of support. His confession had been a seismic event, shaking the very bedrock of trust they had built. But in its aftermath, Mara had seen not weakness, but an act of profound bravery. He had laid bare his past, not to excuse it, but to fortify their present and future. His willingness to confront his shadows, to risk everything for their sake, was a testament to the man he had become, the man she had seen and believed in.

"My friends, my neighbors, my Havenridge family," Mara began, her voice clear and strong, amplified by the plaza's acoustics. It carried over the anxious murmur, cutting through the air like a beam of sunlight piercing through clouds. "The past few cycles have been fraught with challenges. We have faced the demanding gaze of an external delegation, a gaze that sought to impose its will upon our home. We have met their ultimatum with innovation, with unity, and with a fierce determination to chart our own course."

She paused, allowing the familiar narrative to settle. Then, she shifted, her gaze sweeping across the faces, acknowledging the unspoken question, the lingering unease. "This morning, our community council heard a revelation that has undoubtedly shaken us. Eli, a man who has become a pillar of this settlement, a partner in our vision, a friend to so many, has shared a part of his history that many of us did not know. A history that is complex, shadowed by circumstances he has long sought to overcome."

A collective breath seemed to be held across the plaza. Mara could feel the weight of their attention, the collective need to understand, to reconcile the Eli they knew with the one he had revealed. "I understand that such news can be unsettling," she continued, her tone laced with empathy. "We value honesty, transparency, and the courage it takes to confront difficult truths. Eli has given us that courage today. He has not asked for our forgiveness, but for our understanding. He has offered us his past, so that we might better safeguard our future."

Her gaze found Eli again, a silent affirmation of her belief in him. "I have worked alongside Eli. I have seen his dedication, his tireless efforts, his unwavering commitment to the safety and prosperity of every single one of us. His past may be a part of his story, but it does not define the man who stands before us today, the man who has poured his heart and soul into building this haven with us. He has faced down adversaries before, adversaries who prey on fear and division. And he has chosen to face them now, openly, with us, because he believes in us, and because he knows that our greatest strength lies not in hiding from our vulnerabilities, but in confronting them together."

The scent of pine seemed to intensify, carried on a gentle breeze that rustled through the banners hanging from the surrounding buildings. It was as if the very spirit of Havenridge was breathing encouragement, a silent testament to the resilience woven into the fabric of their community.

"We are Havenridge," Mara declared, her voice rising with conviction. "We are a community founded on principles. Principles of resilience, of self-determination, of the unwavering belief that every individual, every settlement, has the right to forge its own destiny. We chose this life, away from the suffocating grip of larger powers, because we believed in a better way. A way where collaboration trumps control, where shared prosperity outweighs individual gain, where the collective good is paramount."

She spread her hands, encompassing the crowd. "Remember why we are here. Remember the sacrifices made to establish this place. Remember the dreams we nurtured, the hope we cultivated. We did not come to the fringes of explored space to be dictated to. We came to build, to grow, to create a future where our children could thrive, free from the machinations of those who seek to control and exploit. The delegation, and the shadowy figures behind them, underestimate this spirit. They see our isolation as weakness, our independence as defiance. They believe they can break us by threatening what is dear to us, by sowing discord, by exploiting any perceived cracks in our unity."

"Eli's past," she continued, her voice firm, "is a tool they intend to wield against us. They believe that by exposing his history, by associating him with their machinations, they can shatter your trust, not just in him, but in the very ideals of Havenridge. They want us to turn on each other. They want us to retreat into fear and suspicion. They want us to believe that our dreams of autonomy are naive, that we are not strong enough to stand on our own."

Mara took a step forward, her gaze piercing and unwavering. "But they are wrong. They have underestimated the strength of our conviction. They have underestimated the bonds that tie us together. They have underestimated the power of truth, even when it is painful. And they have underestimated the courage of a community that refuses to be bowed."

"Eli's confession is not a reason for us to falter," she stated, her words ringing with certainty. "It is a testament to his character, his commitment to us. He has shown us his vulnerabilities, not as a sign of weakness, but as an act of profound trust. He has laid bare the enemy's tactics, their intent to divide and conquer. And now, armed with this knowledge, we can stand even taller."

The crowd was silent, rapt. The anxiety that had permeated the plaza was slowly giving way to a resolute focus. The scent of pine needles, carried on the gentle breeze, seemed to whisper tales of enduring forests, of roots that ran deep and branches that reached defiantly towards the sky, an echo of the resilience Mara spoke of.

"We will not be intimidated," Mara proclaimed, her voice echoing with a new, unshakeable resolve. "We will not be dictated to. We will not allow our home to be seized by those who seek to profit from our subjugation. This is our land, our community, our future. And we will defend it with everything we have."

She extended her hand, palm up, a gesture of open invitation. "We have the ingenuity to adapt. We have the spirit to persevere. And we have each other. This is not just about Eli, or the delegation, or the threats they pose. This is about the kind of future we want to build. A future of freedom, of self-governance, of unwavering solidarity. A future where our children can grow up knowing that their home was defended by the courage of their parents, by the strength of their community."

"Let us not be swayed by fear," Mara urged. "Let us be galvanized by truth. Let us stand together, united in our purpose, unwavering in our resolve. Let us show the delegation, and all those who seek to control us, that Havenridge is not a prize to be claimed, but a spirit that cannot be broken. We are more than just a settlement; we are a testament to what free people can achieve when they stand as one. We are Havenridge, and we will not yield."

Her words hung in the air, potent and powerful. The hushed anxiety that had gripped the plaza began to transform into a palpable sense of shared purpose. Faces that had been etched with worry now showed a glimmer of determination. The whispers of fear were being drowned out by the rising tide of collective resolve, a tide that carried with it the fresh, invigorating scent of pine, a fragrant promise of enduring strength and unwavering spirit. The community, inspired by Eli's vulnerability and Mara's unwavering conviction, was beginning to rally, not just against an external threat, but in defense of the very soul of Havenridge. The path ahead would be challenging, fraught with uncertainty, but in that moment, standing united under the vast, open sky, they were more ready than ever to face whatever reckoning came their way. The wind rustled through the surrounding pines, a sigh of affirmation, and the scent of their needles seemed to deepen, a grounding, earthy perfume that spoke of resilience, of roots that held firm, of a spirit that refused to be extinguished.

The air in Havenridge, once alive with the hum of progress and the murmur of community, now vibrated with a different kind of energy – a potent, focused tension. The words spoken in the central plaza had resonated, transforming apprehension into a shared resolve. The ultimatum from the delegation, a stark declaration of their intent, had served not to break Havenridge, but to forge it into something harder, more determined. Eli, his gaze now holding a steely glint that belied the turmoil of his past, stepped forward as the architect of their defense. He moved with a quiet authority, his every action a testament to the urgency of their situation. The salvaged components, the intricate circuitry painstakingly pieced together from derelict starships and forgotten orbital platforms, were no longer just curiosities of engineering; they were the sinews of their protection.

He stood amidst the growing bustle of the defensive staging areas, his hands, once accustomed to delicate calibrations and intricate repairs, now wielding tools of a different sort. Sparks flew as technicians, their faces illuminated by the harsh glare of welding torches, integrated newly reinforced plating onto the settlement's perimeter shields. Eli moved among them, his voice a low, steady presence, offering adjustments, answering questions, his understanding of the technology almost intuitive. He had overseen the strategic placement of energy dispersal nodes, their glowing conduits a network of latent power ready to be unleashed. These weren't the sleek, polished defenses of a well-funded military; they were a testament to Havenridge's ingenuity, a defiant patchwork of salvaged brilliance born from necessity and a desperate will to survive.

"Ensure the secondary power conduits are shielded against atmospheric disruption," Eli instructed a team calibrating a formidable-looking array of sonic emitters. "They've shown a preference for EMP bursts. We can't afford any blind spots." His mind raced, envisioning the possible vectors of attack, the subtle nuances of the delegation's technological capabilities. He had seen their ships, their weaponry, and he knew that brute force alone would not be enough. Havenridge's strength lay in its adaptability, its ability to weave defenses from the threads of what others had discarded. He had personally overseen the modification of the settlement's atmospheric scrubbers, re-purposing their filtration systems to generate a dense, obscuring aerosol, a tactical fog that could disrupt targeting sensors and provide cover for rapid redeployments.

Across the settlement, the echoes of this frantic preparation were palpable. The rhythmic clang of hammers against metal, the low thrum of energy systems coming online, the sharp hiss of pressurized air – these sounds wove themselves into a new symphony, one of defiance and readiness. The scent of freshly turned earth filled the air, a visceral reminder of the physical preparations underway. Trenches, hastily but diligently dug, crisscrossed the outer perimeters, their earthen walls a testament to the collective effort of every able-bodied individual. Farmers, their hands roughened by years of tilling the soil, worked alongside engineers, their movements synchronized by a shared purpose. It was a sight that filled Mara with a profound sense of pride and a gnawing worry.

Mara, her focus divided between the immediate and the long-term, moved through the settlement with a different kind of authority. Her role was not to wield the tools of war, but to nurture the foundations of their resilience. She oversaw the meticulous rationing of supplies, ensuring that every nutrient paste packet, every water purification tablet, was accounted for. Her calm demeanor was a balm to the underlying anxiety that still lingered, a subtle undercurrent beneath the surface of their focused activity. She had established reinforced subterranean shelters, their entrances camouflaged and their air filtration systems robust, designated as safe zones for the elderly, the very young, and those deemed non-essential for the immediate defense.

She checked on the medical teams, their bay filled with a sterile scent mingled with the antiseptic tang of potent healing compounds. Volunteers, their faces etched with concern but their hands steady, were practicing rapid wound dressing techniques, their movements rehearsed and efficient. "Ensure the bio-regeneration units are fully charged and accessible," Mara instructed the chief medic. "And have the shuttle bays prepped for emergency evacuations. We need to be ready for any contingency." Her mind was a constant whirl of logistics, of contingency planning, of ensuring that the heart of Havenridge – its people – remained protected. She understood that while Eli focused on repelling the physical threat, her responsibility lay in safeguarding their future, in ensuring that even in the face of utter devastation, the spirit of Havenridge would endure.

She walked through the marketplace, its usual vibrant energy replaced by a focused determination. Stalls were being dismantled, their wares carefully stored in the communal depots. Children, their faces a mixture of awe and apprehension, were being guided by their parents to the designated safe zones, their small hands clutching treasured possessions. Mara paused, her gaze resting on a young girl, no older than seven, who was meticulously packing a small, crudely fashioned wooden bird into a sturdy satchel. The girl looked up, her eyes wide, and Mara offered a gentle smile. "You're keeping your special things safe," Mara said softly. The girl nodded, a flicker of bravery in her gaze. "So we remember when it's all over," she whispered, her voice barely audible. Mara's heart ached, but she saw in the child's solemnity a reflection of the community's unwavering spirit.

The rhythmic clang of metal, the low hum of activated systems, the scent of earth and industry – these were the sounds and smells of Havenridge preparing for the storm. Eli, with his intricate understanding of technology and his growing strategic acumen, was meticulously weaving a net of defense. Mara, with her unwavering focus on the well-being of their people, was fortifying the very heart of their community. They were two sides of the same coin, their efforts intertwined, each dependent on the other. The community, once a collective of individuals pursuing their own paths, was now a unified force, their every action, from the digging of a trench to the calibration of a shield, a testament to their shared commitment. The earth beneath their feet, the very ground they were so determined to defend, seemed to thrum with their collective defiance, a silent promise of resistance.

Eli stood at the central observation post, the holographic displays before him a swirling tapestry of real-time sensor data. He traced the projected flight paths of their modified survey drones, their cloaking technology enhanced to an unprecedented level. These weren't just scouts; they were the eyes and ears of Havenridge, relaying critical intel on the delegation's movements. He had overseen the integration of a repurposed deep-space communication array, now tuned to intercept and analyze enemy transmissions. The information gleaned was vital, allowing them to anticipate troop deployments and probe for weaknesses in the delegation's formations. "Report on the energy signature from the asteroid belt," Eli commanded into his comm unit, his voice calm and steady despite the immense pressure. "I need to know if they're attempting a flanking maneuver through the debris field."

His attention shifted to another screen, displaying the status of Havenridge's primary shield generator. It was a hulking behemoth of salvaged technology, its core a fusion of components from three different derelict vessels. Eli had personally overseen its most recent recalibration, pushing its output to its theoretical limits. "Maintain shield integrity at ninety-five percent," he instructed the engineering team monitoring the generator. "We'll need every joule for the initial engagement. And prep the surge capacitors for a directed energy burst, should the need arise." He knew that the delegation's capital ships were formidable, their offensive capabilities vast. Havenridge's defense had to be a multifaceted strategy, a combination of deterrence, evasion, and localized, overwhelming force.

He had also implemented a network of seismic sensors buried deep within the surrounding terrain. These were designed to detect subsurface troop movements, the subtle tremors of approaching ground forces. Should the delegation attempt an orbital bombardment or a direct ground assault, Havenridge would have precious seconds, perhaps even minutes, to react. Eli's mind, a finely tuned instrument of analysis and prediction, was constantly evaluating probabilities, calculating risks, and devising countermeasures. He understood that this was not just a physical battle; it was a war of attrition, a test of endurance, and a race against time. He had even commissioned the construction of a series of mobile defense platforms, jury-rigged from decommissioned cargo haulers, their weapon systems modified for rapid deployment and surprising agility. These would serve as a mobile defense, able to reinforce weakened sectors or launch targeted strikes against vulnerabilities.

Mara, meanwhile, was coordinating the final stages of the civilian evacuation to the subterranean shelters. She moved with a quiet urgency, her presence a comforting reassurance to those she encountered. She personally inspected the life support systems in the deepest shelters, ensuring that the air purifiers were functioning optimally and that the emergency power reserves were fully charged. Her focus was on the psychological well-being of the evacuees as much as their physical safety. She had organized teams of storytellers and musicians to provide comfort and distraction, ensuring that the youngest among them wouldn't be overwhelmed by the fear of the unknown.

She met with the heads of the various guilds – the farmers, the engineers, the artisans – ensuring that their essential skills were accounted for and that plans were in place for their rapid reintegration into the community once the immediate threat had passed. "Maintain communication lines with the surface teams as much as possible," Mara instructed a technician overseeing the comms hub. "We need to know the status of the defenses in real-time. And ensure the emergency medical supplies are distributed to all designated safe zones." Her organizational skills were the bedrock upon which Havenridge's resilience was built, a testament to her ability to manage complexity and maintain order amidst chaos.

She walked through the hydroponic gardens, their verdant growth a stark contrast to the grim reality of their preparations. Here, under the artificial glow of nutrient lamps, the future of Havenridge was being nurtured. Mara paused, her hand brushing against the cool, smooth surface of a ripening fruit. This was what they were fighting for – not just their lives, but the continuation of their way of life, the promise of growth and sustenance. She had overseen the doubling of their seed reserves and the fortification of the garden's protective domes, anticipating the possibility of orbital bombardment. Every detail, no matter how small, was being considered.

The rhythmic clang of metal continued, a constant pulse beneath the surface of their organized chaos. The scent of ozone, a byproduct of the activated energy shields, began to mingle with the earthy aroma of the trenches. Eli's meticulous planning and Mara's steadfast leadership were creating a formidable defense, not just of fortifications and technology, but of a unified will. The community, once a disparate collection of individuals drawn together by a shared dream, was now a single, resolute entity, their actions a symphony of defiance. The earth itself seemed to breathe with them, a silent witness to their unwavering commitment to protect their home, their way of life, and the fragile future they had so painstakingly built. Every action, every sound, every scent, was a testament to Havenridge's refusal to yield, a prelude to the reckoning that was inevitably on its way.

The air in Havenridge, thick with the scent of ozone and anticipation, crackled with the unspoken question that hung over every inhabitant. The delegation's ultimatum, delivered with chilling efficiency, had stripped away all pretense of negotiation. It was a stark dichotomy: surrender their hard-won autonomy and become a mere cog in the delegation's vast, indifferent machinery, or stand their ground and face an onslaught that threatened to obliterate everything they had built. The choice, presented with brutal finality, was a choice between the illusion of security offered by subjugation and the terrifying, exhilarating embrace of freedom.

Mara stood on the central promenade, the holographic projections of the delegation's fleet shimmering ominously in the twilight sky. They were a stark, metallic scar against the bruised canvas of the heavens, a constant, undeniable reminder of the power arrayed against them. Beside her, Eli's silhouette was etched against the glow of the command center's main display. His usual focused intensity was now underscored by a profound gravity, a reflection of the immense weight he carried. They had navigated treacherous waters together, their partnership forged in the crucible of shared challenges and nascent hope. Now, they stood at the precipice of a decision that would define not only their future, but the very essence of Havenridge itself.

"They're waiting for our response, Mara," Eli's voice was a low murmur, barely audible above the subtle hum of the settlement's defensive systems coming online. "Their sensors are already registering our increased energy output. They know we're preparing for *something*." He gestured towards the tactical display, where the delegation's fleet movements were meticulously tracked. "Our intel suggests they're not interested in a protracted negotiation. They want compliance, swiftly and decisively."

Mara's gaze swept across the faces of the Havenridge residents who had gathered, a sea of anxious but determined individuals. There was fear, undeniably, etched into the lines around their eyes and the slight tremor in their hands. But beneath the apprehension, a resolute spirit flickered. They had chosen this life, this fragile existence on the frontier, seeking an escape from the suffocating control of larger powers. To yield now, to trade their independence for the sterile safety of servitude, would be to betray the very reason they had come to Havenridge in the first place.

"And what do you believe, Eli?" Mara asked, her voice steady, though her heart hammered against her ribs like a trapped bird. "What is the 'something' they expect from us?"

Eli turned to her, his eyes, usually so full of analytical detachment, now held a flicker of raw emotion. "They expect us to be rational, Mara. To understand the futility of resistance. They expect us to choose the path of least resistance, the path of survival, however diminished." He paused, a grim smile touching his lips. "They don't understand Havenridge. They don't understand what it means to build something from nothing, with nothing but grit and a shared dream."

The weight of that dream, of the sacrifices made to nurture it, pressed down on Mara. She thought of the barren plains they had transformed, the rudimentary shelters that had blossomed into a thriving community, the bonds of kinship that had formed between strangers united by a common purpose. This was more than just a settlement; it was a sanctuary, a testament to the human capacity for creation and self-determination. To surrender it would be to extinguish the light they had so bravely kindled.

"Stability," Mara mused, the word tasting like ash on her tongue. "They offer us stability, a place within their order. But it's the stability of a well-maintained cage. And we are not meant for cages, Eli."

Eli nodded, his gaze returning to the holographic fleet. "The cost of that stability is our identity. Our right to make our own choices, to chart our own course. They will integrate our resources, our labor, our very existence into their system. We will become another nameless, faceless designation in their grand galactic ledger." He looked at her, a silent question passing between them. "Can we afford to pay that price?"

The question hung in the air, heavy and pregnant with unspoken consequences. The delegation's fleet was a formidable force, their military might a well-documented terror. Havenridge, with its jury-rigged defenses and its collection of salvaged technology, was a defiant David against a Goliath. The odds were astronomically stacked against them. Yet, the alternative, the slow erosion of their spirit, felt like a death sentence of a different, more insidious kind.

"We have prepared, Eli," Mara said, her voice gaining strength. "We have built our defenses. We have reinforced our shelters. We have organized our people. We have done everything in our power to be ready for *this* day." She met his gaze, her own resolve hardening. "The decision is not ours alone to make, not entirely. It belongs to every soul who calls Havenridge home. We must present them with the choice, the stark reality of what lies before us, and let them decide."

The news spread like wildfire through the settlement, carried by hushed whispers and urgent pronouncements from community leaders. A mass gathering was called for the following cycle, a convocation to address the delegation's ultimatum. As the sun dipped below the horizon, casting long, spectral shadows across the plazas and pathways, an unprecedented stillness fell over Havenridge. The usual sounds of communal life – the laughter of children, the hum of workshops, the distant murmur of conversation – were replaced by a profound, almost reverent silence. It was the quiet before the storm, the collective holding of breath before a momentous decision.

Eli and Mara spent the remaining hours in the command center, poring over tactical readouts, refining defensive protocols, and simulating potential scenarios. Every calculation, every projection, pointed towards a grim reality: a direct confrontation would be devastating. The delegation possessed overwhelming firepower, advanced weaponry that could breach Havenridge's shields with relative ease. There was no illusion of outright victory, no naive belief that they could simply repel the invaders through sheer force of will.

"We can inflict damage, Eli," Mara said, her voice strained as she reviewed the projected casualty figures from a simulated ground assault. "We can make them pay a price. But the cost to us..." She trailed off, unable to voice the horrifying numbers. "We need a strategy that doesn't just focus on repelling them, but on enduring them. On surviving whatever they throw at us."

Eli ran a hand through his hair, his frustration evident. "Their primary objective isn't annihilation, Mara. It's subjugation. They want to incorporate us, not obliterate us. That's our only real leverage. The threat of our complete destruction might be a deterrent, but the threat of... inconvenience... might be more effective." He tapped a schematic of Havenridge's core infrastructure. "If we can demonstrate that integrating us will be more trouble than it's worth, that our destruction would cripple key systems they rely on, perhaps they'll reconsider."

This was a dangerous gamble, relying on the delegation's pragmatism rather than their mercy. It meant presenting a unified front of defiance, but also subtly hinting at the chaos and disruption that resistance would unleash. It was a tightrope walk between signaling a willingness to fight and an implicit threat of mutually assured destruction, albeit on a vastly unequal scale.

"So, we make them choose between a controlled acquisition and a chaotic, potentially damaging fight," Mara summarized, the implications of such a strategy settling in her mind. "We make them understand that their prize might be less valuable if it's shattered in the process."

"Precisely," Eli confirmed. "We highlight our value – the unique resources, the specialized knowledge we possess – but we also emphasize the difficulty of controlling something that refuses to be controlled. We make them weigh the cost of our submission against the cost of our annihilation, and hope they find the former to be the lesser of two evils."

As the gathering commenced in the main plaza, a hushed anticipation filled the air. Thousands of faces, illuminated by the soft glow of the settlement's lighting, turned towards the elevated platform where Mara and Eli stood. The holographic fleet still hung in the sky, a silent, imposing presence that served as a constant reminder of their precarious situation.

Mara stepped forward, her voice amplified to reach every corner of the plaza. "My friends, my neighbors, my family," she began, her gaze sweeping across the assembly. "You know why we are gathered here today. The delegation has presented us with a choice. A choice that will define our future, and the future of Havenridge."

She explained, with unsparing clarity, the terms of the ultimatum: complete capitulation, loss of self-governance, and assimilation into the delegation's vast network. She spoke of the potential consequences of refusal – the overwhelming military might that stood ready to enforce their will. There were gasps, murmurs of fear, and the quiet sobs of children clinging to their parents.

"They offer us security," Mara continued, her voice ringing with conviction. "A guaranteed place within their order, a life free from the constant struggle for survival that has been our lot. They offer us stability, predictability, and an end to the uncertainty that has defined our existence since we first set foot on this world."

A wave of murmurs rippled through the crowd. The promise of an end to hardship was a potent lure, especially for those who had borne the brunt of Havenridge's struggles. The weight of their daily burdens, the constant need to innovate and adapt, the ever-present threat of scarcity – these were realities that even the most ardent proponents of freedom found wearying.

"But this stability," Mara's voice grew firmer, imbued with a quiet power, "comes at a price. The price of our freedom. The price of our autonomy. The price of our very identity. If we accept their terms, we cease to be Havenridge. We become merely a resource, a designation, a footnote in their grand design. Our choices will no longer be our own. Our future will be dictated, not by our dreams, but by their directives."

She paused, allowing the gravity of her words to sink in. The fear that had been a palpable presence in the plaza seemed to solidify, morphing into a grim understanding. This was not a negotiation; it was a surrender of their souls.

Eli stepped forward, his presence a steady anchor beside Mara. "We have built Havenridge with our own hands, from the salvaged remnants of others' discards. We have forged a community here, based on trust, on shared effort, and on the radical idea that we can create our own destiny." His voice, usually calm and analytical, now carried a fierce passion. "This place is more than just a collection of buildings and systems. It is a testament to what humanity can achieve when it is free to pursue its own vision."

He gestured towards the holographic fleet. "The delegation sees us as a resource to be managed, a problem to be solved. They underestimate our ingenuity, our resilience, and our unwavering commitment to the principles on which Havenridge was founded. They believe that by threatening us with destruction, they can compel our submission. But they fail to grasp that the destruction they threaten is not the end of our story, but the potential end of *their* ambition."

A hush fell over the crowd as Eli's words, laced with a subtle but potent threat, resonated through the plaza. The implication was clear: Havenridge might be outmatched in a direct confrontation, but it was not powerless. If forced into a corner, if its very existence was threatened, it could unleash a torrent of chaos that would make subjugation a far more costly endeavor than the delegation might imagine.

"We have fortified our systems, we have prepared our defenses, and we have, most importantly, united as a people," Eli continued. "We will not bow down. We will not surrender our freedom. But neither do we seek a senseless war of annihilation. We seek to preserve what we have built, and to continue charting our own course."

He turned to face the delegation's orbital presence, his voice carrying a message of defiance and calculated risk. "We are willing to demonstrate the strength of our resolve. We are willing to make them understand the true cost of their demands. We will not yield our autonomy, but we will also make it unequivocally clear that the destruction of Havenridge would be a pyrrhic victory, a self-inflicted wound that would reverberate far beyond our small corner of the galaxy."

The crowd remained silent, absorbing the weight of their leaders' words. The choice was no longer simply about surrender or resistance. It was a complex calculation of risk, of sacrifice, and of the enduring power of self-determination. Mara and Eli had laid bare the stark reality, offering not a guarantee of safety, but a path forward defined by courage and unity.

The decision, however, was not entirely theirs to unilaterally make. While Eli and Mara had articulated their stance, the ultimate commitment had to come from the people themselves. Each inhabitant of Havenridge, from the youngest child to the oldest elder, had to weigh the cost of their freedom against the terrifying prospect of conflict.

As the gathering dispersed, a new kind of energy permeated the settlement. The fear had not vanished, but it was now tempered with a resolute purpose. Conversations, once filled with apprehension, now buzzed with discussions of strategy, of resource allocation, and of the unwavering commitment to protect their home. The choice between freedom and control had been laid bare, and Havenridge, with bated breath, was preparing to embrace the consequences of its decision. They understood that stability could be found in servitude, a predictable existence under the thumb of a larger power. But that stability was a gilded cage, a surrender of the very spirit that had drawn them to this frontier in the first place. True stability, they realized, was not the absence of risk, but the courage to face it, together.

The coming hours were a testament to Havenridge's collective spirit. While the external threat loomed, the internal discourse was as vital as any defensive measure. Mara, moving through the settlement, engaged with individuals and small groups, her calm presence a conduit for their fears and their hopes. She listened to the anxieties of parents, the pragmatic concerns of engineers, the quiet determination of the farmers who had cultivated life from the barren soil. Each conversation was a reinforcement of their shared purpose, a reminder that their unity was their most formidable weapon.

"We cannot guarantee victory, not in the traditional sense," Mara confided to Elara, the lead botanist, as they surveyed the reinforced hydroponic domes. "But we can guarantee that we will not be conquered without a fight. And we can guarantee that if the worst comes to pass, our spirit, our knowledge, our legacy will endure."

Elara, her hands stained with the rich soil of Havenridge, nodded, her eyes reflecting a fierce resolve. "These plants," she said, her voice resonating with a deep affection, "they are our future. They are the promise of sustenance, of continuation. We will defend them, and what they represent, with everything we have."

Eli, meanwhile, was engaged in a series of rapid-fire simulations, pushing the boundaries of Havenridge's technological capabilities. He worked with his engineering teams, fine-tuning the energy dispersal nodes and calibrating the sonic emitters. Each adjustment, each optimization, was a deliberate act of defiance, a calculated step in their strategy of making resistance a costly proposition for the delegation.

"If they attempt a direct orbital bombardment," Eli explained to a senior technician, his finger tracing a complex energy flow diagram, "we overload the primary shield capacitors. Not to destroy them, but to create a massive, localized energy surge that will scramble their targeting systems and potentially damage their orbital platforms. It's a desperate measure, but it buys us time, and it sends a message."

The message was clear: Havenridge would not be a compliant acquisition. It would be a thorny, dangerous prize, one that would demand a significant investment of resources and risk to control. Their strategy was not about brute force, but about calculated disruption, about leveraging their unique technological ingenuity and their profound understanding of their own systems to create an unpalatable level of resistance.

As the cycle drew to a close, a palpable sense of shared destiny settled over Havenridge. The fear was still present, a low hum beneath the surface of their resolve, but it was no longer paralyzing. It had been transmuted into a steely determination. They had chosen freedom, a path fraught with peril, but one that honored the very essence of their existence. They had looked into the abyss of control and chosen the exhilarating, terrifying uncertainty of self-determination.

Mara and Eli stood together at the edge of the main plaza, watching as the last of the community members returned to their homes, their steps no longer hurried by apprehension but steadied by a newfound purpose. The holographic fleet remained, a stark silhouette against the nascent dawn, but it no longer held the same aura of absolute power. It was now a challenge, a gauntlet thrown down, and Havenridge, united and resolute, was ready to pick it up.

The dawn that broke over Havenridge was not a harbinger of peace, but of a reckoning. The choice had been made, and the consequences, whatever they might be, would be faced together. The fragile hope that had sustained them through the darkest hours now burned brighter, fueled by the unwavering belief that a future defined by their own choices, however difficult, was infinitely more valuable than a life dictated by the will of others. They had chosen freedom, and in that choice lay their greatest strength, and their most profound hope.

Chapter Twelve
The Stand

The holographic projection of the delegation's fleet, a stark lattice of metallic threats, shimmered above Havenridge, a silent, unyielding sentinel. Within the council chamber, the air, heavy with the residue of debate and the scent of ionized particles from the bustling command center, now thrummed with a different kind of energy – the quiet, resolute hum of a decision made. Mara stood tall, her gaze steady, the weight of the community's collective will settled upon her shoulders. Eli, his expression a canvas of focused determination, stood beside her, his presence a silent testament to their shared journey. The ultimatum, delivered with the cold precision of a surgeon's scalpel, had been a stark proposition: surrender their hard-won autonomy, their very essence, or face annihilation. Yet, Havenridge had chosen not to bleed, but to stand.

The council members, a diverse cross-section of Havenridge's skilled populace – engineers, xenobotanists, geologists, artists, and philosophers – had deliberated long and hard. They had weighed the chilling arithmetic of the delegation's military superiority against the immeasurable value of their freedom. They had debated the merits of subservience versus the terrifying allure of self-determination. Each voice had contributed to the chorus of consensus, a symphony of defiance forged in the crucible of shared experience. Now, it was time to formally communicate that unified refusal.

"We have considered your proposal," Mara's voice, amplified to resonate through the chamber and beyond, carried a quiet authority. It was not the strident cry of a warrior, but the measured pronouncement of a leader who understood the gravity of her words. Her gaze swept across the faces of her people, etched with a mixture of apprehension and unwavering resolve. "We acknowledge the power you command, and we understand the implications of our response."

She paused, allowing the weight of her statement to settle. The delegation's envoy, a stoic figure whose face remained impassive, sat across from them, a study in controlled impatience. Beside him, a more junior officer fidgeted, a tell-tale sign of the undercurrent of tension that permeated the room. The faint scent of ozone, a byproduct of Havenridge's active defensive systems, seemed to amplify the charged atmosphere.

"Havenridge was founded on the principle of self-governance," Mara continued, her voice gaining a subtle strength. "We sought a haven, a place where we could chart our own course, build our own future, free from the dictates of distant powers. We have poured our sweat, our ingenuity, and our very souls into making this world our home. We have overcome countless challenges, not through the imposition of will, but through collaboration, innovation, and a shared commitment to our collective well-being."

She gestured towards Eli, his hand resting lightly on the console beside him, a subtle reminder of the technological prowess Havenridge possessed. "We are not a threat," Mara stated, her tone firm but devoid of aggression. "We are a community seeking peaceful coexistence, a beacon of what can be achieved when individuals are empowered to contribute their unique talents and perspectives. We believe in the inherent worth of every sentient being, and we extend that belief to our interactions with all civilizations."

Eli stepped forward, his voice a clear, resonant baritone that echoed the sentiments Mara had so eloquently expressed. "Your ultimatum demands that we surrender that which is most precious to us: our autonomy. It asks us to become cogs in a machine, our individuality subsumed, our dreams relegated to the footnotes of your grand design. We cannot, and will not, comply with such a demand."

He looked directly at the delegation's envoy, his gaze unflinching. "We respect your right to exist, to pursue your own objectives. However, we will not allow those objectives to come at the cost of our fundamental right to self-determination. We have spent cycles building a society based on mutual respect and the freedom to make our own choices. To abandon those principles now would be to betray ourselves, and to invalidate everything we have strived to achieve."

The envoy's expression remained unchanged, but the subtle clench of his jaw, the almost imperceptible tightening of his hand on the armrest of his chair, betrayed a flicker of something beneath the veneer of composure. He had expected a plea, perhaps even a desperate negotiation. He had not anticipated such a quiet, yet unyielding, rejection.

"However," Eli's voice took on a more somber, yet equally determined, tone, "while we seek peace, we are not naive. We understand the power you wield, and the potential consequences of refusing your demands. We have, therefore, made preparations. Our systems are robust, our defenses are operational, and our people are united. We do not seek conflict, but we will not stand idly by while our home, and our freedom, are threatened."

He paused, allowing the unspoken implication to hang in the air. Havenridge, though smaller and less technologically advanced in terms of sheer destructive capacity, was not defenseless. They had invested heavily in their infrastructure, in their defensive grid, and in their ability to make themselves an unpalatable target. They possessed knowledge, ingenuity, and a fierce protectiveness of their home that the delegation might be underestimating.

"We offer you a choice, envoy," Eli continued, his voice resonating with a quiet power. "You can attempt to force our submission, a path that will undoubtedly result in significant cost and disruption for both sides. Or, you can acknowledge our right to exist as we are, a sovereign entity capable of contributing to the galactic community on our own terms. We are willing to engage in dialogue, to explore avenues of mutual benefit, but only from a position of equality, not subjugation."

The envoy finally spoke, his voice a low, gravelly rumble that seemed to scrape against the polished surfaces of the chamber. "Your defiance is... disappointing," he stated, the word laced with a chilling undertone. "Havenridge has proven itself to be a valuable asset. Your systems, your resources, your technological innovations – they are all ripe for integration. We offered you a place within a larger, more stable framework. A framework that would ensure your survival and prosperity far beyond what you can achieve on your own."

He leaned forward, his eyes, the color of polished obsidian, fixed on Mara. "Your refusal is illogical. It is a rejection of pragmatism, a gamble with your very existence. Do you truly believe your jury-rigged defenses can withstand the might of the delegation? Do you truly believe your disparate technologies can stand against our unified fleet?"

A low murmur ran through the council members. The envoy's words were designed to sow doubt, to remind them of their precarious position. But Havenridge had weathered storms far greater than mere threats. They had built their society from the ground up, their resilience forged in the fires of necessity.

Mara met his gaze, her own eyes reflecting the quiet fire of conviction. "We do not underestimate your power, envoy. We acknowledge the vast disparity in our military capabilities. However, you underestimate the value of what you seek to control. Havenridge is not merely a collection of resources to be harvested. It is a living, breathing entity, populated by individuals who have chosen to build a life here, a life they are fiercely protective of. To subdue us by force would be to shatter the very prize you seek to acquire."

She continued, her voice steady and clear, "You speak of integration, of stability. But what you truly seek is control. And control, when imposed through coercion, breeds resentment, inefficiency, and ultimately, instability. We believe that true prosperity lies in cooperation, not domination. We are willing to cooperate, to share our knowledge and resources, but only as equals, not as subjects."

The air in the chamber grew thick, the subtle scent of approaching rain outside, carried on a nascent breeze, seemed to mirror the brewing storm of conflict. The tension was almost palpable, a silent standoff between two vastly different philosophies of existence. The delegation saw a resource to be claimed, a system to be absorbed. Havenridge saw a home to be defended, a dream to be nurtured.

"We have made our decision," Eli stated, his voice firm. "We reject your ultimatum. We will not surrender our autonomy. We wish for peace, and we are open to dialogue, but that dialogue must be conducted on the understanding that Havenridge is a sovereign entity. If you choose to pursue a path of aggression, then you will find us united, and we will defend our home with every means at our disposal."

The envoy rose slowly, his movements deliberate, almost predatory. The junior officer beside him mirrored his posture, his hand instinctively moving towards a concealed sidearm. "Your defiance will not be tolerated," the envoy declared, his voice now devoid of any pretense of civility. "The delegation does not accept refusal. You have made your choice, Havenridge. Now, you will face the consequences."

With that, he turned, his obsidian gaze sweeping across the assembled council members one last time, a silent promise of retribution in his eyes. He and his accompanying officer exited the chamber, their footsteps echoing on the polished floor, each click a harbinger of the approaching storm.

As the heavy doors swung shut behind them, a profound silence descended upon the council. The weight of their decision, of the path they had irrevocably chosen, settled upon them. The faint scent of rain intensified, the first fat drops beginning to spatter against the chamber's reinforced windows, a mournful prelude to the tempest that was undoubtedly on its way. Havenridge had stood its ground, its rejection of the ultimatum a testament to its spirit, but the true test of that spirit was yet to come. The quiet dignity of their refusal had been met with open hostility, and the illusion of negotiation had dissolved, leaving only the stark reality of inevitable conflict. The gamble had been made, the die cast. The future, once a horizon of possibility, now loomed as a battlefield. Yet, even in the face of such daunting odds, a nascent sense of pride, a quiet exultation in their shared courage, began to bloom amongst them. They had faced the dragon, and though the fight was far from over, they had not flinched. They had chosen to remain themselves, whatever the cost.

Eli's mind, a tempest of calculations and stratagems, had already moved beyond the confrontation. The envoy's departing footsteps were a mere echo; the true battle was now waged in the invisible currents of data and perception. While Mara's measured words had formed Havenridge's shield of defiance, Eli's work would be its unseen sword. He'd anticipated this outcome, of course. The delegation, arrogant in its perceived superiority, would not accept a polite refusal. They would see Havenridge as a prize to be taken, a resource to be exploited. And that, Eli knew, was where their fatal flaw lay. They operated on assumptions, on the predictable patterns of conquest. He intended to shatter those patterns.

He moved with a practiced urgency, his fingers dancing across holographic interfaces, weaving a tapestry of digital illusions. The faint scent of ozone, a byproduct of the sophisticated network he was manipulating, prickled his nostrils, a constant, sharp reminder of the immense forces at play. This wasn't about brute force; Havenridge couldn't match the delegation's fleet in a direct confrontation. This was about leverage, about making the cost of aggression prohibitively high, not in terms of military expenditure, but in terms of strategic advantage and potential gains. It was about making them hesitate, making them question, making them *doubt*.

"Mara," he murmured, his voice low, a focused hum that barely disturbed the charged atmosphere of the command center. "Initiating Phase One. The phantom signatures are being seeded."

Mara, standing beside him, her gaze fixed on the central display that now showed a complex, ever-shifting web of Havenridge's defensive grid, nodded. Her own hands moved with a subtle grace, inputting commands, cross-referencing data streams. She was the anchor, the steady presence that ensured his intricate designs remained grounded in reality, or at least, a carefully constructed version of it. "Sensors are showing nominal readings on the outer perimeter. The diversionary drones are deploying on schedule. Their initial trajectories are calibrated to mimic geological survey units."

"Good," Eli replied, a ghost of a smile touching his lips. "The delegation's intelligence likely flagged those as benign. They'll see a routine geological survey, nothing to worry about. It buys us time. But the real trick will be in the comms traffic." He tapped a sequence on his console, and a new window bloomed, displaying a dense stream of encrypted data. "I'm injecting a series of modulated bursts, designed to look like internal communication failures on our end. Glitches, dropped packets, the kind of technical hiccups that would frustrate any automated system trying to analyze our network for vulnerabilities. They'll waste cycles trying to decipher ghost signals, assuming we're struggling to maintain our own infrastructure."

The deception was layered, intricate. Eli wasn't just creating noise; he was crafting a narrative. A narrative of a struggling, less-than-perfect system that was a far cry from the unified, sophisticated defense the delegation might have anticipated based on their initial scans. This played into their inherent arrogance, their belief that any civilization capable of resisting them would be technologically superior in a way they could easily understand and overcome. By presenting an image of chaotic imperfection, Eli aimed to lull them into a false sense of security, to make them underestimate the true depth of Havenridge's resilience.

"And the fleet projection?" Mara asked, her eyes scanning the holographic display of the delegation's ships, now a more distant, menacing presence. "Are we feeding them the updated battle readiness reports?"

Eli's fingers flew, his focus unwavering. "Yes. I'm subtly altering the energy signatures of our primary defensive arrays. Not enough to trigger immediate alarms, but enough to suggest we're powering up, increasing our readiness. Simultaneously, I'm layering in false positives in their sensor sweeps, suggesting anomalous energy readings from the *outer* sectors of our system. Things that look like pre-attack staging, but are actually just our deep-space research outposts performing routine atmospheric analysis."

He leaned back for a fraction of a second, a weary sigh escaping him. "It's a delicate balance, Mara. We need to make them think we're preparing, but not so aggressively that they launch a preemptive strike. We need them to believe they have the initiative, that they are in control of the pace of engagement. We're planting seeds of doubt, not waving a flag of war."

The command center, usually a hive of activity, felt amplified by the unspoken tension. The hum of machinery, the soft clicks of consoles, the almost imperceptible whir of the life support systems – all seemed to underscore the precariousness of their situation. Every byte of data Eli manipulated, every signal he sent or rerouted, was a gamble. One miscalculation, one flaw in the illusion, and the delegation's fleet could descend like a thunderclap.

"The delegation's primary objective is likely resource acquisition and strategic positioning," Mara mused, her brow furrowed in thought. "They see us as an underdeveloped world with valuable, untapped potential. They'll expect resistance, but probably a predictable, easily overcome kind. They won't expect us to try and outthink them on a strategic level, to play a game of deception."

"Exactly," Eli agreed, his eyes gleaming with a fierce, almost manic energy. "Their strategic doctrine is built on overwhelming force, on rapid subjugation. They don't account for asymmetric warfare, for a smaller, more agile force that can leverage information and misdirection to create uncertainty. If we can make them believe that attacking Havenridge will be more costly and complex than they initially calculated, that the potential intelligence gained will be compromised by our countermeasures, they might reconsider their immediate approach."

He gestured to a section of the display showing a simulated projection of the delegation's fleet movements, based on their projected arrival times and likely deployment patterns. "I'm creating phantom fleet movements in their long-range scans. Small, evasive signatures that appear and disappear in the void between star systems. Enough to make their navigation and targeting algorithms work overtime, enough to make them question whether they're being tracked, whether there are other, unseen forces at play in this sector."

This was the core of Eli's gambit: creating an illusion of a larger, more complex threat than Havenridge actually posed. By making the delegation expend valuable resources and attention on phantom entities, he aimed to disrupt their planning, to sow discord within their command structure, and most importantly, to buy Havenridge precious time. Time to consolidate their defenses, time to rally their people, and perhaps, time for a diplomatic solution to emerge, however unlikely it seemed at that moment.

"The risk," Mara stated, her voice calm but firm, "is that they'll see through it. That they'll recognize the deception and use it as justification for an immediate, overwhelming assault."

"They might," Eli conceded, his gaze never leaving the screens. "But their arrogance is our greatest ally. They *want* to believe they're the smartest, the most powerful. They'll likely interpret these anomalies as evidence of a sophisticated, albeit struggling, defense system. They'll spend time analyzing, trying to find a weakness, rather than assuming outright deception. And the more resources they pour into analyzing our 'phantom' threats, the less they'll be focusing on our actual capabilities. It's a calculated risk, but it's a risk we have to take. We can't afford to be predictable."

He initiated another sequence, a subtle manipulation of Havenridge's atmospheric sensor data. "I'm introducing minor, yet persistent, fluctuations in the upper atmosphere readings. Nothing that would suggest a catastrophic environmental shift, but enough to make their orbital bombardment calculations slightly inaccurate, enough to suggest that our atmospheric defenses might be more robust or unpredictable than their models predict. It adds another layer of uncertainty to any direct assault."

The command center buzzed with Eli's focused energy. He was a conductor, orchestrating a symphony of digital deception. Mara provided the crucial counterpoint, her steady hand ensuring that the illusion remained plausible, that no element clashed jarringly with the established reality of Havenridge's capabilities. She'd spent cycles working alongside him, understanding his unique brand of technological warfare, and her trust in his abilities was absolute.

"The diversionary drones are now entering the delegation's projected sensor range," Mara reported, her voice a calm counterpoint to the digital storm Eli was conjuring. "Their mission parameters are to transmit low-level, coded distress signals, designed to mimic autonomous probe failures. Standard protocol for our deep-space exploration units."

"Excellent," Eli breathed, a slight tremor of adrenaline coursing through him. "They'll log those as malfunctions, perhaps even dismiss them as background noise. But to a highly analytical delegation, looking for patterns, for vulnerabilities, even minor anomalies can become significant. It's the accumulation of these small, 'unexplained' events that will begin to wear down their certainty."

He paused, watching the intricate dance of data unfold on the screens. The delegation's fleet was still a distant specter, a promise of violence yet to be delivered. But Eli was already engaging them, striking at their perceptions, their assumptions, their very confidence in their own intelligence. This was not a battle of laser cannons and plasma torpedoes, at least not yet. This was a battle of minds, of strategic wit, fought in the silent, invisible realm of information.

"The comms blackout protocol is now active across non-essential civilian networks," Mara confirmed. "This will further enhance the perception of internal instability if they attempt any deep network probes."

"And the energy redirection is complete," Eli added, a triumphant note in his voice. "Our primary energy conduits are now operating at seventy percent efficiency, a deliberate drop from optimal levels. This is to simulate a strain on our power grid, as if we're diverting everything to defensive systems. It will make them believe we're pushed to our limits, that our capacity for sustained combat is diminished." He grinned, a flash of fierce pride. "They'll think we're on the verge of collapse, when in reality, we're just making them think that. The true power reserves are still intact, ready to be deployed if absolutely necessary."

He was building a sophisticated lie, a narrative of a civilization struggling under immense pressure, a facade of frailty designed to mask their true strength and their unwavering resolve. The delegation, accustomed to dealing with straightforward adversaries, would be looking for direct confrontations, for clear displays of power. Eli was offering them a confusing, contradictory picture, a labyrinth of deceptive signals that would force them to slow down, to second-guess, to expend valuable time and energy unraveling a mystery that he, and only he, controlled.

"The objective is to create a state of strategic paralysis," Eli explained, his voice resonating with conviction. "To make them pause, to initiate a deeper intelligence-gathering phase, to question the immediate viability of a swift, decisive assault. If we can force them to divert resources to understanding these phantom threats, to analyzing our 'communications failures,' to recalibrating their targeting solutions based on our simulated power fluctuations, then we've already won a significant battle."

He knew the stakes. The faint scent of ozone, the constant hum of the advanced systems, the watchful gaze of Mara – they were all reminders of the gravity of his actions. But he also felt a surge of exhilaration. This was what he was built for. To take the raw materials of technology and weave them into a shield, a weapon, a means of survival. He was a strategist in the truest sense, using the very tools of advancement to protect the principles of freedom and self-determination.

"They'll likely initiate probe missions, both physical and digital," Mara predicted, her analysis mirroring Eli's own. "They'll want to verify our internal status, to assess the effectiveness of our defenses firsthand."

"And we'll be ready for them," Eli confirmed, his fingers already flying across the console, preparing the next layer of his intricate deception. "Our actual defensive systems are in place, calibrated and ready. The phantom signals will serve to draw their attention *away* from the real threats, to make them look in the wrong direction. They'll be so busy chasing shadows, they might not see the lions lurking in the bushes."

He worked tirelessly, fueled by a potent cocktail of adrenaline and the unwavering belief in Havenridge's right to exist. Each keystroke, each data packet, was a testament to his ingenuity and his commitment. The delegation saw a simple conquest; Eli saw a complex puzzle, and he was determined to solve it, not with brute force, but with the sharp edge of his intellect. The fight for Havenridge had begun, not with a bang, but with the subtle, insidious whisper of a thousand digital ghosts.

The weight of impending confrontation pressed down on Havenridge, a tangible chill that seeped into every corner of their lives. While Eli worked his strategic magic in the sterile glow of the command center, his mind a battlefield of algorithms and phantom signatures, Mara moved through the heart of their community, a beacon of quiet strength. Her presence was a balm, a steadying hand against the rising tide of anxiety that threatened to engulf them. She didn't command fleets or orchestrate digital illusions, but her role was no less critical. She was the guardian of their spirit, the silent architect of their collective will.

She began in the Central Commons, a space usually vibrant with the laughter of children and the hum of daily commerce, now hushed by an expectant stillness. Families were gathered, their faces etched with a mixture of apprehension and fierce determination. Mara moved from group to group, her steps purposeful, her voice a melody of calm reassurance. She didn't offer false promises of an easy victory, nor did she dwell on the potential for loss. Instead, she spoke of resilience, of the strength they possessed not as individuals, but as a unified community.

"We have faced challenges before," she said, her gaze sweeping across the assembled faces, meeting each one with a steady, unwavering focus. "We have weathered storms, both natural and those that threatened our very way of life. And each time, we have emerged stronger, more united. This is no different."

Her words were simple, unadorned, yet they carried the weight of conviction. She shared small anecdotes, not of grand battles, but of everyday acts of courage and kindness she'd witnessed in the preceding days. The farmer who had meticulously reinforced his home against potential damage, not for his own sake, but to provide shelter for his neighbors. The artisan who had painstakingly crafted new tools for those whose equipment had been damaged in the recent tremors, working through the night without complaint. These were the true stories of Havenridge, the quiet heroism that formed the bedrock of their community.

As dusk began to settle, painting the sky in hues of bruised purple and fiery orange, Mara initiated a new rhythm. The air, once heavy with unspoken fear, began to carry the comforting aroma of woodsmoke. She had coordinated with the communal kitchens, ensuring that supplies were distributed equitably and that the familiar ritual of a shared meal would commence. This wasn't just about sustenance; it was about connection, about reminding everyone that they were not alone, that their struggles were shared, and their strength was in their togetherness.

"Tonight, we eat together," she announced, her voice carrying through the quietening commons. "We share stories, we share laughter, and we share our resolve. Let the scent of our shared meal be a reminder of what we are fighting for: a Havenridge that is united, strong, and free."

As the fires were lit and the communal tables were laden with fragrant stews and freshly baked bread, a palpable shift occurred. The anxious whispers began to subside, replaced by the murmur of conversation, the clinking of cutlery, and the occasional burst of genuine laughter. Mara moved through the gathering, her presence a silent sentinel. She paused beside an elderly couple, offering a warm smile and a comforting hand on the woman's shoulder. She spoke with a group of younger residents, listening attentively to their concerns and offering practical advice on how they could best contribute to the community's defense efforts.

"Your skills in engineering are vital," she told a young woman named Lyra, her hands stained with the grease of her recent work repairing defensive mechanisms. "Every repair, every reinforcement, is a brick in our wall of resistance. Don't underestimate the importance of your contribution."

Lyra, her face usually alight with youthful exuberance, now bore a more somber expression. But as Mara spoke, a flicker of pride returned to her eyes. "I... I will do my best, Mara. For Havenridge."

Mara's gaze lingered on the faces around her, absorbing their quiet strength, their unwavering hope. She saw not fear, but a resolute determination hardening their features. She saw not despair, but a deep-seated love for their home, a fierce protectiveness that transcended individual anxieties. This was the essence of Havenridge, a spirit forged in the crucible of shared experience and a deep-seated connection to their land.

Later, as the stars began to prick the darkening sky, Mara found herself on the outskirts of the main settlement, near the agricultural sector. The scent of damp earth mingled with the lingering woodsmoke, creating a uniquely Havenridge aroma, one of resilience and groundedness. She walked through the neatly tilled fields, the silhouettes of the protective domes stark against the celestial canvas. Here, the farmers, their faces illuminated by the soft glow of portable lanterns, were engaged in their own quiet acts of defiance. They were not soldiers, but their labor was as crucial as any weapon.

She spoke with old Silas, his hands gnarled and weathered by years of working the soil, his eyes twinkling with a wisdom that seemed as ancient as the stars above. "The harvest is good, Mara," he said, his voice a low rumble. "We've secured as much as we could. Enough to see us through. And what we couldn't bring in, we've protected as best we can. The land will endure."

"Your dedication is inspiring, Silas," Mara replied, her voice soft. "You are the heart of Havenridge, ensuring that even in the darkest hours, life continues to bloom."

Silas chuckled, a dry, rustling sound. "Life always finds a way, child. It's our job to give it a little help, that's all. Just like you're doing, keeping our spirits strong."

Mara continued her rounds, her presence a silent affirmation of their shared purpose. She checked on the communal shelters, ensuring they were prepared and stocked. She spoke with the medical teams, offering words of encouragement and support, reminding them of the vital role they played in caring for their community. Every interaction, however brief, was a reinforcement of their unity, a quiet testament to their collective strength.

Eli's intricate digital defenses, while essential for Havenridge's survival, were a solitary endeavor. Mara's work, however, was deeply human. It was about connection, about empathy, about weaving a tapestry of hope from the threads of individual fear and uncertainty. She understood that even the most sophisticated defenses could crumble if the spirit of the people faltered. Her mission was to ensure that Havenridge's spirit remained unbroken, a flame that refused to be extinguished, no matter how fierce the winds of adversity blew.

The scent of woodsmoke, a comforting anchor in the encroaching darkness, began to weave its way through the entire settlement. It was a smell that spoke of shared meals, of communal warmth, of a people gathered together in the face of an unseen threat. Children, their faces no longer contorted with fear but softened by the day's shared experiences, played quietly near the glowing hearths, their innocence a precious commodity that Mara was fiercely determined to protect.

She paused at the edge of a gathering, watching as a group of elders shared stories with the younger generation. Their voices, though hushed, were filled with a steady cadence, a rhythm that spoke of generations of resilience. Mara felt a profound sense of peace settle over her. They were not simply waiting for a battle; they were actively building their defense, not just with steel and energy shields, but with the unbreakable bonds of community.

As the first stars began to emerge in the inky blackness above, Mara knew her work was far from over. The delegation's fleet loomed, a distant threat, but within Havenridge, a different kind of power was blooming – the quiet, unwavering strength of a united people. And Mara, with her steady gaze and her unwavering heart, was its fiercest guardian. She was the embodiment of their collective resolve, the living proof that even in the face of overwhelming odds, hope, and the will to survive, could burn brighter than any star. The air, still carrying the scent of woodsmoke and the promise of dawn, felt charged not with fear, but with a resolute, unyielding determination. They stood together, a community ready to face whatever came their way, their spirits as unshakeable as the ancient mountains that cradled their home.

The first tremors of conflict arrived not with a thunderous roar, but with a series of insidious whispers, a subtle yet unmistakable tightening of the external pressure. The delegation, their veiled threats now solidifying into tangible actions, began their probing assault. It wasn't an all-out invasion, not yet. Instead, it was a calculated series of tests, designed to gauge Havenridge's response, to pry open any perceived weakness in their carefully constructed defenses.

Eli, hunched over his console in the dimly lit command center, felt the shift in the atmospheric pressure before the first alert even pinged. His fingers danced across the holographic interface, his gaze a laser-like focus on the cascading data streams. The air hummed with a low, resonant frequency, a subtle disturbance that Eli recognized instantly as an energy manipulation signature. "Power grid," he murmured, his voice a low growl, barely audible above the whirring of the servers. "They're trying to destabilize the primary conduits. Standard diversionary tactic, but they're being more aggressive than anticipated."

On the main screen, intricate lines representing Havenridge's energy network pulsed with a faint, agitated glow. Tiny red indicators began to flicker along the edges, signaling unauthorized energy incursions. These weren't brute-force attacks, but sophisticated attempts to overload and reroute power, aiming to plunge sections of the settlement into darkness and sow chaos. Eli's team moved with practiced efficiency. Technicians, their faces illuminated by the stark blue light of their displays, rerouted energy flow, bolstered shield matrices, and isolated the compromised sectors. The goal was containment, a surgical strike against the digital invaders.

"Deploying localized energy dampeners, sector Gamma-7," announced Lena, her voice clear and steady. "We're seeing their signature trying to piggyback on our civilian communication frequencies. Clever, but not clever enough."

Eli nodded, his eyes never leaving the tactical display. "Acknowledge. Maintain passive monitoring on all civilian channels. No direct interference unless absolutely necessary. We don't want to give them any excuse for escalation." He knew the delicate balance they walked. Every defensive maneuver had to be precise, calculated to neutralize the immediate threat without providing justification for a more severe response. Their strength lay not just in their technology, but in their restraint.

Across Havenridge, the distant hum of the power grid faltered momentarily, a collective intake of breath from the populace as lights flickered. Mara, who had been overseeing the final preparations in the communal shelters, felt the subtle shift. It was a faint tremor in the fabric of their daily life, a reminder of the unseen struggle unfolding on the fringes. She didn't need to see the readouts or hear the technical jargon to understand. She felt it in the subtle tension that rippled through the gathered residents, in the way their eyes darted towards the sky.

She moved through the crowds with her usual calm assurance, her presence a grounding force. "A momentary flicker," she announced, her voice amplified just enough to carry through the hushed halls. "A minor test. Our engineers are already addressing it. Everything remains stable." She offered a reassuring smile to a group of children huddled near their parents, their small faces wide with apprehension.

"Think of it as a quick nap for the lights. They'll be back, brighter than ever, in no time."

Her words, simple and direct, seemed to soothe the immediate unease. Yet, the distant sounds, faint but undeniable, began to punctuate the air – sharp crackles, muffled thuds, the alien whine of energy discharges. These were the sounds of the first wave, the delegation's initial foray into demonstrating their intent. Havenridge's outer perimeter sensors were screaming, and Eli's team was engaged in a constant dance of deflection and neutralization.

"They're attempting to breach the orbital blockade," Eli reported, his voice tight with concentration. "Several scout vessels have made passes through the secondary exclusion zone. Our drones are engaging, but they're persistent."

The main screen now displayed a more dynamic battlefield. Tiny, almost microscopic icons representing Havenridge's defensive drones zipped across the starfield, intercepting even smaller, rapidly moving aggressor craft. The engagements were swift, precise, and remarkably bloodless. Havenridge's drones employed targeted EMP bursts, kinetic disruptors that disabled propulsion systems, and precisely aimed energy pulses designed to overload shields without penetrating hulls. The objective was clear: disable, disarm, and deter.

"Three scout vessels incapacitated," came a report from a tactical officer. "Returning to base for regrouping. Their propulsion is failing, they're drifting. No hull breaches, no casualties."

Eli allowed himself a brief, almost imperceptible nod. This was the strategy. They were a fortress, not an invading force. Their technology was designed for defense, for repelling aggression without succumbing to the temptation of annihilation. The delegation, accustomed to different rules of engagement, would likely find this approach... frustrating.

Mara continued her rounds, a constant reassuring presence. She checked on the medical teams, ensuring their supplies were replenished and their teams rested. She spoke with the logistics coordinators, verifying food and water reserves. Her role was to be the anchor, the steady hand that kept the community grounded while Eli's team fought the unseen battles in the digital and orbital realms. She felt the distant reverberations of the conflict, not as a direct threat to her person, but as a tremor that threatened the stability of their home.

"Are they... are they going to attack us, Mara?" a young boy named Finn asked, his voice small and trembling. He clutched a worn fabric toy, his knuckles white.

Mara knelt beside him, her gaze meeting his directly. "They are trying to make us afraid, Finn," she said softly. "They want us to believe we are alone, that we are weak. But look around you." She gestured to the faces of the people in the shelter, the quiet determination etched on their features, the shared sense of purpose. "We are not alone. We are Havenridge. And we are strong because we stand together."

She then turned her attention to the ventilation systems, ensuring the air filtration was operating at peak efficiency. The faint scent of ozone, a byproduct of energy discharges, was beginning to subtly permeate the deeper levels of the settlement. It was a reminder that the conflict, however distant, was real and present.

Back in the command center, Eli's team was dealing with a new challenge. The delegation, realizing their direct probes were being effectively neutralized, shifted tactics. Instead of attacking the power grid directly, they began to target the external sensor arrays that monitored Havenridge's perimeter and the surrounding space. These were crucial for early warning and for tracking the delegation's movements.

"Multiple targeted strikes on the northern hemisphere sensor cluster," reported a technician, his voice strained. "They're using focused energy beams, precise enough to cause localized EMP damage without triggering our broad-spectrum defenses. We're losing visual and energy signature tracking in that quadrant."

Eli's jaw tightened. This was a more sophisticated move. It wasn't about overwhelming force, but about insidious erosion, about blinding them piece by piece. "Prioritize repairs on the northern cluster," Eli ordered. "Deploy aerial maintenance drones. And increase passive sensor sweeps from the secondary arrays. We need to compensate for the blind spot."

The sounds of minor skirmishes continued to echo faintly, a constant, low-level thrum of conflict that permeated the community. These were the sounds of Havenridge's automated defenses engaging the delegation's probes, of energy shields deflecting stray fire, of kinetic rounds impacting the hulls of disabled drones. It was a constant, low-grade fever, a sign that their defenses were active, that they were holding the line.

Mara felt the subtle shifts in the ambient noise, the distant percussive sounds that were becoming a grim soundtrack to their lives. She understood that Eli and his team were engaged in a relentless, high-stakes game of technological chess, pushing the boundaries of their defensive capabilities. Her role was to ensure that the human element, the very heart of Havenridge, remained unyielding.

She initiated the next phase of her plan: a series of community-wide briefings, delivered through the public address system and in person at key gathering points. These weren't reports of casualties or dire warnings, but rather affirmations of their resilience and detailed explanations of their ongoing defensive measures, presented in accessible terms.

"We are experiencing external probing," Mara's voice resonated through the commons, calm and steady. "These are attempts to test our readiness, to find weaknesses. Our technological defenses, under the brilliant direction of Eli and his team, are performing exceptionally. They are neutralizing threats with incredible precision, disabling aggressor craft without causing unnecessary harm. They are our shield." She paused, letting the weight of her words sink in. "And you, each and every one of you, are the heart of that shield. Your continued calm, your cooperation, your unwavering resolve – that is what truly protects us."

She then outlined the steps they were taking to reinforce the community's internal infrastructure, explaining how power was being rerouted and critical systems were being protected. She spoke of the ongoing efforts to maintain food and water supplies, and the vigilant work of the medical teams. It was a narrative of strength, not of fear.

"The sounds you may hear are distant," she continued. "They are the sounds of our defenses at work. They are not a sign of immediate danger to our homes or our loved ones. We are prepared. We are secure. And we will not be intimidated."

Across the settlement, residents listened, their anxieties momentarily assuaged by Mara's confident tone and the clear, logical explanations. They understood that the true battle was being fought on multiple fronts, and that their participation, even in passive roles, was crucial. Farmers continued their work in the protected agricultural domes, artisans refined their crafts, and families maintained their routines as much as possible, their resilience a silent testament to the community's spirit.

Eli, meanwhile, was facing a new surge of activity. The delegation, seemingly frustrated by their inability to breach Havenridge's primary defenses, was now attempting to create diversions. Multiple energy signatures flared on the edge of their sensor range, hinting at larger fleet movements, while smaller, more agile craft continued their persistent attempts to probe weaker points.

"They're trying to spread us thin," Eli observed, his gaze sharp. "Multiple vectors of attack, all designed to draw our resources away from the core." He tapped a command, and a holographic projection of the surrounding space materialized, showing a swarm of tiny red icons representing the delegation's fleet, encircling Havenridge like sharks.

"Allocate a minimal drone response to the peripheral flares," Eli instructed his team. "Maintain primary focus on the direct infiltration attempts. Lena, I want continuous analysis of their energy signatures. We need to identify any patterns, any weaknesses in their new offensive protocols."

Lena, her fingers flying across her console, confirmed. "Already on it, Eli. They're using a modified plasma conduit technology. It's powerful, but it seems to generate a detectable harmonic resonance when overstressed."

"Good," Eli replied, a flicker of grim satisfaction crossing his face. "That resonance will be our guide. Track it. Pinpoint it. And then... we neutralize it."

The distant sounds of conflict continued, a low thrum beneath the surface of their daily lives. The crackle of energy discharges, the dull thud of kinetic impact, the whine of disabled propulsion systems – these were the sounds of Havenridge's stand. They were not the sounds of a collapsing society, but the sounds of a resilient one, fighting back with precision and purpose.

Mara, in the heart of the settlement, felt these sounds as a constant reminder of the stakes. She saw the quiet determination in the eyes of the people around her, the way they continued their tasks, their hands steady, their resolve unbroken. This was not just about technology or strategy; it was about the unyielding spirit of a people defending their home.

"They are testing our resolve," Mara said to a group of elders gathered in a communal lounge, the faint sounds of distant skirmishes a subtle backdrop to their conversation. "But our resolve is deeper than any probe they can send, stronger than any energy beam they can fire. We have faced challenges before, and we will face this one, together."

The delegation's initial wave of confrontation was a carefully orchestrated display of force, designed to intimidate and to probe. They had attempted to disrupt power, to breach blockades, and to blind Havenridge's senses. But with each attempt, they met the same calculated, defensive precision. Eli's team countered with non-lethal countermeasures, disabling technology rather than destroying it, rerouting energy and reinforcing defenses. They were proving that Havenridge was not a target to be easily overcome, but a fortress to be respected. And in the calm, steady heart of the community, Mara ensured that their spirit remained as unbreachable as their technological defenses, a constant, unwavering beacon in the face of encroaching conflict. The distant sounds of minor skirmishes served as a stark, visceral reminder that their stand had begun, a grim chorus to the quiet courage of Havenridge.

The subtle tremors of the initial probes had evolved into a persistent, unsettling hum, a constant reminder of the external pressures testing Havenridge's resilience. The delegation, their probes met with unwavering, precise countermeasures, had shifted their tactics from outright aggression to a more insidious form of psychological warfare, a slow erosion of confidence and unity. Yet, in the face of this growing threat, something remarkable was happening within the heart of Havenridge. The cracks that had once seemed so significant, the divisions that had threatened to fracture their nascent society, were beginning to mend, not through deliberate policy, but through the undeniable crucible of shared adversity.

Eli, his gaze still fixed on the cascading data streams in the command center, noticed the anomalies not in the energy signatures or the orbital trajectories, but in the communication logs. Encrypted messages, previously focused on individual concerns or departmental updates, were now peppered with offers of assistance, requests for collaborative problem-solving, and simple, heartfelt expressions of solidarity. He saw a message from Lena, his second-in-command, requesting an override for a non-critical system to reroute auxiliary power to a sector experiencing minor disruptions due to the delegation's continued atmospheric interference. The request was routed through, but what caught Eli's attention was the addendum: a personal note from a technician in Sector Epsilon, offering to remain on standby to assist Lena's team should their workload become unmanageable. This was not the usual protocol; it was a spontaneous act of mutual support.

"They're... they're working together," Eli murmured, a strange sense of wonder seeping into his voice. He'd expected fear, panic, perhaps even infighting, as the delegation's subtle campaign of disruption continued. Instead, he was witnessing the emergence of something far more potent: a quiet, unyielding solidarity. He zoomed in on a visual feed from the agricultural domes, a sector that had always been a point of contention regarding resource allocation. He saw Elara, the head botanist, a woman known for her fierce independence and occasional aloofness, not only supervising the automated nutrient delivery but also personally instructing a group of younger trainees on emergency blight containment procedures, procedures that had been developed in response to simulated threats during recent drills. The trainees, in turn, were working with an unusual level of focus and efficiency, their earlier rivalries seemingly forgotten in the shared task.

Mara, her rounds taking her through the increasingly busy communal spaces, felt this shift most acutely. The air, once tinged with the subtle anxiety of a community still finding its footing, now carried a palpable sense of purpose, a quiet determination that hummed beneath the surface of everyday life. She saw it in the way neighbors, who had previously only exchanged polite nods, were now sharing meals, their conversations flowing easily from the latest developments in defense protocols to the simple comfort of shared laughter. A baker, whose stall had often been overlooked in favor of the more established food vendors, found himself with a queue stretching down the concourse, his expertly crafted nutrient bars and energy biscuits in high demand. He, in turn, was quietly sharing his excess stock with the families of those working on the front lines of Havenridge's defense, their gratitude a silent, powerful exchange.

One evening, as the faint sounds of the delegation's probes continued to echo in the distance – the low thrum of energy shields deflecting atmospheric disturbances, the occasional distant pop of a disabled drone – Mara found herself in the residential sector, checking on a family that had recently relocated from a less secure area. The parents, who had expressed significant anxiety about their children's well-being just weeks prior, were now engaged in a makeshift science lesson with their neighbors' children, using salvaged components from outdated technology to build rudimentary communication devices. The children, their faces alight with curiosity and focus, were demonstrating a level of cooperation that Mara found deeply moving.

"It's... it's incredible, isn't it?" the mother, Anya, said to Mara, her voice soft. "Before all this, we barely knew our neighbors. We kept to ourselves. Now... now it feels like we've known them our whole lives." She gestured towards the children, their small hands busy with wires and circuits. "They're teaching each other. Sharing their knowledge. We're sharing our food, our skills. This... this place, Havenridge, it's more than just a home now. It's a family."

Mara nodded, a profound sense of hope swelling in her chest. This was the true strength of Havenridge, a strength that transcended technology and strategic planning. It was the strength of human connection, forged in the fires of shared challenge. She saw it in the repurposed workshop where skilled engineers, once focused on optimizing individual projects, were now collaborating on reinforcing the settlement's atmospheric processors, their laughter and focused chatter echoing through the repurposed space. She saw it in the communal garden, where individuals from all walks of life, their previous social strata blurring into insignificance, worked side-by-side, tending to the vital crops that sustained them all.

Eli, while engrossed in the complex dance of defensive maneuvers, also began to recognize these subtle shifts. The efficiency of his team, usually a testament to their individual skill and rigorous training, was now amplified by an unspoken synergy. Technicians who had once worked in silos were now anticipating each other's needs, offering assistance before it was requested, their communication concise and effective, imbued with a deeper understanding of their shared objective. He even observed a rare moment of collegiality between two department heads who had historically held opposing views on resource allocation. They were seen huddled over a holographic display, not arguing, but brainstorming solutions to a shared problem, their usual friction replaced by a grudging respect.

"We're seeing a significant uptick in cross-departmental collaborative problem-solving requests," Eli reported to Mara during one of their infrequent comms checks, his voice laced with an unfamiliar tone of pleasant surprise. "Resources are being shared more freely, expertise is being volunteered without hesitation. It's... it's like they've all collectively realized that their individual success is directly tied to the success of everyone else."

Mara smiled, a genuine, unburdened smile. "That's the essence of unity, Eli. Adversity has a way of stripping away the superficial, of reminding us of what truly matters. And what matters is protecting each other, protecting our home." She then recounted the story of the makeshift science lesson, the shared meals, the collaborative spirit blooming in the repurposed workshop. "They are no longer just individuals living in Havenridge, Eli. They are becoming Havenridge itself."

The delegation's continued probes, though still a source of concern, had inadvertently become a catalyst for this profound internal transformation. Each attempted disruption, each subtle act of intimidation, served only to reinforce the need for collective action. The fear that the delegation sought to sow was being transmuted into a shared resolve, a collective determination to stand firm. The whispers of doubt that the delegation attempted to plant were being drowned out by the chorus of mutual support, by the quiet affirmation that they were not alone, that they were stronger together.

Even in the sterile environment of the command center, the tangible scent of this newfound unity began to permeate. It was not an olfactory sensation, but an energetic one, a subtle shift in the atmosphere that spoke of shared purpose and unwavering commitment. Eli noticed that his team's morale, which had been tested by the sustained pressure, had not only stabilized but was actively improving. There was a lightness in their interactions, a shared understanding that transcended professional courtesy. They were no longer just colleagues; they were comrades, bound by the invisible threads of shared struggle and mutual reliance.

Mara continued her work, her presence a steadying force throughout the settlement. She facilitated the sharing of specialized tools and equipment between different sectors, ensuring that no team was hindered by a lack of resources. She organized informal gatherings, not for formal briefings, but for simple human connection, creating spaces where individuals could decompress, share their experiences, and reaffirm their bonds. These were not moments of levity designed to distract from the ongoing threat, but rather essential opportunities to nurture the very foundation of their resilience.

She witnessed a formerly isolated craftsman, renowned for his intricate metalwork, teaching a group of younger residents how to repair essential structural components, his hands, usually so delicate, now working with a sturdy efficiency born of necessity. He spoke not of the artistic merit of his work, but of the critical importance of structural integrity, of how each rivet, each weld, contributed to the overall safety of their community. His passion for his craft was now channeled into a larger purpose, his skills a vital contribution to their collective defense.

The delegation's attempts to destabilize Havenridge were failing on a fundamental level. They had targeted their technology, their infrastructure, their defenses, but they had failed to account for the most powerful force of all: the indomitable human spirit, amplified by the bonds of community. The shared experience of resisting the delegation's aggression had done more to solidify the foundations of Havenridge than any construction project or security protocol ever could. Individuals who had once been divided by differing perspectives or isolated by circumstance now found an unbreakable common ground in their fight for survival and autonomy.

Eli and Mara observed this profound transformation with a mixture of awe and quiet satisfaction. They saw neighbors supporting each other, sharing resources with an unhesitating generosity, and contributing their unique skills selflessly. The adversity they faced had, paradoxically, strengthened their community, forging a unity far more profound and enduring than any they had achieved during times of peace. The scent of determination, of shared purpose, of an unyielding collective will, hung palpably in the air, a testament to the enduring power of unity forged in the fires of adversity. Havenridge was no longer just a settlement; it was a testament to what people could achieve when they stood together, not in forced conformity, but in genuine, heartfelt solidarity.

CHAPTER THIRTEEN

A Future Together

The faint, metallic tang of ozone, a lingering ghost of Havenridge's defensive efforts, was slowly dissipating, yielding to a different, more delicate atmosphere. It was the scent of cautious hope, of diplomatic overtures, a subtle fragrance that began to weave its way through the corridors of the command center and into the communal spaces. The immediate crisis had passed, not with a definitive victory in the traditional sense, but with an undeniable display of resilience and capability that had evidently given the delegation pause. Their probes, once aggressive extensions of their will, now seemed hesitant, their advance blunted not by overwhelming firepower, but by the quiet, unyielding strength of a united community.

Eli stood by the main viewport, gazing out at the now quiescent expanse of space. The data streams, which had pulsed with the urgent rhythm of imminent conflict, had settled into a more measured cadence. The delegation's orbital platforms, previously a constant, looming presence, had adjusted their positions, a subtle but significant shift that spoke volumes. It wasn't retreat, not yet, but it was a clear signal that their initial strategy of brute force had proven counterproductive. The wider galactic community, even if indirectly, was a factor, and the optics of Havenridge being aggressively subjugated by a more powerful entity would not serve the delegation's interests. This realization, coupled with Havenridge's surprisingly robust defense, had created an opening, a window of opportunity that Eli was determined to exploit.

"They're circling," Eli murmured, a faint smile playing on his lips. "Like predators who've found their prey is more formidable than anticipated. They haven't backed down, not completely, but the aggression has been... recalibrated." He turned from the viewport, his gaze meeting Mara's as she entered the command center, her presence bringing with it a sense of calm assurance. The lines of fatigue were still etched around her eyes, but they were softened by a growing sense of resolve.

"Recalibrated is a polite way of putting it," Mara replied, her voice carrying a note of weary satisfaction. "They threw their best at us, and we weathered the storm. Now, they're assessing their next move, and I suspect it's not one they're particularly comfortable with." She walked over to the central console, her fingers hovering over the holographic displays. "The word from the periphery is that their transmissions have shifted. Less demanding, more... probing. Not in a military sense, but in a conversational one."

Eli nodded, accessing the latest intercept logs. "Precisely. They're no longer issuing ultimatums. They're asking questions. About our intentions, our long-term goals, our capacity for... autonomy." He scrolled through a series of translated communications, the stark demands of mere hours ago now replaced by more nuanced, albeit still self-serving, inquiries. "They're trying to gauge our willingness to negotiate, and more importantly, what terms we might accept.

They're hoping to find a compromise that allows them to save face, to avoid a wider conflict that could draw unwanted attention."

"And we should give them that opportunity," Mara stated, her gaze steady. "But from a position of strength, Eli. Not from a place of desperation. We've proven we can defend ourselves. We've shown them that subjugating Havenridge would be a costly, perhaps even impossible, endeavor. This isn't about seeking peace out of weakness; it's about securing our future from a position of undeniable capability." She met his gaze directly. "We need to approach these renewed negotiations with clear objectives, objectives that go beyond mere survival. We need to define what sovereignty truly means for Havenridge, and we need to articulate it in a way that is both firm and irrefutable."

"I agree," Eli said, leaning forward. "Their initial aggression was a test, an attempt to gauge our resolve and our willingness to capitulate. They expected fear, division, perhaps even a desperate plea for mercy. What they found instead was unity and a potent defense. This has clearly forced a strategic re-evaluation on their part. They're likely facing internal pressure from their own leadership, a need to justify their resources and their presence here without escalating into a full-blown war that could have significant diplomatic repercussions across the sector." He tapped a specific data point on the screen. "Their probes have also been less intrusive in the last cycle. Fewer atmospheric disruptions, more passive observation. It's as if they're waiting for our cue."

"Then we shall provide it," Mara said, her voice firm. "But we must be deliberate. Our terms cannot be simply about warding off further aggression. They must be about establishing a lasting peace, one that guarantees our right to exist, to develop, and to govern ourselves without external interference. We need recognition of Havenridge as a sovereign entity, not as a territory to be claimed or a resource to be exploited."

Eli's mind was already racing through the possibilities, the strategic implications of such a negotiation. "Recognition is paramount. Beyond that, we need clear delineations of our territorial claims, both on this planet and in orbit. Any delegation presence must be clearly defined and limited. Their access to our resources, if any, must be strictly regulated and mutually beneficial, not exploitative. And crucially, we need a framework for future disputes, one that avoids the kind of unilateral action we've just experienced."

"And the safety of our people," Mara added, her hand resting on his arm for a brief, grounding moment. "Any agreement must include robust security protocols, ensuring our inhabitants are protected from any future threats, whether they originate from the delegation or elsewhere. We cannot afford to be vulnerable again. This experience has taught us that our greatest strength lies in our self-reliance, but that self-reliance must be acknowledged and respected by others."

"So, we're looking at a multi-faceted negotiation," Eli mused, sketching out the key points in his mind. "Sovereignty, territorial integrity, regulated interaction, and assured security. It's a significant shift from their initial demands, but one that their current predicament necessitates. They've gambled on intimidation, and that gamble has failed. Now, they must negotiate."

He brought up a secure communication channel, the interface glowing with a soft, inviting light. "The scent of ozone is fading,

Mara. It's time to introduce the aroma of diplomacy. I believe it's time for us to send a formal communication, not an offer, but an invitation to discuss terms of mutual coexistence, framed within the context of our newly established defensive capabilities."

Mara met his gaze, a shared understanding passing between them. "Let's draft it carefully, Eli. Every word will carry weight. This is not just about avoiding conflict; it's about building a future. And that future must be built on a foundation of respect and recognition."

The drafting of the communication was a meticulous process. Eli and Mara, along with a small, trusted team of advisors, worked through the night, carefully selecting each word, each phrase, to convey Havenridge's unwavering resolve while also signaling a willingness to engage. The tone was to be firm but not aggressive, assertive but not hostile. It was a delicate dance, balancing the need to acknowledge their recent defensive success with the desire to open a path towards a stable, long-term resolution.

"We need to emphasize our commitment to peace," Mara suggested, reviewing a draft. "But also our preparedness to defend that peace. It's a dual message. We don't seek conflict, but we will not shy away from it if our sovereignty is threatened."

Eli nodded, highlighting a sentence. "This phrase here, 'Havenridge stands as a testament to the will of its people to forge their own destiny,' that captures it perfectly. It's a statement of fact, not a boast. It acknowledges our right to self-determination."

The communication was then broadcast on a secure, encrypted channel, addressed directly to the highest echelon of the delegation's command structure. It was a carefully worded invitation to establish a dialogue, to explore avenues of mutual understanding and cooperation, contingent upon the full recognition of Havenridge's independent status and territorial sovereignty. The emphasis was placed on the mutual benefits of a stable and cooperative relationship, one built on respect rather than coercion. It was an olive branch, but one that was firmly rooted in the iron will they had so recently demonstrated.

As the communication was sent, a palpable shift occurred in the command center. The tension that had been a constant companion for days began to dissipate, replaced by a quiet anticipation. The hum of the defense systems, though still active, seemed less urgent, less resonant with imminent danger. The scent of ozone was now truly gone, replaced by the fainter, yet more pervasive, aroma of hope and the subtle, complex fragrance of diplomacy taking root.

Days turned into a week, and the delegation's response was, as expected, measured. They did not immediately capitulate, nor did they dismiss Havenridge's overture. Instead, they acknowledged the communication and proposed a preliminary meeting, not on Havenridge, but on a neutral orbital station, a sign of their continued caution and their desire to control the setting. The delegation leadership, having reassessed their strategy, now understood that outright conquest was too costly and too risky. They had underestimated the resilience and unity of Havenridge, and now they were forced to engage on terms that were significantly less advantageous to them than they had initially envisioned.

Eli and Mara, along with a carefully selected delegation of Havenridge's leaders, prepared for the meeting. The stakes were incredibly high. This was not merely about repelling an invasion; it was about forging a lasting peace, about securing Havenridge's place in the wider galactic community as a sovereign and self-determined entity. The experience had forged an unbreakable bond between the inhabitants of Havenridge, a unity that Eli and Mara were determined to preserve and strengthen.

"They'll try to probe for weaknesses, for any sign of disunity," Eli warned as they reviewed their talking points. "They'll offer concessions, but always with a hidden agenda. We need to remain focused on our core objectives: recognition, sovereignty, and security. Anything less is a step backward."

Mara nodded, her expression resolute. "We've come too far to compromise on the fundamental principles of our existence. We are not a prize to be claimed or a pawn to be manipulated. We are a people who have defended our home, and we will negotiate from that unshakeable foundation. The people of Havenridge have demonstrated their strength, their unity, and their unwavering commitment to their future. This negotiation is not just for us; it is for them, and for all those who will come after."

The journey to the neutral station was a quiet one. The inhabitants of Havenridge watched their leaders depart with a mixture of hope and trepidation. They had placed their trust in Eli and Mara, and in each other, and now it was time for diplomacy to take center stage. The echoes of the defense systems had faded, replaced by the hushed whispers of negotiation, the subtle scent of peace offerings intertwining with the lingering, yet diminishing, aroma of ozone. The future of Havenridge, once so uncertain, now hung precariously, yet hopefully, in the balance of words and intentions. The true negotiation, the one that would define Havenridge's place in the galaxy, was about to begin, not with the clash of weapons, but with the careful calibration of language and the unwavering strength of a unified will.

The delegation, finding their initial aggressive approach thwarted, now found themselves in a delicate strategic predicament. Their attempts at intimidation had not only failed to break Havenridge's spirit but had also inadvertently broadcasted their aggressive posture to a wider audience. The potential for regional condemnation, or even intervention from established powers who favored stability, was a considerable deterrent. It was a gamble that had not paid off, and the subsequent assessment of their own intelligence suggested that further direct confrontation would be counterproductive, risking not just failure but also significant political fallout.

Eli, observing the shift in the delegation's tactical approach, recognized the opportune moment for a change in Havenridge's own strategy. The initial phase of defense had been about demonstrating capability and resolve. Now, the objective was to leverage that demonstrated strength into a diplomatic victory. "Their probes have changed their tune," Eli observed to Mara, his voice low and measured as he monitored the intercepted communications. "The overt threats have been replaced by thinly veiled inquiries. They're testing the waters for negotiation, fishing for concessions, but they're doing it from a position of tentative weakness, not absolute dominance. This is precisely the shift in the power dynamic we anticipated."

Mara, standing beside him, her gaze fixed on the same data streams, nodded in agreement. "They're trying to recover from their miscalculation. They underestimated us, and now they're seeking a way to extricate themselves without appearing utterly defeated. This is our chance to define the terms of engagement, to ensure Havenridge's security and sovereignty are not just protected, but formally recognized." Her hand rested on the console, her touch gentle but firm, mirroring the resolve she felt. "The scent of ozone is fading, Eli, but the lingering scent of their aggressive intent remains. We need to replace it with something far more substantial. The aroma of a carefully crafted peace offering, one that is not born of fear, but of strength and foresight."

"Precisely," Eli affirmed, a sense of purpose sharpening his focus. "Renewed negotiations are in order, but this time, we dictate the initial parameters. Our proposals must be clear, unambiguous, and geared towards long-term security and recognition of our autonomy. We've proven we can defend ourselves, and that fact must be the bedrock of any future dialogue. They cannot afford to simply dismiss us any longer. The cost of continuing their aggression has become too high, both in terms of resources and potential galactic repercussions."

Eli initiated a secure communication protocol, his fingers moving with practiced efficiency across the holographic interface. "We need to formalize this invitation for dialogue. Not as a plea, but as a strategic proposal. We will outline the essential conditions for coexistence, emphasizing mutual respect and defined boundaries. The focus will be on establishing a framework that guarantees our sovereignty and prevents future incursions. Their current predicament, their need to avoid wider conflict, means they are more likely to consider terms that would have been unthinkable just days ago."

Mara leaned closer, her eyes scanning the draft communication forming on the screen. "We must ensure our terms are comprehensive. Recognition of Havenridge's independent status, clear territorial demarcation, mutually agreed-upon protocols for any future interaction, and ironclad guarantees of our non-interference in their affairs, and vice-versa. This isn't just about de-escalation; it's about de-escalating towards a recognized and respected independence." She paused, her brow furrowed in thought. "We also need to consider the implications of any resource sharing. If they propose it, it must be on our terms, with fair compensation and strict oversight, ensuring they cannot exploit our planet for their own gain. We cannot allow our hard-won autonomy to be undermined by future economic dependencies."

Eli nodded, incorporating her points into the draft. "Agreed. Their initial probing was a classic tactic to gauge our desperation. Now that they've found resilience instead, they're looking for a more palatable exit strategy. We can offer them that, but it comes with a non-negotiable price: the formal acknowledgment of Havenridge as a sovereign entity. No more probes, no more atmospheric interference, no more implied threats. Just a clear, defined relationship based on mutual respect for established borders and autonomy." He keyed in a final command, sending the encrypted message. "The ball is in their court now. Let's see if they're ready to engage in diplomacy rather than coercion."

The subsequent days were a tense waiting game, but the atmosphere within Havenridge had perceptibly shifted. The lingering fear had been replaced by a quiet confidence, a collective understanding that their united front had yielded tangible results. The aroma of peace offerings, though still nascent, was beginning to mingle with the fading scent of ozone, creating a fragrance of cautious optimism that permeated every level of their society. The delegation's response, when it finally arrived, was not a capitulation, but a calculated agreement to preliminary talks, held on neutral ground. It was a concession, albeit a carefully worded one, and a clear indication that the delegation was indeed re-evaluating their approach, forced by Havenridge's demonstrated strength to consider negotiation over domination. The era of overt aggression had passed, and the era of de-escalation and negotiation had begun.

The lingering scent of ozone, once a sharp reminder of Havenridge's desperate struggle for survival, was gradually giving way to something softer, more hopeful. It was the perfume of newly turned earth, of seedlings tentatively pushing through the soil, a delicate fragrance that spoke of renewal and the painstaking process of rebuilding. The immediate threat had receded, leaving behind not scars of defeat, but a profound sense of shared resilience. Now, the true work began: stitching the fabric of Havenridge back together, mending the fraying threads of trust and community that had been tested to their limits.

Internally, Mara found herself navigating a landscape as intricate as any diplomatic negotiation. The initial unity forged in the crucible of defense was a powerful force, but beneath the surface, old anxieties and new vulnerabilities lingered. The delegation's presence, though no longer overtly hostile, cast a long shadow. Some citizens, having witnessed the raw power wielded by the outsiders, harbored a deep-seated fear, a constant vigilance that bordered on paranoia. Others, pragmatic and weary, simply craved a return to normalcy, their focus already shifting to the practicalities of rebuilding their lives and livelihoods.

"We can't pretend the threat is entirely gone," Mara explained to Eli during one of their hushed late-night strategy sessions, the soft glow of the viewport illuminating the lines of fatigue on their faces. "The memory of their probes, the chilling efficiency of their technology – it's not something easily forgotten. We need to acknowledge that fear, not dismiss it. Our people need to know that their concerns are heard and validated."

Eli nodded, his gaze thoughtful. He understood the delicate balance they had to strike. "And yet, we cannot let fear dictate our future. We've earned this moment of peace, this opportunity to solidify our independence. If we allow ourselves to be consumed by apprehension, we risk becoming prisoners of our own anxieties, undermining the very freedom we fought for." He gestured towards the holographic projections of newly planted agricultural sectors, green shoots reaching towards the artificial light. "Look at this, Mara. This is what we're fighting for. Not just to repel an aggressor, but to cultivate a future. That requires more than just defense; it requires growth, prosperity, and a belief in what we are building."

Their approach to rebuilding trust was multifaceted, weaving together overt gestures of reassurance with subtle, persistent efforts to reinforce their shared identity. Mara initiated a series of community forums, not for grand pronouncements, but for open dialogue. These sessions, held in communal halls and open-air plazas, became vital spaces for citizens to voice their fears, share their experiences, and offer their own ideas for recovery. Eli, meanwhile, focused on the tangible aspects of rebuilding, overseeing the rapid deployment of resources to repair damaged infrastructure, restore essential services, and support those who had lost their homes or livelihoods. The replanted gardens, a symbol of their commitment to renewal, became focal points for communal work, drawing people together in a shared endeavor that was both productive and cathartic.

"The soil is still warm from the defense systems," a farmer named Lyra remarked one afternoon, her hands caked with earth as she carefully placed a seedling into the ground. "But it's good to feel the sun on my face again. Good to be planting, not preparing for battle." She looked up at Mara, who was observing from a nearby pathway, a gentle smile on her face. "We needed this, Mara. We needed to remember what life was like before. To feel that sense of continuity."

Mara knelt beside Lyra, her own hands instinctively reaching for a fallen leaf. "Continuity is important, Lyra. But so is evolution. We have faced a profound challenge, and we have emerged stronger, more unified. We are not simply returning to the way things were; we are building something new, something better, on the foundations of what we have learned." She picked up a small, smooth stone from the rich soil, turning it over in her fingers. "This stone was disturbed by their probes. Now, it is part of a new garden. A testament to resilience, to the power of growth even after disruption."

The internal healing was a slow, organic process, much like the slow unfurling of leaves in the spring. It required patience, empathy, and a consistent affirmation of Havenridge's core values: community, self-determination, and mutual respect. Eli and Mara made a conscious effort to be visible, to be accessible, to embody the very principles they were advocating. They shared meals with repair crews, consulted with community leaders from all sectors, and actively participated in rebuilding efforts, their presence a constant reminder that they were in this together, shoulder to shoulder with every citizen of Havenridge.

Externally, the diplomatic landscape presented a different, yet equally complex, set of challenges. The delegation, having been rebuffed in their aggressive overtures, had recalibrated their approach. The initial communication from Havenridge, carefully crafted by Eli and Mara, had opened a door to dialogue, but it was a door that swung both ways. The delegation was eager to negotiate, not from a position of strength, but from a place of strategic necessity. They needed to salvage their reputation, to avoid further escalation that could draw the attention of larger galactic powers, and, perhaps, to secure access to Havenridge's unique resources or technologies under more palatable terms.

"They're offering terms that sound generous on the surface," Eli reported after a particularly taxing virtual meeting with the delegation's representatives. "Trade agreements, joint research initiatives, even a non-aggression pact. But the underlying current is still about control, about ensuring our long-term compliance with their interests." He sighed, running a hand through his hair. "They're trying to buy our compliance, to lull us into a false sense of security with promises of economic prosperity, all while subtly reinforcing their claim as the dominant regional power."

Mara listened intently, her gaze sharp and focused. "We must not be swayed by the allure of immediate gain. Their offers of partnership are only meaningful if they are rooted in genuine respect for our sovereignty. We need to define what 'partnership' truly means for Havenridge, and ensure it aligns with our own long-term vision for self-governance and independent development." She walked over to the viewport, gazing out at the star-speckled canvas. "Remember the scent of the new gardens, Eli? That's our guiding principle. Growth, not subjugation. Cultivation, not exploitation."

Their strategy was clear: to engage in diplomacy from a position of established strength, leveraging the hard-won respect garnered from their successful defense. They meticulously crafted their counter-proposals, focusing on establishing clear boundaries and mutually beneficial, yet rigorously defined, areas of cooperation. Formal recognition of Havenridge as a sovereign entity was paramount, non-negotiable. This was the bedrock upon which any future relationship would be built. Beyond that, they sought to establish specific, time-bound agreements for any proposed resource sharing or technological exchange, ensuring these were conducted with full transparency and provided demonstrable benefits to Havenridge, not just the delegation.

"We are not simply warding off an invasion," Mara stated during a meeting with their own advisory council, a diverse group of individuals representing various sectors of Havenridge society. "We are laying the groundwork for our future in the galactic community. This requires us to be not only strong defenders but also astute diplomats. Our engagement with the delegation must be guided by our founding principles, ensuring that any alliance or partnership enhances, rather than compromises, our independence."

The advisory council, a testament to Havenridge's commitment to inclusive governance, debated heatedly but constructively. Some argued for a more cautious approach, advocating for minimal engagement with the delegation, fearing any interaction might reignite past tensions. Others, particularly those from the burgeoning technological and resource sectors, saw potential for significant advancement through carefully managed collaboration. Eli and Mara facilitated these discussions, ensuring all voices were heard and that the final diplomatic strategy reflected a broad consensus.

"The delegation is not a monolith," Eli pointed out during one such council session. "There are factions within their own leadership, some who genuinely see the benefit of a stable, independent Havenridge as a partner, and others who still harbor expansionist ambitions. Our approach must be nuanced, acknowledging these internal dynamics and playing to our strengths, which are unity and a clear, unwavering vision for our own future."

Their diplomatic efforts extended beyond the immediate delegation. Havenridge also began discreetly reaching out to other established powers within the region, seeking to cultivate relationships based on shared interests and mutual respect. This proactive outreach served a dual purpose: to bolster Havenridge's standing on the galactic stage and to create a network of potential allies should the delegation's intentions ever shift back towards aggression. These overtures were subtle, emphasizing Havenridge's commitment to peace, its unique contributions to intergalactic discourse, and its unwavering dedication to self-determination.

The scent of freshly planted gardens became a pervasive and welcome aroma across Havenridge. It was a constant reminder of their collective effort, a visual and olfactory testament to their commitment to rebuilding and to growth. Children, who had cowered in shelters during the crisis, now played amongst the burgeoning plants, their laughter a sweet counterpoint to the distant hum of atmospheric processors. Families worked together, tending to their plots, sharing seeds and stories, reinforcing the bonds of community that had been so vital to their survival.

One such family, the Kaelens, had lost their home during the initial skirmishes. They were now housed in temporary but comfortable modular units, but their focus was on rebuilding their small horticultural business. Mara visited them often, not as a leader issuing directives, but as a fellow citizen offering support and solidarity.

"It's hard to see the old homestead gone," Mrs. Kaelen said, her voice tinged with sadness as she weeded a row of vibrant, alien flowers. "But these new seedlings... they have a good spirit about them. They want to grow." She smiled, a genuine, hopeful smile that reached her eyes. "Just like us, Mara. We want to grow. We want to thrive, not just survive."

Eli, overseeing the construction of new communal living structures designed to be more resilient and self-sustaining, echoed Mrs. Kaelen's sentiment in his own way. "We're not just rebuilding walls and roofs," he told his construction crews. "We're building futures. Every beam we place, every conduit we connect, is an act of faith in Havenridge's continued existence. And that faith is our greatest asset."

The diplomatic negotiations with the delegation were slow and deliberate, a painstaking process of crafting agreements that would safeguard Havenridge's autonomy without alienating a potentially powerful neighbor. Eli and Mara, alongside their chosen diplomatic team, approached each session with meticulous preparation, armed with data, historical context, and an unshakeable understanding of their people's will. They proposed a phased approach to any collaborative ventures, allowing Havenridge to build trust and confidence incrementally, ensuring that any integration of their systems or economies would be on their terms.

"They're accustomed to outright dominance," Eli observed after a particularly lengthy negotiation session. "The idea of a true partnership, where both parties hold equal standing and mutually define the terms of engagement, is clearly challenging for them to grasp. We must be patient, persistent, and unwavering in our core demands. Our sovereignty is not a commodity to be bartered; it is the foundation of our existence."

The delegation, observing Havenridge's steady progress in rebuilding and its burgeoning diplomatic outreach, began to recognize the strategic advantage of a stable, cooperative relationship. The cost of continued aggression had proven too high, and the potential benefits of a mutually respectful partnership, particularly in terms of access to Havenridge's unique knowledge and resources, began to outweigh their initial desires for outright control.

As the weeks turned into months, the scent of ozone faded further, becoming a faint memory, an almost mythical tale of a time of great peril. In its place, the rich, earthy aroma of the revitalized gardens flourished, a testament to Havenridge's enduring spirit. The fragile seedlings, once vulnerable and new, were now growing taller, stronger, their leaves unfurling towards the light. This growth was mirrored in the community itself, as trust, both internally and externally, was slowly, painstakingly, but surely, being rebuilt, one hopeful seed at a time. The future, once a terrifying unknown, was now taking shape, nurtured by courage, unity, and the unwavering commitment to cultivate a life of freedom and self-determination.

Eli's integration was not a mere formality; it was the organic flowering of trust, a natural progression born from shared trials and a profound understanding that blossomed between him and Mara, and indeed, the entire populace of Havenridge. The echoes of his confession, the raw vulnerability he had displayed when revealing the depths of his past misjudgments and the subsequent arduous journey of redemption, had resonated deeply. It was not the confession itself that had secured his place, but the unwavering commitment he had demonstrated in the aftermath, a commitment that had been tested and proven in the crucible of Havenridge's fight for survival. His subsequent actions, his tireless dedication to rebuilding, his insightful strategic counsel, and his genuine empathy for the citizens had woven him inextricably into the fabric of their newly forged society.

Mara observed this integration with a quiet satisfaction that settled deep within her bones. She had championed Eli's cause, had seen the potential for good within him when others had been hesitant, and her faith had been rewarded tenfold. Now, as she stood beside him, looking out at the sprawling expanse of Havenridge – a place once teetering on the brink, now humming with the vibrant energy of reconstruction and renewed purpose – she felt a profound sense of solidarity. The scent of pine, carried on the crisp, clean air from the surrounding forests, was a constant, grounding reminder of their shared home, a home they were now collectively nurturing towards a brighter tomorrow.

Eli's presence in leadership was a vital counterpoint to Mara's own strengths. Where Mara possessed an innate understanding of people, an almost intuitive grasp of their emotional landscapes and communal needs, Eli brought a sharp, analytical mind, a wealth of experience from his past in more complex, often ruthless, political systems, and an unparalleled ability to translate vision into tangible action. He understood the intricacies of resource management, the delicate art of inter-community relations, and the practicalities of establishing long-term stability in a way that Mara, while growing rapidly, was still developing. He was the architect who could map out the structural integrity of the future, while Mara was the visionary who painted its vibrant hues.

One crisp morning, as they surveyed the progress on the new hydroponic farms – a critical initiative designed to ensure food security and reduce reliance on vulnerable external supply lines – Eli turned to Mara. His gaze, usually so direct and focused on the task at hand, softened as it met hers. "The projections for yield are exceeding expectations, Mara. We're looking at a surplus within the next cycle, which means we can begin allocating resources to the outer settlements, bolstering their defenses and improving their infrastructure. It's a tangible sign of our progress, a testament to everyone's hard work."

Mara smiled, a genuine, unburdened smile. "It's more than just projections, Eli. It's the hope in the eyes of the farmers, the pride in their voices as they show off the first burgeoning fruits. That's the real surplus we're cultivating." She gestured towards a group of children, their faces smudged with dirt, as they helped to carry small watering cans. "They're learning not just how to grow food, but how to contribute, how to be part of something bigger than themselves."

Their leadership dynamic was a carefully orchestrated dance, a seamless blend of shared decision-making and autonomous execution. They established a rhythm, a flow that allowed for both the meticulous planning of long-term strategies and the swift, decisive action required in the day-to-day realities of governance. Their strategy sessions were no longer hushed, clandestine affairs born of crisis, but open, collaborative dialogues held in the bright, airy council chambers, the scent of fresh pine mingling with the faint, metallic tang of advanced holographic displays.

"The delegation has responded to our latest proposal regarding resource sharing," Eli reported, his brow furrowed in concentration as he manipulated the holographic interface. "They're... amenable. More than amenable, actually. They're proposing a joint scientific expedition to the Xylos nebula, citing mutual interest in studying its unique energy signatures. This could be a significant opportunity, Mara, for us to gain valuable data and establish a more scientific, less politically charged, connection."

Mara considered this, her fingers tracing the outline of a nebula on the display. "A scientific expedition. It sounds... benign. But we know their reputation for 'mutual interest' often translates to exploitation. What are their proposed terms for intellectual property and data sharing? And what resources are they expecting Havenridge to contribute?"

"They're offering their advanced astrogation and data analysis capabilities, essentially covering the operational costs of the expedition on their end," Eli explained. "In return, they want access to our deep-spectrum sensor readings from the anomaly during the recent crisis. They claim it's crucial for understanding the broader phenomenon. Our contribution would be primarily in personnel – xenobotanists, geologists, perhaps a specialist in gravitational anomalies. They're framing it as a chance for our scientists to work alongside some of their brightest minds, to foster cross-cultural collaboration."

Mara's eyes narrowed slightly. "The 'anomaly'. They're still so focused on that event. It was a consequence of their actions, not a prelude to their arrival. We must be exceptionally careful. While the opportunity for scientific advancement is tempting, we cannot allow them to reframe our history to their advantage. Our participation must be contingent on their acknowledgment of the circumstances surrounding the anomaly and a clear, unwavering commitment to the principle of independent scientific discovery. No data, no research, no collaboration that could be twisted to imply Havenridge was the aggressor or the anomaly's origin."

Eli nodded, his expression mirroring her caution. "Agreed. My counter-proposal will emphasize clear protocols for data ownership and publication, ensuring that any findings are attributed equitably and that Havenridge retains the right to independent research based on the shared data. Furthermore, I will stipulate that their acknowledgement of the event as a consequence of their initial probing actions be a prerequisite for our full participation."

This was the essence of their partnership: Mara's unwavering commitment to Havenridge's narrative and self-determination, coupled with Eli's pragmatic understanding of galactic politics and his ability to negotiate complex agreements without compromising their core values. He understood the subtle language of diplomacy, the art of the concession that was not a surrender, the strategic positioning that maximized their leverage.

Beyond the external negotiations, Eli was instrumental in solidifying Havenridge's internal governance structures. He helped to refine the electoral processes, ensuring representation across all sectors of society, from the agricultural cooperatives to the burgeoning technological guilds. He advocated for a comprehensive system of community mediation, establishing neutral grounds where disputes could be resolved amicably, thereby preventing the festering of resentments that could undermine their hard-won unity. His experience with bureaucratic systems, honed in a galaxy far more hierarchical and often corrupt, allowed him to identify potential pitfalls and implement safeguards that protected Havenridge's nascent democracy.

He often spoke with the younger generation, the children who had known only fear and uncertainty for so long. He would tell them stories, not of war, but of resilience, of how a single seed, when planted in fertile ground and nurtured with care, could grow into a mighty tree. He shared his own journey, not as a tale of heroic redemption, but as a testament to the power of choice, the possibility of change, and the enduring strength of the human spirit to seek and find its way towards the light. He made himself approachable, a figure of wisdom and experience, not distant authority. He would often be found in the communal gardens, his hands not afraid to get dirty, sharing stories and laughter with the very people he now served.

"It's remarkable, Eli," Mara remarked one evening, as they watched from a balcony overlooking the main plaza. The plaza was alive with activity – families sharing meals, musicians playing lively tunes, artisans displaying their crafts. The scent of pine was a comforting backdrop to the vibrant tableau. "The way people have embraced you. You've become a pillar of this community, as much a part of Havenridge as any of us who were born here."

Eli turned to her, a quiet pride in his eyes. "They welcomed me, Mara. They saw not my past, but my present and my commitment to our future. That's the real strength of Havenridge. It's not just about defense; it's about its capacity for inclusion, for growth, for second chances." He paused, his gaze sweeping across the scene below. "And it's about you. Your vision, your empathy... you created the fertile ground for this community to thrive, for individuals like me to find a place to belong."

Their partnership was more than just a functional alliance; it had evolved into a deep, abiding friendship, a bond forged in mutual respect and shared purpose. They understood each other's unspoken thoughts, anticipated each other's needs, and found solace and strength in each other's presence. The pressures of leadership were immense, the challenges multifaceted, yet they navigated them together, their shared glance conveying a deep understanding, a silent acknowledgement of the burdens they carried and the unwavering commitment they shared.

One of the most significant challenges Havenridge faced was the reintegration of individuals who had been deeply affected by the conflict. Trauma, fear, and displacement had left their mark, and Eli, with his grounded pragmatism, and Mara, with her profound empathy, worked in tandem to address these needs. Eli helped to establish support networks and resource allocation for psychological counseling and community reintegration programs, drawing on his knowledge of various therapeutic models. Mara, in turn, ensured these programs were delivered with sensitivity and understanding, fostering an environment where healing was not just encouraged but actively facilitated.

They initiated a program that paired individuals who had experienced significant loss with those who had been instrumental in the defense efforts. The idea was to bridge divides, to foster understanding and to create a sense of shared experience and mutual reliance. Eli, observing a session where a former civilian engineer was discussing rebuilding strategies with a member of the defense force, felt a surge of hope. "It's about rebuilding not just structures, but connections," he remarked to Mara later. "Every successful connection, every moment of shared understanding, strengthens the foundation of our society."

The diplomatic landscape, while no longer fraught with immediate peril, remained a complex negotiation. The delegation, recognizing Havenridge's resilience and its growing network of regional contacts, had shifted from overt pressure to a more subtle strategy of influence. They continued to propose joint ventures, ostensibly for mutual benefit, but always with an underlying aim of increasing their economic and technological leverage. Eli and Mara, by this point, had developed a sophisticated approach to these negotiations. They were adept at identifying the delegation's true objectives, dissecting proposals with meticulous care, and formulating counter-offers that prioritized Havenridge's autonomy and long-term strategic interests.

"Their offer for a joint venture in asteroid mining has a very attractive headline profit margin," Eli mused, reviewing the latest proposal. "But the fine print reveals a clause that would grant them preferential access to the resulting mineral wealth for the next fifty cycles, essentially locking us into a long-term supplier role rather than a true partnership. And the environmental impact assessment is suspiciously vague."

Mara leaned over the display, her brow furrowed. "We've seen this before. They offer the bait of prosperity, but the hook is control. We need to counter with a proposal that focuses on shared ownership and equitable distribution of resources, with strict environmental protocols that we ourselves define and enforce. Our expertise in sustainable resource management is a significant asset, and we should leverage that in our negotiations."

Their collaboration extended to the very air they breathed, or rather, the systems that maintained it. Havenridge, with its advanced atmospheric processors, was a marvel of bio-engineering and technological integration. Eli, working with the planetary engineers, ensured that these vital systems were not only robust but also adaptable, capable of withstanding unforeseen external pressures. He understood the fragility of even the most advanced technology and the critical importance of redundancy and foresight.

"The new filtration units are online and operating at peak efficiency," reported Elara, the lead atmospheric engineer, during a technical briefing. "We've also implemented a secondary bio-filter system that draws on native flora to process trace atmospheric contaminants. It's a more organic, sustainable approach, and thanks to Eli's foresight in securing the necessary bio-samples and his support in fast-tracking the research, it's already proving highly effective."

Mara looked at Eli, a flicker of admiration in her eyes. He had a knack for anticipating needs, for seeing the interconnectedness of systems, be they technological, social, or diplomatic. This holistic understanding was precisely what Havenridge needed as it navigated its place in the wider galaxy.

The integration of Eli was a testament to Havenridge's evolving philosophy. It was a society that had learned from its near-destruction, a society that understood that strength was not solely derived from isolation but from the intelligent and discerning embrace of capable individuals, regardless of their past. Eli, with his proven loyalty, his invaluable skills, and his deep commitment to their shared future, had become an indispensable leader. He stood not as an outsider, but as an integral part of the leadership, his presence a symbol of Havenridge's capacity for growth, its unwavering hope, and its determination to build a future together, a future scented with the enduring promise of the pine-scented forests and the boundless potential of their united spirit. He and Mara, side-by-side, were the embodiment of that promise, their shared glance a silent vow to guide their people towards that brighter horizon.

The air, usually crisp with the scent of pine, carried a new, softer fragrance tonight. It was the delicate perfume of the night-blooming cereus, its pale, luminous petals unfurling in the twilight, a subtle yet persistent reminder of the cyclical nature of life and the quiet magic that Havenridge held within its embrace. Mara breathed it in, a contented sigh escaping her lips as she stood beside Eli on the observation deck, the sprawling settlement a tapestry of soft lights below them.

"It's more than just a place, isn't it?" Eli's voice was a low murmur, his arm a warm presence around her shoulders. "Staying here. It feels... different now."

Mara leaned into his embrace, her gaze sweeping over the familiar landscape. "It is different. It's not just about putting down roots, Eli.

It's about actively cultivating them. It's about tending to the soil, fighting the weeds, and celebrating every new bloom." She turned her head to look up at him, her eyes reflecting the faint starlight. "Staying has become a verb. An action. It's a choice we make, every single day."

He nodded, his thumb gently stroking her arm. "A choice to defend, to rebuild, to innovate. A choice to believe in something bigger than ourselves. I remember when 'staying' felt like a concession, a survival tactic. Now…" He trailed off, a hint of awe in his tone. "Now it feels like a victory."

"A victory earned," Mara agreed, her voice soft but firm. "We've faced down extinction, Eli. We've stared into the void and chosen to create light. And we've done it together. You and I, and everyone in Havenridge." She thought of the early days, the fear that had clung to them like a shroud, the desperate scramble for resources, the constant threat of discovery. They had been a fragile ember, easily extinguished. Now, they were a steady flame, casting a warm, protective glow.

"When I first arrived," Eli confessed, his gaze distant for a moment, "I saw Havenridge as a refuge. A temporary harbor until the storms passed. I didn't fully grasp the depth of what was being built here, the sheer resilience of its people. And I certainly didn't anticipate finding… this." He tightened his hold on her, his gaze returning to hers, filled with a profound tenderness that always made her heart flutter. "Finding you. Finding a home."

Mara's smile was a soft curve of her lips. "You didn't just find a home, Eli. You helped build it. You brought your own unique strengths, your wisdom, your… stubborn refusal to give up, even when the odds were stacked impossibly high. And in doing so, you became as much a part of Havenridge as the ancient pines that surround us." She gestured to the dark silhouette of the trees against the star-dusted sky. "They've always been here, enduring. And so have we."

The night-blooming cereus, sensing the shift in the atmosphere, released another wave of its intoxicating fragrance, a subtle endorsement of their reflections. It was a flower that bloomed in the darkness, a testament to finding beauty and life even in the most unexpected of moments. Much like their own journey.

"It's not just about the external challenges either," Eli mused, his voice deepening. "It's about the internal ones. The moments of doubt, the lingering shadows of past mistakes. 'Staying' means confronting those shadows, not letting them consume us. It means choosing to be better, even when it's difficult." He looked at her, his eyes holding hers with an intensity that spoke volumes. "You've always been so good at that, Mara. At seeing the potential for light, even in the darkest corners."

"And you've been my anchor," she countered, reaching up to cup his cheek. His skin was warm beneath her touch, a grounding sensation. "When I faltered, when the weight of responsibility felt too heavy, you were there. You reminded me of why we were fighting, of what we were striving for. You grounded me when my idealism threatened to float away."

Their love, she realized, was not a passive force, but an active participant in their growth. It was the catalyst that had spurred them to face their deepest fears, to overcome their individual limitations. It had allowed them to see each other not just as leaders, but as partners, as soulmates who had found each other amidst the chaos of a shattered galaxy.

"Remember that first council meeting after the ceasefire?" Eli chuckled softly, a warm sound that resonated through the quiet night. "You were so fiercely determined to implement that universal childcare initiative. The elders were... skeptical, to say the least. They saw it as a drain on resources, a distraction from rebuilding the infrastructure."

Mara smiled at the memory. "And you, with your diplomatic flair, managed to frame it as a long-term investment in Havenridge's future, emphasizing how it would foster innovation and ensure a stable, educated workforce for generations to come. You took my passion and gave it your strategic genius."

"And you took my pragmatism and infused it with your compassion," he replied. "We're a good team, Mara. A very good team."

The satisfaction that settled in her heart was profound, a quiet hum of contentment that resonated deeper than any outward triumph. It was the knowledge that they had chosen this path, that they had built this life together, brick by painstaking brick, dream by audacious dream. They had not merely survived; they had thrived. They had taken the ashes of their past and forged a future that was brighter, more resilient, and more beautiful than they could have ever imagined.

"The cereus," Mara said, nodding towards the delicate blooms. "They bloom for only a few hours, but their fragrance is unforgettable. It's a reminder to cherish the present, to savor the moments of beauty and peace, because they are precious."

"And they'll bloom again," Eli added, his gaze steady and full of promise. "Just as Havenridge will continue to bloom, and just as our love will continue to grow. 'Staying' isn't just about holding on, Mara. It's about blossoming. Together."

He kissed her then, a slow, deep kiss that tasted of starlight and the sweet, lingering perfume of the night flowers. It was a kiss that spoke of shared victories, of unwavering commitment, and of a future that stretched before them, boundless and full of hope. The scent of blooming night flowers was no longer just a fragrance of accomplishment; it was the sweet, indelible scent of their enduring love, forever intertwined with the destiny of Havenridge. The quiet satisfaction in their hearts was a testament to the profound meaning of 'staying,' a meaning they had not only found but had created, together. They were home, not just in Havenridge, but in each other's arms. And that, they knew, was the greatest discovery of all. The journey had been arduous, fraught with peril and uncertainty, yet it had led them to this precipice, this moment of perfect clarity, where the choice to 'stay' was not a burden, but a boundless joy. It was the realization that their love was the soil, their shared vision the sunlight, and Havenridge the fertile ground where their dreams could take root and flourish, forever reaching towards the heavens.

The last rays of the setting sun painted the sky in hues of apricot and rose, casting a warm, golden benediction over Havenridge. From their vantage point on the newly reinforced observation deck, Mara and Eli watched as the settlement below transformed, its utilitarian structures softened by the gentle twilight. Lights flickered on, tiny beacons of warmth and life against the deepening indigo of the encroaching night. The air, still carrying a faint whisper of the night-blooming cereus from earlier, now mingled with the comforting aroma of hearth fires and the distant, cheerful clamor of evening routines.

"It's beautiful, isn't it?" Mara's voice was hushed, a soft melody in the quiet expanse. She rested her head on Eli's shoulder, her fingers tracing the intricate patterns of the reinforced railing they had helped design. It was a symbol, she thought, of their collective efforts – a blend of necessity and elegance, a testament to building not just for survival, but for enduring comfort and grace.

Eli's arm tightened around her, his presence a solid, reassuring weight. "It is. More than beautiful, Mara. It's... earned." He exhaled slowly, the sound imbued with a deep sense of peace. "I can still remember the early days, when 'home' felt like a fragile concept, easily swept away by the next crisis. Now, looking down there, it feels like something truly rooted. Something permanent."

Mara nodded, her gaze sweeping over the familiar contours of their settlement. The hydroponic farms, now lush and verdant, pulsed with a soft, internal glow. The community workshops, once centers of desperate innovation, now hummed with the quiet efficiency of ongoing projects, of art and craftsmanship flourishing alongside essential repairs. The children's play areas, once cleared spaces for safety drills, now echoed with the joyous shouts of laughter, a sound that never failed to send a tremor of pure, unadulterated happiness through her. Havenridge wasn't just a collection of buildings and people; it was a living, breathing entity, a testament to their shared will to not just survive, but to flourish.

"It's the resilience, I think," Mara murmured, her thoughts coalescing into words. "The sheer, stubborn refusal to give up. We've faced down threats that would have shattered lesser communities.

We've navigated internal conflicts, resource shortages, the constant hum of external uncertainties. And through it all, we've learned to lean on each other. To trust. To build something together that is far greater than the sum of its parts." She turned her head, meeting Eli's gaze. His eyes, reflecting the nascent stars, held a depth of understanding that always made her feel seen, truly seen. "We didn't just find a place to survive, Eli. We found a place to *live*. And we built that life, hand in hand."

He smiled, a gentle crinkling at the corners of his eyes. "And what a life it is. Remember when we were debating the expansion of the arboretum? So many argued it was a luxury, a drain on resources we desperately needed elsewhere. They didn't see the psychological impact, the importance of beauty and nature in fostering a sense of normalcy, of hope." He squeezed her shoulder. "But you did. You saw beyond the immediate needs, to the long-term well-being of our people. You argued for it with such passion, such conviction."

Mara's heart swelled with a familiar warmth at his remembrance. "And you, with your steady logic and unwavering belief in our collective potential, found the solutions. You secured the extra energy conduits, negotiated the material allocations, and ensured that the expansion not only happened, but was integrated seamlessly into our existing infrastructure. You always knew how to bridge the gap between my idealism and practical necessity." She paused, her gaze drifting to the distant, star-dusted horizon. "It's that balance, isn't it? That synergy. It's what has allowed us to not only weather the storms, but to learn and grow from them."

The journey had been a crucible, forging them and their community into something stronger, something more profound. There had been moments of crushing doubt, of near despair, when the weight of responsibility had felt like an insurmountable burden. But in those darkest hours, they had found solace and strength in each other, in their shared vision, and in the unwavering spirit of Havenridge.

"I think about all the compromises we've made," Eli mused, his voice a low rumble. "The sacrifices. The personal dreams deferred for the good of the whole. There were times, I'll admit, when I wondered if the cost was too high." He turned to face her fully, his hands finding hers, his touch a familiar comfort. "But then I look at this," he gestured broadly with his free hand, encompassing the entirety of Havenridge spread before them, "and I see the faces of our people, happy and secure, and I know, without a shadow of a doubt, that every single sacrifice was worth it."

Mara squeezed his hands, her heart overflowing. "It's not just about the absence of war, or the presence of security. It's about the abundance of connection. Of shared purpose. We've built a society, Eli, not just a settlement. A place where people feel seen, valued, and empowered to contribute. Where the elderly are cherished for their wisdom, where children are nurtured with boundless love, where every individual's talents are recognized and utilized for the betterment of all." She thought of the recent harvest festival, the joyous camaraderie, the palpable sense of gratitude that had permeated the air. It wasn't just a celebration of a good yield; it was a celebration of their collective survival, their collective triumph.

"The integration program for the refugees," Eli continued, his gaze thoughtful. "That was a significant undertaking. Concerns about resources, about cultural assimilation, about potential friction. It would have been so much easier to turn inward, to focus solely on our own needs."

"But that wouldn't have been Havenridge," Mara finished for him, her voice firm. "We learned long ago that isolation is a precursor to decay. True strength lies in embracing diversity, in weaving new threads into the fabric of our community. And the way they've embraced us, the way they've contributed their unique skills and perspectives... it's enriched us beyond measure." She smiled, remembering the vibrant musical performances by the newcomers, the innovative agricultural techniques they had introduced, the fresh energy they had brought to every aspect of life in Havenridge.

The vast, open expanse of the sky above them seemed to echo the boundless potential that lay before them. The stars, now beginning to prick through the twilight, were not distant, unreachable lights, but familiar constellations, mapping out their shared heritage, their shared future. The challenges had been immense, the path arduous, but they had navigated it together, their love and commitment a constant beacon.

"We've proven that it's possible," Eli said, his voice filled with a quiet triumph. "That even after devastation, after loss, after the brink of annihilation, humanity can rebuild. Not just physically, but emotionally, spiritually. We can choose to create something beautiful, something lasting."

"And that choice," Mara added, her gaze meeting his, a silent understanding passing between them, "is the most powerful act of defiance there is. A defiance against despair, against cynicism, against the very forces that sought to break us." She leaned her forehead against his, the gentle friction a soothing caress. "We've built more than just a home, Eli. We've built a legacy. A testament to what can be achieved when love, resilience, and a shared vision coalesce."

The setting sun dipped below the distant, jagged peaks, painting the western sky in a final, spectacular burst of crimson and gold. The light, though fading, was a promise. A promise of a new dawn, a new beginning, and countless tomorrows to be faced, and to be cherished, together. Havenridge, nestled in the valley below, glowed with a peaceful, steady radiance, a beacon of hope in the gathering darkness. It was a future they had fought for, a future they had dreamed of, and a future they would continue to nurture, side by side, their love the enduring foundation upon which it all stood. The quiet hum of contentment that settled over Mara was profound, a deep, resonant peace that spoke of a journey's end, and a new beginning, embraced with open hearts and unwavering hope. This was not an end, but a grand, magnificent unfolding, a symphony of shared dreams played out under an endless, star-strewn sky. Their partnership, forged in the fires of adversity, had bloomed into a love that was as sturdy and enduring as the ancient pines that guarded their sanctuary, and as vast and full of possibility as the cosmos itself. They had found their haven, not just in a place, but in each other, and in the vibrant, thriving community they had so painstakingly brought into being. The final glow of the sun was a warm kiss upon their faces, a gentle affirmation of the enduring strength and beauty of their shared future, a future that was, at last, unfolding before them in all its boundless, hopeful glory.

Chapter Fourteen
Vocabulary

Cereus, Night-Blooming: A flowering plant known for its large, fragrant white flowers that open only at night. In Havenridge, its cultivation is both aesthetic and symbolic of hope and new beginnings.

Havenridge: The name of the protagonist's settlement, signifying a place of safety and enduring community.

Hydroponic Farms: Systems that grow plants without soil, using mineral nutrient solutions in a water solvent. Essential for sustainable food production in challenging environments.

Observation Deck: A vantage point within Havenridge designed for both security and community gathering, offering views of the settlement and the surrounding landscape.

www.ingramcontent.com/pod-product-compliance
Lightning Source LLC
Chambersburg PA
CBHW030055310726
48970CB00004B/1015